KING OF CAMPUS

JENNIFER SUCEVIC

ALSO BY JENNIFER SUCEVIC

Campus Heartthrob

Campus Player

Claiming What's Mine

Confessions of a Heartbreaker

Crazy for You (80s short story)

Don't Leave

Friend Zoned

Hate to Love You

Heartless

If You Were Mine

Just Friends

King of Hawthorne Prep

Love to Hate You

One Night Stand

Protecting What's Mine

Queen of Hawthorne Prep

Stay

The Boy Next Door

The Breakup Plan

The Girl Next Door

CHAPTER ONE

Ladies, and a few guys as well, ;) keep those Roan King sightings pouring in. Especially the ones of him at football practice. Hot, sweaty, with an extra shot of gorgeous is exactly how I take my Roan King. Don't mind me while I type away with one hand... KingOfCampus.com

"*Honey,*" I holler at the top of my lungs before kicking the door shut, "*I'mmmm home!*"

Those words are met with a loud shriek as Lexie flies around the corner before hurtling her small curvy body at me. I'm given roughly two seconds to drop my bags in anticipation of impact. She's lucky I have fairly decent—

The breath gets knocked out of me as we both go crashing to the floor.

Apparently, reflexes are no match when that much force and weight are careening toward you at the speed of light. Physics, I'm guessing, is exactly how I end up sprawled on my back with my best friend and roommate spread out on top of me in our brand-spanking-new apartment. There's a completely manic light filling her big brown eyes. Matching the look, I can't help but beam up at her because it is so freaking good to see her gorgeous face.

It's been precisely fifteen months since we've been in the same room together. Actually, it's been fifteen months since we've been on the same continent. I spent my sophomore year of college studying abroad in Paris.

Needless to say, it was as amazing and spectacular as you'd imagine it would be. Even thinking about it leaves me with a tiny pang of nostalgia for the life I'd left behind.

"Damn, now that's hot! Can I snap a shot for my wallpaper?"

We turn to stare at the tall, good looking male grinning...or maybe the correct term would be—*leering* down at us. His eyes slide oh-so-slowly over our entwined bodies as if he's trying to singe this moment into his memory for all eternity. But it's not in a pervy way...what the heck am I saying? Of course, it's in a pervy way. Which is precisely when I realize that my dear friend, Lexie, seems to be missing the lower half of her outfit.

Yep...she's only wearing panties.

She smothers a giggle before clearing her throat. Rather impressively, her voice whips out in a perfect imitation of a mother scolding her three-year-old toddler. "You damn well better not snap a picture or you won't be seeing this ass for a very long time." To emphasize this point, she gives it a little shake and her boyfriend groans in response.

"Please?" There's a whole lot of whine filling his deep masculine voice. Which is kind of hilarious because he's well over six feet tall and is seriously broad in the chest and shoulders. This one is definitely all man. Lexie, of course, filled me in via Facetime on the football playing boyfriend she acquired about seven months ago. Needless to say, she wasn't exaggerating.

He's pretty damn hot.

If you're into big and muscly.

Which I'm not going to lie... I am.

"The mental snapshot you're burning into your brain will have to suffice."

Folding his muscular arms in front of an equally solid looking chest, he grumbles under his breath, "You always have to be such a hard ass."

Lexie gives me a little wink. "You wouldn't have it any other way, babe."

"True," he sighs in agreement, "very true."

Since Lexie isn't showing any indication of removing herself from my person anytime soon, I'm forced to point out the obvious. "You might want to get off me before your boyfriend has an embarrassing moment in his shorts."

I'm joking, of course.

Sort of.

"You don't have to get off on my account," he quickly chimes in as he continues to ogle us.

Lexie rolls her eyes at me.

"Have I mentioned just how hot you look in that thong?" His voice sounds all heated up and I'm seriously considering shoving Lexie off me before something unfortunate, not to mention awkward, happens and I'm no longer able to look this dude in the eyes again.

"Jeez, Lex, did you have to molest me while only wearing a thong?" No wonder her boyfriend is all but sporting a woody over there.

"Be happy you didn't arrive ten minutes later, I wouldn't be wearing anything at all."

I shake my head to loosen that mental image from my brain. "That wasn't something I needed to know."

Continuing to grin, Lexie smacks my lips with a big wet sloppy kiss. "Goddamn but I missed you, Ivy." Then she does her damnedest to squeeze the very life out of me before rolling gracefully to her side.

"I'm glad to be back, too." As the words automatically spill from my mouth, I realize that I don't necessarily mean them. There's a large part of me that wishes I were still living my life in Paris. With an ocean between me and my dad, I didn't have to dwell on him and the new family he created for himself so quickly after Mom died.

Dad's life carried on while mine fell apart. Even though it's been five years since she died, the ache still feels painfully tender. Returning to Barnett means that I no longer have an excuse not to visit them.

Shaking those thoughts away, I realize I'm still sprawled on the carpeted floor. I blink my eyes a few times as a handsome face peers down at me before crinkling into a large friendly smile. I don't bother hoisting myself up just yet. Instead, I say in my most formal tone, "Mr. Sullivan, I presume."

His grin intensifies, making him appear even more striking than I'd originally thought. Lexie had gushed about how gorgeous her new guy was. And it's not like I didn't believe her, but it's obvious she wasn't exaggerating.

Like at all.

Because Dylan Sullivan is seriously hot.

Golden blond hair, deep brown eyes, sculpted jaw, and athletic body.

According to Lexie, he treats her like a total princess. Which is exactly how it should be. Lexie deserves someone who appreciates how smart, loyal, and gorgeous she is. She's a damn good friend and I'm lucky to have her in my life.

"The one and only," he beams in response, throwing a flirty wink in for good measure.

Oh, this guy is totally dangerous.

Could they be more perfectly suited to one another?

I absolutely love it.

"Umm, isn't your father Dylan Sullivan the first?"

He shrugs his broad shoulders. Self admittedly, I'm kind of a shoulder and arm girl myself. And Dylan Sullivan certainly has nicely chiseled ones.

"Shhh, you're ruining the moment, babe."

That being said, Dylan offers me a hand, which I grab hold of, before being hauled off the floor and set back onto my sandaled feet. I dust my backside off before my gaze slides to Lexie. The unexpected glassy sheen of tears shining in her big brown eyes has my own widening in confusion.

"Lex, why are you—"

I don't get a chance to wrap my lips around the last word before she's hurtling herself in my direction. Her arms slip around my body before tugging me close.

"I missed you, Ivy-girl," she whispers fiercely against my ear, "so damn much! Fifteen months is a long time to stay away. Don't ever leave me like that again."

I'm not normally an emotional person, but her heartfelt words have me choking up and I squeeze her to me.

She pulls back to search my eyes before admitting quietly, "I was afraid you might decide to stay over there."

That just goes to show you how well Lexie knows me. What I don't mention is that I tried my damnedest to make that happen. To finish out college, find a permanent place to live, a dance gig, all so I could postpone coming home indefinitely. Being back here, even though this is a new apartment, still reminds me that my mom is dead, and my dad has moved on and I no longer have a home to return to.

Not one that feels like home used to feel.

"I'm just so glad you're finally back."

"Me, too," I whisper as hot licks of emotion prick the back of my eyes. I hug her tightly one last time before releasing her.

Lexie and I have been best friends since fourth grade when her family moved in down the block from mine. We made it through middle and high school with our friendship intact and decided to apply at some of the same colleges so we could room together. Luckily, Barnett was on both of our short lists. It has a highly regarded fashion design program for Lexie and a kickass dance program for me.

There's absolutely no one in this world I can count on like Lexie Abbott. I'm actually a little ashamed of myself for failing to remember that. In trying to escape all the painful memories, I forgot about the good stuff, too.

Lexie backs up until she's standing directly in front of Dylan. As soon as she's close enough, he wraps those huge arms around her before pulling her flush against the front of his body. Looking ridiculously contented, he settles his chin on top of her head like he's done it a hundred times before.

Like it's the most natural thing in the world.

I can't help but feel thrilled that Lexie has found someone who appreciates the amazing woman she's grown into.

Unwilling to get anymore sappy than I already have, I shake my head. "Do you two come with barf bags? I've only been here for ten minutes and you're already making me sick to my stomach."

They both flash big cheesy grins at me. I want to roll my eyes before sticking my finger down my throat like I'm going to puke. "I suppose you're going to be practically living here with us?" Yep, I can already see how this will go. Dylan will be our unofficial apartment mascot.

With big innocent eyes, she says, "Didn't I mention that Dylan lives in the apartment next to us with two guys from the football team?"

"Nope," I shake my head, "you definitely did not mention that. I guess that makes things convenient."

"Totally convenient," Dylan adds with a sly grin aimed in my direction.

This time, I actually roll my eyes. "So which room is mine?"

In her exuberance, Lexie all but jumps out of Dylan's arms before leading me down a short hallway. As I trail after her, I'm reminded that she's only wearing a thong.

I mean, sure, she has a great ass but still...

"Er, maybe you should put your shorts back on before you give me the grand tour." Out of the corner of my eye, I see Dylan open his mouth. My narrowed gaze slices to his. "Don't even say it," I warn.

Biting her lip, Lexie stifles another laugh before dashing into her bedroom. In twenty seconds flat she rejoins us sporting tiny white shorts. Then she leads the way into a sunny little room before doing her best auto show model imitation as she gestures with wide sweeping movements to all the wonderful amenities my room has to offer.

She points toward the two large windows lining the wall. "Look at all the gorgeous sunlight that pours in!" Then she throws open the bi-fold closet doors. "And a humongous closet for all the clothes you brought back from Paris." Her arms drop to her sides as she swivels toward me. Her auto show model imitation is forgotten in lieu of possible new stylish European clothing. "You *did* bring me back some clothes, right?"

For a moment, my eyes travel around the room, taking everything in. It's not huge by any means but after living in Paris, it sure feels like it is. I'm used to about a third of the space. So this feels pretty damn luxurious. I can't imagine what I'm going to do with all this space to myself. Then my eyes fall to the double sized mattress shoved up against the far wall and my heart actually swells with unfettered joy.

Oh my god, it's so big! I've been sleeping on a twin bed for the last fifteen months. I literally can't wait to spread out on that huge mattress. Maybe roll around a bit. Make some snow angels...minus the snow. Already I'm looking forward to hitting the sheets tonight.

I spent a little more than eight hours on a plane with a two-hour layover in Amsterdam. And France is six hours ahead of us. So, I'd like nothing more than to fall into bed for a nice long nap.

When I don't respond, a thread of worry weaves its way through her voice. "Ivy?" Her concerned tone snaps me right out of my thoughts.

"Of course I did," I say. "There's a short, thigh length pleated skirt, two hand woven scarves, one cashmere sweater, a gorgeous black knit top and these creamy trouser pants that your ass will thank me for."

If watching Lexie sprawled out on top of me, wearing nothing more than a lacy little thong and a tank top is Dylan's idea of a wet dream, hearing about all the beautiful clothes I brought back from Paris is hers. We're talking flushed cheeks and dilated eyes.

And yes, it's entirely possible Lexie could have an embarrassing moment in her shorts. Although I hope not.

"Oh, I can't wait to see them," she squeals in delight, practically jumping up and down with unbridled enthusiasm.

Fashion design is Lexie's life. She was a budding fashionista way back in middle school before I ever cared about what top went with what bottoms. Thank goodness for Lexie or I probably would have been much more of a walking fashion disaster than I was.

I scraped together enough money and perused a few vintage boutiques to find unique pieces I knew she wouldn't be able to get here in the States. I hope she loves them half as much as I think she will.

"What about some hot French lingerie?" her boyfriend asks.

Since Dylan is standing directly behind Lexie, she doesn't bother turning around to admonish him. Instead, she rams her elbow into his gut. He grunts in response. If she hadn't done it, I probably would have.

"Just stand there and look pretty," she mutters under her breath.

My lips twitch because he is definitely pretty.

Lexie gives me a little wink as if she can read my mind. "Don't let his good looks fool you, he's smart, too."

Of course he is.

Because gorgeous and smart are exactly the kind of guys Lexie attracts. While I, on the other hand, had the sad misfortune to fall for a hot athletic jerk who assured me he was going to remain faithful to his study-abroad-girlfriend when in actuality, he started hooking up with other girls as soon as above-mentioned-girlfriend was out of the country.

I've had the last fourteen and a half months to get over Finn McKenzie. And I have. I am totally over him. Unfortunately, he's been calling and texting almost relentlessly for the last week, which means he's been occupying my thoughts way more than I'd like.

Perhaps I should say he's been *trying* to call and text. I haven't bothered to pick up his calls or respond to his rather lengthy and apologetic text messages. I mean, can you seriously believe that? The guy has some nerve reaching out to me after what he did. Is he so delusional as to think we're going to pick up where we left off now that I'm back at Barnett?

Apparently, he is.

We'd been together for about six months before I left for Europe. And yes, I knew having a long-distance relationship would be difficult, but I was willing to give it a shot. I'd grown to like Finn. I hadn't been gone more than two weeks when Lexie Facetimed me about what Finn had been busy doing...which had been, in case you're wondering, other girls.

And that, my friends, had been the end of that.

Lexie's advice was to forget about my cheating asshole of an ex by hooking up with a bunch of hot French guys.

I hooked up with two semi-hot French dudes and buried myself in dance which was the reason I'd been accepted to study at the Conservatoire de Paris in the first place. After a few months, my heartache lessened. I stopped thinking about Finn, my dad, his new wife, their kids, and I concentrated on soaking up everything I possibly could.

It took some time to adjust but after two months, I found myself with an amazing new life in a city renowned for its art and culture. There was no way I was going to allow anything to ruin this once in a lifetime opportunity. Right around the year mark, I stopped thinking about Lexie and returning to Barnett University and started wondering if maybe I could live here for the rest of my life.

Or, at the very least, the next few years.

When I mentioned this possibility to my dad, he made it perfectly clear that he would not be footing the bill for a life in Paris and said, in no uncertain terms, he wanted me back at Barnett come August. Undeterred by his directive, or perhaps because of it, I'd searched for enough scholarship and grant money to pay for me to continue studying in Paris. Needless to say, I hadn't been able to pull it off which is exactly why I was back at Barnett for my junior year.

"So, do you like it?"

My eyes swing back to Lexie who is standing there with all this hopeful expectation lighting up her face. A tiny smile tugs at the corners of my lips because it really is good to see her after all this time apart. "It's absolutely perfect."

Looking very much like the best friend I left behind fifteen months ago, a huge grin spills across her beautiful face before she hurtles herself at me for a third time.

CHAPTER TWO

Hang onto your panties, ladies, because Roan King is kicking off the first day of the fall semester by stripping off his shirt...and yeah, it's definitely a majestic sight to behold. Is it possible that he's even more ripped and gorgeous than last year? Someone hand me a napkin, I'm starting to drool over here... KingOfCampus.com

How could I have forgotten that jet lag is a total bitch?

It should really be called *ass lag* or maybe even *ass drag* would be a more accurate description because my ass is literally dragging on the ground and it's only nine fifty in the morning. I have a whole freaking day stretched out ahead of me.

Oh god, that thought makes me want to weep.

I want to lie down right here in the middle of campus and cry.

And no amount of highly caffeinated beverages seems to be helping with that affliction either. I've been steadily pouring them down my throat since I pried open my blurry eyes this morning. My fingers are tightly wrapped around drink number three as we speak.

I hate to say it, but it already feels like I'm off to a crappy start.

Here it is the first day of classes and I'm practically running clear across campus because I'm late. Why exactly did I think packing up my entire life in France and traveling home the day before fall semester started was such a brilliant idea?

Oh, that's right...I had wanted to squeeze every single moment I possibly could out of Paris. Which, come on, you can't blame me for. Because of that, I'd spent all of yesterday unpacking and organizing. Basically running around like a chicken with my head cut off before collapsing onto my lovely double sized bed at midnight. Then I'd slept for eight solid hours.

Yeah. Eight blissful, dead-to-the-world hours.

And I'm still dragging like I haven't slept a single wink.

Hauling my ass out of bed this morning had been a monumental accomplishment on my part. I'd wanted to pick up my books at the campus bookstore before they ran out which actually happened to me freshman year. Unfortunately, the line at the bookstore had been way longer than I'd anticipated which has now made me late for my ten o'clock Business Ethics class.

I can't believe what a bunch of freaking procrastinators go to this school!

I, on the other hand, have a completely legitimate reason for waiting until the last minute to get my books. Okay, fine. I could have *technically* ordered them online. But I hadn't wanted to think about Barnett until absolutely forced to. Thinking about Barnett meant I had to accept the life I'd created in Paris would be coming to a screeching halt.

So now here I am, trying to hustle my way across campus.

In dire need of something to pull me out of this mental fog, I hoist the Frappuccino to my lips. Instead of giving me a much-needed jolt of energy, it makes me feel even more jittery than I already am. My sunglasses are sitting on the bridge of my nose, shielding my eyes from the overly harsh sunshine that I would be all but basking in on any other given day. My super-sized iced coffee is in one hand while my phone is in the other because it keeps pinging with incoming messages. My bag is slung across my chest. As I move along the wide sidewalk toward Adler Hall, it feels as if I'm fighting exhaustion with every step I take.

I honestly don't know how I'm going to make it through an entire day like this without falling into some kind of narcoleptic state. My eyelids are on the verge of drooping when I crash into a hard body. Instinctively, I clutch my phone in one hand as my half-filled coffee gets dumped all over the person who has the misfortune to end up colliding with me.

I may not have been fully awake before this unexpected collision, but I certainly am now. My mouth falls open in shock and a fair amount of horror as I watch icy brown droplets course their way down a male T-shirt covered chest.

"Oh my god," I finally squeak. I'm all but dying of mortification as hot licks of embarrassment set fire to my normally pale cheeks. "I'm so sorry." Now would be a perfect time for the sidewalk to crack open and swallow me whole.

Yup, right now.

Right now, damn it.

What makes matters worse is that he has yet to utter a single word. The last thing I want to do is force my gaze up and make eye contact. At this very moment, I'm desperately racking my brain for an exit strategy. Like sprinting away from the humiliating mess I've caused in the middle of campus. I hear people laughing in the background. It's like the dull roar of an ocean filling my ears.

Just when I think I might die of total shame, a deep voice rumbles, "I generally enjoy when a girl soaks me, but not like this."

I have to shake my head as his words slowly filter their way through my brain.

Wait a minute...

Did he...did he seriously just say that?

I have to be imagining the innuendo, *right?*

Embarrassed or not, my head whips up as my widened gaze snaps to his.

Inhaling a sharp breath, it gets stuck in my throat before I pretty much swallow my tongue. If I hadn't been stunned into silence by the whole god-awful predicament playing out, that face would have done me in because the guy standing before me is absolutely gorgeous. He makes Lexie's boyfriend, Dylan, look like some hideous troll in need of a bridge to hide under.

He's got tousled black hair and the most vibrant turquoise-colored eyes I've ever seen. Frozen in place, I'm powerless to look away. As I continue studying the unique hue of his eyes, I realize they hold a knowing smirk. I can't help but notice that his lashes are long and thick enough to make any woman gnash her teeth in jealousy. High cheek bones and beautiful full lips complete the picture.

Even though I'm finding it rather difficult to look away from his stunning face, my gaze falls to his wide, strapping chest which is high-lighted rather nicely by an incredibly tight fitting red cotton T-shirt that hugs him in all the right places.

As if this guy has any wrong places...

Because, trust me, he doesn't.

I'm seriously starting to feel lightheaded over here. Like I need to sit down and put my head between my knees so I can breathe through this whole ordeal. That's when I notice the huge brown stain marring that perfectly chiseled chest. His jeans, which seem to be riding rather low on his lean hips, are also dripping with my chilled coffee.

This feels like one of those horrendous, first-day-of-school night-mares that people jolt awake from in an icy cold sweat. Then, once they realize it's nothing more than a terrible dream, they fall against their pillows in relief.

Except this is actually happening to me.

Which makes it a thousand times worse.

I'm about to open my mouth and stutter out yet another lame apology, when I hear, "Hey, King, what the hell happened to you?"

Hearing those words thankfully breaks the strange spell that has fallen over me at the sight of him as I blink my eyes a few times before giving my head a bit of a shake. I'm hoping the movement will somehow jump start my brain into action. That's when I realize this little incident is drawing a whole lot of unwanted attention. Thank god I'm wearing huge sunglasses that cover my eyes and face. Other-wise this guy would get a good look at me.

Anonymity is the only thing getting me through this moment.

"I-I...maybe I have a napkin in my bag." Not that a napkin or Kleenex is going to do anything to clean up that drippy mess but it's the only thing I can think of. Other than running away and never seeing this gorgeous guy again. Which is a shame. As I slide my phone into my bag, I rummage around in it.

But it's a pit in here. My fingers come in contact with books, a calculator, an extra pair of tights for dance class, a few hair bands (also for dance class), a pair of ballet shoes (yep, you guessed it—dance class), ChapStick, hand lotion, sanitizer, my wallet, a protein bar, pain medication, a tampon...

Apparently, I have everything except something to help clean him off.

"Don't worry about it, sweetheart."

Well, I have to hand it to the guy, he's definitely taking this like a champ. If someone had spilled an entire drink on me, I'd be pissed as hell.

My gaze lifts in time to see him whip off the snug fitting T-shirt leaving an amazingly bare chest in its place. My mouth dries as my sunglass-hidden eyes widen before licking over every exquisite sun-kissed inch of him.

Oh.

My.

God.

Someone must have chiseled this guy from marble. It takes everything within me not to reach out and stroke my fingers over him. Because that's exactly what I want to do.

And maybe lick him as well.

Yes...I definitely want to run my tongue over his lustworthy pectorals.

And those abs...

Six pack?

Ha!

Try an eight pack on for size.

This guy's definition is literally amazing.

As someone who uses their body for artistic expression, I can appreciate the utter beauty of a well sculpted form.

God, can I...

"See something you like, gorgeous?"

Even when that cocksure tone hits my ears, I can't stop my eyes from eating him up. He uses the now wadded T-shirt to wipe away some of the wetness that has trickled down his stomach.

Yes, I'm definitely feeling woozy.

And it's not the jet lag that has my brain taking a mental pause either.

As much as I'm having my very own private moment with this guy's amazing body, I can't help but become aware of the catcalls and whistles coming from all directions. Glancing around me, I realize there are pockets of girls who have also stopped to admire the bare-chested Adonis.

The tips of my ears reignite with heat. Wanting to distance myself from the calamity, I take a hasty step backward.

Then another.

"I really am sorry," I mumble again, all the while continuing to back away from him. He's on the verge of opening his mouth when I turn and bolt down the wide sidewalk. As I do, I can't resist throwing one last look over my shoulder. Our gazes lock for just a moment before he's swallowed up by a surging crowd of onlookers.

His blue-green colored gaze stays fastened to me as I hightail it to my ten o'clock class which I'm now late for. Not that there's anything good about what just occurred, but I'm sure as hell wide awake now. I suppose that's an unexpected bonus regarding the disaster I'm currently sprinting away from. Raising a hand to my cheeks, I realize they're still burning with humiliation.

The only thing I can do is shake it off and move on with the rest of my day.

Barnett has about twenty thousand students, so the chances of running into that guy again are slim to none. At least that's what I keep telling myself because it makes me feel decidedly better.

It takes all of five minutes for me to bust through the heavy doors of Adler Hall which is one of the business buildings here on campus. I glance at my schedule. Room 305. I jog up two flights of stairs before heading down a long echoing corridor until I finally find the room. It's a small class. Probably around twenty-four students since this is a higher-level business course.

Luckily, the professor is still talking with a student and hasn't officially started class. Breathing out a heavy sigh of relief, I slide into a desk at the far side of the room and drop my bag to the floor before repositioning my sunglasses on top of my head. I'm winded and frazzled by what happened with that guy.

But that's over with now. Other than to fantasize about that amazing chest of his (probably late at night when I'm feeling sexually frustrated), I never want to think about him or the whole mortifying incident ever again.

As far as I'm concerned, it never happened.

As Professor Paulson begins class, I take out my laptop and start typing away. Fifteen minutes into it, my pulse has settled and I'm no longer thinking about spilling an entire drink on some unsuspecting stranger when the door to the classroom creaks open and in strolls Mr. abs of steel himself. Eyes bulging out of my head, I do a double take because I can't believe it's really him. The entire class turns to stare. Even the professor halts her lecture mid-sentence.

Unconsciously, I slump in my chair before subtly shielding my face in a lame attempt to hide even though I know there's absolutely no way in hell he'll recognize me. I mean, I had on huge sunglasses that swallowed up my entire face. And he's not even looking in my direction.

I wait for the professor to lay into him for disrupting her class. Carefully peeking through my fingers, I notice he's now wearing a bright blue T-shirt and his denim has been changed as well. Which probably means that him being late to class is entirely my fault.

Thankfully, he's still staring at the professor. I'm clear across the room, parked near the windows several rows over from where he's standing.

"Sorry, Dr. P, I was delayed on the way over."

I'm going to wager that this is the part where Dr. Paulson rather embarrassingly rips him a new one in front of the entire class. I almost cringe waiting for it to happen because obviously I'm the one to blame for his tardiness. Not that I'll be apologizing any time soon. I don't plan on conversing with this guy ever again.

My body tenses as I wait for her to make some humiliating example out of him to scare everyone else into being prompt for the rest of the semester.

Wait for it...

Here it comes...

Much to my surprise, Dr. Paulson going off the deep end in a scary tirade revolving around promptness and respect never happens.

Slowly my brows draw together in confusion.

The woman almost looks like...

Um...is she...is she actually *blushing*?

That can't be.

For goodness sake, our professor has to be at least forty. If not older. I squint as if I can't quite believe what I'm seeing. Yup, she's definitely blushing like some kind of tween coming face to face with one of the dudes from One Direction. Now she's tucking a stray piece of mousy brown hair behind her ear as she shifts from one orthopedic shod foot to the other.

"Don't worry about it, Mr. King. See me after class and I'll get you caught up to speed on what you missed."

In response, he dazzles her with a full-blown smile. Even though the look isn't directed at me, I'm embarrassed to admit that my panties flood with heat. I think a good number of the females surrounding me sigh in response as well.

"Thanks, Dr. P." He gives her a little wink. "You're the best."

This guy is totally shameless.

I quickly cover my face as he glances around the room before sauntering up the first row closest to the door and parking himself near the front. All the girls in his general vicinity gravitate toward him as if he has some kind of magnetic pull. All the guys give him fist bumps and back slaps.

It's all a little ridiculous.

Who the hell is this guy anyway?

"You don't know who Roan King is?"

Surprised, I turn toward the girl sitting in the row directly across from me. Unless this chick is a mind reader, I must have muttered the question out loud. I shake my head.

She gives me an odd look, like I must have crawled out from under a rock just to attend this class. Which prompts me to say with a touch of defensiveness, "I did a study abroad program last year. I just got back to town yesterday."

Apparently, this makes perfect sense and I am no longer a huge loser who hides under rocks.

"That's Roan King, a senior. He's a football playing god who redshirted his freshman year. He was such a stud on the field, that he's been a first-string wide receiver since he was a sophomore." She leans toward me as if she's about to reveal top secret information no one else on campus is privy to. Getting caught up in the moment, I angle my body toward her as if I'm all ears. Which apparently, I am.

"Word is he'll be entering the draft in January even though he could play at Barnett for another year." Her eyes dance with unmitigated excitement as if she has a personal stake in that occurring. Then she sighs rather dreamily, "And just look at him, he's totally gorgeous."

My gaze slides to the eye candy currently being discussed. She's right, he's definitely gorgeous. But I'd also lay odds he's a cocky douchebag as well. I mean, come on, he's a football player. Who looks like some kind of freaking Adonis.

"If you're interested," she gives me a look that says—*and who wouldn't be,* "there's a website solely devoted to all things Roan King. And there are some seriously hot pics of him to drool over."

Now that my Roan-King-haze has started to dissipate and my hormone levels are once again evening out, my brows snap together in disbelief. "Are you telling me this guy created a website so he can promote himself?" Oh, that's going too far even for a gorgeous football playing god like him. I almost wince at my unchecked thoughts.

Football playing god?

Did I seriously just think that?

Guilty.

So, so guilty.

She shakes her head. "Of course not. Roan King has a major following here at Barnett. Whoever created the sight allows people to track and post Roan King sightings and gossip. If you ever want to know what he's up to, check out the website. I always look to see where he is throughout the night so maybe I can run into him."

Umm...right.

I think this girl wants to do more than *just* run into him. What she's describing is borderline stalking. I can't believe she's actually admitting it to a virtual stranger. How embarrassing. Of course, that thought leads me to wonder if she's fucking with me because he's not a freaking celebrity.

He's just some college athlete.

Albeit a really *hot* college athlete.

With my eyes narrowed in skepticism, I ask, "And this is all because he plays football?" I'm having a really hard time wrapping my mind around this. And I certainly haven't ruled out the whole- *I'm-being-fucked-with scenario* either.

Giving me that- *do-you-live-under-a-rock look* again, she shakes her head. "No, he doesn't just *play* football, he *is* football here at Barnett. Like I said before, he's entering the draft in January. And well...just look at him." She flicks her hand in his direction. "He's the hottest guy on campus. Roan King is going places, and everyone is interested in where those places are."

With that, she swivels in her seat, so she's turned fully toward the professor. And Roan King.

For the next thirty-five minutes I do my best to focus on what Dr. Paulson is discussing, but I would be lying if I didn't admit that my gaze keeps straying across the room to rest on Barnett's legendary football star. Every time I catch myself staring at those wide shoulders, bulging T-shirt clad biceps, and inky black hair, I have to mentally chastise myself before refocusing my distracted attention. After the seventh time, I'm more than a little irritated with myself for acting like the rest of these silly little twits who are practically drooling all over their desks.

Even though I was here for my freshman year, I don't recall hearing anything about Roan King. Instead of paying attention to Dr. Paulson as she outlines what we'll be learning this semester, I'm too busy racking my brain trying to remember any little tidbit of information about this guy.

But I keep drawing blanks.

Which shouldn't surprise me because I've never really cared for football. I know absolutely zero about it. And furthermore, I have no interest in learning anything about it either. When forced to attend high school homecoming games with Lexie, I distinctly remember being bored off my ass.

My eyes narrow as I continue contemplating him.

I'd hazard a guess to say there's not much going on beneath all that gorgeousness. And if our professor is any indication, he's probably been coasting through the last three years of college on his hotness and football playing skills.

That is if playing football can actually be considered a skill.

Every time I've been forced to watch a game, the guys on the field don't seem to do anything more than run around throwing some oblong shaped ball to each other. And the game is constantly being stopped which only makes it even more mind-numbing. Like they're deliberately trying to torture all the fans that have filled the stands.

Seriously, how much skill can something like that possibly take? It's not like executing a perfect pirouette or adage or ballonne. That takes years of relentless practice and dedication.

So even though I don't know Roan King personally, he's obviously someone to steer clear of. And not that Mr. football has any interest in me whatsoever, but after what happened with Finn last year, I have zero interest in getting tangled up with another jerk.

I mean jock.

Especially some football playing Neanderthal who obviously thinks he's god's gift to the female population of Barnett University.

Ugh.

Thanks, but no thanks. I'll pass.

CHAPTER THREE

With my head bent forward, my caramel-colored hair falls over my face like a thick curtain, shielding it from view. Tapping my foot nervously, I wait until Mr. abs of steel swaggers his way up front to speak with the professor. As I'm about to make a break for it, he saunters back to his desk before picking up his backpack and strolling out the door like he has all the time in the world.

I have no idea how he was brought up to speed so quickly on what he missed. Regardless, I just want to put as much distance as I can between Roan King and myself. Once he's gone, my whole body deflates.

I think as time goes by, he'll forget about the whole iced-coffee-spilling-fiasco. Or, at the very least, he won't remember me specifically as the one who caused it. That's my hope. And I'm going to cling to it until proven wrong.

Other than the professor who is reading through some papers at the front of the classroom, I'm the last lingering student. He has to be gone by this point which means it's safe for me to finally get out of here. Gathering up my bag, I jog down the two flights of stairs, mentally running through my schedule for the rest of the day.

I have a French and dance class every Monday, Wednesday, and Friday. I was lucky enough to snag a job at the local dance studio in town teaching ballet and tap to four and five year olds. The less money I have to grovel to my father for, the better off I'll be.

Plus, its dance which I live and breathe. So, teaching for about ten hours a week works out perfectly for me. It's only about a mile from the apartment which is totally walkable if I can't bum a ride from Lexie.

Lost in thought, I push through the double doors leading outside before walking down the wide cement stairs. As I do so, I slide my sunglasses over my eyes. Today is a bright and gorgeous August day. With autumn on its way, I know this kind of weather won't stick around forever. It needs to be soaked up and thoroughly enjoyed before the chill of September sets in.

"Hey, coffee girl!"

Since my name is most definitely not *coffee girl*, I don't bother glancing around. I keep on moving. Unfortunately, I forgot to pick up a supplemental reading guide, so I need to head back to the bookstore for—

"Hey, coffee girl!"

This time, the words are nearly shouted. People are craning their heads to see what's going on. I feel bad for whoever this poor *coffee girl* is. How embarrassing to be spoken to like that. She's probably some unfortunate barista who works at one of the coffee shops on campus. Seriously. Some people are so damn rude. Which is exactly why I turn glaring eyes on the A-hole shouting it.

Imagine my shock and dismay when I see freaking Roan King smirking at me as our gazes collide. Great. That's when it occurs to me that *I'm* the poor and unfortunate coffee girl. Unconsciously, because— damn it, he seems to have that god-awful effect on me—my feet grind to a halt and I can't help but stop and stare at him like some kind of idiotic fangirl.

Thankfully, I've gotten used to his dazzling good looks and don't feel completely gob smacked. Plus, he's once again wearing a shirt. No gorgeous chest to lose my mind over.

In my best haughty tone, I yell back, "Are you talking to me?"

The smile grows, which has me gnashing my teeth together painfully because that was so not the response I was going for. "Ah, she speaks."

This has my face coloring. "My name isn't *coffee girl*," I finally ground out.

Revealing bright white teeth, he leisurely pushes away from the brick wall he was leaning against. That's when I notice him turn toward the thick crowd surrounding him.

How did I not notice the huge group he's standing in the midst of? And it's not just girls who make up his fan club either, but guys as well. This dude definitely has the strangest effect on me. I don't like it at all. I'm not used to feeling so tongue-tied and awkward.

I'm really not.

I have no idea what he says to them. His lips move and then the crowd reluctantly disperses before he closes the distance that separates us. The way he carries his powerful body has all the saliva in my mouth instantly drying. He's so big and muscular. So unexpectedly graceful. I wish I didn't appreciate the beautiful lines of his sharply defined body, but I can't seem to help myself. As he jogs toward me, shards of inky colored hair fall over those brightly sparkling eyes. When he's about two feet away, he slows to a stop before flicking a chunk of hair out of the way.

The look he aims in my direction is so well-honed I nearly gasp.

Oh...this guy is completely dangerous. And he's clearly aware of the effect he has on the opposite sex.

That's for damn sure.

Thankfully, it's enough of a slap in the face to have me straightening my spine all the while trying to wrestle my traitorous hormones into submission. Which is no easy task when faced with...well...*him*.

His gaze holds mine for a long silent moment. It's almost as if his eyes are caressing mine. Which is completely ridiculous, I know. But still, that's exactly the way it feels. My heart stutters in response to all that sexiness packaged up so prettily in front of me.

He cocks his head as if waiting for me to give him an answer. God, I hope he hasn't asked a question and I've been too busy drooling to realize it.

"So what's your name if it's not *coffee girl?*"

I glance pointedly at the growing group of girls who are avidly watching our exchange before my gaze arrows back to his. For just a moment, I feel like *Alice in Wonderland* tumbling down the rabbit hole. My belly dips as if I'm truly falling.

How is that possible?

"Does it really matter?" Okay. Good. That came out cool enough to sound unaffected. Even though I am totally and unequivocally affected.

Following my gaze, another devastating smile slides its way across his handsome face before he shrugs those powerful shoulders basically telling me that—*no, it really doesn't.* Instead he steps closer, invading my personal space until my heart is slamming almost painfully against my chest.

Those beautiful eyes of his continue holding mine, ensnaring them. Like he's capable of some kind of crazy voodoo magic. "I have two hours to kill until my next class, why don't we head back to your place for a bit."

Head back to my place?

Two hours to kill?

Wait just a minute...

That sounds suspiciously like he's asking me to—

My spine stiffens so quickly, it's as if someone has rammed a massive pole up my ass.

I'm pretty sure my eyes flare open to the point of popping out of my head. "Are you suggesting we go back to my place for a few hours and have," I pause as my voice lowers, because there are, after all, about a dozen people watching our exchange, "*sex?*"

Those lovely bow-shaped lips lift into a knowing smile. "Yeah, babe, I am." Then his eyes meander down my body. I can all but feel them licking over every single inch of me. On their slow perusal back up to my face, they stop at my chest.

I think my nipples just tightened under the intense scrutiny of those turquoise-hued eyes. I'm seriously cursing myself for not bothering with a padded bra this morning. Instead, I'm wearing a sports bra because it's so damn comfortable.

Thankfully, he hasn't made any noises that would lead me to believe I have the dreaded headlight effect going on, so maybe it's not as bad as I'm imagining. There's certainly no way I can glance down and see for myself because that would only draw attention to my nips. Instead, I keep my gaze focused steadily on his face.

He tilts his head just a bit before admitting, "I usually like a girl with a little more going on upstairs, but you'll do."

Outrage slams through me, making me gasp.

I have never, and I do mean *never*, had anyone talk to me like this before.

With my nails digging into my clenched fists, I take a step closer to him. My narrowed eyes feel as if they're blazing fire, as if they could burn him alive with one single look. Unable to control myself, I stab a finger at his gorgeous, rock solid chest.

Gritting my teeth, I hiss, "I don't know who the fuck you think you are and quite frankly, I don't give a shit. But don't you ever talk to me like that again! You've apparently mistaken me for one of the groupies you're used to screwing anytime you please. Make no mistake, *asshole*, that's not me."

If he's at all surprised by my unexpected outburst, he doesn't say one damn word. Instead, his bright gaze holds mine, almost as if he's assessing me with a bit more interest.

My breath continues to come out in short choppy pants. Like I've just run a marathon. Still frothing at the mouth, I give him one last frosty glare that will hopefully shrivel his balls before stalking away.

The nerve of some people!

"See you around, coffee girl."

Even though I can't help the growl that escapes from my lips, I don't bother dignifying that last parting shot with a comment. Mr. abs of steel can go screw himself for all I care.

CHAPTER FOUR

There's a ton of back-to-school parties happening tonight. Will Roan King be making an appearance at any of them? Stay tuned to find out! KingOfCampus.com

Sticking my brand-new brass key in the lock, I push open the door to our apartment. It's well after seven and I've just come home from my first day of teaching dance at *On Pointe*. Spending two hours with all those little cuties was just enough balm to soothe away my run in with a certain douchebag jock earlier in the day. It literally kills me that we have a class together and I'm going to have to endure his presence three days a week for the entire semester.

Ugh.

Avoid. Avoid. Avoid.

That's the plan henceforth.

"Lexie-Lou," I sing-song loudly from the front hall. God, it feels so good to be home again. My ass is seriously dragging. All I can imagine is taking a long hot shower, curling up in bed, and reading a book or watching a little mindless TV before crashing.

Hmmm. That's strange. No answer. Although, I don't exactly wait for one either. Even thinking about that obnoxious asshole has everything within me prickling with irritation.

I toss my keys in a little ceramic bowl since I am notorious for losing them. Apparently, the colorful little dish set right next to the door in our entryway is supposed to cure that affliction.

We'll see.

I'm not holding out too much hope.

I repel keys in much the same way I repel nice guys.

One of the first things I did today was get two copies of the apartment key made. My plan is to give one to Dylan since he oh-so-conveniently lives next door. Hopefully, his roommates aren't total creepers that will have me reassessing that decision.

Glancing through the mail stacked neatly besides the key bowl, I yell, "I had the distinguished honor of meeting the campus douchebag today."

I could have sworn that when I came through the door, I heard the TV. I assumed she was in the living room watching it. When I don't receive a response, I continue in a louder voice, wondering if maybe she's in her bedroom. "Talk about a total asshole! Roan fucking King! Seriously, that's his name. I've been informed that he's Barnett's very own golden boy."

Except he's dark as sin and sexy as hell.

Damn it.

Where the heck did *that* thought come from?

Unwrapping the sweater I had thrown over my black leotard after teaching ballet class, I pad down the hall before stepping into the living room. As I do, my feet grind to a halt as three sets of gazes fall on me.

And not one damn set belongs to my roommate either.

How embarrassing.

They're all male, too.

Figures...

This freaking day has been nothing more than one humiliation after another. I'd seriously give anything to be back in Paris right now.

Stuffing my mouth with a yummy pastry. Instead, I'm suffering through yet another mortifying moment.

The first guy my gaze collides with is Dylan. For some strange reason, I notice he's paused the Xbox game he's in the middle of playing. Which is odd. I know enough about guys and video games to realize this is highly unprecedented behavior. The sinking sensation in the pit of my gut continues to grow. Then my gaze slides to—

Oh.

Hell.

No.

What the hell is *he* doing here?

"What the hell are *you* doing here?" I practically spit the words at him as my temper ignites. Why is this guy sitting on my couch? In *my* apartment?

A huge smile moves across his chiseled face before he chuckles. "So you're the roommate from France, huh? Perfect."

Gnashing my teeth together at his amusement, my narrowed gaze slices back to Dylan. He visibly pales as my eyes land on him again. Which, under different circumstances, I'd actually get a kick out of. He is, after all, a huge hulking guy. I weigh a buck thirty soaking wet. My best guess is that he weighs a solid two forty or so.

Slowly, as if he doesn't quite understand what's going on, he says, "Umm...I take it you've already met, Roan. He's one of my roommates." He jerks his head toward the other guy sitting quietly on an overstuffed armchair. My gaze slides toward him. "And that's Sam. He also lives with us."

I give a stiff nod to Sam who rather smartly doesn't utter one damn word.

My attention arrows to Dylan before I grit out, "Where's Lexie?"

"Shower. We're heading out soon. You coming?"

Even though I had zero intention of going out tonight, my gaze slides to a still smirking Roan before I jerk my thumb in his direction. "Is he going?"

Dylan shifts uncomfortably in his seat. "Ummm, yeah."

"Then no," I shake my head emphatically, "I'm not."

He shoots a questioning gaze toward Roan before muttering under his breath, "Lexie won't be happy about that."

As if on cue, the bathroom door opens and out billows a ton of steam along with my roommate. She's wrapped in an oversized tan-colored towel. Dylan yanks his gaze from the TV screen before quickly jumping to his feet. "I'm going to help Lex get dressed."

"Hey, babe." Unaware of the thick tension that has descended upon us, she commands, "Go get changed, girl. We're hitting a couple first-day-of-school parties. Plus, we have to celebrate you finally getting your ass back to America." She makes a few hand gestures which are meant to send me scurrying to my room to change. "Shoo now...go on and be quick about it."

Feeling absurdly aggravated that the bane of my existence is sitting in my living room, grinning at my obvious irritation, I shake my head. "No thanks. It's been a long day and I'm feeling jet lagged." Although I'm pretty damn sure I could have been cajoled into going out for a drink or two to celebrate my return to Barnett. But there's no way in freaking hell I'm going anywhere with that tool bucket.

That being said, I head to my room before closing the door softly behind me. Even though I want to slam it so the door rattles on its hinges, I don't. The last thing I want is to give that egomaniac out there the satisfaction of hearing me slam my bedroom door like some two-year-old in the midst of a temper tantrum.

But it's hard.

Slumping onto my bed, it finally sinks in that I'm going to be constantly running into this guy. It's totally unavoidable. Having a class with him for the rest of the semester is bad enough. Now I find out that he lives next door? And his friend is going out with my best friend?

Perfect.

Just fucking perfect.

God, this day keeps getting shittier and shittier. Every time I think I've reached rock bottom, I somehow manage to jackhammer to a new level. It's enough to have moisture gathering in my eyes. Five minutes later, there's a gentle knock on my door. Not waiting for an answer, Lexie pushes it open before peeking her head around the corner.

"Come on, Ivy-girl, you have to come out with us. We can't celebrate your return to Barnett without you." Her lips tug up into a small smile before she adds, "Well, we can but it won't be half as much fun."

Meeting her eyes, I halfheartedly say, "I'm really tired. I think I'm going to shower, watch a little TV, and hit the sack. We'll celebrate this weekend for sure."

Silently she searches my eyes as if sifting through them for the truth. Without another word, she steps into the room before closing the door behind her. Then she plunks herself down next to me on the bed. The mattress dips under our combined weight.

Lexie and I have been best friends for a really long time. She knows me well enough to understand that something isn't right. Plus, I'm pretty much betting that Dylan filled her in while *helping* her get dressed. Honestly, I'm surprised they're out so quickly.

"What's the deal with Roan? What happened today?"

Before I can deny it, she arches a brow and cuts me off. "Dylan said you two had some kind of run in," she pauses, her lips twitching, "and it didn't go well?"

Rolling my eyes, I launch into the whole embarrassing coffee debacle. By the end of my story, her lips are doing way more than twitching. Clearly, she's having a hard time keeping a straight face.

I raise a brow before gritting out with as much outrage as I can muster, "He's a total self-absorbed tool who propositioned me for sex."

Those words have her bursting out in laughter.

Which only ratchets up my annoyance. "It's not funny! It's insulting," I sniff before adding, "for all womankind." Neither of us mention that I'm not exactly a hard-core feminist.

After her laughter subsides, she holds up a hand. "I know, I know. You're absolutely right. Totally insulting. Not just for you, all womankind should be highly aggrieved by what happened."

My eyes narrow. "But you're still laughing," I point out. "And you don't look the least bit aggrieved by what happened to me."

She schools her features so that she looks mildly distressed. Although it should be noted that Lexie took a drama class in high school, so I'm kind of thinking she might be drawing from those skill sets instead of actual aggravation at how I've been mistreated by her boyfriend's friend. "No, you're right. He shouldn't have done that. But—"

Oh my god...is she actually going to defend him?

"Don't you dare defend him," I cut in sharply. "Asking me to take him back to my place and have sex is indefensible." My cheeks actually heat with embarrassment when I think about him telling me that *I would do.*

I would do!

He doesn't even want to know what *I would do* to him! He'd be lucky to limp away with his balls still intact.

Yup...still seething over here.

She shrugs. "I'm not trying to make excuses for him, I'm really not. If you had been around last year, you would understand. Girls follow him everywhere. It's like he's a rock star or something. It's totally ridiculous."

Grabbing a tissue from the nightstand next to my bed, I pretend to dab at a few tears. "Oh, poor Roan...so much attention. How does he stand it?" Then I roll my eyes. I'm sure he loves being Barnett's golden boy. Having all those girls panting after him like dogs in heat...

She laughs. "I'm sure he was expecting you to be thrilled with the offer."

"Well, I wasn't," I grumble. What girl would seriously want to be spoken to like that? He couldn't have cared less what my name was either. He made some half-assed attempt to find out before admitting that it didn't matter.

My mind tumbles back to the groups of girls who were standing around with him as well as the ones in class. They were all drooling. Even the freaking professor looked a little starstruck by his presence.

And the fact that there's a website dedicated solely to him and what he's up to is completely asinine. I'm sure it helps feed his immense ego.

"I would hazard a guess to say that you made your thoughts on the subject perfectly clear by the fact you were moments away from slicing off his balls and ramming them down his throat. I'm sure he won't bother you anymore."

My lips lift. "If he enjoys his balls being attached to his body, he'll steer clear of me."

"Okay. Good. I'm glad that's settled. Roan King is no longer an issue. Now you can come out with us tonight and we can celebrate my best friend getting her ass back home where she belongs." Knowing exactly how to get what she wants, Lexie gives me a pleading look. "It'll be so much fun. The party we're hitting is going to be a mob scene. You won't even see Roan there. You'll do your thing and he'll do his. Trust me."

CHAPTER FIVE

For anyone who's interested (which is pretty much anyone with a labia), a Roan King sighting has just been confirmed at the massive house party on Hudson Street. Get your asses over there, people. KingOfCampus.com.

Trust me...

I should have known better.

I mean, of course I should have known better. This day started out as a massive clusterfuck and apparently, it's going to end as one.

Right now, I'm squashed in the backseat of Dylan's truck, tucked tightly between Roan and Sam. And they're both big muscly guys. I'd have to guess they each weigh well over two hundred and thirty pounds. Although, oddly enough, I'm barely touching Sam, even though I keep trying to scoot my way toward him on the bench seat.

I think I scared him when I came in earlier tonight. He probably thinks I'm a total psycho and is trying to get through this ride without making eye contact. Roan, on the other hand, is all but plastered against my side. Just when I think it can't get worse, he casually slings an arm across the back of the seat, so it's stretched out behind me.

And yeah, in case you're wondering, he smells damn near edible.

I grit my teeth, trying my damnedest to ignore him. But it's impossible. I'm hyperaware of his powerful body shifting next to mine.

Damn him, damn him, damn him...

"So, about today..."

His breath feathers softly against the delicate shell of my ear. A slight shiver works its way through me. For goodness sake, I can't even tolerate the guy. Why is my body reacting to him like this? It's completely aggravating. The last thing I want is to feel attracted to him.

Unwilling to look his way, I continue staring straight ahead. "Let's just forget it ever happened."

The alternative is to talk about it in a car full of people.

Umm, no thank you.

"Are you sure?" Even though I don't make eye contact, he sounds dubious. Like maybe I'm trying to pull a fast one on him and he's smart enough not to fall for it.

"It's already forgotten," I mutter under my breath.

And yes, I am a big fat liar pants because I will never forget what he was rude enough to say to me. One of my worst qualities is that I have a hard time letting things go. But it doesn't really matter because we aren't going to be friends. As far as I'm concerned, Roan King doesn't exist.

Something settles in me as I reassure myself with those comforting thoughts.

A moment later, I feel the firm pressure of his fingers as they brush against my shoulder. The reverberation of it arrows right down to my nether regions. Unconsciously, my thighs clench as something suspiciously similar to desire floods through me.

Son of a-

Snapping my head in his direction, I hiss, "*What do you think you're doing?*"

One side of his mouth slides its way upward. "Nothing."

Pressing my lips into a thin tight line, I give him a murderous glare before turning away. But his fingers don't budge from my shoulder. Not one damn bit. They're still there, softly strumming over me. I can feel the tips of them through the thin top I'm wearing.

It's all but driving me crazy.

This car ride feels excruciating, like it's going to last forever. I seriously need to get away from this guy. I'm almost to the point of telling Dylan to pull over so I can jump out and walk the rest of the way.

Clearing my throat, I angle my body toward Sam. Since I'm squashed against Roan, my boob grazes his chest in the process which has the bud instantly tightening in response to the contact. My gaze flies to his to see if he's noticed.

I'm really hoping he hasn't.

His blue-green colored eyes are already latched onto mine when our gazes collide.

Yup...the boob graze has not gone unnoticed.

Grrrr.

I can't win today. I should have stayed home and skipped the party. Going out was a huge mistake. I give him another icy glare before my gaze swivels to the guy on my other side.

"So, Sam, you're a senior, too?"

His gaze swings to mine before flickering toward Roan who is now seated behind me since I have turned my body completely away from him. Although his damn hand is still on my shoulder and no amount of shrugging it off has dislodged it. I'm still very aware of him. I don't think I've ever been more hyperaware of anyone in my life. And I certainly don't want to think about the reasons for that either.

"Yup," he answers rather succinctly before turning toward the window.

Seriously?

That's it?

Can't this guy work with me for a few minutes?

Hoping to draw him out, I ask about something I care nothing about. "And you play football with Dylan?" I'm pretty sure that's what Dylan mentioned earlier. Sheesh. I'm working way too hard for this.

This time, he doesn't even bother glancing my way. "Yep."

Feeling exasperated, I find myself snapping before I can stop the words from flying out of my mouth, "You're a man of few words, aren't you, Sam." It's not even a question. More of a frustrated observation.

His deep blue eyes jerk back to mine before narrowing. Just when I think he's going to turn away yet again, he finally cracks a smile. And I realize in that moment that he's rather good looking. Dirty blond hair with a bit of curl to it, ocean blue colored eyes and a muscular body that has been honed from years of football practice and working out. Amusingly enough, I think I would have realized it sooner except it's kind of hard to notice anyone else when Roan is in the vicinity. It must suck being his wingman.

"No, not really."

A small smile touches my lips in response.

Finally.

We're actually getting somewhere here.

Again, his attention slides over my shoulder before the smile disappears and he silently turns to the window.

I'm about to question what the hell is going on when Dylan pulls the truck over to the curb. Damn near ecstatic that we're finally parking, my eyes sweep the immediate vicinity. People are scattered all over the sidewalk in big groups. Everyone is heading down the block. The house in question looks to be already bursting at the seams. The front lawn is overflowing as college students spill onto the sidewalk and street. Already I can hear the low bass of the music as it pumps from the open windows.

Maybe Lexie was right. With so many people, there is no way I'll run into Roan again for the rest of the evening. Since Sam is sitting on the side next to the curb, I slide toward him. I'm actually a little surprised when his hand reaches in to help me exit the truck. As soon as my feet are safely planted on the green grass, Sam lets go of my hand.

"Thanks."

Our gazes lock and hold for a moment as he gives me another crooked smile along with a quick nod before the five of us head up the sidewalk toward the party. Lexie and Dylan are ahead of me and Sam is behind them. I'm about to hasten my step when a heavy arm is slung across my shoulders all but halting my progress. The little zing of electricity that races through me only adds to my growing annoyance.

Is this guy for real?

Doesn't he get the hint that I'm not interested in becoming one of his little groupies? What do I need to do? Send him a notarized letter?

"What are you doing?"

He gives me a brilliant smile before stating the obvious. "Walking with you."

I give a pointed look to his massive arm draped across me. *Again.* "Is it possible for us to walk to the party without you accosting me along the way?"

His grin broadens and something unwanted pings in the bottom of my belly. I don't like the way he makes me feel. Especially since I don't like the guy. Someone needs to inform my body that we're not supposed to be getting turned on by him.

"I'm not accosting you. Merely trying to make nice with my new neighbor."

I try wiggling out from under his arm but it's impossible. It's like he's anchored himself to my side and no amount of fighting it helps to free me from him. The fact that I'm trying to get away has him chuckling before he hauls me closer. The woodsy scent of his cologne assaults my senses. Without realizing it, I inhale another lungful before my eyes drift shut to savor the scent.

Could I seriously be more pathetic?

Don't think so.

"I taste even better than I smell."

My eyes fly open when I hear those huskily murmured words right next to my ear. His gaze is sparkling with both mischief and humor and I realize he's teasing me. Instead of acting all pissy and bitchy, I decide to roll with it and not let him ruin my night.

I have no doubt what he's saying is absolutely true. But I have zero interest in finding out firsthand.

Oh, who am I kidding?

Of course, I want to find out if he tastes as delicious as he smells but I'm smart enough to know when not to play with fire and Roan King is a veritable house set ablaze. I would only hate myself in the morning for hooking up with a guy who is nothing more than a womanizing man whore. It's almost a certainty that he would immediately forget I existed, and I'd be nothing more than one of his pathetic fangirls kicked to the curb.

No thanks.

I need to treat Roan like he's one big walking venereal disease.

For all I know, he is.

He's probably slept his way through most the girls at Barnett. And he'll be busy working his way through the rest this year. I've never been one of those girls and I'm certainly not going to start now...even though he's tempting as hell. I almost cringe as that thought rolls through my head.

"I'm surprised you can walk upright with such a massive ego."

A grin lights up his face. "Don't kid yourself, sweetheart, that's not the only massive thing about me. And I walk around with both just fine."

So damn cocky.

I can only shake my head before rolling my eyes.

Let's see—so far, he's called me gorgeous, babe, and now sweetheart.

So typical...

I can't resist asking, "Do you even know my name?" I'm sure this guy doesn't bother learning any girl's name. I mean, why should he?

Before I can crank myself up, he says rather simply, "Ivy."

Completely shocked, my gaze flies to his. He holds it with those gorgeous blue-green colored depths as a smirk settles over his lips.

His eyes take on a sly, knowing look. "Didn't think I knew it, did you?"

"Nope."

His arm tightens around me. "I did a little recon."

The admittance surprises me. I'm almost afraid to ask... "And what exactly did you find out?"

"Let's see, you studied abroad in Paris last year and you're into dance." Heat flares in his eyes as they slide their way down my body. "Can't deny that I wouldn't mind getting a private lap dance."

My mouth tumbles open. Before I can summon the words to blast him with, he continues, "And you're double majoring in dance and business."

Well color me stunned.

And slightly frightened.

My eyes narrow. "Why?"

He quirks a brow like he doesn't understand the question.

With my mind whirling, it's slowly I ask, "Why would you bother finding out anything about me?"

His gaze ensnares mine as we continue walking down the sidewalk. Instead of looking at where I'm going, my head is turned and I'm staring at Roan. Which is almost like staring straight at the sun. It kind of hurts my eyes. There are tons of people surrounding us, jostling past, laughing and talking, but I'm not aware of them. I wish it was the jet lag that had me feeling so befuddled, but I know it's not.

It's Roan freaking King. My confusion can be laid entirely at his feet.

It's actually a relief when he shrugs those amazingly broad shoulders. "Just curious about my new neighbor."

I blow out the breath that has become lodged in my throat. A little curiosity is fine. Anything else would be damn scary. Not to mention disastrous.

As we reach the front porch, people seem to realize that the king of Barnett has decided to grace them with his esteemed presence, and we're descended upon by at least a dozen fans. Back slaps, fist bumps, people clamoring for his attention as if his popularity or football prowess will somehow rub off on them. The guy is like a one-man circus sideshow act.

I take this as the perfect opportunity to get the hell away from him and find Lexie who has already disappeared inside the house. Since I don't want to lose her, I hustle my ass through the front door. As I do, I can't help but toss a glance over my shoulder. Roan has been swallowed up by a frenzied crowd of admirers.

It's actually a relief to get away from him.

At least, that's what I tell myself as I maneuver my way through the front hall.

Pushing Roan from my mind for what feels like the billionth time today, I search the jam-packed living room for Lexie. I'm starting to wonder if I'm ever going to find her when I catch sight of her fiery auburn hair which is piled high on top of her head in a messy bun.

After a few minutes of pushing and shoving, I grab hold of her arm to get her attention. She turns to me with a beer in each hand.

"Double fisting it already?" Hell, if anyone should be double fisting it for having a lousy day, it's me.

"Nope, sharing one with my bestie," she says right before handing me a red plastic Solo cup filled with frothy golden liquid.

With the amount of people crammed inside this house, not to mention the ones outside, I have to admit I'm fairly impressed with her beer retrieval skills. "You certainly work fast."

She nods her head to the left. "Gotta love the freshman football players. Poor newbies."

When my brows slide together, she goes on to explain, "It's pretty much their job to keep the more senior players on the team happy. Which means Dylan. And since its Dylan's job to keep me happy, that extends to me." She grins before taking a huge gulp. "And you." Tilting her cup toward me, she says, "Cheers to you being home where you belong!" Then she knocks it into mine. Beer sloshes over the rims of both our cups.

Taking a healthy drink, I feel everything within me relax. This day has been a total shit show. But I'm not going to dwell on that. I'm going to focus on cutting loose and having fun. "Thanks, Lex, I missed you, too."

My eyes stray to all the gyrating bodies writhing away in the dining room. The music is pumping, the lights are low, and I'm totally feeling it. Downing the rest of my beer in one fell swoop, I grab hold of Lexie's hand before dragging her toward the makeshift dance floor.

Yep, this night has nowhere to go but up.

CHAPTER SIX

Roan King was just spotted disappearing upstairs with three lucky ladies. It's nice to see that the king of campus is back in full force and spreading the love around! KingOfCampus.com

Roan

At this point, I've pretty much stopped trying to tear my gaze away from her. Every time I make a concerted effort to do so, it somehow finds its way back again.

The attraction humming through my body is completely baffling. This girl isn't even my usual type. Like at all.

For one thing, she's got a ton of attitude. Can't exactly say I've ever stumbled across that before. And she doesn't want anything to do with me either. Which is another first. I probably shouldn't enjoy needling her as much as I do. But I can't seem to help myself, it's so damn easy. Not to mention entertaining.

Trying to be objective, I allow my gaze to slide over her body. The girl is all long lean lines with a high tight ass. I'm the first to admit that I usually go for a girl with a lot of soft curves. Big breasts, small nipped in waist, and a nicely rounded ass. This one— Ivy—isn't built like that at all.

She looks kind of...well...*flat*.

Plus, there's no ass to speak of.

But she's got legs for miles. I think they might actually start under her armpits.

And yet there's something about her. Something that has my gaze constantly shifting back to her. Like a puzzle I can't quite solve. Apparently, I won't be letting this go until I either figure it out or fuck her.

As much as I would like to fuck her and move on, I don't think that's going to happen. Although I could be wrong. For all I know, this could be some big show she's putting on. Playing hard to get or some shit like that.

You know what the most hilarious part of today has been?

As soon as I'd walked into my business ethics class, I'd spotted her with her hand covering her face like she was trying to hide from me.

Even now my lips twitch as I think about it.

Fucking cute as hell. Seriously.

"Dude, I don't like the look on your face."

My gaze slides to Dylan, who has sidled up to me while I was zoning out.

Going for nonchalant, I shrug. "What are you talking about?"

He nods toward the girls who are currently out there dancing their proverbial asses off. Even though Dylan self-admittedly doesn't have any moves whatsoever, he isn't about to leave his woman out there unattended. They've already drawn quite a crowd of horny guys.

And who can blame those dudes?

Both of them are sexy as hell. Lexie with all her sweet curves and Ivy with her tight athletic body moving with so much grace that it's mesmerizing.

Well, *I'm* mesmerized by it.

I take a quick peek around, noticing that I'm not the only one checking her out. My hand tightens around the green glass bottle I'm holding.

"Screwing around with her, dude, it's a bad idea."

I take a long pull from my beer not really wanting to hear what Dylan has to say on the subject. In all honesty, Dylan doesn't give a damn if I fuck Ivy. He only cares that fucking her could somehow inadvertently effect his relationship with Lexie. If I screw over her friend, he's going to end up hearing about it.

Apparently, my poker face isn't what it used to be because he keeps on yammering. "Lexie will kick your ass if you mess with Ivy. You know that, right?"

Yeah...he's not lying either.

Lexie will seriously do it. She might be small and pixie-like, but she can get her crazy on. I've seen her go ape shit. Plenty of times. It's not pretty. Although, if it's not happening to you specifically, then it's hilarious. You can just sit back and enjoy the show.

Been there, done that.

Even though I should deny it, I hear myself asking, "What if she's into it?"

Because come on... they're *always* into it. I've yet to meet a girl not into getting it on.

My gaze slides over her for the umpteenth time. The fluid way she moves her body has my balls tightening and my cock stirring with interest. I bet she's a freaking wildcat in bed. I wonder if she can bend her body into a whole bunch of sexy positions.

I should probably stop thinking about that while I'm standing around with Dylan.

He chuckles before lifting the bottle to his lips and taking a long pull. "Yeah. She's into you all right. I've never seen a girl want you *less*. It's actually pretty fucking hilarious. Don't think I'm not totally loving it, dude." He laughs again before his brows snap together and the smile falls clean off his face. "That's it, isn't it?"

I shoot him a look. "What the hell are you talking about?"

"She doesn't want you." He groans, "Christ...she's a challenge."

Since I can't deny that he's wrong, I don't say anything at all. It's called plausible deniability.

"Hey, King."

A pretty little blonde wraps herself around me. I give her an easy smile as my gaze flicks over the rest of her. Now this girl is definitely my type. Curvy and filled out in all the right places. A tight pink T-shirt with Greek letters stretches its way over her nicely rounded titties all the while showcasing a fair amount of cleavage.

I should totally be into this girl.

And yet, for some reason, my attention strays to the writhing bodies about twenty feet away from me. Specifically zeroing in on Ivy. Some dude has come up behind her and has his hands on her narrow waist. Instantly forgetting about the blonde nestled against me, I almost stalk over there when I see Ivy wiggle out of his grasp before sliding away.

"King?"

Blondie strokes her delicate hand over my chest as my gaze settles on hers.

She's certainly pretty, I'll give her that. And on any other night, I'd be giving her a lot more than that. But I'm just not feeling it tonight. Which is definitely strange, to say the least.

Unsure what to do, I take another drink of my beer. Normally, this would be the point in the evening where I wait for a chick to come on to me before finding a room upstairs to fool around in.

Already I know that's not going to happen.

For whatever reason, this girl who isn't even my type, is throwing off my whole game. I don't like it. I think Dylan is right—she's the first girl in I-don't-know-how-long, maybe ever, who isn't interested in being boned by me. Which, unfortunately, has me losing interest in all the other willing prospects craving my attention. Of which there are many.

That's some seriously perverse shit...right?

I'm no psychology major, but I'm pretty sure there's a name for wanting something you can't have. Although, quite honestly, I plan to have her. Hopefully tonight. This—whole I-don't-want-you shtick she's got going on is probably just that—*a shtick*.

"Hey, King, missed you over the summer."

Another hot chick has sidled up to me and is currently pressing her double D's against the side of my arm. I'm not complaining, I'm just saying. They both stare at me with longing and promise in their heated gazes.

I should take the pair of them upstairs and give them what they want.

Except...I know it's not really me they want. They want Roan King—the Barnett football star. The guy who will hopefully go in the first round of the NFL draft later this year. They want a piece of my notoriety. They want to be balled by the king of campus.

Yeah, yeah... I know, boo-hoo. Poor fucking Roan.

You know what? A year ago, two years ago, that shit wouldn't have bothered me at all. It didn't make one damn bit of difference why these girls were spreading their legs so easily. I just enjoyed that they were.

Trust me, I enjoyed it every single weekend. Sometimes more. Now it feels old and tired. If you can believe that. I know, it's difficult to wrap your mind around.

All these faceless strangers wanting to hang out with me all the time. But they don't know me. Hell, they don't know anything about me. Not the *real* me. I could be a freaking serial killer for all they care. They wouldn't give one damn shit.

Do you know how seriously messed up that is?

My gaze moves from the blonde clinging to me to the gorgeous brunette curled up under my other arm. It's obvious they would be willing to screw me together. Hell, they'd probably get off on it. One would be snapping action shots while the other was getting her brains fucked out. And the photos would end up plastered across that dumbass website that shadows my every move.

I'm not going to lie, just like all the easy chicks and my NFL prospect notoriety, the website devoted solely to me was flattering at first. Now it just irritates the hell out of me. I've had my ass chewed out by Coach on more than one occasion for pictures of me partying or getting it on with some random chick that were posted to that site or someone's Instagram.

So now I have to be more careful. I've started wearing a ballcap so I can move around campus unnoticed. It's completely ridiculous.

Even I know I'm not that fucking interesting.

I came here tonight prepared to celebrate the kickoff to yet another great year of college. Probably my last. I was going to down a few beers, maybe get laid, but I don't think that's going to happen anymore. Even though I have two beautiful women wrapped up in my arms, screwing them is the last thing on my mind.

Like a heat seeking missile, my gaze zeros in on the reason for my disinterest.

That's the moment I see that fuckwad lacrosse player, Finn McKenzie, dragging Ivy away. Damn, I should have never taken my eyes off her.

"Hey," Blondie gasps as I pull away from the pair of them without any explanation.

"King!" the brunette whines, "where are you going? I thought we were going to—"

Not wanting to take my gaze off her again, I throw a halfhearted apology over my shoulder. "Sorry, ladies. A friend needs me."

Well...that statement is up for interpretation.

What I've learned about Ivy is that she can be prickly and isn't impressed by my status like everyone else seems to be. Until I get a handle on what my game plan is, I'm not about to watch some douchebag player like Finn McKenzie swoop in and steal her away. Now, once I'm finished, he's more than welcome to take her off my hands.

Even though this party is jammed packed, the crowd parts so I have a clear path leading straight to Ivy. People are slapping my shoulder and back in greeting as I pass by. I don't bother acknowledging any of them. My eyes are totally focused on the way Finn is manhandling her upper arm.

I don't like it. Not one damn bit.

That's just one of the many differences between McKenzie and me. He's all brute strength and I'm finesse. Unless I'm on the football field. Then I'll pound your ass for looking at me sideways.

In case you haven't realized it yet—I don't care for Finn McKenzie. The guy is a total tool. He's a lacrosse player and thinks he's a big shit around here. Clearly, it chafes his ass that I'm the bigger shit. The dude thinks everything between us is a pissing match. And normally, I'm more than happy to oblige and give him a run for his money.

But that's not going to happen with Ivy. Until I get my head wrapped around her, she's mine. I'm calling dibs.

The music is loud, and people are laughing, talking, and shouting all around us. I slide in beside Ivy before snaking an arm around her. Finn blinks in surprise at my sudden arrival on the scene. I can't help but smirk in return.

Sure, there's a part of me that doesn't want to see Ivy get messed up with Finn and then there's another part that enjoys fucking with him. Sometimes it really is the simple pleasures in life you have to take the time to enjoy.

Finn's eyes narrow at me before sliding angrily back to Ivy. "Do you know this guy?"

I almost grin but don't, because even though I rode to the party with this girl and had my arm wrapped around her, she's blinking at me as if she doesn't know who the hell I am. Which would really make me look like some dipshit loser in front of Finn.

That's not a risk I'm willing to take.

I pull her against me before cutting in, "Ivy and I have a class together." Then I add a slow sly smile meant to get under his skin. "And we also happen to be neighbors."

If it's possible, his eyes narrow further until they're practically slits. If the sudden tick in his jaw is any indication, then, yeah, I'm totally getting to him.

"Well, that's great but we're having a *private* conversation. So, why don't you take off, King. I'm sure there are a dozen groupies waiting in line to get laid by the king of campus."

Ivy flinches at the ugly words.

My gaze drills into Finn's as I ask her in a tightly strung voice, "Is this guy bothering you, sweetheart?"

The endearment has Finn's face turning an ugly mottled shade of red like he's on the verge of blowing a gasket. I can't say his reaction doesn't please me.

He nods his head toward the door. "Let's get out of here, Ivy, so we can talk without all this noise."

Over my dead body is that happening. Unconsciously, my hold on her tightens.

For the first time since I've slid my arm around Ivy, she finally speaks up. "Now's not really a good time, Finn."

Frustrated by her answer and probably by the fact I'm here with my arm around her, Finn grits out, "You won't return any of my calls or text messages. How can we talk when you keep ignoring me?"

Hmm. That sounds suspiciously like they know each other. Since Ivy just returned from a trip abroad that had her out of the country for more than a year, I'm guessing they must have had a relationship prior to her leaving.

She shifts from one foot to the other before finally saying, "We'll sit down and talk this week, okay? I don't really want to get into it right now."

"Why not?" His eyes darken as he glares. "You suddenly part of King's pussy posse?"

Gasping, her eyes flare wide right before narrowing. I would have thought her voice would be cutting and angry, like it was when she dealt with me today. But it's not. She actually sounds hurt.

"Is that really what you think of me, Finn?" She waits a beat before adding with a little more heat, "If you do, then I don't understand why you're trying so hard to get back together with me."

He has the good grace to flush before shaking his head. Which is kind of hilarious, because Finn McKenzie is a big dude who tops out around six foot two with broad shoulders. Although I'm six three with broader shoulders.

What? I'm just saying...

Unfortunately, what I've gleaned from this conversation has confirmed my suspicions about their prior involvement. I'm curious about what happened between them for Ivy not to return his calls or text messages.

I'm about to run my hand over Ivy's slender back when she ducks out of my arms before stalking off without so much as a single word. She totally leaves us standing there with our dicks in our hands like a couple of douchebags.

Although that certainly doesn't mean we aren't going to take a few parting shots at each other. Old habits die hard.

Finn steps into my space, his eyes hardening. "Stay the fuck away from her, King."

Amused, I raise a brow at his tone. Is this guy serious? Does he really think he can scare me off like I'm some damn freshman pussy who's intimidated by the likes of him?

Fat fucking chance of that happening.

I'm not worried about getting into a fight with freaking McKenzie. I've got a good thirty pounds of muscle on him. And in case you're wondering, Finn's no slouch in the muscle department. I just so happen to have more. Neither of us are afraid to throw a punch which means this could explode into one hell of an ugly brawl in the blink of an eye.

"And if I don't?" My words are quietly spoken but he hears them well enough over the noise pressing in on us.

"I'll fucking come after you so hard, you'll have to skip the draft this year."

Hands tightening at my sides, my eyes narrow as heat and rage leap into them. God, I would love to kick this guy's ass. It would be cathartic. "You threatening me, McKenzie?"

He takes a step away, an unexpected smile gracing his lips. "Nope. Just telling you to back off. Ivy's not one of the trashy groupies you're constantly dipping your dick in. She's way too good for someone like you."

With that he leaves me standing there...dick in hand.

As I watch him go, I suddenly wonder what the hell I'm doing. I don't know this Ivy chick at all. I've only just met the girl today. Why does she have me wound so tightly around the axel? Shaking my head, I turn around only to find Dylan watching me.

Yep. He definitely looks pissed off.

Fuck.

Maybe I need to get laid after all. Maybe that'll be enough to wipe this girl from my thoughts. As the crowd parts, three girls I recognize cling to my arms.

Yeah.

I think this is *exactly* what I need.

Ivy who?

That's right...

That's *exactly* right.

CHAPTER SEVEN

Were you one of the lucky ladies Roan was with Monday night? If so, be a doll and give us all the down and dirty details so we can live vicariously through you. Come on now, you know you're dying to share them... KingOfCampus.com

I'm sorry. Forgive me?

Biting my lip, I stare at the newest text from Finn. He's been blowing up my phone for days. He wants to get together and talk. Which probably means he wants to work things out. The problem is that he really hurt me, and I don't know if I can let that go. Rather stupidly, I'd thought we had something special and within a week or so of me leaving for Paris, he was already hooking up with other girls.

Lexie had never cared for Finn to begin with, so she'd been more than happy to send me a photo every time she saw him out with another girl. Needless to say, I have about forty pictures.

I'm not really sure what to do about the Finn situation. Deciding to ignore the text, I shove the phone back into my bag. It's Saturday morning and I've just taught three tap and ballet classes back-to-back. I should be tired. Teaching fifty-five-minute-long classes to four and five year olds is exhausting. I'd forgotten just how short their little attention spans could be. But they're so dang adorable and full of life that their energy is infectious.

I throw a light pink, off-the-shoulder T-shirt over my leotard before pulling on black leggings and a pair of leopard print ballet flats. Grabbing my bag, I wave goodbye to Donna, the owner of the studio, before pushing my way through the door into the brightly shining sun which strokes my skin with warmth.

I'm not more than two steps from the studio when I spot Finn leaning against the wall of the building with his hands shoved deeply into the pockets of his cargo shorts. He straightens to his full height as soon as our eyes connect. Surprised to find him here, my feet grind to a halt.

"Hi, Ivy."

A tentative smile slides its way across his face as if he's unsure of what my reaction will be. It makes him look boyishly sweet and hesitant. His normally overconfident, cocksure self is notably absent. Which is probably for the best. The expression tugs at something deep inside, reminding me how good-looking Finn is and how easy it was to fall for him freshman year. It's that side of him that drew me in.

"I was hoping we could maybe grab a coffee," he clears his throat, "that is if you're not too busy."

Lexie and I are planning on doing a little apartment shopping after lunch which means that—yes, I do have time to grab coffee but that doesn't necessarily mean I'm ready to sit down with Finn and hash out our past.

When I remain silent, his expression turns pleading, making him look downright adorable. Like a cuddly puppy dog I want to wrap my arms around and squeeze tight.

"Please, Ivy? I just want to talk."

His imploring expression has me folding like a shaky house of cards before I'm able to think better of it. I can only comfort myself with the fact that at some point, we would have probably sat down to talk about what happened between us. So, if not now, then later. Better to get it over with.

I give him a tight nod before hugging my oversized bag closer to my body. "Okay, but I can't stay long. I have plans later." It's not that I'm trying to play games but what I do with my time is no longer Finn's concern. Just like what he does isn't any of mine.

Emotion flares in his hazel eyes before he quickly tamps it down. Instead of fishing for information, he inclines his head toward the shop on the other side of the street. "How about a smoothie?"

Damn but he knows me so well.

After being in the studio for three solid hours with only water to hydrate with, a smoothie sounds absolutely fantastic. I have to admit there's something comfortable about falling back into a friendship with someone who knows all the little things you enjoy. I give myself a mental slap, because that's definitely not a reason to get back together with Finn.

"Okay, sure."

Wordlessly we cross the street before heading inside the shop and ordering our drinks. I get a pomegranate berry smoothie and Finn orders a strawberry banana one which is exactly what we always ordered when we were together. Once we have our drinks, we head outside to sit at one of the little café tables in front of the brick build-ing. It's gorgeous out. I want to soak it all up before the nice days are few and far in between.

With the sun beating down upon us, we both sit, sipping from our straws for a moment before Finn finally says, "Look Ivy, I want to apol-ogize for my behavior the other night. I honestly didn't mean to piss you off." He glances away before quietly continuing. "It took me by surprise that you seemed so chummy with King. That you're already on his radar. I mean, you just got back from France."

Not that I owe him any kind of explanation, but I guess it feels somewhat warranted. We did date for about six months during my freshman year before I left Barnett. "Honestly, I don't know Roan at all." I give a little shrug. "He lives next door and he's in one of my classes. So we've run into each other. That's the extent of our rela-tionship."

Looking slightly agitated, Finn runs a hand through his thick mahogany colored hair which is cut short on the sides and left longer on top as his greenish-brown eyes drill into mine. "Do me a favor and stay away from him, Ivy. Roan is nothing more than a douchebag player and everyone at Barnett knows it. He'll nail anything with a heartbeat, and he doesn't look back once he does. You're way too good for that."

I can't figure out if it's jealousy or genuine concern that has him issuing the warning. "I appreciate the advice, Finn, but I have zero interest in the guy."

Okay...so that isn't altogether true because he's absolutely gorgeous but after that first run in with him (and obviously the second), I'd already figured out he was the worst kind of trouble there is. And in the subsequent days since, my opinion has only solidified. People naturally flock to him. Especially girls. Every time I catch a glimpse of him around campus, there are at least three or four girls vying for his attention.

Thankfully, we haven't had any more exchanges since that party. Not only have I been avoiding Finn, I've been avoiding Roan as well. It also helps that I'm taking eighteen credits, working ten hours a week at *On Pointe*, and spending every spare moment I can in the dance studio working on chorography.

I don't have time to dwell on a cheating ex-boyfriend or the campus demigod.

Apparently satisfied with my answer, Finn's big shoulders relax as he settles back in his chair. His gaze probes mine before he quietly admits, "I really missed you, Ivy." Now that we've settled the whole Roan King issue, the sad puppy dog look is back in full force.

I almost snort. All those damn photos filed away in a computer folder titled—*douchebag ex-boyfriend* tell a different story. I'm not sure why he's bothering to go back down this road again.

Instead of responding, I raise a brow and suck my straw.

His gaze falls to my lips and remains there for a long drawn out moment before swinging back up to mine. "I know I broke things off right after you left for Paris." His brows draw together as he pauses. "I guess it was just too hard to think about having a long-distance commitment when we'd only been together for about six months."

I'd been plagued with the same thoughts. I'd really liked Finn and had wanted to try and make things work between us. Rather foolishly, I had hoped he liked me enough to want that as well. Instead, he'd baled within two weeks (if not sooner), leaving me to feel disconnected and depressed.

Which, in hindsight, had been just plain crazy because I'd been in Paris, for god's sake. Who the hell can be all sad bastard in Paris? Well...yeah, me apparently. After a few weeks of moping around, I'd pulled myself out of the funk I'd slid into by walking around the city and immersing myself in the rich culture.

"I was kind of hoping we could give it another shot, you know? Pick up where we'd left off." Slowly he reaches across the table before laying his hand over mine. "I still care about you, Ivy." Something changes in his eyes. A look of vulnerability fills his gaze that I find almost impossible to ignore. "Do you still have feelings for me?"

I stare at our stacked hands as I contemplate the question.

Do I still have feelings for Finn?

We broke up almost fifteen months ago and were basically incommunicado the entire time I was gone. I had relegated Finn McKenzie to the *just a guy I had once dated* category. No one was more surprised than me when he started bombarding me with text messages about a week before I came home.

After the way he'd hurt me, there was no way I was responding. In fact, I believe the words—*he can go screw himself* were bandied about in my conversations with Lexie more than a few times.

And yeah, part of me does still feel that way...but I can't deny that I'm torn. I mean, we were together for six months. Not to mention those pathetic puppy dog eyes he keeps casting my way.

I can practically feel myself caving.

Taking a deep breath, I force it out slowly before replying truthfully, "I don't know, Finn." My eyes fasten onto his as I allow him a small glimpse of my heartache. "The way you ended things," I begin softly, "I was away from everything, everyone I knew, trying to get acclimated to a totally different culture. What you did was devastating." Even thinking about it brings back a surge of anger and sadness within me.

Looking remorseful, he nods as if he completely understands what he did was wrong. And maybe he really does.

Who knows...

"I want a chance to show you that I'm not the same guy I was back then." Angling his body toward me, he leans closer. His gaze pleading with mine. "I'm sure you've grown and changed in the fifteen months you were gone...well, so have I. Give me a chance to prove that to you. We were so good together, Ivy." His eyes search mine. "Weren't we?"

Hundreds of unbidden memories tumble their way through my head as we sit and talk. We did have fun together. I'd fallen really hard for Finn freshman year. With my front teeth sinking into my lower lip, I mull over the possibility of starting something up with him again.

If Lexie knew I was contemplating the idea of giving Finn another chance, she would string me up alive. For whatever reason, she'd never liked him. Not even in the beginning when I'd started seeing him. She thought he was nothing more than a cocky player who was running a game on me.

I'd never felt that way. Well, not until she started sending me all those pictures.

He'd been so sweet. Taking me out to eat. Walking me to class. Showing up with flowers. Little things like that. Gestures that had burrowed easily under my skin. And I guess, because of the situation with my dad, I'd been desperate to find someone to love. Someone to feel connected to since I didn't necessarily have that with my family.

When I'd first arrived at Barnett, even though Lexie and I were rooming together, I'd still felt a bit lost. The death of my mom when I'd been fifteen had all but devastated me. And my dad remarrying six months later had only made the situation worse.

Right before the end of first semester, I'd met Finn at a party, and he had literally swept me off my feet. I mean, everyone on campus knew who Finn McKenzie was. Superstar stud lacrosse player. He was bright and handsome and well liked.

The fact he'd sought me out to spend time with had made me feel special during a time when I hadn't felt special to anybody. Not since my mother had died. In the six months we were together, not once had I ever suspected he might be cheating or seeing other girls behind my back.

Not until Lexie started bombarding me with all those photos. After a while, I stopped looking at them. I kept them in a file and watched the number of pictures grow until everything I'd felt for Finn was gone.

And now here he is. Fifteen months later. Wanting a second chance.

Had he changed?

Had he matured?

He definitely *looked* more mature. In the time I'd been gone, he'd lost the last of his cute boyishness. His handsome face was all chiseled planes and angles. His body was bigger. Shoulders wider. Waist tapered. He was even more attractive than when I'd first met him two years ago.

Were the changes more than physical in nature? Did it matter anymore if they were? I couldn't help but admit there was something easy about falling back into a relationship with a guy who had once meant something to me. A person who knew what I liked and didn't like. By the same token, that relationship already had baggage attached to it.

I needed to figure which one outweighed the other.

"I don't know," I finally murmur. Not because I'm trying to be coy or play games but because I genuinely don't know what to do.

His hazel gaze burns into mine. "I'm asking for a chance, Ivy," he finally says, "just one to prove that I've grown and changed."

Unable to hold his eyes any longer, my gaze falls to our connected hands. All of the good times we'd had swim through my head and before I realize it, the words are tumbling out of my mouth. "Okay. One date."

His lips pull up at the corners as he gently squeezes my hand. "You won't regret it, I promise."

I have the feeling that I probably will regret giving him another chance...

Especially when I tell Lexie.

CHAPTER EIGHT

I just heard that some lucky girl got partnered up with our very own legend on the football field in a business ethics class. Damn... I knew I should have stuck it out with that major... KingOfCampus.com

"For the next six weeks, you're going to work with a partner on a project that will be worth sixty percent of your final grade." She pauses as shocked gasps ripple throughout the room. Apparently expecting just such a reaction, Professor Paulson nods her head as if to reconfirm what we're all hoping we somehow misheard. "Yes, that's right. *Sixty percent.* It will be worth more than anything else you do in here, so keep that in mind when working on it. Not only does the topic need to be well researched, it will have to be completely fleshed out, so it supports the main idea of your project."

Another round of groaning along with disbelieving chatter grips the class. Her eyes slowly encompass all of us. "The end result of your time and energy spent researching will be a thought-provoking paper twenty pages in length." Holding up her hand, she cuts off the sudden conversations that have sprung up.

"Okay, quiet down. Quiet down, please." She clears her throat before glancing at the clipboard she's holding in her hand. "I'm going to run through the class list and pair everyone up today. We're going to spend about ten minutes going over my expectations in more depth and then you'll have about fifteen minutes of class time to work with your partner."

Feeling just as stupefied as the rest of the class, I sit silently in my seat as Professor Paulson runs through the list of students enrolled in her course. After she reads off the second set of names, it becomes apparent that she's pairing people up alphabetically. Something in my heart clenches as she reads off my name. Unless there's someone else that falls between Kaster and King, I'm—

"Ivy Kaster and Roan King."

—*screwed.*

My gaze reluctantly cuts across the room to Roan. I'm startled to realize that he's already angled his body toward me. There's a hint of a smirk sliding its way across his handsome face.

I gulp.

No.

No. No. No.

I can't work with him.

This is a massive project and there's no way in hell I'm going to get stuck doing all the work by myself. With the eighteen-credit course load I have and working ten hours a week, I don't have the time it would take to complete a project of this scope and magnitude on my own.

Before I can work myself into a tizzy, Professor Paulson hands out a packet to each of us regarding what we're going to be working on for the next six weeks. My heart sinks further when I read through the expectations.

Shit.

Sixty percent of my grade is riding on Roan King. I almost laugh at such an absurd thought. The freaking king of campus, with his—what did Finn call them? Oh, that's right...his *pussy posse*, is holding my grade for Business Ethics in his huge hulking hands.

Nope. I can't allow that to happen. I need to work with someone who actually gives a damn about their grade and is going to do their fair share of the workload. I need someone who is serious about this class...and school, for that matter.

And I just don't think that's the resident demigod football player.

I mean, he barely takes notes in class while all I do is tap away on my laptop from the very start to the end of class. My guess is that he's probably here on a football scholarship. From what I've heard, he's not even going to finish up his degree before he turns pro. He probably doesn't give a crap if he passes or fails.

But I do.

I'm here on an academic scholarship and I can't afford to lose it.

Once Dr. Paulson goes through the packet, and we're allowed to get together with our partners, I scurry toward her desk. Not wanting to catch Roan's eyes, I keep my gaze trained straight ahead.

That unfortunately, doesn't work.

"Hey, where you going?" he calls out as I hustle toward the front of the room.

Guilt floods through me as I shoot him a quick look, not allowing my eyes to linger. "I have a few questions for Professor Paulson. I'll be right there."

Once beside her, I give her an apologetic look because this is only the second week of school and I don't want her to think I'm difficult. On the other hand, there's no way I'm getting stuck with deadweight either.

I really hate group work.

Sitting at a desk off to the side, she glances over the black frames of her glasses. "Question, Ms. Kaster?"

Awkwardness descends at the thought of discussing this with Roan sitting twenty feet away from me. "Um, well, I was wondering if it's at all possible to be reassigned to a different partner."

If the slow blinking of her light blue eyes is any indication, then I've completely thrown her for a loop. She'd probably assumed I had scurried up here to thank her for partnering me with him. She couldn't be farther from the truth.

"Do you have a problem working with Mr. King?"

At the mention of his name, I can't help but hastily glance over my shoulder to where Roan is sitting. My face floods with heat as my eyes catch his quizzical ones. Turning back toward her, I lower my voice before admitting my concerns. "I, ah...this is a really huge project and I want to be paired with someone who is going to do their share of the work." When she doesn't immediately respond, fresh nerves spiral through me as I shuffle from one foot to the other.

One brow slowly hikes up her forehead as she contemplates me for a long silent moment that leaves me filled with unease. Her words are sharp and low when she finally asks, "And you already know that Mr. King won't be able to contribute his fair share to the project?"

If I weren't already blushing, I would be now. My gaze slides away from hers before I force it back. "Um, well, I just thought—"

Abruptly her slim hand slices between us and my words fall off. "There will be absolutely no reassignment of partners for any reason other than someone dropping the class. And I do not believe Mr. King will be dropping this class." If it's possible, her eyes harden even more until they resemble cold little chips of ice.

"A hard truth you apparently need to learn, Ms. Kaster, is that we don't always work with the people we want to. Bosses, co-workers...we often find ourselves at odds with them but still, we must find a way to compromise and work together for the greater good." She levels me with one last frosty glare that leaves me wilting beneath it.

"I suggest you find a way to work with Mr. King for the greater good of this project otherwise both of your grades will suffer for it." She glances rather pointedly at the thin gold watch adorning her wrist, signaling that this subject has been firmly closed. "Now, I suggest you use the next ten minutes wisely to discuss possible topics with your partner."

Feeling very much like a recalcitrant child, I nod before skulking down the aisle to where Roan is sitting with his long legs spread out in front of him. There's a slight frown marring his face as his focus burns into me. Even though my gaze is lowered, I still feel him staring.

"Get everything squared away?" There's a distinct edge to his normally lazy sounding voice.

With my face flushed, I force my eyes to his. "Yep."

Glancing at the five-page packet stapled together, I clear my throat uncomfortably. It's pretty damn obvious I'm going to be the brains of this operation. And, unfortunately, the labor as well. Roan will add his name to the byline after the project has been completed and that, apparently, will be his big contribution.

Even though I've been all but chastised by Professor Paulson for trying to switch partners, I'm starting to work myself up all over again because my scholarship rides on being able to maintain a 3.5 grade point average. I can't afford to lose it. And I'm certainly not going to let getting stuck with this Neanderthal as a partner stand in the way of getting an A in this course. So, if that means I'm going to have to do the workload of two people to eek out that A, then that's exactly what I'm going to do.

"I was thinking we could go the case study route instead of the informal content analysis." Because the main component to analyzing a case study would be research. And research is something I can handle on my own. Even though it'll take a lot of time I don't have. But there isn't another choice. I can't drop this course, it's a requirement. I need it to graduate.

Roan continues staring at me through semi-narrowed eyes before nodding his head in agreement. "That sounds fine to me."

Since Roan probably won't be contributing anything more than that, I'm not really sure what else we have to discuss. Glancing at the clock on the wall, I notice we have about five minutes. I don't see a point in sticking around any longer. I'm meeting Lexie for lunch and then I have French and dance. And I—

"You're leaving already?"

His words snap me right out of my thoughts. "Um, well, yeah."

I'm shoving the packet into my bag when he asks, "Don't you want to discuss what kind of case study we're going to focus on or when we can get together and work on it?"

For a moment, I stand there gaping at him in surprise. "Ummm, is that what you want to do?"

The hard line of his jaw tightens as his normally smirking mouth settles into an annoyed slash across his handsome face. "Yeah, Ivy...it is. This is a massive project worth more than half the points in this class. I have a tight schedule with my course load, practice, games, and working out, so I'd like to get something firm nailed down as soon as possible. I can't afford to wait until the last minute."

I blink, feeling totally blindsided by what he's said because it kind of sounds like he actually plans on contributing to this project.

When I don't immediately respond, he leans forward, his heated blue-green eyes sparking with anger. "You don't have to look so damned shocked. Contrary to what you believe, I have every intention of doing my share of the workload."

My mouth tumbles open before I snap it shut. He gathers up his books, shoves them into his backpack and stalks out of the room before I can stutter out an embarrassed apology. As soon as he does, three girls huddle around me, blasting me with rapid fire questions all the while gushing about how lucky I am to be working with Roan King.

I can only smile halfheartedly before collecting my stuff and leaving. I think I just made a huge tactical error regarding this guy. Is it possible that Roan isn't the dumb jock I pegged him to be? I almost wince because I usually don't make snap judgements about people. For some reason, I assumed Roan was coasting through college on his football prowess and good looks.

Maybe that's not the case.

Maybe there's more to him than I'd initially suspected.

CHAPTER NINE

Anyone get invited to the little get together happening at Roan King's apartment? If so, someone needs to share the four-one-one with all of us. Pictures are, as always, welcomed and appreciated. Preferably naked ones...
KingOfCampus.com

"When are you planning to come home for a visit, Ivy? You've been back in town for about three weeks now and we still haven't seen you."

I'm standing on the tiny balcony off our living room, facing the western sky. I didn't think I would enjoy having an outdoor space as much as I do. Whenever I'm home in the evening, I somehow find myself out here when the sun is setting. I love watching all the varying shades of red and pink that paint their way across the horizon. It usually brings me a certain amount of peace. My very own little bit of Zen.

That, unfortunately, is not the case tonight.

"Ivy, are you still there?"

"Um, yeah." Then I add, "Just thinking about my schedule. School and work are crazy busy right now." This is completely true. "I really want to find some time to get together with you guys." I think we all know this one is a whopper of a lie. As much as I love my dad, I have zero interest in spending time with his wife and their kids. "I'm just not sure when I can get away. I'll look into it and get back to you."

"Sure, honey, that sounds good."

I wince at the disappointment that weaves its way through his deep voice. I honestly wouldn't mind if he came here and grabbed dinner or something like that but Leah, his wife, finds it necessary to be included in everything we do. It's annoying to deal with her in order to have a relationship with my dad. It's like she can't bear to be left out even though she's with him twenty-four seven. They have a set of four-year-old twins. Nora and Nolan. They were still toddlers when I left for Europe. I can only imagine what an obnoxious handful they are now.

"How's your apartment? Is it nice?"

Slowly turning around, my gaze skims over the now decorated walls of our living room. The cozy tan couch and matching armchair that were cast offs from Lexie's parents and the forty-inch TV which Dylan promptly bought an Xbox for. I almost shake my head. Right there should have been my biggest tipoff that he would be, for the most part, shacking up with us. "Yeah, it's really nice. There are two bedrooms, one bathroom, a small kitchen, and a living room. There's even a balcony big enough for a small table and two chairs."

"Are you in a safe area? I know you have to walk to your job."

Not that he can see it, but I almost roll my eyes. I lived abroad for more than a year and somehow managed to survive without any parental involvement. I think I can handle living at Barnett again. "It's perfectly safe. Our apartment is two blocks from campus and my job is about a mile away. The dance studio is located downtown, so there are always plenty of people walking around. And a lot of times, Lexie drives me."

"That's good. I'm glad everything is working out for you, Ivy."

That being said, we lapse into an awkward silence. The distance between us feels palpable. And living abroad for almost a year and a half has only made it more so. Just as I'm racking my brain for something to say, obnoxiously loud music is blasted from the apartment next to us.

"Did you just turn your stereo on?"

I snort.

A small smile tugs at the corners of my lips. "No one has a stereo anymore, Dad. And no, it's the guys who live next to us." Stepping toward the edge of the tiny space, I lean over the black iron railing, trying to see past the privacy wall that separates our balcony from Roan, Sam, and Dylan's.

"Well, it's certainly loud."

"Yeah, it is." A sliding door opens and closes before boisterous voices fill the air. "I'd better get going, Dad, I still have some work to finish up." Since it's Friday night, I don't plan on doing anything school related. But it's a good excuse to pull the plug on this conversation. "I'll talk to you soon."

"Just think about coming home for a visit, okay? Leah's excited to hear all about your apartment and trip to Paris. She picked up a house-warming gift for you and Lexie."

"Okay. I'll let you know." I'm thinking *never* would be a good time. Even though I know I'll have to plan a trip home at some point, my strategy is to put it off for as long as possible. Like Thanksgiving.

We both say I love you before disconnecting. A moment later, Lexie sticks her head out the sliding door. "Whatcha up to, Ivy-girl?"

Talking with my dad always puts me in a maudlin mood. It never fails to remind me that we're no longer the tight knit family we once were. And that's a bitter pill to swallow on the best of days. Having to watch Leah snuggle up to my dad is still a painful reminder that he moved on in the blink of an eye.

Nolan and Nora were born almost a full year after my mother's death, so I know they must have gotten together almost immediately after Mom passed away. And once Dad sat me down and dropped the bomb that he'd knocked up his co-worker, she moved right on in.

I never really gave Leah much of a chance.

I mean seriously...how could I?

Every time I looked at her or those kids, all I could think about was how she slid unwantedly into our grieving family before my mom's dead body was even cold.

Setting my phone down on the small glass café-style table, I shrug as if it's no big deal. "Just talking to my dad."

Lexie's eyes widen. She knows all about the unresolved issues my dad and I are still struggling with. Lexie was there when my mom got sick in eighth grade. And she was there to comfort me when Mom died the summer before my sophomore year. She was also there four months later when my father announced out of nowhere that he had impregnated Leah and was now getting remarried.

After that, I spent as much time as I could camped out at Lexie's house. I would have moved in with her family if I could have, but Dad wouldn't allow it. So, I was stuck living with him, his baby mama, and their squalling twins that were born before the start of my junior year of high school.

My dad's modus operandi is to sweep all the ugliness from the past neatly under the rug and pretend everything is hunky-dory. Both he and Leah walk around with their heads up their asses and I'm the fly in the ointment that refuses to go along with it. It's just easier for all involved to have these fake conversations and keep my distance until I'm finally able to support myself.

Her pretty face fills with compassion. "Everything good with him?"

"Always sunny and perfect in John Kaster's la-la land." I give her a mocking smile that feels brittle around the edges. "Come on, you know that."

One side of her mouth hitches in sympathy as she folds her arms across her ample chest. "Is he coming here for a visit? It's been about sixteen months since you've seen him."

Glancing away, I murmur, "I told him I'd check my schedule and get back to him with a date that works."

Because she knows me so well, she snorts. "Do you actually have any intention whatsoever of getting back to him?"

"Nope." I pop the P at the end.

Rather sadly, she shakes her head. "I didn't think so." Lexie moves from the doorway to the small table that is almost too big for our teeny tiny balcony before pulling out a chair and throwing herself down. Gently she says, "Maybe it's time for you to let it go, Ivy. I mean, you've already lost one parent, do you really want to lose him, too?"

Her words catch me so off guard that it feels like I've been sucker punched in the gut. My eyes instantly well with unspent emotion. When I'm finally able to wrap my lips around the words, they sound all rough and gravelly. "Are you really saying that to me?" She, out of everybody, knows what I've been through. She knows how my dad moved on with his life and expected that I would do the same.

She winces but holds my gaze in a forthright manner that only someone who knows you inside and out can do. "Yeah," she sighs, "I guess I am. Look, you know how much I loved your mother. She was like a mom to me, too. What your father did sucked big time. There's no question about it. And you can certainly continue freezing him out or you can finally make amends and try to rebuild your relationship into a better one. *A real one*."

Unconsciously my hand rises to rub at the flesh over my heart which now throbs harshly with grief. "How can I even begin to forgive him, Lex?" Even though it feels impossible, I force out the words. "It's like he didn't care about my mom at all. How do you hookup with someone within months of your wife," my voice catches on the last word, "*dying?*"

She shakes her head before admitting softly, "I don't know. But maybe it's something the two of you need to talk about. Maybe it's time to finally discuss all the shit you both have been trying to ignore for years."

The thought of doing that has my skin prickling with unease. I can't imagine just such a conversation. Instead of entertaining the idea, I shut it down. "Thanks for the advice, Dr. Phil. I'll think it over."

I have absolutely no intention of considering Lexie's words or fixing what is broken between us. Dad obviously doesn't give a shit about me or he wouldn't have married someone else so quickly.

Thankfully, we're saved from further conversation when Dylan leans around the barrier separating our balconies.

"Hey, gorgeous." He gives Lexie a big goofy grin. If I didn't love Lexie like a sister from another mister, I'd be jealous of just how into her Dylan seems to be. And I love it. Love that she's found someone who cares so much about her.

She gives him a little wink along with a sassy smile in return. "Right back at you, hot stuff."

And just like that, we've once again veered toward puke-ville.

"You two lovely ladies gonna get your asses over here or what?"

I shoot Lexie a questioning look. Of course, with all that loud music, I can pretty much guess what's going on over there. These guys seem to have people coming and going all the time. Not that I'm paying attention or anything (although it's hard not to) but a lot of them just so happen to be women. And when that's the case, Dylan clears out and spends time at our apartment, hence the brand-new shiny Xbox we have.

Lexie raises a brow at me in silent inquiry before saying, "Yep, we're on our way."

"See you in a few." And with that, Dylan disappears back around the privacy fence.

Once we're alone, she says, "They're having a few people over. You coming?"

I wouldn't mind hanging out for a bit, but I know Roan will be there. We haven't spoken since he verbally handed my ass to me a few days ago in our Business Ethics class. So, that kind of feels like an awkward situation waiting to explode in my face.

And I'm damn tired of that happening when it comes to him.

At some point, we're going to have to work together on this project. Since I'm the one who assumed he was nothing more than a meathead jock, I guess it should probably be me who sucks it up and extends an olive branch so we can smooth things over and move on with our lives.

God, but I so don't want to do that.

Is there anything worse than having to eat crow?

Nope, not really.

"Yeah, I'll come for a little bit," I mutter.

With a smile lighting up her face, she looks pleasantly surprised by my easy capitulation. "Awesome." She pops to her feet before heading toward the sliding doors. "I'm going to change and then we can get moving."

"Sounds good." I look down at the comfy shorts and tank I'm wearing. I suppose if I'm going to eat crow, I should probably change into something a little nicer.

Fifteen minutes later, we're ready to head over to the guy's apartment. It sounds as if there are about a hundred people crammed inside it. Lexie is wearing black short shorts with a red sleeveless shirt that accentuates her bustiness. A pair of black wedge sandals gives her some extra height. Her long auburn hair is piled on top of her head.

Lexie is a fashion major. She's already rifled through the clothes I brought back from Paris and pulled ones that she is *borrowing* indefinitely. Which actually means in Lexie-speak that I shan't be seeing them again.

She enjoys assessing what I've chosen and then sending me back to my room to change into what she thinks I should wear instead. In what I now recognize to be an error in judgement, I humored her the first couple of times it happened which has now established a pattern of behavior I'm finding difficult to break.

As expected, her mouth slides down at the corners as her narrowed eyes sweep critically over the selection I've thrown on for the evening. "I was hoping you would wear the little blue skirt with the floral off-the-shoulder short sleeve blouse." Her eyes light with excitement. "And then the pink ballet flats you have." She actually claps her hands together with enthusiasm. "Oh my god, that would look so good! You *have* to go change!"

Because she's so dang excited and she's probably right anyway, I head back to my room. When I reappear five minutes later, she practically jumps up and down in her wedges. "I knew that would look amazing!"

I hate to admit it, but she's right. And since she usually is, I seldom bother arguing with her. I try to look at this as having my own in-house stylist and that makes me feel marginally better. Because the skirt is short and I have fairly long legs, I can get away with wearing flats which I absolutely love. Dancing, especially ballet, is hard on your feet. I'll take flats over heels every single time. So, I appreciate her taking this into consideration.

Now that we're ready to go, Lexie links her arm through mine as we walk down the well-lit hall toward the guy's apartment. She doesn't bother knocking but pushes open the door instead. All of the laughter, chatter, and music from inside comes pouring out into the hallway. Most of the tenants in this building are college-aged students, so obnoxiously cranked up music and noise on a Friday night is the norm and therefore perfectly acceptable.

Stepping inside, I weave my way through all the people standing around in clumps talking. As soon as Dylan catches sight of Lexie, he pushes through the thick crowd toward us. Once he reaches her side, he pulls her into his arms, kissing her soundly on the mouth. They stay fused together for a good minute before I actually have to clear my throat. And yeah, there's a whole lot of tongue action happening.

Which isn't awkward at all...

Finally coming up for air, Lexie gives me a sheepish grin as Dylan continues holding her close as if he can't stand to be parted from her for even a moment.

I can't resist admitting, "You guys are totally sickening. You know that, right?"

Lexie's smile intensifies a couple thousand watts until I can barely stand to look at her. "Don't worry, we'll find a guy for you, too. That's one of my missions this year."

I really hope she's joking about that. "I don't need a guy," I groan. The last thing I want is for Lexie to try working her voodoo matchmaking magic on me. Been there, done that. It never works out in the end. I suppose if I get desperate enough, I could always tell her about the date I have tomorrow night with Finn.

Since I know exactly what type of ugly response that will elicit, I decide to keep my mouth shut. I'm hoping I'll be able to sneak out without telling her about it since the last thing I need is for her to pull up all those pictures she snapped of him last year in some desperate attempt at tough love.

"Sure, you do."

I shake my head. "Nope, I really don't." Needing to escape this conversation before she actually starts dragging guys over for an impromptu version of *the Dating Game* (FYI—she likes to bring up embarrassing stories from our childhood), I mumble, "I'm going to get something to drink." The words barely make it out of my mouth before I'm walking away.

The crowd is elbow-to-elbow in here. There has to be at least fifty people jammed into their living/dining room combination. And the noise level is just shy of deafening. Looking around for a familiar face, I realize that most the guys here have big bulging muscles. And more than a few look to have no neck whatsoever. Which is always a weird phenomenon. So, I'm guessing these are fellow teammates.

And the girls...I've noticed there are way more females than guys present and a lot of them are scantily clad and clinging to any male they can find.

In pairs.

I almost roll my eyes. It's doubtful I'll be hanging out here for long. As I grab a beer from the fridge, I catch a glimpse of Roan in the living room. Because of his height, he's hard to miss. Of course, he's surrounded by a thick group of people at least two deep.

And yes, most of them are female with teeny tiny shirts over big round breasts and micro skirts that barely cover their asses. God help them if they need to bend over.

We're talking beaver galore...

My intention in coming here had been to work up the courage to apologize for jumping to conclusions about him. So that's exactly what I'm going to do and then I can get the hell out of here. This really isn't my scene. And quite honestly, before Lexie started dating Dylan, it wouldn't have been hers either.

We usually hang with a more artistic-minded crowd.

Slowly making my way toward him, I mentally rehearse a short but sweet apology that will smooth things over between us. When I'm about fifteen feet away, our gazes collide. More surprising than that is the way they hold as I force myself to close the distance separating us. A little shiver of awareness skitters its way down my spine as his turquoise-colored eyes impale me.

A moment later, he breaks away from the crowd still clamoring for his attention. Everyone's eyes focus on him as he makes his way to me.

"Hey." Slowly his gaze runs down the length of me. For a heartbeat or two, they linger on my bare legs. People have told me that I have legs up to my ears because of their length. I'm comfortable with it now, but when I was a kid, I was constantly outgrowing my pants. My mom had a hard time finding the longer lengths I needed which meant there were times when I looked like I was waiting around for a flood to roll through.

"Looking good, Ivy."

"Thanks." All of a sudden, my throat feels dry and scratchy. Damn him for always having this kind of effect on me.

With his gaze locked on mine, he takes a slow pull from the green bottle in his hand. I feel caught in the crosshairs of his attention and it's an odd feeling. I want to hold my breath until he releases me from his gaze. But he's not looking away and I'm unable to hold my breath indefinitely.

Even though there are tons of people milling around, jostling or knocking into us, it feels as if it's just the two of us. I swear I can feel the enticing lure of him. As if I'm somehow drawn to him against my will. There's something indescribable about Roan that attracts both men and women and holds them captivated.

Needing to break the spell he's woven around me, I shake my head to clear it before ripping my attention away from his. I need to force out my apology and then get the hell out of here before my brain turns to mush. The way his gaze licked over my body is enough to have me spontaneously combusting on the spot. Liquid heat is already gathering in a place I'd rather not think about. To have all that smoldering sexiness aimed right at you for even twenty minutes would be as addicting as a drug.

No wonder they all want a piece of him.

No matter how small it is.

Trying to tamp down my body's natural reaction to him, I keep my eyes trained directly over his shoulder. Every once in a while, my gaze flickers toward his. As soon as they catch, mine skitters away nervously.

Clearing my throat, I force out the words. "I'm sorry about the other day."

He cocks his head before lifting the bottle to his lips again. As he takes another long pull, his focus stays glued to me. When he finally lowers the beer, he steps closer. So close that I can see all the ridiculously beautiful shades and flecks of green and blue that make up the brilliant hue of his eyes.

It's completely mesmerizing.

Even though the party surrounding us is loud, his voice is pitched low. "What exactly are you apologizing for?"

It feels as if my mouth has been stuffed full of cotton and I gulp painfully before answering. How does he do that? How does he twist me up into these tiny knots every time?

"I didn't think you were interested in pulling your weight on the project."

Something flashes in his eyes but it's there and gone so quickly I'm not able to identify the emotion that caused it.

Sounding deceptively flip, he comments, "You thought I'd leave you hanging, so you could do all the work by yourself, huh?"

Uncomfortable being put on the spot, I shift from one foot to the other before glancing away. "Yeah, I did."

He invades my personal space before strong fingers settle under my jaw. Slowly he turns my face until my eyes are ensnared within his brightly burning ones.

"You figured I was some dumbass jock who got passed along because of football." It's not a question. We both know that's exactly what I'd assumed.

The force of his hard-edged gaze feels relentless. I can't tell if it's anger propelling all that churning emotion within it or not.

"Yes," I whisper when I can't stand the intensity a moment longer, "that's what I thought." When I try ripping my attention away, he jerks my chin until it slides back to where he wants it.

On him.

He leans toward me before murmuring, "I'm more than football, Ivy." As those words drift over my ear, his fingers fall away. As they do, I inhale a huge gulp of air. Needing to put some physical distance between us, I scramble back a step. For some reason, my heart feels as if it's going to explode out of my chest.

Whatever this is between us...I don't like it.

I know damn well this is a game he's running on me. For goodness sake, he has this effect on everyone. I bet if he asked every single girl in this room to drop their panties right here, right now, the majority of them would actually do it. I'm nothing special to him and the last thing I want is to fall under the spell he's able to cast over me so easily.

In my haste to distance myself from him, I stumble backward. As my arms pinwheel, Roan grasps my biceps before jerking me toward him.

Neither of us say a word as his arms snake around me. It takes a moment to realize that I'm being all but crushed against that massive chest of his. Oh god, it's as hard and granite-like as I'd suspected. This sends my pulse skyrocketing as I quickly untangle myself from him before stepping neatly out of his embrace.

"Sorry," I mumble. I really need to get out of here before I become any more of a bumbling idiot and embarrass myself even further than I already have. For some reason, I'm acting exactly like one of the silly little twits that are constantly pawing at him.

And I'm not going to bother lying to myself by saying that I'm not attracted to Roan because clearly, I am. I was enthralled from the moment I spilled my coffee all over him. You would have to be blind not to think he's one of the most attractive men you've ever seen in your life. The problem is that he's aware of how good looking he is. He's used to girls hanging all over him. He uses them for his own selfish pleasure without any thought to their feelings at all.

Not that I'm feeling too much in the way of sympathy for these women. They know exactly what they're getting into when they hookup with him and that's nothing more than bragging rights.

And yeah, he's telling me he'll do his share of the workload for this project, but does that necessarily mean it's going to happen? Or that it'll be quality work?

Nope.

As much as I want to believe him, I don't. Not yet. All he's done up to this point is surprise me. Time will tell if he actually changes my opinion of him.

Holding out his palm, he says, "Give me your phone."

Now that my sexual haze has cleared enough for my braincells to function again, my brows snap together. There is absolutely no way in hell I want him adding my number to his contact list of conquered co-eds.

Umm, no thanks.

I shake my head. "I don't think so."

Quirking a brow, a smirk tips the edges of his lips upward. "I want your number so we can figure out times to get together and work on our ethics project. That's it."

My face heats. It never occurred to me that he would want my number for that purpose. Now who looks like a total jackass? Feeling irritated, with him as well as myself, I hand over my phone and watch as he programs his name and number into my contacts. Then he calls his cell before handing it back to me.

"There. How does Sunday afternoon work for you? We need a few hours to sit down and generate some ideas about the case study we're going to consider for the project."

I stare at my phone before glancing back at him. "Sunday afternoon is fine."

My breath hitches as he steps toward me until we're so close that I have to tip my face up to hold his gaze.

"I'll text you with a time and place."

Nodding, I take a careful step away. As I do, two girls slide between us before wrapping themselves around him. With his gaze focused on me, he drapes an arm around each of them.

"I'll be seeing you, Ivy."

There's a slightly mocking tone to his words that immediately has my eyes narrowing. Without another word, I spin around, pushing my way roughly toward the door of the apartment. I need to get out of here and away from him.

Roan King is nothing more than a player.

I realized it way before Finn ever tried warning me off. I'm never going to be a card-carrying member of the *I want to sleep with all the campus athletes* club. That's not who I am. And whatever happened between us back there, I don't want it happening again. I'm not interested in playing these ridiculous cat and mouse games with him.

I want to work on this project and be done with it.

Be done with him.

CHAPTER TEN

*It's been said that Roan King kisses and fucks just like he plays football—with an amazing amount of skill, finesse, and single-minded determination. *big sigh* Oh, how I'd love to find that out firsthand... KingOfCampus.com*

"Are you being serious with me right now?"

Lexie is lying on her stomach in the middle of my bed flipping through the latest issue of *Vogue*. *Vogue* is her fashion bible and she treats everything written within there as if it were gospel. Since I get a free stylist out of it, I'm not going to complain. Lexie is as passionate about fashion as I am about dance. So, we have a pretty good understanding of each other.

Trying to be sneaky, I offhandedly mentioned my date with Finn while she was immersed in her magazine. I was hoping she wouldn't be paying too much attention. Unfortunately, she heard me loud and clear. As soon as I mentioned the *F-word*, she bolted up into a sitting position before skewering me with a hard-edged glare.

I ended up telling her about him waiting outside the studio last

Saturday and us sitting down over smoothies and hashing things out. The bottom line is that he wants another chance and after a fifteen-month separation, maybe we've grown up enough to try again.

I had really liked Finn.

I'd been attracted to him.

I still am.

Why shouldn't I give our relationship another shot?

With determination, she climbs off the bed. "You've left me no other choice but to pull up all the pictures I sent you."

"Let's not go there." Turning toward her, I hold her eyes before continuing. "I appreciate you trying to look out for me. I really do. But it's just dinner, we're not getting back together. We're talking things out."

Her lips sink into a frown. With eyebrows practically meshed together, she mutters, "I don't like Finn. He's arrogant and a real douche for hooking up with those other girls behind your back. How can you forget about all that?"

I can't exactly disagree with what she's saying. He *is* a douche for doing that.

Like I said before, maybe he's changed. I know I have. And it's just dinner. Nothing more. "I don't even know if I'll see him again after this. So chill out."

In answer, she rolls her eyes at me.

Turning and twisting, I take a good look at myself in the mirror. "Do you like this shirt with these shorts?" Even though it's the beginning of September, it's still warm out. At least eighty degrees. So I'm wearing a little white halter and pale blue shorts along with a pair of silver sandals that have a small heel.

Taking my question seriously, her eyes travel over me and then back up again. "Yeah, but I would pull your hair up into a messy bun and add some chunky earrings." She purses her lips before squinting her eyes thoughtfully. "Maybe your big silver hoops."

Grinning, I rummage through my jewelry box before finding the earrings she's talking about. Once I gather my hair up into a bun, I turn to her with my hands outstretched in silent question.

"Yep. Totally hot." Then she grunts, "Not than Finn deserves any of the effort."

"Yes, yes...you've made your feelings on the Finn subject perfectly clear. You don't have to say another word about it, okay?"

Shrugging, she says quietly, "I don't want to see you get hurt again. Even though you were in Paris and I wasn't there to help you through it, I remember how devastated you were when he ended things."

Exhaling a breath, my shoulders fall before I say with equal softness, "I know. And I appreciate you looking out for me, I really do. You're a good friend, Lex, the best. But it's just dinner. That's it."

Still looking skeptical, she nods her head begrudgingly in acceptance. "Okay."

Not a moment later my phone dings with an incoming text. It's Finn telling me that he's waiting downstairs in his Jeep.

I must mumble the words under my breath because Lexie suddenly says, "What, Mr. romantic can't be bothered to walk his ass up here and pick you up?"

I shoot her an exasperated look before gathering up my purse and heading for the door. "It's not a big deal. I'll see you later."

"Okay. Text me when you get back if I'm not here," she calls after me.

Opening the door, I yell back, "Will do. Have fun tonight."

Stopping right outside my door, I smooth down my shorts and straighten my top. As I'm about to start down the hall, the apartment door next to us opens and out walks Roan. For a long moment, neither of us say a word as our gazes catch.

Not sure what to do, I hold up my hand in silent greeting as he walks toward me. His eyes, like last night, ensnare mine, refusing to let go. When he stops two feet away from me, his gaze takes a leisure tour of my body before coming up to meet mine. I feel the heat of a blush stain my cheeks at his perusal.

Why does this guy have such an effect on me?

I don't even like him.

In all fairness, I don't know him well enough to make that kind of statement, but what I do know, I don't particularly care for. And yet, he tangles my insides up every time I see him. It's maddening.

"Looking sexy, Ivy."

"Thanks," I mumble under my breath. "I've got to get going." With that, I try making a hasty get away but he's right there beside me. His long-legged strides shortening to match mine. Apparently, I'm not going to be able to shake him loose so easily.

"Hot date tonight?"

It's so much better when we're both facing forward, and his gaze isn't able to capture mine. Even though I can feel him watching me, it's nowhere near the full effect and therefore I'm still able to keep my wits about me.

"Umm," I pause for a beat, "just getting together with a friend."

He nods as we continue walking. As silence settles over us, I find myself asking, "What are you up to?" Not that I care.

"Going to work out at the gym, then I'll probably head out with Sam."

I allow my gaze to slide over him. He's wearing long athletic shorts and a black tank top that does incredible things for his arms. I've said it before, but it bears repeating—those arms of his are literally amazing. Huge. They have to be at least seventeen inches around. I'm not kidding. Roan has massive biceps. I can't help but remember what it felt like last night to have them wrapped around me.

I definitely shouldn't be thinking about that right now.

Or ever.

I'm doing my damnedest to put out fires, not enflame them.

Arriving at the elevator, I quickly stab the down arrow button since we're on the third floor. As we wait, I look everywhere but at him. Even though I don't allow my eyes to stray toward him, I feel the heat of his gaze licking over me. I'm practically squirming as my unease continues ratcheting up to unprecedented levels. I just want the damn elevator to arrive so I can get the hell away from Roan and his gorgeous body.

Damn it! I really have to stop thinking about Roan's hot body.

But it's a thing of beauty. There's no denying it.

Thankfully, the elevator dings, signaling that the car has finally arrived. As soon as the doors slide open, I rush inside before punching the lobby button about seven times in quick succession. When I glance at Roan, a big grin tugs at the edges of his lips. He's all but smirking at me.

I seriously hate when he does that.

As the doors close, locking us inside, my brows lower as I treat him to a full-on glare. It's so much easier to embrace the irritation than the attraction I'm currently feeling.

Crap.

I don't want to feel attracted to Roan. And I sure as hell don't want him suspecting that I'm drawn to him either. He'd only end up thinking he could use me. And that's never going to happen. "Something funny?"

His blue-green hued eyes slide to mine. "Nope, not at all."

Humor all but simmers within their shining depths. That alone is enough to have me clenching my teeth.

"Spill it, King." This guy seriously aggravates the crap out of me. How is it possible to be so turned on one moment and so completely irritated the next by the same person?

With our gazes locked, he reaches out before hitting the alarm button. I gasp as the elevator jolts to a halt.

"What are you doing," I whisper as my eyes flare wide. My voice doesn't even sound like my own. It's deep and breathy with a bit of shake to it.

"What I've been dying to do ever since you spilled that damn coffee all over me."

Before I'm able to fully realize what those words mean, his arms snake around me, hauling me close to the heat of his hard body. And then his lips are crashing down on mine. Stroking over them with such an intensity that it has everything in me going up in flames. I can't help the stifled moan that escapes as his mouth slides swiftly over mine. It's like an assault on every single one of my senses.

My lips part on a groan, wanting—no, *needing* more of him. As soon as they do, his tongue slips inside before stroking over mine. Caressing me in a way that is so sexy it has my eyes rolling up inside my head. Pleasure explodes like a series of fireworks before ricocheting throughout my entire being.

And then he does the unexpected.

Instead of continuing to pummel my mouth with his, he draws away, holding me at arm's length before searching my dazed eyes. After a long moment, he tugs me back toward him again until he can nibble at the corners of my lips before sucking my bottom one gently into his mouth.

"You taste even better than I imagined."

His low, gravelly words wash over me, banking the fire within. And then his mouth is back to crushing mine and I...can't...think. I don't want to dwell on anything other than the addictive taste of him flooding my senses. The feel of him as he steals each and every breath from me.

It's the shrill ringing of the elevator alarm that startles me into awareness and has Roan slowly backing away. His heated gaze continues holding mine captive as he reaches over to the panel of buttons on the wall and presses the lobby button. As the elevator jolts into a downward descent, he tugs me back to him until I'm once again pressed against that massive chest of his.

"You have to know one taste isn't going to be nearly enough."

I gulp.

What does that mean?

What the hell does that mean?

The confusion I'm feeling must be written all over my face because in the next breath he says, "This is going to happen between us, Ivy."

Almost frantically, I shake my head. "No."

Slowly quirking a brow, he grins down at me. "You didn't enjoy that, sweetheart?" Before I can even formulate an answer, he continues, his voice all low and sexy. The cadence of it strums something deep inside me. "Because I'm kind of thinking you did." He lays a gentle kiss at the corner of my lips before whispering, "You were moaning into my mouth, practically begging me for more."

Lying at this point would only make me look foolish. Not to mention a huge ass liar. And I may be an idiot for allowing this to unfold between us, but I'm not a liar. "It has nothing to do with enjoying that kiss and everything to do with not being the kind of girl you're used to hooking up with."

Even though it's the last thing I want to do, I untangle myself from him as the elevator doors slide open. I'm about to step into the lobby when Roan wraps his fingers around my upper arm to stop me from escaping. As he turns my body toward him, our eyes lock and my breath catches in my throat.

His eyes are full of hot sultry promise. "I could make you feel so damn good."

Inhaling a shaky breath, I force out the words. "I don't doubt that. I'm just not into casual sex." But he tempts me in the worst kind of way. More than anyone else ever has.

His eyes narrow before he finally drops my arm. "And I'm not interested in having a girlfriend. I like to keep things fluid."

Fluid?

He likes to keep things fluid?

I almost start to laugh.

So basically, he's interested in fucking me a time or two. If I'm real lucky—three times and then he's moving on. Because Roan King likes to keep things *fluid.*

What.

A.

Jerk!

I'm a total idiot for allowing things to get so out of hand. I should have pushed him away as soon as he pressed his lips against mine.

But hot damn that was one hell of a kiss!

Unconsciously, my fingers rise to my lips. Not wanting him to see just how affected I am, I force my arm back down to my side.

Turning toward the lobby doors which lead outside the building, I almost chastise myself for feeling...god...am I seriously disappointed? Ugh. I want to smack the hell out of myself right now. The guy basically propositioned me (for a second time, no less) and I'm actually *disappointed* that he dropped the subject as quickly as he did when I told him I wasn't interested in screwing around.

As we walk silently out of the building, I can't get his words out of my head.

Fluid!

This guy is a real piece of work.

I'll give him fluid...right up the ass.

My teeth are tightly clenched, and my hands are balled into fists that hang uselessly at my sides. As soon as we're outside, I scan the parking lot for Finn. He still drives a hunter green Jeep and almost immediately I spot it idling about six spaces from the entrance. As our gazes meet, I have to consciously unlock my tensed muscles before giving him a halfhearted wave and smile.

"Finn McKenzie? Hmmm...now there's an uninspired choice."

Roan's comment has my teeth gnashing together painfully. Straightening my spine, I ignore him as I walk down the cement sidewalk that lines the parking lot.

"I enjoyed our ride in the elevator, Ivy. We'll have to do it again sometime."

My jaw aches from clenching it so tightly. I'm so tempted to give him the finger, but I don't. Not unless I want to explain what happened to Finn.

It irritates me to no end that I've allowed this guy to crawl under my skin. *Again!* For goodness sake, I should know better. It's been obvious from the get-go that Roan is nothing more than a man whore looking for an easy lay.

And I refuse to be that for any guy.

Yanking open the door to the Jeep, I make a concerted effort to smooth out my features along with my jangled nerves. "Hi."

Finn smiles before his gaze slides to Roan who is walking past us. His brows lower. "Were you two together?"

I can't help but glance at Roan. It's as if my gaze is irresistibly drawn to him against my will. Like an idiotic moth to a flickering flame. As our gazes collide, he gives us a huge shit eating grin. Jerking his chin in acknowledgement to Finn, he keeps on walking. When he's about ten feet past us, he turns, walking backward a few steps before calling out, "Looking forward to seeing you tomorrow afternoon, Ivy." Apparently not satisfied that he's needled Finn nearly enough, he adds a little wink before disappearing inside a huge black SUV.

The smile Finn had been wearing moments ago melts into an irritated scowl as he continues watching Roan through narrowed eyes that spark and snap with anger.

Clearing my throat, I mutter, "No. I told you he lives next door to us. I ran into him in the hallway when I was walking out."

Even though he continues glowering, he says nothing in response.

Not wanting this to ruin our evening, I try making light of the situation. "Finn, I barely know the guy." My mind tumbles back to the elevator ride and his lips sliding deliciously across mine. To the feeling of electricity that shot clean through me. For some reason, it occurs to me as my gaze involuntarily falls to Finn's mouth, that he's never made me feel that way.

Out of control and completely turned on.

It's like comparing a light spring shower to a tsunami. It can't be done.

Knocking me out of my silent reverie, Finn grumbles, "I don't like how familiar he is with you."

I'm so tempted to roll my eyes. This date with Finn isn't exactly off to a great start. The last person I want to talk about is Roan. Sliding onto the front seat next to Finn, I try placating him one last time. "Like I said before, I barely know the guy. He's just a neighbor."

With a scowl, he watches me suspiciously, as if I'm lying to him. Which...I guess...I am. "You two are meeting up tomorrow?"

I suddenly remember that we are indeed getting together tomorrow. Shifting uncomfortably in my seat, I say in the most offhanded tone I can muster, "Oh...um, yeah. We're partners on a project for our Business Ethics class. We need to start working on it."

"Did you ask to be partnered with him?"

It takes a moment to remember that Finn and I aren't together. I have nothing to feel guilty about. Not even for the kiss that happened five minutes ago. Finn is the one who ended things between us. Not me. I don't owe him any explanations as to what I'm doing or who I'm spending time with.

Raising a brow, I say in a no-nonsense voice, "Actually, I asked the professor if I could change partners. It's a huge project and I want to work with someone who's going to pull their share of the workload, but she wouldn't let me switch."

Finn snorts in response before reaching out and tangling his fingers in my hair. "I think the guy's a real dumbass. You were smart to try and get rid of him. You'll probably get stuck doing most of the work."

Even though I no longer think that's true, I don't bother correcting him. I'm kind of wondering what his problem with Roan is. It's clear they don't care for each other. I could sense it at that party a few weeks ago.

But I don't want to talk about Roan King any more tonight. I'd rather have a nice evening with Finn and see where it takes us.

CHAPTER ELEVEN

Roan

"Hi," I give the older woman sitting behind the front desk a full wattage smile, "is Ivy around?"

She blinks a few times before a cheeky grin pulls up the corners of her mouth. "Well, hello there, handsome."

I can't help but laugh in response.

Wanting to get a better look at me, she leans across the front desk. Her gaze takes a leisure tour before coming back to rest on my face. "I know who you are."

For one ridiculous moment, I wonder if Ivy has mentioned me to this woman. Don't ask why the notion of her talking about me sends a little thrill slicing through me, but it does.

"You're Roan King. Wide receiver for the Barnett Bulldogs. I just read an article about you in the newspaper. First game of the season yesterday and you all but crushed Ohio."

I smile even though something that feels suspiciously like disappointment careens through me. "Yup, the team is really vibing right now. Got our eyes focused on winning games and working toward a championship."

Still smiling, she shakes her head. "Can't remember the last time there's been so much buzz about the football team. You've got the whole city talking."

Right...no pressure there.

I continue smiling before clearing my throat. "So, Ivy?"

"Ah, yes, Ivy," her mouth stretches into a wider grin, "she's just finishing up with a ballet class." She points toward a hallway with several doors. "Last studio on the left."

With one last smile, I thank her before taking off down the hall. We agreed to meet at the library around one o'clock, but when I stopped over at the girls' apartment this morning with Dylan, Lexie told me Ivy was teaching a few classes at the studio downtown. Apparently, she usually walks to and from her job and since it's about a mile from the apartment, I decided to swing by and pick her up so we can get right to work.

Since I know Ivy would shoot down any overtures I made, I didn't bother asking.

That seems to be her usual modius operandi where I'm concerned.

She clearly couldn't care less that I'm Roan King. Barnett University's very own golden boy. The wide receiver who's looking to turn pro at the end of the year and has a damn good shot at going as a first-round draft pick.

At least, that's what my agent keeps telling me.

So far, this girl has spilled her drink on me, tried to ditch me as a partner because she thinks I'm a complete dumbass, all the while shooting down all my hookup attempts.

If I had any brains whatsoever, I'd steer clear of Ivy Kaster. Unfortunately, I already know that's not going to happen. As much as I hate to admit it, the girl totally intrigues me. The mere fact I'm standing outside the studio she's teaching in because I started feeling impatient to see her only slams that point home with a ruthlessness I wasn't expecting.

I mean, what the hell is up with that?

Peeking inside, I watch as she leads a class at the front of a mirrored room. Her fingers are wrapped around a wooden barre that sits about waist high and spans the entire wall. There are six little girls in pink leotards and tights standing alongside her. It's apparent to even me, that each and every one of them is trying to mimic exactly what she does. And while they're all wearing sheer little skirts, Ivy is wearing nothing more than a black leotard.

My mouth dries as my eyes skim down her long lean length.

God...did I really think she wasn't my type?

That she didn't have any curves to speak of?

Standing there in nothing but Lycra and tights, with her hair pulled up into a tight bun on the top of her head, she couldn't look any sexier if she tried. I listen intently as she instructs the class to follow her movements. The heels of her feet are pressed together as she bends at the knees and sinks gracefully to the floor. One arm is still holding the barre while the other is stretched out straight. The girls standing alongside her in a neat little row try to copy what she's doing.

I can't help the smile that twitches around the corners of my lips. Normally, I'm not one who thinks kids are charming or cute. The most interaction I have with squirts this age are when they clamor for me to sign their footballs and programs. Or when the team puts on a clinic for kids in the community.

Otherwise, I generally steer clear of the little beasties.

Ivy asks them to hold their poses as she comes around to check their positioning. Smiling, she praises each one.

Even though her smile isn't aimed in my direction, it still arrows through me. I've never seen Ivy smile like that before. And certainly, never at me. It makes me feel as if I've been somehow cheated.

Clapping her hands, all the girls break their poses before swarming her. She speaks quietly to them before they all nod their heads in unison. Then she gets a small bowl from the front of the room and without being told, all of the girls rest their hands on top of their heads as she comes around with stickers that she places on them.

In the blink of an eye, all the little half pints are scampering away. A few of the parents stay to speak with Ivy. Asking questions, I'm guessing. She looks so completely serious as she explains whatever-the-hell-it-is-she's-taking-the-time-to-explain to them.

When all the girls and their parents have finally cleared out of the studio, Ivy walks to the front of the room and grabs a bottle of water before taking a long drink from it. I'm still loitering in the hallway and she hasn't seen me yet. I should let her know I'm here, but I don't.

Not quite yet.

For some reason, I want to stand here and watch her for a little bit longer while she's unaware. Ivy is so full of grace and polish. Setting down the bottle, she goes to the barre and places both hands on it before leaning forward and stretching one leg out in back of her. After holding the pose for a long moment, she does a few more stretches before moving to the middle of the wooden floor.

Holding out both arms, she executes a series of leaps and jumps that span the length of the space. There is no music playing but there must be some kind of beat in her head because all of her movements are rhythmic and purposeful. Just when I feel like I couldn't be more impressed with the sheer flexibility she exudes, she performs what looks like the splits midair. As she comes out of it, she rolls onto the floor in a somersault before popping up and then spinning around on one foot.

I'm pretty sure my jaw is on the floor.

I can't take my eyes off her as she bends and tucks and rolls. Somehow making her body do whatever the hell she wants it to. I've never seen someone with so much physical command over themselves. It may be totally unmanly to admit this, but my breath actually catches at the back of my throat as I continue watching her. Hell, I don't think I could rip my gaze away if I tried.

I'm completely blown away by what she's able to do. I mean, yeah, sure...I'd heard she danced, but I had no idea she could perform like *this*. That she was *this* good. Like a...professional or something.

And then the spell is broken.

All movement ceases as our eyes collide. I hadn't realized I'd stepped inside the room instead of hovering outside the door, but here I am.

Her breath comes in fast little pants as her eyes take me in. She looks confused.

"What are you doing here? I thought we were meeting at the library in about forty-five minutes?"

Is it wrong to say that watching her do whatever-the-hell-she-just-did is a huge turn on? And that body-hugging leotard certainly isn't helping matters either. That scalding hot kiss from yesterday crashes through my head. It takes everything I have inside not to close the distance separating us and haul her into my arms so I can kiss the hell out of her again.

"Roan?" Her voice rises as if she knows exactly what's tumbling through my head.

Clearing my throat, not to mention those unruly thoughts, I reply, "I, ah, thought you might need a ride home."

Cocking her head, she watches me. Almost as if the offer might be some sly bit of trickery on my part. "How did you know I was here?"

Before I even have the chance to formulate a response, she mutters, "I'm going to kill Lexie."

I can't help but flash a grin. "Oh, don't be too hard on her. I weaseled it out of her before she had her first cup of coffee."

A slight smile curls around the corners of her lips. "Well, I guess that would explain it."

Since Dylan and I have been roommates since freshman year, I met Lexie when they started hanging out last year. She's a cool chick. I like her. And she's slept over enough times in the past for me to know that she has a major caffeine addiction problem. If you ever need to get info out of her, hit her hard before that first cup in the morning. She's usually so groggy she'll tell you anything you want to know.

Hence me finding out where Ivy was this afternoon.

I also took the opportunity to do a little more digging into the Finn McKenzie situation. I was decidedly unhappy to learn that they were together for about six months before he dumped her ass while she was in France. Clearly, he's looking to patch things up with her.

Am I bothered by this newly gleaned information?

Yeah, I think I actually am. Mostly because I can't stand that prick. The guy is a major asshole. And a huge player.

I understand how that could come off sounding a bit hypocritical, but still...

When I hook up with a girl, I'm completely clear about my intentions. It's a onetime deal. I'm not in the market for a girlfriend. I have way too much going on. Which in no way means that I don't enjoy getting laid with a fair amount of frequency. It just means I don't want the aggravation of having a girl whining at me about what I'm doing, where I'm going, and that I'm not spending enough quality time with her. I don't have time for that bullshit. I have to stay focused on football and school.

But Finn...I've heard some not-so-good things about that dude. He dates girls and then screws around on the side. I have zero respect for that. If you want to nail anything that moves, anytime you want, then don't have a girlfriend. It's as simple as that.

Not knowing what else to say, I shove my hands into my pockets. "You ready to head out?"

Looking conflicted, she doesn't move a muscle. There's just a hint of confusion written across her features as if she's not quite sure she should take me up on my offer. And the fact that I kissed her in the elevator last night probably isn't helping matters either.

Neither of us say a word as our gazes continue to hold. It's so quiet I can almost hear the clock on the wall ticking. Apparently deciding I'm an acceptable mode of transportation, she finally nods her head. "Yeah, just let me grab my bag and we can go."

Unable to help myself, my gaze slides appreciatively over her body as she turns away from me. A few seconds later, she's jogging over to the corner of the studio where her bag is lying against the wall. She slips off her black ballet shoes before pulling on an oversized T-shirt and pair of leggings. Sliding her feet into a pair of shoes, she then shoves the ballet slippers into her bag.

I seriously can't believe how hot this girl is. And watching her dance, that only kicks it up a hundred notches. Unfortunately, I have a semi-aroused situation going on in my jeans. God forbid I actually stiffen all the way up while we're walking out of here. It's doubtful that Ivy would be flattered by my lust. She'd probably refuse the ride back to the apartment.

I try focusing on things that are in no way related to Ivy...or dancing...or long caramel colored hair...or skintight leotards.

Damn it.

Instead, I focus on the season opener we played yesterday. I think about the arms and chest workout I need to run through tonight. My attention turns to the time-consuming Business Ethics project Ivy and I need to start working on.

Hmmm.

That only brings me back to spending more time with Ivy.

Which has me thinking about her long lean body.

And those freaking splits she did midair.

Fuck...I bet she's limber as hell.

Now I really need to shift my junk around. This isn't good at all.

As we're walking out, the woman who greeted me when I first came into the studio looks like she's getting ready to close up for the day.

"Bye, Donna," Ivy says. "I'll see you tomorrow night."

"Bye, honey." Donna's gaze shifts before giving me a saucy little wink. "And it was certainly nice to meet you, Roan. Good luck with the rest of your season." Her gaze swings speculatively between us.

I give her a wave in acknowledgement. "Thanks, nice to meet you, too."

And then we're pushing through the front door into the bright sunshine. Even though I picked Ivy up so we could get right to work, that idea doesn't necessarily appeal to me at the moment. Noticing the shop across the street, I point toward it. "You want a smoothie or something? You must be hungry after that."

I sure as hell know how I feel after working out. Fucking famished.

She pauses, her gaze sliding to the vibrant yellow and orange shop across the street before arrowing to mine. Just when I think she'll agree, she shakes her head instead.

But I know she wants one. As soon as I mentioned the word *smoothie*, her green-colored eyes lit up with interest. "Are you sure?" I cajole, "Because I could seriously go for a pomegranate and berry one." Now that I'm saying the words out loud, I realize how true they are. I really *could* go for a smoothie right about now. It would be the perfect pick me up before heading to the library for a few hours.

Uncertainty flickers across her face as her gaze shifts to mine again. "Really?"

One side of my mouth twitches up. Instead of replying, I grab her fingers before tugging her across the street toward the small building. As we make our way to the counter, I ask, "So what kind are you in the mood for?"

Her gaze catches mine before skittering away. She does that a lot. "Same as you."

My lips curve even more and when it's our turn, I order for both of us. The guy behind the counter does a double take before a massive grin overwhelms his face. "No problem, King!"

With raised brows, Ivy's gaze slides to mine as the guy calls out our order to someone else who will make our drinks. Before I can try to engage her in conversation, the dude is back.

Shaking his head, he leans across the counter as if settling in for a nice long chat. "That was one hell of a game yesterday." He quickly glances over his shoulder before inching closer to me. "I've got to watch my language around here. The manager would write me up if he heard that."

Even though I nod like I'm completely fascinated by what he's saying, I'm really wishing this guy would just go away. Instead, he continues as if totally oblivious to the fact that I might be trying to spend some time with the girl standing next to me. Not once does he glance in Ivy's direction. He probably doesn't even realize she's there.

"We all went crazy when you caught that fifteen-yard pass and then made it through like five guys before scoring that touchdown! It was the most amazing play I've ever seen in my life!" Grinning like a lunatic, he shakes his head again. "Only you, King! Only you could do something like that."

I smile tightly as he continues yammering on about one of the upcoming games. Ivy is watching the whole exchange with a curious stare as if we're primates at the zoo. I don't like it. I don't want her watching me like I'm part of some damn circus act.

I get that enough as it is.

It suddenly occurs to me that I actually like that Ivy isn't caught up in all the football hype and BS. In the few conversational exchanges that we've had, not once has she brought up football or the NFL. It's like she's totally oblivious to all of it.

Chad, the dude who took our order and has pretty much yapped my ear off for the last five minutes, hands us our smoothies. I know his name is Chad because he told me like three times. The girl who made our drinks had to clear her throat twice before tapping him on the shoulder to get his attention because he wouldn't stop talking.

Thanking him, I hand Ivy hers before turning away from the front counter.

"Hey, King?"

I almost grit my teeth as Chad calls out my name with a hopeful note tinging his voice. But I don't. That's not the way to handle fans and I know it. These people enjoy watching me play and they spend their hard-earned money at the stadium. I'm appreciative of that fact. Instead, I keep the relaxed expression plastered across my face. "What's up?"

"Um...would you mind signing this piece of paper for my little brother?" His face reddens. "He's a huge fan. And I just know you're gonna go pro this year."

"Of course." I walk back to the counter before taking the pen he's holding out. "What's his name," I ask, preparing to write my usual shtick.

"Oh...um, er, Chad."

My gaze flicks to his. Any moment, his face is going to burst into flames. Zits and all. "No problem." Then I get busy writing so we can get the hell out of here.

Once finished, I hand him the pen before saying goodbye. Glancing around the small shop, I notice a few other people watching me. Placing my hand on the small of Ivy's back, I maneuver her to the exit. When the door closes behind us, I inhale a deep breath of fresh air and continue walking toward my truck which is parked in the lot next to the dance studio.

Ivy doesn't say a word. She continues sipping away on her smoothie. I can't imagine what she's thinking.

When we're close enough, I click the automatic locks and open the door for her. She shoots me a surprised look before murmuring a quick thanks. Then I'm hustling around the front and sliding in beside her.

Is it strange that I like having her next to me in my truck?

You know what's even weirder than that?

I've never driven a girl anywhere in this vehicle.

When I said I was only into hookups, I wasn't kidding. And I don't ever make the mistake of bringing them back to my place either. I did that once and it took forever to convince her that it was time to leave when we were finished knocking boots.

I huff out a relieved breath that we're finally alone in my truck and away from Chad and all the other curious onlookers. Sometimes it really does feel like I'm a monkey at the zoo.

My attention slides to Ivy only to find hers already settled on me as if she's silently assessing the situation. She takes another long pull from her straw. My eyes slip to those ruby red lips. My junk stirs again wondering what it would feel like to have her suck me with such single-minded determination. Yeah...now probably isn't the best time to be fantasizing about a blow job.

I'll save that for another time.

My gaze flicks to hers when she says, "So...you play football, huh?"

I can't help the surprised chuckle that escapes from my lips. As I laugh, a small smile curves her mouth upward. "Yeah, a little bit, but I'm not very good."

The smile grows, transforming her face until she's probably the most gorgeous girl I've ever laid eyes on. And like in the dance studio, when I'd been watching her soar across the room, the breath catches at the back of my throat. It's an odd and unexpected feeling.

"I kind of inferred that from the convo in the smoothie shop. It must suck riding the bench."

I compress my lips together, so I'll stop smiling. But it's not working. Clearing my throat, I finally say, "Yeah, it does. I'm really more of a glorified water boy than anything else."

"Well, just keep working hard, I'm sure you'll improve. With any luck, you could be Barnett's very own *Rudy*."

I almost choke. It takes a moment before I'm able to say, "That's some solid advice. Thanks." *Rudy*...I freaking love that movie. I mean, who doesn't? I watch her with a little more appreciation for being able to work that cinematic gem into our conversation. And trust me, I've been seriously appreciating her ever since I first laid eyes on her this afternoon.

With the tension broken between us, I pick up my smoothie before taking a hearty pull from the straw. Even though Ivy and I have spoken a few times, it never occurred to me that she might have a sense of humor. She's usually glaring way too much to let it show.

With curiosity filling her eyes, she asks, "Does that kind of thing happen often?"

She's kidding, right?

I shrug. Over the years, I've grown used to the attention. Normally, it doesn't bother me at all. But then again, I've never had a girl at my side and our conversation totally hijacked. This is the first time I've ever felt irritated that someone wanted to talk football with me. "Often enough."

A thoughtful expression crosses her face. "And you don't mind all the attention?"

Well, I never have before...

"Not really. It's part of being a high-profile athlete, I guess." It's always been like that. Even back in high school, I was getting noticed for my football playing abilities.

"It must be exhausting."

Instead of replying to that comment, I take another long pull from my straw as her words roll around in my head.

Again, I jerk my shoulders. It's all part of playing ball. Part of being good and having NFL scouts looking, talking, and making predictions about you. It's what I've worked my entire life for. "It doesn't bother me," I repeat, almost as if I'm trying to convince myself instead of her.

Glancing away, she looks over at the smoothie shop across the street. "I think that would bother me. I like being anonymous."

Even in high school, I couldn't go anywhere without people talking to me about football and college and my chances of turning pro.

Hell, Dylan told me a few weeks ago that there was a picture of me disappearing inside the men's room posted on some stupid website.

Can you believe that shit?

Thank god whoever snapped the photo didn't actually follow me in.

Not wanting to discuss my pseudo-celebrity status any longer, I steer the conversation in another direction. "So, we'll head back to your place, you can change, pick up your computer and we can take off for the library."

She takes one last pull from her straw, finishing off her pomegranate berry smoothie before agreeing with my plan. Again, something stirs in my boxer briefs.

Two hours later, we're camped out at the library. We both have our laptops out and are typing away as we formulate a loose outline of what our project will entail. It may sound a little obvious, but we've decided to delve into the Bernie Madoff Ponzi scheme.

That dude couldn't have been more unethical if he tried. There's so much material to work with, it's almost overwhelming. Entire books, along with articles in business journals and newspapers, have been written about this subject, so research is plentiful. And I don't think I'm the only one who finds it interesting either. Ivy has been riveted to her computer screen for the last hour. Every so often, she shakes her head, sharing some tidbit she's stumbled across.

For a moment, I sit back and watch her work. Her light brown hair is still piled high on her head in a messy bun like it was last night. Even thinking about her spending time alone with Finn McKenzie has me gritting my teeth. Her bright green eyes flash with intensity and focus.

Hell, I bet if I packed up all my shit and walked away, she wouldn't even notice.

I almost snort.

That shouldn't turn me on...but damn if it doesn't.

I'm used to girls tripping over themselves and each other just to get to me. Brows sliding together, I rack my brain for a time when I actually had to work to get a girl's attention. Middle school, maybe? It sure as shit wasn't in high school or college. Chicks have always been plentiful. Hell, I'm usually knee deep in pussy any given night of the week.

Being with Ivy is kind of...nice. She's smart. And pretty. Not to mention really limber...

Because what happened at the smoothie shop has made me more cautious, we're buried in the stacks on the second floor. The last thing I need is to be interrupted by people who want nothing more than to inform me that the football team is off to a great start and ask how I think we're going to fair next weekend against Buffalo, one of our biggest conference rivals.

I also grabbed a ball cap from my apartment and now have it pulled low over my brow. My lips twitch thinking about meeting Ivy earlier in the hallway when we were leaving for the library. She had looked me over before asking if this was what the Roan-King-version of incognito looked like.

Not bothering to answer, I grabbed her hand and towed her to my truck.

Like I said before, I like her sense of humor. And I like that she's finally allowing me to catch a glimpse of it. I feel like she's actually showing me who the real Ivy Kaster is.

Finally surfacing from the impressive amount of research she's gathered, Ivy glances up from her computer screen before our gazes catch and hold. It's probably for the best if she doesn't realize that I've been staring at her for a good five minutes.

Something like that could potentially creep her out.

I swear she becomes more attractive every time I look at her.

Someone needs to seriously explain how that's even possible.

Something inexplicable tightens in the pit of my gut before I finally clear my throat. "I think we've made a good dent with all the research we collected today. Plus, we have a solid game plan regarding the direction we're going to take this project in."

She nods, her teeth sinking into that plump bottom lip of hers. Lowering her eyes from mine, she shifts in her chair before murmuring, "I'm sorry for assuming that you weren't serious about this project."

Not saying a word, I lean back in my chair before stretching my long legs out in front of me. I'm actually a little surprised she's bringing this up. Her eyes lift hesitantly before catching mine. "I didn't want to get stuck with someone who wasn't equally invested in putting the time in to both this class and the project."

Since I'm genuinely curious as to how she jumped to that conclusion without knowing me, I keep my tone neutral. "Why would you think that?"

She jerks her narrow shoulders into a tight shrug.

I can't resist pushing for an answer. "Because I'm good at football, you assumed I didn't have much going on upstairs?" As soon as the words shoot out of my mouth, red stains flag her cheeks.

"Well...it's not like I ever see you taking notes in class."

She thought I wasn't taking this class, or my entire freaking college education for that matter, seriously because she's never seen me take notes? "I record all the lectures on my computer, and it transcribes them for me so I can actively listen to the lecture and participate in class discussions. That's what works best for me."

Her mouth tumbles open.

For some strange reason, I feel the need to prove this to her, so I click on the file that has all my classes listed in order. Then I turn the computer toward her before using the touch screen to open up our Business Ethics class. Her gaze scans through the list of dated notes before bouncing up to mine.

If she didn't look so appropriately chastised, which—damn it, is hot, I'd be a hell of a lot more pissed off. "I'm really sorry, Roan. I jumped to conclusions about you that obviously weren't true."

I cock a brow. "You mean the stereotype that all jocks are stupid and get passed through the system because of their athletic abilities and what they're able to do for the university?"

Even though I don't intend the words to sound harsh, she winces. After all, it's nothing I haven't heard before. It just sucks she assumed that about me.

"Yeah, I guess so." Silently she worries her lower lip between her teeth as if she's debating something with herself. Finally, she whispers,

"I asked Dr. Paulson if she would give me a different partner to work with." Ivy holds my gaze steadily as she admits this.

Should I tell her that I already know she tried ditching me?

You know what? I think I'm going to. She needs to understand that I'm not the idiot she thinks I am.

"Yeah, I know."

Her eyes widen until I see all the multifaceted flecks of green that make up the spectrum of hues within them.

Before she can wrap her lips around the words, I continue, "I could tell that's what you were talking about with Dr. P. I'm a pretty decent lip reader."

Instead of looking impressed with my admission, because come on, it's like a talent, she narrows her eyes. "Seriously?"

Making a split decision, I jump out of my chair before closing the distance that separates us. Grabbing her hand, I tug her to her feet. And then we're on the move.

"Where are we going?" Her words sound breathless as I pull her along behind me.

"I want to show you something."

With her free hand, she motions to our computers. "What about all our stuff?"

"No one's over here. We'll only be gone for a few minutes, I promise."

It takes a moment or two before we enter the main part of the library where there are about twenty or so tables clustered together. Pulling my Bulldogs ball cap a little lower, I scan the surrounding area until I see a couple sitting at one of the wooden tables. They have books spread out between them but they're way too deep in conversation to be doing any actual studying. In fact, it looks as though they're in the middle of a heated exchange.

Perfect.

Ivy's fingers are still enclosed in mine and they feel damn good. Kind of like they belong there. She trails behind me as I find a table for us to park ourselves at. Once we're both seated on the same side next to one another, I glance around making sure I've gone undetected.

Leaning toward her, I point to the couple I've scoped out for this little exercise.

"Okay," pausing, I study his lips, "he just asked why she's so pissed off." My gaze swivels to the girl. Moving a little closer to Ivy, I talk in a hushed tone. At first, I think she might balk at how close I am, but then I whisper, "She says she doesn't like the girl who was just over here talking to him." Ivy's body relaxes as I continue. My attention slides back to the dude. "He's saying he barely knows her." I pause. "Oh, she's saying that he seems to know the girl pretty well and if he'd rather be with someone like that, there are plenty of other guys who are interested in being with her." Ivy stifles a small giggle and I can't resist smiling as I continue following their conversation.

Even though Ivy is watching the couple as if they're a TV show, she still asks with a fair amount of skepticism, "Are you really reading their lips?"

Her breath feathers over my ear and it sends a chill scampering down my spine. Taking my gaze off the arguing couple, it arrows straight to hers. God, but she's so damn close. Only inches away. As I search her vibrant green depths, there's a hitch in her inhalation.

I feel it all the way down to my toes. Which is ridiculous.

Almost of its own accord, my body strains toward her. Just as I'm about to go in for a kiss, she gasps, "Look."

I glance at the couple in question in time to see another girl walk past them. Actually, that chick is shaking her hips in more of a sexy saunter. Then she trails a hand lightly over the guy's shoulder as she continues on her way. The girl sitting at the table punches him in the bicep before packing up her things and huffing off toward the main entrance of the library.

"I can't believe you were actually reading their lips."

As I swivel toward Ivy, a grin of satisfaction touches my mouth. Then I grab her hand, pulling her to her feet. "Come on, we'd better get back to our table before someone hijacks both our computers."

With her fingers firmly enveloped in my own, we make our way to the second floor. I like the feel of her soft skin pressed against my calloused palm. I don't want to relinquish the hold I have on her. Once we reach the table, there's no reason for me to keep touching her. Reluctantly, I let her go as she settles across from me.

We both look at our laptops and the papers strewn across the table.

"Well, I think we're off to a good start," she finally says.

"Definitely." Nodding in agreement, I shut down my computer. "So...you don't mind handling the rest of this project on your own, do you?"

Her fingers still before her widened gaze slices to mine. For a moment, she doesn't say a word. My shoulders tremble. I can't hold in the laughter that's already vibrating in my chest.

She shakes her head as a hint of humor threads its way through her voice, "You're such a jerk."

I'm still chuckling. "I've been called worse."

She treats me to a genuine smile. "I don't doubt it."

Rising to my feet, I can't resist holding out my hand for her to take one last time. "Come on, let's get the hell out of here."

CHAPTER TWELVE

Now this is some seriously breaking news—Roan King was photographed several times in the company of a certain brown-haired young woman. Does anyone know who the vixen in question is? KingOfCampus.com

"Oh my god," Lexie squeals before shaking me so hard that a few fillings in my teeth loosen.

I groan and try to knock her off me. "What the hell, Lexie? It's seven in the morning. Get out of here." I attempt to roll away from her sadistic tirade, but she won't stop molesting me.

"Get your ass up! You have to see this!" Her voice rises in decibel.

"In an hour. I'll see whatever it is you have to show me then." I wave my hand toward the bedroom door. "Now get out of my room before I bludgeon you to death." It's not an idle threat either...I'll do it.

With both hands, she shakes me again until it feels like my brain is being scrambled. "You'll want to see this right now," she promises.

Maybe the quickest way to get Lexie to vacate my room is to agree to her demands. The girl is acting like a damn lunatic. Which isn't her usual style.

"I've been getting text messages all morning," she adds.

Still feeling blurry-eyed, I finally hoist myself up into a sitting position. My hair is all over the place and I have to shove it out of my face so I can see her. Plus, I don't have my contacts in. So, even without all the hair in my face, I still can't see a damn thing.

"You woke me up to tell me how popular you are? This is hardly breaking news." I try to lie back down as my eyes feather closed again.

"Wake up or I swear to God, I'll slap you silly. Hell, I'm going to slap you silly for not telling me about this. I can't believe I had to read about it on the freaking internet. Some friend you are," she mutters.

Sure, she's speaking English but it's in no way coherent. What is she even babbling about? It's like she's talking in riddles and I'm losing what little patience I have at seven o'clock in the morning. Which isn't much. "What the hell are you talking about?"

"This!" She shoves the screen of her laptop in my face, but I can barely see without my glasses or contacts.

"Just a minute," I grumble before stretching over to feel around on my nightstand for my black framed glasses. Attaching them to my face, I blink at the screen until it comes into focus.

"How could you not tell me? I thought I was your best friend!" Lexie's voice is pitched somewhere between petulant and irritated. Not to mention screechy. It's starting to hurt my eardrums.

Gradually, the images on her computer screen filter their way through my still groggy brain. As much as I'd like to look away, I can't. It's like a horrific car accident I can't rip my eyes from.

Her hands go to her hips. "Don't deny that it's you."

Oh, there's no denying that at all. The images of me are crystal clear. As are the ones of Roan. There are five of them in total.

What the hell?

What.

The.

Freaking.

Hell!

I shake my head, trying to make sense out of what I'm seeing. Finally, I snap, "You're the one who sent him to pick me up from the studio yesterday." I glare at her before announcing, "I blame you for this!"

"I sent him over so you wouldn't have to walk home." She waves her hand at the computer screen. "*This* looks like way more than working on some class project."

Reluctantly, I admit that she's right. It *does* look like way more than studying.

The first picture is of us walking out of the dance studio together. He's holding the door open for me. Okay. No big deal. Moving on...

The second picture is of him handing me a smoothie.

Again...nothing to see here, folks.

The third is of us sitting in his SUV. It looks like we're having a serious conversation.

So what?

People sit and talk all the damn time. Give me a break.

The fourth is of him holding my hand, dragging me through the library. Which okay...maybe it could be misconstrued as something it's not.

But who the heck cares?

And the fifth...well, that's when we were watching that couple and he was doing his whole lip-reading parlor trick.

Except...we aren't looking at the couple.

Nope.

We're staring at each other and even though Roan has a ball cap pulled low over his eyes, his clothing is the same as in the earlier pictures that were snapped making it completely obvious that it's him. Our faces are so close. Like we're on the verge of kissing.

Oh my god!

Is that really what we looked like?

All heated up?

With a little too much force, I slam her laptop shut. I don't want to look at those stupid, not to mention intrusive, pictures anymore. And I sure as hell don't want to read all the comments. There have to be about three hundred of them.

Seriously? Do people have nothing better to do than sit around trolling the Roan King website for up-to-date info on him? Or posting pictures?

Apparently so, by the ridiculous number of comments that have already been posted and shared and tweeted...

"If it makes you feel any better, they don't know who the mystery girl is," she pauses before adding, "yet."

Yet...

Great.

My eyes arrow to hers.

Very gently, she asks, "Are you sure there's nothing going on between you two?"

I shake my head. "I told you—we have a class together and we're partners for a project. That's it."

Technically, I'm not lying to my best friend. Then I remember Saturday night and the kiss we shared in the elevator. You know...the one where he all but crushed those amazingly talented lips against mine, giving me the best damn kiss I'd ever experienced in my life, right before I went on a date with Finn?

Yeah...*that kiss.*

FYI—that date ended up being a complete dud. Finn couldn't move on from the fact that Roan and I are partnered up for that damn business project or that he lives right next door to me. As ridiculous as it sounds, Roan King wasn't even on that date and yet he dominated the entire freaking evening. By the end of the night, I was relieved to be dropped off at my apartment where I baled from his Jeep before he could get any ideas about walking me to my door.

Plus, I couldn't stop thinking about that sexy-as-all-hell kiss Roan laid on me.

So yeah...maybe there is a little something going on between us. But it's not like anything will happen. He wants a hookup. I need a real relationship. Those two things are never going to mesh.

No matter how many sparks fly between us.

And who said I wanted a relationship with Roan?

Ummm...no one, that's who.

Apparently, everything that's been rolling around in my head has been flickering across my all-too-expressive face.

As Lexie's gaze holds mine, she says, "Be careful, Ivy. Roan is a major player. He's the king of one-night stands. I've never seen him with the same girl more than once or twice."

Heat floods my cheeks because I'm well aware of this. For god's sake, he told me himself that he doesn't *do* relationships. I believe the word he used was—*fluid*. As in—*I like to keep things fluid*. Even thinking about that comment has everything within me solidifying. "There's no reason for me to be careful because nothing is going on between us."

When she finally smiles, it's in obvious relief. "I'm glad to hear that. Roan's a nice guy but not boyfriend material at all. The last thing I want to see is you get hurt again."

"Roan and I are partners for this class. We're going to be spending time together on our project. It's nothing more than that." Not wanting to discuss Roan or those pictures any longer, I shoo her from my room. "Now go. I'm tired. I still have forty-five minutes before I have to get up."

Taking her computer with her, Lexie closes the door softly as she leaves. Only when she's gone, do I release the pent-up breath I've been holding as I flop against my pillows.

I can't believe people actually stalk Roan. How freaking creepy is that? And then to post pictures online for everyone to see? Not to mention, comment upon. Like his life is up for discussion by people who don't even know him. Like they can weigh in on everything he does as if their thoughts on the subject matter.

That's just plain bizarre.

Settling back against my pillows, I try closing my eyes.

At least they don't know who I am. I'm still anonymous in all this. Roan is used to this kind of weird attention. It doesn't seem to faze him at all. But I want no part of it.

I'm on the brink of falling asleep when the first text message rolls in.

CHAPTER THIRTEEN

Ladies, ladies, please...we can't trash this girl simply because she's been seen a few times with the love of our lives. Even though I kind of want to...
KingOfCampus.com

With humongous sunglasses covering my face, I keep my head angled down as I hurry to class. My long golden-brown hair cascades over my shoulders and against my back. Anything to make me look different from the photos that have been splashed across that damn website.

All morning long, I've been fielding text messages from friends who recognized me in the pictures posted online. I honestly thought this whole thing would be a non-issue. I mean, so what if I was photographed with Roan? Who the hell cares? He must get photographed with girls all the time. Right?

Wrong.

Sure, at parties. Around campus. Or in groups with several grinning females (and their monstrous boobs) in the shot. There are tons of those kinds of pics all over the place. But there aren't any of him leaving a dance studio, in a smoothie shop, or at the library. All with the same girl.

For those who stalk Roan King's every move, this is a huge freaking deal.

And the answer to the question of *who actually gives a rat's ass is*—practically the entire campus. Well, the female portion of it. Apparently, because Roan is Barnett's very own crowned prince, that makes him public domain. Anyone photographed with him also, by association, becomes public property to be commented upon and discussed. Or ripped apart. Much to my chagrin, Lexie read through all the comments. Quite a few of the postings were hostile in nature.

Like I-might-actually-have-to-take-out-a-restraining-order hostile.

So, here I am, trying to make my way to class undetected. So far, so good. Hopefully, I don't have to worry about Roanlover565 who said she would (and I quote) *knife that bitch* if she finds out who I am.

I'm unfortunately serious.

"Ivy!"

Hurrying my step, I ignore the person calling my name. I want to get my classes over with and hole up in the studio for a couple of hours and pretend my life is as simple and uncomplicated as it was twenty-four short hours ago.

"Ivy!"

Finally recognizing the voice, I stop and turn as Finn jogs toward me with long-legged strides that eat up the distance between us. It takes approximately fifteen seconds before we're on the move again. Because of his ridiculous reaction to seeing me with Roan Saturday night, I'm hoping he hasn't—

"What the hell is going on between you and King?" This sounds suspiciously like it's going to be a repeat of our conversation from Saturday night. Perfect. Just what I need. His brows lower over his eyes. "You said you barely knew that piece of shit."

I almost wince at his harsh words.

Keeping my head down, I mutter, "Finn, I already told you, there's nothing going on between us."

Or maybe there is but it certainly isn't going any further than it already has. I mean...look at what's going on now! I can't leave my apartment without worrying about being knifed by some overzealous, internet stalking fangirl.

I don't need this kind of drama. And I certainly don't need Finn grilling me about my pseudo-relationship with Roan.

"Look, we need to talk." Not waiting for an answer, he wraps his fingers around my upper arm before pulling me out of the flow of student traffic.

The last thing I need is to be late for class. That will only attract more unwanted attention.

"Finn," exasperation simmers in my clipped tone, "I don't have time for this right now. I need to get to class."

A pissed off expression settles on his face. "I saw the pictures posted online, Ivy."

Behind my oversized sunglasses, one of my brows rises.

His face reddens before he mutters, "Someone showed them to me. That's the only reason I know about the website."

Right...

I can't help but sigh. This whole situation is so ridiculous. "Look, he gave me a ride home from work and we ended up getting smoothies. Then we researched our project at the library. That's it. End of story. Those pictures have totally been taken out of context."

Wanting him to see the seriousness of my expression, I lift the glasses from my face. "I don't know why someone would take pictures of us or post them online, making it look like something's going on when it's not, but that's exactly what they did. It's stupid."

His shoulders relax as some of the tension drains from his body. He grabs my hand, holding it in his larger one. "I had a really good time on Saturday." His earnest hazel eyes search mine. "I want to take you out again, Ivy."

I'm not sure that's a good idea anymore. And no, it has nothing to do with a certain dark-haired football player I shouldn't be thinking about.

Or his toe curling kisses...

Biting my lower lip, I finally hedge, "Right now isn't a good time. I feel like there's so much going on with classes and dance." When his face falls, I find myself hastily tacking on, "Maybe in a few weeks, when everything lightens up."

God, I could really kick myself for saying that. I may have liked Finn freshman year, but I don't think I'm into him the way I once was. And I don't think getting together a few more times is going to change that.

I should have told him the truth.

Disappointment settles over his face. "Sure. That sounds good. I'll text you."

"Okay." Glancing around, I realize the throng of students has thinned which means I'm probably late for class. Great. "Look, I've got to go."

Without waiting for a reply, I take off, hurrying across campus.

As I reach Adler Hall, I catch a glimpse of Roan surrounded by a large group of people. Even though I feel kind of lousy for doing it, I duck my head, hoping to avoid talking with him. We haven't spoken since he dropped me off yesterday afternoon, so I have no idea whether he knows about the pictures that have been posted online.

Regardless, this is business as usual for him.

Me, on the other hand, not so much.

I enjoy the attention and adulation I get from giving a kickass performance on stage. This is nothing like that. It's notoriety simply for being with someone famous.

And I'm not into that.

I'm pulling open the heavy glass door that leads inside the business building when a bulging arm reaches around, doing it for me. I'd recognize that ridiculously huge bicep anywhere. I don't even have to glance over my shoulder to see Roan standing behind me.

Is it bad that I know exactly what he smells like?

I probably shouldn't admit this, but I find his cologne completely intoxicating. Those wayward thoughts have me wanting to gnash my teeth in irritation. My attraction to Roan is pointless. What I need to do is get a firm grip on my unruly hormones before my life spirals further out of control.

"Thanks," I murmur before rushing through.

He falls in line with me. "So, are we still on for tomorrow night?"

I nod, knowing there's no choice in the matter. We have to work on our ethics project and that means spending time collaborating and meshing information. Although we don't necessarily have to go out in public for that to happen...right?

"Um, yeah, but I'm thinking it might be better if we work at my apartment instead of the library."

His arm snakes around my waist before dragging me to his side. His warm breath feathers across my neck. "If you want to be alone with me, gorgeous, just say the word. You don't have to create reasons to lure me back to your place."

He grins devilishly before I shove my way out of his arms. My feet come to a standstill as I glare at him. "I'm not trying to get you alone." I glance around. The last thing I need is more photographs surfacing. Curling my fingers around his wrist, I haul him into a darkened classroom so we can talk in private.

"Look," I can't help but bounce uneasily from one foot to the other before pushing out the words, "I don't want to be seen with you."

The sly grin which had been playing across his face morphs into an expression of shock. It makes me feel like a real piece of shit for being the one to put it there. But what else am I supposed to do? I need to distance myself from him. What I don't need is any more photos making me out to be public enemy number one.

The way his voice fills with disbelief has me wincing. "You don't want to be *seen* with me?"

Oh god, is that hurt I hear threading its way through his words?

Even though I feel like a real bitch, I continue, "Not after all those pictures were posted, I don't."

"What pictures?" He shakes his head in confusion. "What the hell are you talking about, Ivy?"

"Someone took photos of us yesterday and plastered them all over your stupid website."

He looks at me like he doesn't quite understand what the big deal is. "Okay, first off—it's not my website. And second—why is that a problem? I mean, we were studying at the library." Shrugging, he adds, "And we got smoothies. Why are you so upset about it?"

Digging out the phone from my bag, I pull up the website and click on the pictures before shoving it in his face. He takes the cell before slowly scrolling through each picture. It only takes a moment for the corners of his mouth to sink and his brows to draw together. Looking decidedly unhappy, he silently hands the phone back to me.

"Now do you understand why I'm upset?"

He jerks his head into a nod. "Yeah, I get it." Silently he plows his long fingers through his inky black hair.

Still feeling like an asshole, I say, "We don't have time to discuss this right now. We need to get to class."

"Yeah, okay." He looks distracted as we head toward the room. Unfortunately, I can tell by the absence of people in the halls that the lecture is already underway.

Is it too much to ask that we're able to sneak in unnoticed?

Probably.

I should have realized that would never happen. It's a well-known fact that Roan never flies under the radar. For god's sake, there's a website devoted solely to tracking his whereabouts. Like he's been outfitted with a Lojack or something.

Even though we're only a minute or two late, Professor Paulson has already begun lecturing. She doesn't stop when she sees us, but almost everyone turns to catch a glimpse of who hasn't made it to class on time. As my eyes scan all the faces that have swiveled toward us, I see two girls start whispering.

With my head bent, I quickly slink to my desk, but not before a few other girls hold up their phones for what I assume are pictures. My eyes flicker to Roan but he isn't looking at me, he's staring straight ahead.

Sliding into my seat, I do the same.

CHAPTER FOURTEEN

I have it on excellent authority that the girl Roan has been photographed with is nothing more than a partner for a class project. I think we can all breathe a huge sigh of relief that there's nothing going on between those two. I mean come on now...this is Roan King we're talking about. He doesn't do relationships. Thank goodness for that ;) KingOfCampus.com

I'm sitting in the middle of my bed with my laptop and my French book splayed open in front of me. I have an exam in two days and I'm trying to prepare for it when there's a light knock on my bedroom door. Since it's about eight at night, I've already showered and changed into a comfy tank top and pair of shorts.

Glancing up, I figure its Lexie. Although she usually barges in. I mean, too hell with privacy and all that crap... In her defense, I think we both know I'm not in here having some kind of hot monkey sex with anyone.

I suppose that in and of itself should have been the first tip-off that it wasn't Lexie.

"Since when do you bother knocking," I call out in response.

As the door swings open, Roan pokes his head around it. "Since you're already pissed at me, I figured I'd better not push it."

Our gazes collide as his legs eat up the short distance separating us. My room shrinks around him. I hadn't necessarily thought of it as tiny, but it certainly feels that way with him in it.

"Um, hi." I cock my head, racking my brain for our study schedule. "Were we supposed to work together tonight?" I wouldn't be sitting around in a tank top and tiny sleeping shorts...and no bra, if we were.

"No," he moves a little closer to the bed before tentatively settling at the end of it. My book and computer are between us and for some reason, I'm glad about that. The kiss we shared in the elevator flashes its way unwantedly through my head. It's definitely better to have a barrier between us. No matter how small it is. "I thought we should talk...in private."

One side of his mouth hitches into a thin smile.

Straightening, my gaze holds his turquoise-colored ones. God, but his eyes are completely stunning. They're such an unusual and bright greenish-blue hue. As I unconsciously sway toward him, I realize what I'm doing and jerk to awareness.

I clear my throat. "Yeah, that's probably a good idea."

"I," his big hand comes up to scratch at the dark stubble covering his chin before he continues, "guess I should apologize for this mess."

My brows snap together. "Why? None of it is your fault. It's not your website," god, it had better not be, "*right?*" My eyes narrow. If he has something to do with that freaking website, like he's trying to create more hype for himself, I'll punch him.

A few times.

Right in that pretty face of his.

He must see the murderous glint that enters my eyes because he immediately shakes his head. "No, of course not. I barely pay attention to all that crap." Then he amends, "But I know the site is out there. I got myself into a shitload of trouble last year when some pictures surfaced that were taken at a party. So, I know I have to be aware of what I'm doing when I'm out in public. It never occurred to me that picking you up from work and doing a little bit of research at the library would turn out to be such a big freaking deal."

I shrug, wanting to downplay everything that's happened since this morning but it's not easy. It feels like my life has been turned upside down. Other than keeping my distance from Roan, I don't know what else to do about it.

Diplomatically, I say, "I'm trying not to let it bother me."

"For what it's worth, I appreciate you being a good sport about it. Pictures of girls get posted online all the time but there are usually a few of them in the shot." He pauses before lowering his voice. "I guess that's why these photos are a big deal. It looks like more than just a random hookup. And I'm pretty much known for my one nighters."

Charming.

"But we're not going out and we're definitely not hooking up," I emphasize to him. Maybe I say the words for my own benefit as well. Just another reminder that there's absolutely nothing between us. We're partners for this project and that's it.

"I know, Ivy. But the pictures make it look like something is going on. And for whatever reason, people are interested in what I do and who I spend time with."

"Okay, I get that. If we make a concerted effort not to be seen together, then everything should die down, right?" That's what I'm hoping for. People aren't going to sit around talking about us if there aren't any new pictures to fuel speculation.

His gaze burns into mine before he finally admits, "Probably."

Even though this has only been going on for about twelve hours, I already know this kind of scrutiny isn't something I'd want to live with on a daily basis. I'm getting tons of text messages from people I didn't know had my number and my Facebook page has been flooded with friend requests as well as about forty messages asking if Roan and I are now an item. I keep denying it, but that hasn't quashed any of the buzz surrounding this whole ridiculous situation.

"Let me ask you something," he pauses as my gaze lifts to his, "does it really matter if people talk about us? We know what the truth is."

I sit up a little straighter before pulling my knees to my chest and hugging them close to my body. "People think we're like...*involved*. Why would you want that?"

"I didn't say I wanted it. But who the hell cares what people post on some stupid website? They don't even know us." He lets those words hang in the air before asking, "I mean, we're friends, right?"

Giving him a curious look, I can only respond to his question with one of my own. "I don't know. *Are* we friends?"

The corners of his mouth curl up just a bit. "Well, I was kind of thinking we were."

Narrowing my eyes, I ask, "Do you even have girls who are *just* friends?"

When he gives me a wolfish grin, I know that whatever he's about to say is meant to provoke a reaction from me. "Nope, but that doesn't mean we couldn't engage in a little friends-with-benefits action. I'd be totally onboard with that."

He doesn't disappoint.

I shake my head before replying drily, "We're not going to be *that* kind of friends."

His gaze falls to my lips. Then lowers further to my bare legs before rising again to my eyes. His voice deepens as if it's dropped a few octaves and it does something funny to my insides. Something I don't necessarily like or want.

"You sure about that, Ivy?"

My gaze flattens. "Positive. I think we need to keep things strictly platonic."

He leans closer and my heart skips a beat. "You have to admit, that was one hell of a kiss."

My mouth dries because that damn kiss keeps nudging its way back into my consciousness at the most inopportune of times. Instead of admitting how good it was, I clear my throat. "What kiss?"

The smile gracing his lips turns decidedly predatory. My eyes widen as I realize I've made a tactical error. "Maybe I should remind you just how good it was."

In the blink of an eye, I'm off the bed and practically out the door. His smile grows wider. As if he knows exactly what's going on inside my head. I really hate that he's able to tie my insides up into teeny tiny knots. I've never had that happen before. And I'm not quite sure how to handle it or make it go away.

How do you neutralize attraction like this?

"I'm, ah, going to get a bottle of water." I throw the words over my shoulder because I don't want to look him in the eyes again. Maybe I'm afraid he'll see the lie within mine. "You want one?"

I'm already halfway down the short hall when I hear him chuckling. "Sure."

As I walk through the living room, I see Lexie and Dylan snuggled up together on the couch. "Thanks for letting him in," I mutter on my way to the kitchen.

Lexie shrugs before shooting me a look that says it all. "I figured you guys had stuff to talk about."

Grumbling at her answer, I grab two bottles of water from the fridge. While I'm there, I close my eyes before inhaling and exhaling a deep breath. Then another. And then one more for good measure.

Do I want to kiss Roan again?

Ummmm, yeah. Of course I do.

That kiss was spectacular. But I know getting tangled up with him would be a *huge* mistake. He'd eat me alive and spit me out without thinking twice about it.

Once my libido is firmly under control, I reluctantly return to the bedroom. I'm a few feet away from the door when I hear Roan's deep voice. Like he's talking on the phone or something. I'm almost wondering if I should give him a little bit of privacy. Maybe go sit with Lexie and Dylan when I hear what sounds suspiciously like my father's voice.

Brows snapping together, my feet quicken because I have to be mistaken. There is no way in hell that Roan is somehow conversing with my dad.

As I burst through the doorway, I see Roan sprawled out on my bed with a phone—*my phone*—held in his large hand. He's staring at the screen, a wide smile on his face as he discusses the season...*with my dad*.

"No, I've been watching lots of film and I think we're going to be able to take them."

I actually wince when Dad responds enthusiastically. "I hope so. Everyone is talking about how strong both the offensive and defensive lines are this year. And your quarterback has one hell of an arm on him. It's very exciting. Did Ivy happen to mention that I played football my freshman and sophomore year at Barnett?"

His amused gaze slides to mine. "No, she didn't mention it. Anytime you'd like to attend a game, Mr. Kaster, just let me know and I'll get you some sweet tickets on the fifty-yard line."

"That would be great! I might just take you up on that offer, Roan. I think my wife would really enjoy seeing a Barnett football game. Especially this year."

The thought of Leah and my dad at Barnett as guests of Roan spurs me into action.

Oh.

Hell.

No.

Those are the only words careening through my head as I race to the bed. Our gazes continue to cling as I barrel toward him like a freight train.

"Oh, I think Iv—"

That's all he's able to get out before I'm ripping the phone out of his fingers. If I'm lucky, I managed to leave a few claw marks. God damn it! I seriously can't believe this is happening right now! Then I remember to smooth out my features before looking at the small screen. "Ahh, hi, Dad. What are you calling for? You never call on a Monday night. Is something wrong?"

Normally we speak every Sunday afternoon. Except for yesterday because I was busy. If he has any inkling that I'm angry about everything that went down after my mom died, it's not something we discuss. Or even acknowledge. It's all been swept neatly under the rug where it can fester.

At least for me, it does.

"I was hoping that maybe you could come home next weekend and spend the day with us."

Without even thinking about what I have going on, I immediately shake my head. "That sounds great, but I don't think I can make it, Dad. I don't have a way to get home."

Sure, I could probably borrow Lexie's little silver Jetta but I'm not going to ask.

"Oh."

That's all he says as his face falls. The difference in his lighthearted banter with Roan only a few moments ago and mine is a stark reminder that the past sits heavily between us. As difficult as it is, I press my lips together, not saying a word.

After a long uncomfortable silence, he says, "We haven't seen you since you left for Paris and that was almost sixteen months ago. You've been so busy since you came back, and we wanted to give you a little bit of time to settle in."

We.

Him and Leah.

Always him and Leah.

Hearing him say that is like fingernails slowly scratching their way down a chalk board. I almost flinch in response.

"You haven't seen your family in sixteen months?"

I almost shoot Roan a dirty look before remembering that the camera is focused on me and Dad is watching. Instead I ground out, "I was in Paris for fifteen of those months and I've been really busy with school and work. I've only been back here for a few weeks. I'm still getting acclimated." It takes all my self-control not to snarl at him like some junkyard dog on a choke chain.

Silently, Roan cocks his head as he watches me. It's almost like he's trying to sift through the lies shuttered within my eyes. I would dearly love to rip him a new one right now for picking up the phone, but I can't. After I disconnect, Roan is going to get an ass chewing of epic proportions.

"Can you at least try to make it home this weekend, Ivy? The kids would love to see their big sister."

I grit my teeth because their children are not my siblings. They probably don't even know who the hell I am. I haven't seen them since...

I rack my brain. Although it's not difficult to figure out. I marked the fifth year of Mom's death which means the twins just turned four. So, when I left, they were around two or so.

It's doubtful they even know I exist.

"Yeah, I'll try, Dad." My heart feels as if it's going to pound right out of my chest with the uncomfortableness that has settled over us like a heavy blanket. It's one that will end up suffocating the hell out of me one day.

My fingers twitch wanting to hit the red disconnect button and pull the plug on this horrifically awkward conversation. Then, in a day or two, I'll send him a quick text letting him know that it's just not going to work out this weekend.

Oh well...

"Hey, I can drive Ivy home on Sunday."

My mouth tumbles open before my wide eyes swing to Roan. I want to yell—*noooooooo* but I can't. Absolutely no sound comes out at all. Not even a little squeak of protest.

My dad's face breaks into a delighted smile. "That would be fantastic, Roan! Ivy's stepmother and I would really appreciate it." He takes a breath before continuing. "Are you sure it's not a problem?"

Yes, I want to scream, *it's a huge freaking problem*!

This can't be happening. I want to kill Roan! As soon as this call is finished, that's exactly what I'm going to do. And then Roan-fucking-King will be no more.

My eyes narrow as I fume. Just look at him over there...he's totally oblivious to my seething anger. In the very next moment, he squeezes his face in next to mine so that it fills half the tiny screen.

"No problem at all, Mr. Kaster. I look forward to meeting you in person. I can't believe you used to play for Barnett! That's so awesome."

Grrrr.

It feels as if I'm clenching my jaw so tightly that all my teeth are going to shatter.

"Yeah, it'll be a fun afternoon. I'll have to dust off some of the old newspaper clippings I still have." His gaze drifts back to mine. "I can't wait to see you, sweetheart. It's been much too long."

Unable to do anything else, I smile weakly in response until I'm able to disconnect. Then I throw my phone onto the bed before using both hands to shove at Roan's strapping chest with all my might.

I can't believe he did that to me!

Unprepared for my violent assault, he tumbles against my pillows in surprise. His eyes are like huge saucers. The look of cluelessness would be comical if there were anything remotely amusing about this situation. Almost immediately, he props himself up on his elbows so that he's facing me. Albeit from a prone position on my bed as I tower over him in fury.

"Ah, you're welcome," he drawls.

Oh, that is it!

Throwing my hands up in the air, I screech like a pterodactyl, *"What the hell did you do that for?"*

His brows pull together until they're nothing more than a tight line across his forehead, as if he's bewildered by how this is playing out. "Do *what*? What did I do?" His gaze searches mine for a long silent moment before he asks, "You didn't want to go home and see your family? I thought I was doing you a *favor*."

"Well, you didn't! The last place I want to go is home!" Absurdly frustrated, I hop off the bed before pacing. After a few silent minutes, I say, "I'll just tell him you had to cancel at the last minute. It's not a big deal." I'm talking to myself now, trying to fix the mess he's gotten me into.

This is what he's driven me to...actually holding conversations with myself.

As he drags himself to a seated position, Roan watches me as I frantically walk the small space between the door and the bed. "Why don't you want to see your family?" His words are quietly spoken as if he's only now realizing what a colossal mistake he's made.

My footsteps stutter as I turn to scowl at him. "It's a long story," I mutter under my breath, not wanting to share the details of my life with Roan. We're not friends. Even though he said we were, we're not.

Aside from Lexie, I don't do that with anyone.

He stares at me expectantly as if silently trying to prod me into proceeding. Which isn't going to happen. Instead I snap, "Why the hell would you answer my phone?"

He glances at my black encased phone that has an image of tattered pink ballet shoes on the back. "No passcode."

I fold my arms tightly across my chest before searing him with the heat of my glare. "Not having a passcode isn't an invitation for you to answer the damn thing."

His mouth quirks. "Apparently it is. If it had been passcode protected, I couldn't have answered your phone when you decided to turn tail and run instead of answering my question about the kiss. If you think about it, none of this would have happened if you'd just responded." He points to me before saying, "So, this is really your fault."

I gasp.

"Should've had a passcode and shouldn't have run away when we were discussing that kiss."

I look at him in stupefied amazement. "Not only are you demented, you're totally delusional as well."

He chuckles before springing forward and nabbing my hand. Then he pulls me to him until I'm tumbling onto his lap. Not a moment later, his arms wrap around me, pinning me tightly against him. My breath hitches as I stare into those gorgeous eyes of his.

"I don't think I'm delusional at all. That kiss was pretty damn fantastic." He tilts his head before murmuring, "Don't you want to find out if it was as good as you remember it being?"

Someone needs to slap me silly because yeah...I kind of want to find that out. It was a completely spectacular kiss and I'm seriously hoping that I've built up the whole thing in my head. Because if I haven't...well, then...Roan King is the best kiss I've ever had.

And that would be all kinds of depressing.

Not that I'll be mentioning this to Roan, but I let Finn kiss me on Saturday night and it was decidedly lacking. Needless to say, it isn't Finn's kiss I've been fantasizing about for the past couple days.

With my gaze locked on his, I nip my bottom lip between my teeth. "Ummm, I don't know."

God knows I would dearly love to kiss him again but I'm clinging to the knowledge that it's a bad idea. Make that a disastrous idea.

He leans closer until his warm minty breath feathers slightly across my lips. Until the scent of him is nothing short of intoxicating. "It's just a kiss, Ivy."

Just a kiss...

That is true. It would be *just* a kiss because we are definitely not going any further than that.

I gnaw my lower lip with indecision. His gaze drops to my mouth before he groans. I hear it rumble from deep within his chest before escaping through his parted lips. This might be the only way to prove to myself that I've built up that kiss in my head. If it turns out to be nothing special, then I can stop thinking about him and move on.

"Okay," I agree before good sense returns and I chicken out.

Barely do I breathe out the word before his lips are sliding across mine, caressing them with soft yet sure strokes. Without a second thought, I tangle my arms around his neck before dragging his body closer. The growl-like sound he makes in approval fills my ears. His lips never leave mine for long. They may slant this way or that way before nipping at my bottom lip, but they're constantly roving over mine.

I don't know how long we stay fused together, stroking each other before his tongue slips inside my mouth. He caresses me with deep strokes that almost drive me to the brink of insanity. So drunk on the taste of him, I don't realize that I'm straddling his lap, grinding myself against him.

Although, to be fair, he's thrusting against me as well.

If what I'm feeling is a true indication of what lies beneath those jeans, he's huge. But I have no plans to find that out firsthand. And yet, knowing there will never be anything meaningful between us, here I am practically dry humping him in my bedroom. Actually, there's no *practically* about it. I *am* dry humping the guy all the while playing an intense game of tonsil hockey.

It takes effort to fight my way out of the thick fog that has descended with the first slide of his lips against mine. Oh, who am I kidding, I was a goner when he pulled me onto his lap and wrapped those bulging arms around me.

This was just plain stupid.

I'm an idiot for allowing it to happen.

Again.

Slowly I loosen my arms from around his neck before using my palms to reluctantly push against his chest. And yeah, he's as solid as a damn rock. The athlete in me totally appreciates the beauty of all that well-honed muscle. It's obvious he spends hours in the gym working out and training on the field. He's definitely one hell of a beautiful specimen.

Not understanding why I'm pushing away from him, his cloudy gaze lifts to mine. It's a slight consolation that I'm not the only one befuddled by that kiss. His eyes gradually clear before sinking to my mouth. He licks his lips as if seconds away from diving in for more.

In truth, I want that as much as he does. But that doesn't necessarily feel like the best idea right now. Or probably ever.

At the end of the day, he's still Roan King. Resident football god at Barnett. Future NFL prospect. Totally gorgeous man. And he's smart, too. That's clear from the little bit of research we've done together. He sounds almost too good to be true.

But that's the thing.

He is.

Roan isn't interested in being tied down to one girl. He's into hooking up for the night and moving on without so much as a second thought. A laugh bubbles up in my throat as I search his heated turquoise-colored eyes. They are totally mesmerizing in their depth and intensity. I understand why he has inspired legions of women at Barnett to trail after him. To cyberstalk him.

Who wouldn't want to tame a guy like that?

Even I, a girl who considers herself to be above all that BS, feel slightly tempted to try my hand at it. But that's where the logical side of my brain kicks in. I know all too well that trying to bring a guy like Roan to heel rarely works.

Instead, I'll be the one nursing a broken heart and I'm unwilling to take that chance. My ex-boyfriend hurt me enough after I left for my study abroad program. It's obvious that Finn and Roan are cut from the same cloth. Which is probably why they don't seem to like one another. As tempted as I am to take this attraction further, I know exactly how it will end.

And that's badly.

For me.

In silence, I tear myself from his arms before climbing unsteadily to my feet. Even though my heart is racing, and my breathing hasn't evened out, I know I'm doing the smart thing. I can't do a hookup situation which is the only thing Roan is capable of. And that's fine. I'm not judging him for it. I'm just not interested in being a one-night stand.

"Ivy?"

His eyes have cleared but he hasn't moved from my bed.

With my arms wrapped around my middle, I say in a voice that sounds surprisingly husky, "I think you should leave now."

Emotion snaps in his eyes before he rises to his feet. Our gazes lock and hold as he moves toward me. My breath catches. If he takes me into his arms again, I honestly don't know if I'll be able to push him away. It feels as if it took everything I had inside to do it the first time. When our faces are little more than a scant inch apart, his lips ghost over mine.

"Admit it, Ivy, it was a damn good kiss."

Oh, there's definitely no question about it. And I would look like a huge liar if I tried to say differently.

"It was," I agree softly.

Looking slightly surprised by my easy capitulation, his gaze falls to my lips. "Don't you want more?"

The husky cadence of his voice has me biting down on my lower lip in an attempt to stifle the small whimper that is desperate to escape.

"Yes," I finally admit.

Heat flashes in those gorgeous eyes of his.

"So do I," he pauses before saying in a gravelly voice that sounds as if it's been roughed up with sandpaper, "and I want more than just your mouth."

His fingers rise until the pad of his thumb can gently caress my lower lip. The intensity of his gaze is fixated on the leisure movement. It feels as if I'm being burned alive by the fire in his eyes.

Without warning, his hand falls away. I can't help but suck in a ragged breath hoping that maybe he'll finally put a little distance between us and allow me some breathing room to collect my scattered thoughts. Instead, he wraps his hand around the back of my neck before dragging me forward until his lips are fused to mine.

If I were smart, I would step away from him, but I don't. Oh no.

I'm practically melting in his arms as his lips rove over mine before his tongue slips inside my mouth. That soft little mewling noise I was trying so very hard not to make, finally escapes. This only spurs him on. His mouth moves with more intensity as he deepens the kiss.

My fingers curl into the soft material of his T-shirt as he draws away from me. His heavy-lidded gaze holds mine for a moment before he whispers thickly, "I'll be seeing you, Ivy."

Then he walks out of my room without a backward glance. I hear a few murmured words exchanged between Dylan, Lexie, and him before the front door closes. Then I do the only thing I can and sink to my knees on the carpeted floor and wonder how in the hell I'm going to avoid what would most likely be the hottest sex of my life.

CHAPTER FIFTEEN

There are parties going on, but no Roan King. He's been inconspicuously absent from all the festivities. I'm starting to have withdrawals. Does anyone know where RK has been hiding himself? Update ASAP! KingOfCampus.com

"So, are you going to tell me what the deal is with your family?" Roan slants a look in my direction before his gaze arrows to the road in front of him.

Yeah, I probably should. In less than an hour, we'll be there. It's just that...well, I'm feeling conflicted. Not about my family, but about Roan. The guy has knocked me off balance. After sharing that totally hot kiss Monday night, I was prepared for him to come at me hard. It's not exactly a secret that he wants to sleep with me.

But he hasn't.

At all.

Here's the bad part—I don't know if I'm relieved or disappointed by his lack of pursuit. I have the sneaking suspicion that it's not relief coursing through me.

Sure, I saw him in class on Wednesday and Friday. And we spoke briefly. We worked together at the library on Tuesday night and then again on Friday afternoon. Our project on Bernie Madoff and his Ponzi scheme is coming along nicely. The more research I pour over, the worse I feel for all those people who were scammed out of their life savings. Some of them lost everything they had, all of their retirement money.

And for what?

Greed.

Sheer greed.

It makes me sick inside to think about it.

Both of the times we studied together, he was a perfect gentleman. Or friend. Because I guess, rather surprisingly, that's what we are now. It's like those two kisses never happened.

Relief should be coursing through me.

But it's not...

"Ivy?"

"What?" With a light blush tinging my cheeks, I blink back to the present and the question he asked. "Oh...my family. Right." Taking a deep breath, I waffle for a minute or two before deciding to fill him in. Everything in me feels weighted down as I think about Mom and what happened after she died. Honestly, I'd had every intention of cancelling today. Simply telling my dad that something came up with Roan and he wouldn't be able to drive me to their house.

But...

I actually think having him there today will be something of a distraction. For all of us. I've seen firsthand how people react to him, how they gravitate toward him. So maybe I'm using him to ease the tension I know will be there with my family. And if not today, it would have happened sooner or later. Even I realize I can't keep pushing it off indefinitely.

I have no doubt that Roan will end up regretting his little burst of altruism by the end of the day. Which kind of makes me want to snicker. He deserves it for shoving his nose where it didn't belong.

"I'll give you the condensed version."

I have to take another deep breath. It's difficult discussing my mom with anyone. Even though she's been gone for five years, fresh waves of grief roll through me when I think about her. Which is why I usually avoid talking about the topic. It's too painful and other than Lexie, there's no one else I feel comfortable unloading on. My mom's parents are both dead and Dad has apparently closed that chapter of his life and moved on.

Sightlessly, I stare down at my fingers which twist nervously in my lap. It's not until Roan reaches out, slipping my hand into his, that I remember he's sitting next to me.

"You don't have to tell me, if you don't want to." He gives me a gentle squeeze.

Those must be the magic words because once the floodgates open, they don't close until I've purged myself of everything. When I'm finished, I steal another glance at him.

He must sense my curious gaze because his fingers tighten around mine before he clears his throat. "That really sucks, Ivy. I'm sorry I forced you into this."

Laughter gurgles up in my throat. "You're lucky I didn't kill you with my bare hands Monday night."

A slight smile tugs at his lips. "I would have killed me, too. You showed incredible restraint."

Shrugging, my gaze falls to my fingers. *Our fingers.* He's still holding my hand in his larger one and the sight of them together makes my belly prickle with unwanted nerves. "Thanks."

He's quiet for a long moment before asking, "Do you want me to turn around and head back to campus? You could always call and tell them that one of us got sick. I don't know...make something up." His gaze fastens on mine for a heartbeat. "We don't have to do this. I'm sorry for forcing it on you."

I mull over his words. Honestly, I appreciate him offering to turn around and take us back to school. Even though I could have strangled him when he piped up with the suggestion, I've come to realize that it's best this way. I don't have to be alone with them and Roan has already hit it off with my father, so that will help smooth things over for the afternoon. Plus, nothing will get too heavy with him there. Everyone, including myself, will be on their best behavior.

"No. As long as you don't mind, we'll go."

His gaze latches onto mine for a few seconds before sliding back to the black ribbon of highway stretched out in front of us. "I don't mind. I'm the one who opened his big mouth and put you in this situation in the first place."

"Yeah," I agree wholeheartedly, "you did." A tentative smile tugs at my lips.

He shakes his head and mutters, "No good deed goes unpunished."

I can't help but snort with laughter. "You got that right."

Forty minutes later, we pull in front of my dad's house. The one he bought with Leah after they got married so they could have a fresh start. What that translates into is that she hadn't wanted to share a house with my mother's ghost and memories. I can't help but stare up at it dispassionately. It doesn't feel like home at all. Even though I lived here for two years before leaving for college, there are no fond memories to be had.

There's just...nothing.

It's like going to visit a distant relative I have absolutely no connection with.

A fresh wave of sadness rushes over me.

As if sensing my distress, Roan squeezes my hand again and that's when I realize he's been holding it for almost an hour. Gently I slip my fingers free. They feel a little too good wrapped up in his strength. I don't want to feel that because it's not real.

The intimacy between us isn't real.

"You ready?"

Not daring to speak, because if I do, I'll probably ask him to drive me straight back to campus, I jerk my head into a tight nod before unclasping my seatbelt. Taking a deep breath, I open the door and swing my legs out. It's weird that I haven't been back here in almost a year and a half. My gaze roves over the two-story Arts and Craft style house.

Leah had wanted something with character. Lots of wood and built-ins. Everything has been updated but it has stayed true to the original concept and style of the house. Again, it couldn't be more different than the rectangle saltbox I spent the first sixteen years of my life in. Even though Leah and my dad have both told me a countless number of times that this is my home and I should feel comfortable here, I don't.

I'm like a stranger who doesn't quite fit in.

I try not to dwell on the fact that ever since Mom died, I don't feel like I belong anywhere.

As I force myself to walk toward the house, Roan is at my side. I can't help but glance at him, suddenly glad he's here with me which is completely bizarre because we haven't known each other all that long. We're barely friends and yet, here he is, catching a glimpse into something so intensely personal. It leaves me feeling vulnerable and exposed in a way I don't particularly feel comfortable with.

As we're climbing up the cement front stairs, I reach out, taking hold of his hand, halting his progress to the door with its ornate beveled glass window. "Thank you." I gulp out the words. "I appreciate you doing this for me."

His blueish-green eyes burn into mine right before his hand tightens around my fingers. Then he's pulling me to him until I'm flush against his body. "I'm sorry I forced you into this," he whispers, gaze searching mine. "I should have kept my mouth shut." His lips twitch with a spark of humor. "I shouldn't have answered your phone."

The corners of my mouth lift as a brow slides upward and I can't resist asking, "Even though I don't have a passcode?"

He grins. The way his gaze caresses mine has my breath hitching.

"Not being passcode protected," he recites as if he's heard it a million times, "is not an invitation to answer someone's phone...or take a gander at their emails...or text messages...or listen to their surprisingly awful taste in music."

All thoughts of the excruciating afternoon stretched out ahead of us vanishes as I gasp, "You didn't!"

He compresses his lips tightly together looking slightly apologetic before clearing his throat. "I might have peeked through a few things."

It's not like I have intensely personal stuff on there, but still! That's a total invasion of privacy!

Grrrr.

Right as I'm about to blast him, his lips descend until they whisper across mine but never quite touch. More like hover.

After a long drawn out moment, he finally murmurs against them, "How about we focus on the fact that I've learned my lesson and I'll never do it again."

All of the fight that had been brewing in me evaporates as we stare at one another. I'm wondering if he's going to kiss me again when the front door is yanked open. We jerk apart so abruptly that I almost lose my footing which is exactly when Roan slides an arm around my waist. We turn toward my father who stands on the other side of the threshold with a bemused expression on his face as his eyes bounce from me to Roan before settling on me again.

"Ivy." He steps forward and tugs me into his arms. Once they're secured around me, he whispers, "It's good to see you." Then he's pulling back, taking a long look at me. "And you're even more beautiful than before!"

Roan thrusts out his hand for Dad to shake. "It's nice to meet you, Mr. Kaster."

"You, too. Thanks again for driving Ivy home." His gaze bounces between us as if trying to figure out what we are to one another. A speculative gleam enters his eyes. Clearly, he's getting ridiculous ideas about the state of our relationship that I'll have to correct at a later date.

Then we're being ushered inside the house. For a moment, my gaze flies around the living room. It's like stepping back in time. Almost nothing has changed since I left. Some of the pictures hanging on the wall are different, but that's about it.

"Sit down, make yourself comfortable. Can I get you something to eat or drink?"

Now that we've greeted one another, awkwardness descends fairly quickly. "We'll have some water, Dad." I feel like a guest in this house. It sucks. "Thanks."

"Nothing to eat? How about some chips or a sandwich? I know it was a long drive."

We both shake our heads. "Nope, water is fine."

He disappears into the kitchen. I rise to my feet, moving toward the fireplace as restlessness sets in. Above it hangs a huge sixteen by twenty-inch framed family portrait.

Except I'm not in it which makes perfect sense because I don't feel like I'm part of this family. Roan says nothing as he moves to stand beside me. When I continue to stare at the picture, his hand slips into mine and something loosens inside me. For some reason, my chest doesn't feel nearly as constricted as it did a few moments ago.

I study the little girl and boy grinning back from the photograph. I'm guessing since the twins look so much older than when I last saw them, this must be a recent picture. Almost begrudgingly, I admit they're adorable. Nora has long caramel-colored hair which she must have inherited from my father. It looks to be the same exact shade of golden brown as mine. And Nolan has bright blond hair like Leah.

"She looks like you," he comments softly.

Almost dispassionately, I study the picture for another long moment. "A little bit," I finally concede.

Nora's facial features are a mix of Leah and my father. My eyes are similar to my dad's, but my lips and cheekbones are all my mother's. She had a long lean body like I do. She wasn't a dancer, but she could have been. She was tall. Around five eight or so, like me.

Without another word, I turn away, dismissing the picture as my father comes back with two bottles of water. His gaze flits to the professionally taken photograph.

Handing us our waters, he says, "We had that done last spring,"

I turn to stare at the portrait again, feeling more removed from the situation. From them. He may be my father, but he started another family and it's obvious there isn't room for me in it.

"It's a nice photo." Needing something to occupy my fingers, I twist off the cap and take a long swig. We've only just arrived, and already this afternoon feels as if it will never end. I'm a fidgety nervous mess. I want to get the hell out of here.

"We'd like to get another one taken next spring with all five of us," he says softly, as if he can tell my feelings are hurt even though I haven't done or said anything to give him that impression.

Instead of responding, I ask the dreaded question. "Where are Leah and the kids?"

"They had to run a few errands. They'll be back soon, I'm sure."

"Okay." I head back to the couch. Roan sits next to me as my father takes a seat in the armchair across from us.

Awkward tension swirls through the air as my father blurts, "How do you two know each other?"

I glance at Roan from the corner of my eye only to find him staring back at me. There's a slight smile tipping his lips upward and I'm slammed with the memory of colliding into him and dumping my iced coffee down the front of his T-shirt. I almost shake my head because I absolutely do not want to share that story with my dad.

Roan arches a brow as if silently encouraging me to take the lead on this one. Clearing my throat, my gaze shifts to my dad where I force it to stay. "We have a Business Ethics class together and we've been partnered up for a project."

"We also live in the same apartment building," the boy next to me adds. "Lexie is going out with my roommate, Dylan."

"Well, that's nice. You two must see quite a bit of each other then."

I shrug. Obviously, my father thinks there's something going on between us. I'm not sure if I should disabuse him of this notion. Just as I'm contemplating what to do, Roan shifts his body toward mine before sliding an arm around my shoulders. Dad's lips lift as the back door is thrown open and little feet pound their way into the house. It's doubtful a herd of stampeding elephants could make as much noise as those two.

"I guess they're home." Dad rises, going to the kitchen to meet his wife. I hear her ask if we've already arrived and then their voices drop. I'm not sure if we should follow him into the kitchen or not, so I opt for staying put on the couch.

Roan squeezes my shoulder with the hand that's draped across me. "You doing okay?"

I blow out a steady breath, wishing we could make a run for it. "I want to get out of here," I mutter.

He nods as his eyes fill with a mixture of sympathy and compassion. Two emotions I never thought I'd see from him. I feel staggered by the weight of his stare. By what I see reflected within his bright depths.

"I know," he replies. Then he says the most unexpected thing. "But

I'm here with you, Ivy. And so far, everything is going smoothly." Leaning closer, his lips brush against my temple.

If I'd thought I was taken aback by the look in his eyes, his words blow me away. I open my mouth to say something. What exactly, I don't know...but no sound comes out. Which is a first.

Thankfully, I'm saved from myself and the strange emotions he rouses inside me when Dad, Leah, and the kids join us in the living room. Nora and Nolan race from the kitchen, their feet pounding against the hardwood floor with every step they take. Brilliant smiles wreath their faces like its Christmas morning or their birthdays or both, all rolled up into one. They're practically vibrating with pent-up excitement. When they see us sitting on the couch, they skid to a halt which is kind of comical.

My dad says to the twins, "Remember your sister, Ivy? The one who lived in Paris?"

They stare silently at him and my heart plummets to the tips of my toes before jackhammering painfully. Why would he point out in front of everyone that they have no clue who I am?

But then Nora runs over to an end table and grabs a silver-framed photograph with chubby little fingers. Showing my dad and Leah, who both smile at her, she hesitantly shuffles her way toward me with a shy smile curving her cherub-like lips upward.

As I stare at the photo from my high school graduation, she points to me and says, "Ivy."

Why that should have tears welling in my eyes is beyond me. I can't help but give a thin, wobbly smile as I feel Roan softly stroke his hand over my jean clad thigh before giving it a gentle squeeze. Clearing my throat, I say, "Yep, that's me. Ivy."

She bestows a bright smile on me and my heart, the one I thought was stone cold where these two kids were concerned, begins to thaw.

Leah steps forward, her hand going to Nora's shoulder. "We've missed you, Ivy. I'm really glad you were able to make it home today." Then she introduces herself and the kids to Roan.

Apparently not wanting to be left out, Nolan yells, "Cake!"

Leah shushes him and Dad laughs before the twins scamper into the kitchen. They scream wildly before the chanting begins.

"Cake, cake, cake!"

"Well, I guess the cat's out of the bag now." She nods toward the back of the house. "How about we take this to the kitchen? The kids have something to show you."

Roan and I follow my father and Leah. His eyes search mine as if silently asking again if I'm doing okay. I give him a slight smile in response.

As soon as we pass through the door jamb into the sun-filled kitchen, the twins jump up and down, yelling, "Surprise!" Or rather some garbled version of it.

Their excitement and sheer happiness are infectious, and I can't help but grin in earnest as I glance around the room. Roan slides his arm around my waist as I take in all the balloons and the banner hanging up that reads—*Welcome Home, Ivy!* And who could miss the cake in the shape of the Eiffel Tower that now has a huge swipe taken out of it?

"Hey, bud," Roan says, pointing to Nolan's mouth, "I think you got a little something-something on your face."

Nolan wipes the back of his hand across his lips before grinning devilishly at his mother.

"We're having lunch, then cake," she admonishes gently, although she doesn't seem put out by his behavior, "not the other way around."

Overwhelmed, I take in the colorful display of pink and black balloons and the banner that is strung from one corner of the kitchen to the other as well as the beautiful cake. I...I can't believe they did this for me. I really can't. Again, I feel a slight burning sensation against the back of my eyelids before doing my best to blink the unexpected emotion away.

I've been holding on to my anger for so long, I'm not quite sure what to do with it. My gaze slides to Leah in confusion. I can't help but stare at her quizzically, not understanding why she would go to all this trouble for me. I haven't been nice to her over the years. I mean, she barged her way into our lives before I was ready for my dad to move on.

And I took it out on her every chance I could.

The rest of the afternoon progresses in much the same fashion. It's actually...kind of...*nice*. Leah asks me a lot of questions about Paris. Dad and Roan talk football. And the twins run around like their butts are on fire before dragging me and Roan off to their bedrooms to see all the toys they have accumulated in four short years.

As I walk through the upstairs hallway, I peek hesitantly inside the room I lived in for the last two years of high school. It looks exactly the same as the day I left. Which, I hate to admit, feels a little bit like balm against my abraded soul.

Why it should matter, I have no clue. It's not like I'm here often. I visit only when I absolutely have to. Like Thanksgiving and Christmas. Other than that, I've become extremely good at manufacturing excuses to avoid them.

And yet, they kept my room. They could have packed everything up into boxes and given the kids a much-needed playroom, but they didn't. They kept a space for me as if I belong here with them. As if I *am* part of this family.

As tangled up in my thoughts as I am, I know the precise moment Roan steps behind me. His presence is overwhelming and for some strange reason, I feel attuned to him. Silently, his breath feathers across the back of my neck. A slight shiver races through me at his proximity.

"Old room?"

I nod as my gaze slides over what I've chosen to leave behind. The white four poster bed, shelves of dance competition trophies, a pair of well-loved pink ballet shoes hanging from ribbons on the wall, light blue billowy curtains, along with favorite books. The only thing missing is my dresser which I have in my apartment.

As I move further into the room, Roan's eyes seem to take in everything which leaves me feeling oddly exposed. All of this stuff, it's who I am. It's what makes up the jagged pieces of me. On the nightstand table is a framed photograph. He picks it up and studies it.

The picture was snapped about six months before Mom was diagnosed with breast cancer. Every time I look at it, I can't help but remember how good our life was right before it blew up.

Sometimes it's hard to believe that everything can be perfectly fine one moment and then in complete shambles the next. And there's nothing that can prepare you for it, either. It sneaks up on you out of nowhere. And then...nothing is ever the same again.

It never goes back to normal.

Not the normal you used to know and never quite appreciated. It settles into a pattern of tests, chemo, and bouts of sickness as things slowly slide downhill instead of getting better until you finally manage to forget entirely that there ever was a time in your life when you were happy and carefree and...normal.

It sucks.

Cancer fucking sucks.

"You look just like her."

I give him a strained smile knowing it's filled with achy sadness. After all these years, it still hurts to look at that picture which is exactly why I left it in my old bedroom. I can't bear knowing Mom is really gone and isn't coming back. That everything I go through will be without her guidance and advice.

Carefully, he sets the framed photo back on the nightstand. He does it as if it's the most precious thing in the world which leaves my heart feeling raw and defenseless. Roan isn't the guy I originally pegged him to be. He has a softer, gentler side he keeps buried beneath the cocky, I-can-get-as-much-ass-as-I-want football player.

I'm kind of wishing he were the one-dimensional ball player I'd assumed he was. That guy was easily resistible. This guy...the one with me today, he's doing things to my insides that scare the shit out of me. I'm starting to realize that Roan isn't one or the other, but a combination of both.

With his gaze cradling mine, he closes the distance between us until I have to tilt my head to hold his stare. I can't help but inhale a shaky breath as his left hand slides its way across my cheek until he's able to cup it.

"I don't like to see you sad."

"I'm fine," I lie.

His thumb strokes the corner of my mouth as his eyes continue searching mine. Sifting carefully through all the emotion brimming within them. It has me wondering exactly what he sees when he gazes at me. I've never had anyone look at me the way he does. Almost as if he sees the real me.

The real Ivy.

It's a scary prospect.

Feeling oddly disconcerted, I have to remind myself that whoever this guy is, he isn't the real Roan. This is just a small slice of who he truly is.

His brows draw together as he studies me. "What are you thinking about?"

Unwilling to divulge the truth, I shake my head. A tiny smile flits its way across my lips. I have the feeling it looks as bittersweet as it feels. "Nothing."

Even though he doesn't look convinced, Roan doesn't push the conversation any further. Instead, he leans forward until his mouth can stroke over mine. We stand in the middle of my old bedroom with the door wide open. When his tongue nudges my lips, I can't help but open for him.

His kisses are completely addictive. I could easily fall for the Roan King I've been treated to today, but I know deep down that would be a huge mistake. One I'm not willing to make. It hurt when Finn broke up with me and it hurt to see all the girls that filled my spot while I was gone. Which is exactly the way it would be with Roan.

Except worse.

Roan isn't interested in a relationship. He's interested in straight up sex. And that's not something I've done before. I'm not sure if I'm capable of casual sex on a regular basis. As uncomplicated as it sounds, it's anything but.

CHAPTER SIXTEEN

Roan

"Dude, what the hell is wrong with you? You're so fucking quiet today."

My focus is centered on pushing the bar all the way up before bringing it down to my chest. I want to think about bench pressing... not Ivy. Unfortunately, she refuses to vacate the space in my head. Especially after the trip to her house.

For whatever reason, that day feels like a turning point in our relationship.

"I'm trying to concentrate, that's all." I keep my gaze trained on the bar and not on Dylan who spots me from behind. The last thing I need is for him to catch a whiff of my growing interest in Ivy. I already know how that would go over.

"Is it a chick?"

Unconsciously my brow furrows before I can stop it. A dead give-away, but I smooth it out before he can—

"Christ, it *is* a chick. Since when do you have female problems?" He's almost giddy with the prospect. The biggest issue I usually have with women is getting them to back off after we've had sex. I've never had a girl work her way under my skin. Ivy is a first. An itch that is all but impossible to scratch. And I don't like that one damn bit. I'm kind of hoping I can just ride this one out and my interest in her will wane with enough time.

It could happen, right?

"Who's the chick?" He grins until I get the urge to punch the smirk off his face. "I'm dying to know."

The only reason he's *dying to know* is so he can run his pussy whipped ass back to his girlfriend and crow about how I've fallen for some female.

"There's no girl," I grunt, pushing upward again. I practically growl out the next words, wanting him to drop the subject. "Can you stop running your fucking mouth and focus?"

He snorts. "Since when don't we talk shit when lifting?"

Well, he's got me there. We usually talk shit. A whole bunch of it. And lifting is the perfect time to do it, too. The music is blasting and talking helps pass the time. If I'm going to get this asshole off my back, then I need to play this a lot cooler. "Look, there's no girl. I just have a lot on my mind."

He makes a noncommittal noise deep in his throat as if he doesn't believe me, which let's face it, he probably doesn't. Dylan and I have roomed together since freshman year. Between that, playing football, and working out together, we know each other pretty damn well.

He's the first one to call bullshit when it needs to be called.

Which is both a blessing and a curse.

I flick a glance at him as I lower the bar. His eyes are narrowed speculatively and if I didn't know better, I'd say the little hamster upstairs was busy spinning on its wheel as he tries to figure this one out. I see the precise moment his brain locks on to an idea and almost swear under my breath.

"This better not have anything to do with Ivy."

Once again, I focus on raising the bar. "Why would you say that?"

"I know you, dude." His gaze darkens. "You like a challenge and that's exactly what Ivy is—a fucking challenge. She doesn't want a damn thing to do with you."

He's not wrong about that. I do love me a good challenge, but I think my interest in Ivy goes a little deeper than that. Maybe in the beginning, the fact that she wasn't interested was like a red flag being waved in front of me, but it's morphed into something more.

Ivy seems to be the only person at Barnett who doesn't give two shits about who I am and the status that comes from being one of my friends or sleeping with me. She never talks about football. Hell, I think she admitted last week that she doesn't like the sport. Never watches it. Doesn't even go to the games.

You'd think hearing that would be a major turn off. But damn, it's the opposite. I kind of like that we don't have to discuss football. It doesn't seem to matter one bit to her that I'll be entering the draft in a few short months.

And no one can say that she's falling all over herself to get my attention or be with me either.

You know what I like best?

After my initial—*let's get it on* and her subsequent—*go take a flying fuck*, we've kind of settled into a...well...friendship. I've never spent time with a girl without the intent of getting laid at the end of the evening. And Lexie doesn't count. If Dylan wasn't there, I wouldn't be hanging with her either.

Of course, the girls I sleep with aren't friends. They're more like groupies. One of the many perks of being an athlete. It's more like an exchange of goods/information. I'm able to get laid on a regular basis and they get to brag to all their friends that they were boned by Roan King.

It works out for all parties involved. And I make it perfectly clear at the onset that this is strictly a one-time deal. Every so often, I'll screw someone twice, but I don't make a habit of it. Once you do that, you enter into the murky territory of a quasi-relationship and I'm not getting involved in one of those. I've got too much on my plate to screw around with shit like that.

And yet Ivy has my thoughts cautiously turning in that direction. I can't have her without some form of a commitment and the thought of her with anyone else pisses me off. So clearly, I have a dilemma on my hands.

"It's not about her being a challenge," I grit out. By the fifteenth rep, my arms are seriously killing me.

"Damn," he shakes his head, "I knew this contemplative mood had something to do with her." He plows a hand roughly through his golden blond hair. "Shit. Lexie is going to fucking kill you." He screws his face up. "And I'm not going to get laid."

I set the bar in place and sit up on the padded bench. Dylan is full-on glaring now. He doesn't like the idea of Lexie withholding sex and I can't say I blame him for it. After all, that has to be the major advantage of a committed relationship, right?

You take away the anytime-you-want-to-have-it sex and what's left? *Exactly.*

With a towel in hand, I wipe the sweat from my brow. "Chill the fuck out, man. I'm not after Ivy." I get up so we can change positions. As Dylan settles on the bench, he continues to scowl as if he doesn't believe me.

Hell, I'm not sure *I* believe me at this point, but I also know I can't just fuck this girl and walk away because he's right. Lexie will beat the piss out of me. Plus, Ivy lives next door and we kind of have the same friend group. Which is where that old saying—don't shit where you eat comes into play. And I really don't want to cause problems for Dylan.

Now, if you pressed me to add one more item to the list of reasons why I should keep this thing with Ivy strictly on a friends level, I'd have to say it's because I have zero interest in having a girlfriend. I need more pressure heaped on me like another hole in the head and that's exactly what a girlfriend would be.

Over the years, I've found females to be fairly superficial creatures. They want to be with me for my looks or my athletic status. Not a damn one of them has ever asked me what I plan to do if football doesn't pan out. Nor do they care that I'm a straight A student. Or that I scored a thirty-three on my ACT when I took it at the end of my junior year in high school.

Nope.

I could be dumber than a freaking fence post and they wouldn't blink an eye. I could treat them like a piece of shit smeared across the bottom of my shoe and it wouldn't matter one bit. Although I would never do that because my mom would slap me upside the head if I treated a girl disrespectfully which is exactly why I'm always courteous and upfront about my intentions. If they aren't into it, then they aren't into it. No big deal. But let's be real here, other than Ivy, I've never come across a girl who wasn't into it.

They get to be with Roan King and that's all that seems to matter. They get their friends to snap lots of pics which are posted by the time I'm done fucking them. So, I don't feel bad for banging all those faceless females and not bothering to tie myself down to one in particular. As far as I'm concerned, I'm better off on my own than dealing with some mercenary chick who only wants me for my status. I have to wonder if I'd be getting as much ass if I weren't looking to turn pro this year. If I weren't on my way to making millions.

Not that I've spoken to anyone about this, but I'm starting to waffle about entering the draft this year. I redshirted my freshman year which essentially means I was on the team and practiced but didn't play in any games. NCAA guidelines only allow players four years of college eligibility. I've used three. The redshirt season doesn't count. Technically, I'm able to stay at Barnett and play for one more season even though I'm currently in my senior year.

The plan has always been to use these four years to earn my degree and enter the draft if it looked like I could potentially go in the first or second round. There's been a lot of hype and that only seems to be growing. So, I'm in a really good position right now.

Possibly the best I'll ever be in.

Except I switched majors last year and that set me back credit-wise. Plus, with football, I haven't always been able to take fifteen credits a semester. There have been times when I've had to lighten my load.

I've been playing around with the idea of staying for a fifth year. I haven't spoken to my family about it because they're not going to like it. In the back of my head, I know that I need a plan B in case things don't work out. I'm all too aware that most guys who go pro only play for an average of three years. It can be cut shorter if they sustain an injury. In football, that's always a possibility. It's highly doubtful this will be the only thing I do with my life.

So finishing up my degree is important.

Dylan picks up the bar and the two hundred-pound weights added to it. He grits his teeth before slowly raising it above his chest. After the fourth rep, the grunting begins. I almost shake my head. Dylan is ridiculously loud when he works out. Unfortunately, that also carries over into the bedroom...if you catch my drift.

I know this because the walls of our apartment are paper-thin. And Lexie spends the night frequently. That dude can be loud as fuck.

"You need to stay away from her." He holds my gaze. "I'm serious. Everything is going well with Lexie. I don't need you fucking up my relationship because you can't stand to be denied."

I roll my eyes. "Give me a damn break. What am I, like two? I'm not going after her because she isn't interested, okay?"

Although I think Ivy is, in fact, interested. But I'm not going to admit that to him.

Dylan focuses on his workout until he hits fifteen reps. Then he sets the bar in place before sitting up. "There are plenty of other chicks out there clamoring for your attention. Do me a favor and leave this one alone."

We move onto the next station.

I should drop the subject.

I shouldn't say one more damn word about Ivy.

But...

I can't seem to help myself. Ever since Sunday, there have been all these thoughts rolling around in the back of my head and they refuse to go away.

"What if it was more than a quick fuck?"

Dylan picks up sixty pound weights and starts bicep curling. "What the hell are you saying? That you suddenly want a relationship?" He snorts as if that's the most ridiculous thing he's ever heard come out of my mouth.

And maybe it is. After all, I've never been interested in being tied down and hell, I'm not even sure I want that now. But I can't stop thinking about her. I can't stop thinking about how nice it felt to spend the day together.

I liked knowing that she needed me. That being there with her actually made things a little easier to deal with. And I liked having my arms wrapped around her and making sure she was okay. The situation had all these protective instincts hurtling to the surface. I've never felt that way before.

"Maybe."

Dylan shakes his head as a chuckle escapes from his lips. "Dude, stop trying to make me laugh, I'm working out here."

My brows draw together as I pick up weights. Seventy-pound ones. Fuck that guy. Aggravation burns through me as I curl the dumbbell toward my chest. "Maybe I do want a girlfriend. What's wrong with that?"

The smile drops clean off his face and he's back to giving me the stink eye. "You're only interested in nailing as much pussy as you can." Before I can argue, he continues, "And that's fine. Hell, I applaud your efforts to plow your way through the female population at Barnett." He smirks. "If I had your pretty face, I'd be doing the same damn thing."

Why those words piss me off, I don't know. But they do.

"They all want a piece of you before you hit the big time." His voice turns shitty as he sneers, "They all want to fuck the king of campus."

My eyes narrow. Dylan and I are bros. We have each other's backs. And we've been friends since freshman year orientation. His dream is to play in the NFL, but I'm not sure that will happen. He hasn't generated the amount of attention that I have. Plus, he tore his rotator cuff last year and I suspect it still bothers him. Every so often, I catch a fleeting glimpse of pain on his face when he thinks no one is looking.

Even though we're friends, I think there's a little bit of frustration that my rise has been seemingly easier than his. I've never been injured. Nor have I ever had to sit out for any length of time to recover. And playing football is like second nature to me. It's more of a natural instinct. I just get it. I can look at the field and think a few steps ahead. It's kind of like playing a faster paced game of chess. It's that ability which has thrusted me to the top of my college football career. And people have sat up and taken notice. Especially scouts and coaches.

Dylan doesn't seem to have developed that skill or it's not as intrinsic as it is for me.

Instead of tackling the real issue sitting between us, I say, "If I recall correctly, you got your share before meeting Lexie."

He grunts. "Yep."

"So, I'm not sure what your point is."

He skewers me with a hard-edged glare. "The point is that I don't want you messing around with Ivy. Steer clear of her. You're not after anything more than a piece of ass for the night. You're not the relationship type, King. Find your kicks elsewhere. I don't need you fucking up my relationship with Lexie so you can nail some chick because she isn't falling onto her back and spreading her legs wide for you."

Instead of jumping down his throat, I look away while curling my seventy-pound dumbbells. I'm so pissed at what's spewing from his mouth that I've lost count of my reps. Gritting my teeth, I start all over again.

After five minutes of uncomfortable silence, Dylan starts yapping about something else and because I don't want there to be a problem between us, I let go of my anger. I mean, Dylan is probably right. My fascination with Ivy has everything to do with her disinterest. No one ever turns me down. That has to be the reason why she's occupying so many of my thoughts lately. Maybe I need to get laid and then everything else will fall neatly into place and I can spend my time concentrating on football and classes and less time thinking about Ivy Kaster.

See?

This is exactly the problem with getting involved with females. You spend way too much damn time thinking about things that aren't important all the while losing sight of the goals you've set for yourself.

I can't allow myself to get distracted.

Not when I have everything to lose.

CHAPTER SEVENTEEN

Hmmm, is it just me or is our legendary wide receiver, Roan King, not spreading around the love like he used to? What's up with that? All I know is that there are an awful lot of sexually deprived women out there clamoring for a little Roan King. If you're reading this, RK, be a dear and give us what we want...
KingOfCampus.com

We sip our drinks, slowly meandering our way down the sidewalk of a local outdoor mall. Lexie has three bags in hand. I have zero. There are a few reasons for this. One—nothing interesting has caught my eye. And two—I don't have money to throw away on useless crap I don't need. Although my dad did shove a hundred dollars into my hand when Roan and I were leaving his house on Sunday. Stunned by the gesture, I tried giving it back, but he wouldn't take it. I figure I'll sock it away in case of an emergency.

"Let's stop in here," Lexie says.

We stroll into a lacy underwear store and right away, she starts rifling through the racks. I have enough underwear, so I don't bother looking for anything until a sexy little bra and panty set in pale pink lace captures my attention.

Before I realize it, I'm walking over to the rack and staring at it for a long minute. It's seriously the most gorgeous little confection I've ever seen. Sheer and delicate are the best ways to describe the material. It would pretty much reveal just about everything but damn, you'd look hot wrapped up in it.

Lexie sidles up beside me. "Oh, you definitely have to try that on."

I shake my head. It's not like I have anyone to wear it for. As much as I try to keep Roan's gorgeous face from materializing in my mind, it does. I have the feeling that guy will be the death of me.

"Why not?" Lexie pulls the set off the hook before inspecting it. "It'll be fun, come on."

I cock a brow, grasping at any straw that will get me out of this. "Trying on something that will only emphasize that I have zero curves for it to cling to isn't my idea of fun." I throw my arms up before glancing down. Like I said before, I'm fine with not having a curvy little body, but having to look at myself in lingerie that's supposed to showcase that nonexistent form will only drive home the point.

Do I need that?

Not really.

Lexie has four bras in her hand. And I would bet money they're all D cups. That girl has curves galore. She looks like a sex bomb waiting to explode and she's extremely good at playing up her finer assets. That's one reason she's so driven to go into fashion design. There are so many styles out there for women who are slender. If you're tall and thin, you can pretty much wear anything and look fabulous doing it. But what if you're shorter with lots of curves? What then? Lexie has actually designed a few outfits for herself and I can't believe how flattering and professional they look.

She checks the size before shoving it at my chest. "This should fit you perfectly." Then she herds me toward a narrow hallway. Since I know when to pick my battles, I allow Lexie to corral me into a fitting room. Then she disappears into the one next to me.

"Don't think I'll be showing you what this looks like," I grumble under my breath. It's not that I'm shy about my body. I've spent my entire life working out religiously in a dance studio. Every line and muscle has been elongated and perfectly sculpted. Plus, I'm always wearing tight leotards that are made of body-hugging Lycra. I've also had my fair share of seamstresses run their hands over me, taking measurements. Not to mention changing costumes in front of other dancers. When you dance, that's just the way it is. After a while, you stop being self-conscious.

Stripping out of my shirt and jeans, I leave my panties on while unclasping my bra. Then I pull on the frothy pale pink thong before clasping the bra and sliding it into place. I would expect the material to feel scratchy and uncomfortable. Rather surprisingly, it doesn't. It's actually quite comfy. My breath gets lodged in my lungs as I lift my eyes to the floor-to-ceiling mirror before forcing myself to take a long look.

God, this almost makes me—

Before I can wrap my mind around what I'm seeing, Lexie barges into the room without knocking or giving me a damn bit of warning. I'm so struck by the sight in front of me, that I don't bother to cover myself. It's not like she hasn't seen me naked a hundred times before. We've been friends since fourth grade and lived together freshman year. We both have the same equipment. Although granted, Lexie is much softer and feminine looking than I am.

Her feet grind to a halt in the open doorway before her eyes nearly pop out of her head. "You look amazing!"

I can't help the way my lips bow up at the compliment. I'm not one to self-congratulate myself or anything like that but I think she might be right. The pale pink bra and panty set is gorgeous.

And it makes me look—

"I can't believe it—you *actually* have tits and an ass!" This is stated with as much exaggeration as she can muster. Like maybe she wasn't sure about it before this very moment.

I smother a chuckle as I turn this way and that, trying to check out the ass I apparently have. As I get a good look in the mirror, I can't help but notice that she's right.

I have an ass!

I'm the proud owner of a bootie.

A passing sales girl stops before taking a long look at me. "Oh, honey, you'd better buy that little number. The man in your life will thank you for it." She gives me a cheeky grin before moving on.

Unfortunately, that comment is all the reminder I need not to buy this gorgeous little set. Why would I? I don't have a man in my life. And I don't see that changing any time soon.

"No, no, no," Lexie begins. When my gaze shoots to hers in silent question, she continues, "You don't need a guy in order to treat yourself to something that makes you feel beautiful and sexy." She flicks her hand in my direction. "And that stunning piece of barely-there-lace makes you feel both. You should definitely buy it."

I shake my head.

What's the point?

It's not like I'm going to buy this and stand around in front of a mirror admiring myself. Okay, so I might do that a few times.

"If I looked that hot, I'd wear it every freaking day just to boost my self-confidence."

I roll my eyes before stating the obvious. "You don't need any help in that department."

She grins. "Neither of us do. But I can tell you feel amazing in it, and that my friend, is worth its weight in gold." Before I can deny what she's saying, she barrels on, "Listen, your birthday is coming up, and *that's* what I'm buying for you."

My shoulders droop as my gaze slides to the mirror.

"That bra does wonders for your boobs." She snickers. "It actually makes you look like you have some."

I can't argue with that. It really does. I'm a B cup. Somehow this gives the illusion of a C cup. Or a really full B. My hands go to the undersides of my breasts, trying to figure out what exactly is going on. "I guess it's kind of a push-up bra." The tricky little bugger is pushing things from the sides to create cleavage.

"My advice is to invest in more of them. A push-up bra is clearly your best friend." Then she grins. "Other than me, of course."

I'm not going to tell Lexie this, but I usually wear a basic black sports bra that flattens the girls out more than they already are. It's super comfortable and I've never bothered with anything else. This little get up is a real departure from what I normally wear. Which kind of makes me want to own it.

"Okay, you've twisted my arm."

She claps her hands together in delight.

"But *I'm* buying it."

"I'll buy it for your birthday," she cuts in.

"Nope. You're right, I love it. Even though I don't have anyone to wear it for, I'm going to splurge."

Lexie arches a brow. "Clothes are meant to make the person wearing them feel good about themselves. If you feel amazing, *that's* what matters."

This little bra and panty set *does* make me feel amazing. So, I guess she's right. That decided, I'm ready to change. "All right, get out," I say, pointing to the hallway.

Obviously proud of herself for talking me into something I normally wouldn't buy, Lexie beams before closing the door behind her. Five minutes later, I'm in my own panties and sports bra. And feeling none too sexy about it, either.

"Did you find anything?" I ask.

Lexie holds up three bras in a spectrum of different colors along with three matching thongs. As we move toward the sales counter, I peek at the price tag and nearly gasp. So much for saving the money my father gave me.

But Lexie's right—I love the way I look in the matching set. I might not have anyone to wear it for, but that's okay. Once we've been rung up, we take our purchases and stroll down the sidewalk.

After a few moments, I realize Lexie has grown quiet. She's never been an incessant chatterbox, but she usually isn't silent either. As I think about it, I realize she's been a little off today.

"Everything okay, Lex?"

We pass by two storefronts before she flashes a smile my way. "Yup, all good. I have something on my mind, but it's probably nothing."

My brows draw together. If something is bothering her, I'm surprised she hasn't already shared it with me. "What's going on?"

There's a tiny park with playground equipment for small children along with a few benches. Finding one that's empty, we sit down before setting our bags next to us.

When she doesn't immediately launch into what's going on, I nudge her along. "Fill me in."

Her body deflates as she nibbles her lower lip. Instead of beating around the bush, she blurts, "A couple of weeks ago, Dylan and I were having sex and," she pauses as her voice drops, "the condom broke."

My eyes widen in understanding. The only thing worse than a ripped condom is a positive pregnancy test. "What does Dylan think?"

She hesitates for a beat. "Obviously, he knows about the broken condom. I wasn't all that concerned when it happened, but I'm pretty sure I should have gotten my period by now."

"You haven't told him that you're worried?"

She bites down on her lip before shrugging. "I wanted to wait until I was sure," her troubled gaze flickers to mine, "one way or the other."

Anxiety is eating away at her and it makes me feel like a shitty friend for not realizing there was a problem. I hate that she's been dealing with this all by herself. "Should we buy a home pregnancy test? Or maybe go to a clinic?" I slip my phone from my pocket before glancing at it. "It's still early. If you want, we can head over to the clinic on campus."

It takes a moment before she admits, "I bought a test yesterday, but haven't taken it yet. I think you have to wait until you've actually missed a period and I've never been very good at keeping track. It just feels like I should have gotten it by now."

I nod, guilty of the same thing. I don't always keep track of my monthly bill. Of course, I haven't been having sex...*at all*...so it seems kind of pointless to keep track of things.

"If you're not sure about a timeline, then maybe you aren't late. Maybe stress is throwing your body off." I'm trying to come up with any plausible explanation other than the obvious.

She glances at the jungle gym equipment where a few small children are running around and playing. Their exuberant voices drift over us. I'm instantly reminded of Nora and Nolan. "I guess, but I feel like my boobs are achy and that's a sign of pregnancy."

"I think that can happen when you're getting your period, too." I consider what would make me feel better if I were in the same predicament. "We should go home, and you can take the test. If it's negative, we'll wait a few days. If you still don't get it, we'll get another test or go to the clinic."

She stares off for a moment or two before jerking her head into a nod. "Okay."

Without further words, we rise to our feet and walk to the parking lot. Our mood is more somber than it had been in the lingerie shop. I'm relieved Lexie finally told me what's going on. And I'm glad that I'm here, able to lend my support. This is really the first time since getting back from Paris that I've felt this way.

We slide into her silver Jetta and drive to the apartment in silence. Now that she doesn't have to pretend everything is all right, she's seems distracted and worried.

As we head toward the lobby entrance, Roan and Dylan catch up to us. Right away, Dylan wraps his beefy arms around Lexie, hauling her off her feet in greeting. She wrinkles her nose, attempting to push him away.

"Ewww!" she screeches, *"you stink!"*

This makes him laugh before gathering her even closer.

"Dylan, that's so gross! Get the hell away from me!" She squeals, still trying to escape from his hold.

"That's manly sweat, baby. Take a good whiff." He jokingly squashes her face into his arm pit.

"Ugh! I think I'm going to be sick!" She makes gagging noises like she's going to throw up.

When he finally releases her, Lexie scrambles away before turning back to give him the stink eye along with a one fingered salute. "Now I'm going to have to fumigate these clothes. You've funktified me with your putrid stench."

He gives her a wide grin. "How about I shower and then we can grab something to eat? Sound good, babe?"

I see the moment reality crashes over her and she remembers the reason we cut our shopping excursion short. All of the laughter and happiness drains away.

Averting her eyes, she nods. "Yeah, that's fine. Like an hour or so?"

Dylan is so finely attuned to her moods that he notices the change in her demeanor. As we enter the lobby, Lexie reaches the elevator first before pressing the button. Dylan comes up behind her and loosely wraps his arms around her body before whispering in her ear.

I hang back, wanting to give them a bit of privacy. Roan falls in line with me.

When I don't offer up a greeting, he nudges my shoulder with his bigger one. "Hey."

I smile as my gaze settles on him. "Hi."

We haven't seen much of each other since our trip home last Sunday. We've both been busy. Plus, it seemed like a good idea to distance myself. Spending the day together was nice. And the kiss we shared in my old bedroom was even nicer. Truth be told, I can't stop thinking about it.

Or him.

I could easily fall for *that* guy. But I know *that* guy isn't who Roan really is.

"Have you been able to work on the project at all?" he asks, breaking into my thoughts.

"Not since Friday. I haven't had any extra time this week. I'm hoping that maybe tomorrow I can hit the library again."

He nods. "I was able to squeeze in a little more research. I'll email the PDF's and you can take a look at what I was able to dig up and see if it fits with the general theme we're going for."

"Great."

I'm reminded of how far off the mark I was in my snap judgement of Roan. I'm almost embarrassed that I listened to Finn when he said Roan wasn't very intelligent. Now that we've had class together for a couple of weeks, I've seen firsthand how easily Roan jumps into discussions with well thought out comments and questions. It's obvious from the amount of work he puts in that he cares about his grades.

He's the farthest thing from a meathead jock there is. I'm actually pretty happy that we were partnered up for this project. He has suggested angles I probably wouldn't have considered exploring on my own.

I just need to keep our relationship platonic.

Which means no physical contact.

Which *definitely* means no more kissing.

Unconsciously, my gaze falls from those gorgeous turquoise-colored eyes to his mouth. Roan is, hands down, the best kiss I've ever experienced. I won't bother lying to myself by saying that I'm not interested in doing it again. Just thinking about it has my tongue slipping out to moisten my lips.

The sound of a throaty growl filling the air has my startled gaze snapping to his.

When his voice rumbles forth, it's all low and heated. "It drives me fucking crazy when you stare at me like that."

I gasp, a flush stinging my cheeks. I know exactly what was running through my mind when I was studying his mouth. Which probably means I was all but eating him up with my eyes. Lowering my gaze, I try to wrestle my runaway thoughts back under control. It's no easy task.

I do the only thing I can to salvage a tiny shred of my pride and lie through my teeth. "I wasn't looking at you any kind of way."

Liar, liar, pants on fire...

Roan steps closer, invading my personal space until my heart feels like it's wedged in the middle of my throat. "I never took you for chicken shit, Ivy."

Our gazes clash for a long, drawn out moment. One that has lust and need arrowing right down to my—

"Cluck-cluck," is all I can manage to choke out.

A wide grin sweeps across his face as the elevator door rattles open and Dylan and Lexie step inside. But Roan's eyes haven't deviated from mine and I find that I'm unable to break the connection binding us to one another.

"Saved by the bell," he whispers when I show no sign of moving.

Unaware of what's going on between us, Dylan yells impatiently, "Are you guys coming or what?"

I clear my throat. It's drier than the Sahara. "Yup."

Yanking my gaze from his, I scurry onto the elevator. As the doors close, I keep my attention focused straight ahead even though Roan has moved to stand next to me. I can practically feel his gaze crawling over me as if he's blatantly staring. When we reach the third floor, it takes forever for the doors to slide open. As soon as they do, I shoot out of the elevator toward my apartment like the hounds of hell are nipping at my heels.

His low chuckle fills my ears as I hastily unlock the door before slipping inside.

CHAPTER EIGHTEEN

Mmm, mmm, mmm, I love me some freshly showered Roan King. Oh, who am I
kidding? I'd happily take that boy all dirtied up. Hell...the dirtier, the better ;)
KingOfCampus.com

Safely locked inside my apartment and away from Roan and his damn
pheromones, the neurons in my brain once again start firing properly.
God, I'm seriously no better than all the other salivating groupies that
stalk him around campus. All I have to do is look at him and my mind
turns to mush.

It's completely frustrating.

Not to mention demoralizing.

I assume Lexie told Dylan what's going on because those two
immediately holed up in her room and haven't come out except to use
the bathroom. Which probably means they're doing the pregnancy
test she bought. Even though I want to be there for her, I'm glad she
shared her concerns with Dylan. This is an issue he needs to be
involved in.

Once my hormones settle, I pull out my project notes to read over.

As I'm doing that, I get an email from Roan with the attachments we discussed earlier. Skimming over them, I'm impressed by what he was able to dig up regarding the Ponzi scheme and Bernie Madoff.

I shoot him a quick email telling him that. I feel like a jerk for wanting to dump him as my partner. At this point, I think he's plowed his way through more research than I have. And Roan is in the middle of his football season, so it's not like he has a ton of down time. And yet, he still manages to do quality work.

Yup, I'm a complete asshole.

I shouldn't have assumed that Roan was only attending college as a steppingstone to the NFL. I have the tendency to look at some of the higher profile athletes on campus, especially the football players destined for NFL greatness, and assume they're just here killing time before moving on to bigger and better things.

It doesn't take long for Roan to respond, mentioning a few more resource leads he wasn't able to check out. I fire off another email saying that I'd be happy to look into those. He replies that we should get together in a few days with all the research we've gathered and sift through what we want to include in our paper.

This might sound kind of nerdy, but I'm stoked as to how this project is shaping up. The downfall of Bernie Madoff was big news and the amount of money he stole from people had far reaching consequences for those who mistakenly placed their trust in him.

A few moments later, there's a knock on the door. Since Lexie and Dylan are still locked away in her room, and it's been at least forty minutes, I jump off my bed to answer it.

A freshly showered Roan greets me from the other side of the threshold. His damp locks look even glossier than usual. He's wearing a black Barnett football T-shirt that hugs the chiseled muscles of his chest and biceps as if it was specially made for him. His hands are shoved into the pockets of faded jeans which hang loosely from lean hips.

I'm in the crosshairs of his beautiful blue-green hued eyes. Something deep within me snaps to attention. I totally understand why the entire female population of Barnett trails after him. The fact that he's intelligent and more than likely turning pro makes him the complete package.

It takes everything inside me not to reach out and bury my fingers in all that silky, ebony-colored hair. To pull his face to mine so I can feel his mouth rove gently over me.

I inhale a shaky breath and realize that the bastard has done it.

He's finally gotten to me.

I have zero interest in being one of the many women he's knocked boots with but there's no denying that I'm sexually attracted to him in the worst way possible. His attentiveness at my dad's house last Sunday was the clincher.

Unaware of the inner turmoil roiling through me, Roan says, "I thought it would be easier to talk face-to-face instead of emailing back and forth."

Yeah...that doesn't necessarily seem like the best idea given how I'm feeling.

I want to slap myself silly for allowing this to happen. Instead of slamming the door in his face like every instinct within is screaming for me to do, I clear my throat. "Um, sure." I retreat a step, allowing him into the apartment.

Silently, he heads straight to my room. He nods his head toward Lexie's closed bedroom door. "Are Dylan and Lexie in there?"

"Yeah." Unconsciously, my eyes slide in that direction. I can't help but wonder what's going on. Is Lexie pregnant? Is she okay?

Roan stops in his tracks before turning with a slight frown marring his handsome face. "You haven't heard any loud grunting, have you?"

My brows slide together. I was expecting some crying if the test turns out to be positive but not grunting.

"No," I say carefully, "I haven't heard anything like that."

A look of contemplation comes over his face as he narrows his eyes. "Maybe we should head out and grab dinner instead. I don't want to be here when the grunting and moaning starts."

Is he serious?

A gurgle of laughter threatens to escape from my lips. "What are you talking about?"

The corners of his mouth tug upward before he jerks his head toward the closed door. "Haven't you heard them have sex before?"

"Oh my god, no!" Now I am laughing and he's chuckling, too. "I try very hard *not* to hear that. They're called earbuds, dude. You need to invest in some if you're being subjected to that."

He snorts. "Trust me, *dude*, I use them all the time with those two."

I can't help but shake my head. "I don't really want to hear this."

"Then we should definitely leave before it starts."

Considering the information Lexie shared with me this afternoon, it's highly doubtful there will be any grunting going on tonight, but I can't tell Roan that.

"Okay. Let me grab my purse and we can take off." Even though I know spending more time alone with Roan isn't going to dampen any of the feelings that have unexpectantly sprung up inside me, I can't bring myself to turn him down.

For better or worse, I'm going out.

With Roan King.

God help me.

CHAPTER NINETEEN

Ohhhh, a sighting at Peppino's has been made and (gasp!) he's with the same girl from the photos previously published on this very site! I'm sad to say that whatever is going on over at that table looks pretty damn serious...
KingOfCampus.com

Roan takes me to a popular pizza joint located in the middle of town. I haven't been here since I left for Paris. It's actually one of my favorite restaurants. To return after nearly a year and a half has nostalgia wrapping around me like a thick comfy blanket.

We grab a booth and are given menus. Although I don't bother to glance at mine. I know exactly what I want.

"Ready to order?" he asks.

"Yep. Mushroom, sausage, and pepperoni." It's my favorite. I especially love the way they prepare it here. The sausage is cut paper thin and the mushrooms are ridiculously huge. The crust is New York style which means it's super thin. A lot of people like to eat it by folding the slice in half. My mouth waters even thinking about it. I'm suddenly glad Roan suggested the place.

"That's my favorite, too." He gives me an odd look. "Did you know that?"

I snort. Is he seriously suggesting that I've been what—*cyberstalking* him? You know…in case we grabbed a pizza together which, let me remind you, was entirely his idea.

"No, that's what I always order." A hard edge creeps into my voice. "You can ask Lexie if you don't believe me."

Agreeing to this dinner with Roan now seems like a colossal mistake. This guy has one hell of a massive ego.

"Open the menu and look at the specialty pizzas." His suggestion is stated mildly as if he realizes his question has rubbed me the wrong way. Guess I have to give him points for being astute. Although it's begrudgingly…

Annoyed that he thinks I'm some creepy closet Roan King fangirl, I don't question him. I'm much too busy seething across from him to do that. The second page of the menu has a list of different styles of pizza you can order. Without another word, my gaze scans the list. Hawaiian. Supreme. Veggie. Margherita. The King. The Henry Winkler. The Works…

Wait a minute.

The King?

My attention snaps back up. Mushroom, sausage, and pepperoni.

Oh, come on…are you kidding me?

Even though I already know the answer, I ask flatly, "They seriously named a pizza after you?" At my favorite place. The injustice of it all…

Roan flashes a grin and something dangerous pings in my belly. Damn him for being able to do that. "Yup." His eyes twinkle with unfettered glee. "Glad to see you're finally a fan of something of mine."

The waitress arrives with two tall glasses of water. Clearly, these two are well acquainted because she gives him a wink. Roan orders us an extra-large King. I roll my eyes when he says it. He must notice because he looks like he's trying to rein in his laughter as the waitress asks if we need anything else. Almost as an afterthought, Roan tacks on an order of garlic knots.

Which, yeah, I love as well.

But I won't be telling him that.

Once she disappears, he takes a long drink of his water, draining the entire glass. When I raise my brows, he explains that he only wolfed down a protein bar before leaving for the gym and that was a couple of hours ago.

He leans forward as if about to say something when an older man approaches the table with his wife. Roan breaks eye contact before glancing at the elderly couple and giving them a friendly smile as if they're already acquainted. Except I notice that it's different than the smiles he beams in my direction. There's not a devilish curl to his lips or a humorous twinkle in his eyes.

"Young man, I hope you don't mind the interruption, but we couldn't resist coming over and congratulating you on how well the season is going." The couple has to be in their late seventies, maybe even early eighties. They're so cute together.

"Thank you, sir." Roan nods politely to the man's wife. "Ma'am. The whole team is playing well."

The man's face crinkles in response. "Yes, they certainly are, but it's you who keeps catching all those passes. Can't say I've seen anything like it in a good decade. You sure are something to watch out on the field."

Nodding again, Roan accepts the compliment graciously. "Thank you, sir. But I couldn't catch any of those passes without Liam Garrison throwing them right to me."

The man agrees easily before laying a weathered hand on Roan's shoulder. "Garrison's a solid quarterback. He has a good arm on him." He pauses for a moment before his sparkling brown eyes take on a decidedly cagey look. "Been hearing rumors about you turning pro after this season. Won't be sticking around for another year, huh?"

With an expression of contrition, Roan dips his chin in acknowledgement. "That's the way it looks."

"Well, I sure hate to see Barnett lose you. There'll be quite a hole in the program when you leave."

"I appreciate you saying that but there are a number of talented players coming up through the ranks. I don't doubt they'll be able to fill the open spots left by this year's graduating seniors."

The man smiles but it's obvious he has a differing opinion regarding the issue. Instead of addressing Roan's statement, he says instead, "Good luck to you, son." For the first time since he arrived at the table, the man's warm eyes slide to mine before he tips his head. "You two kids enjoy your evening. Get rested up for the big game on Saturday."

Roan says goodbye to them before his attention settles on me. Once the couple leaves the restaurant, I ask, "Doesn't that get old after a while?"

As he gazes around, I notice quite a few people staring in our direction. I'm reminded of Chad from the smoothie shop and the pictures that ended up online.

With a look of resignation, Roan shrugs before reaching behind him and pulling out a well-worn ball cap before tugging it onto his head and pulling it down low. It's the same one he wore the afternoon we headed to the library. He must carry it around with him when he doesn't want to be recognized. Not that it does the trick. Whether you're able to see his face or not, people would still stare.

Roan is so tall. He must be about six three or four and he's broad in the shoulders and chest. When he's wearing a T-shirt like he is now, where it hugs his upper body...well, he'd draw attention for that alone.

The guy is seriously built like a Roman gladiator. He's all thick chiseled muscle. Add that gorgeous face to it and you have girls tripping all over themselves to turn those turquoise-hued eyes in their direction.

I know firsthand. As much as I don't want to, I feel the same draw myself. Something in me clamors for his attention.

"Comes with the territory. If I wasn't a good ball player, people wouldn't give two shits about me."

That's debatable. Whether Roan played ball or not, women would still find him ridiculously attractive.

I snort. "I don't think that's true."

He levels me with a hard look. "Yeah, it is. People care about me because of my talent on the field. It's always been that way."

"I'm sure your parents care about you for *you*, not football."

His eyes soften. "Yeah, they do. But everyone else just wants a piece of me." He peers around the restaurant before pitching his voice lower. "Ever since I picked up a football, it's what my life has been about. Consequently, it's all people want to talk about. Or maybe they think it's all *I'm* capable of discussing." His lips curl with derision. "Like I'm just another dumb jock with no other interest outside of the sport I play."

Surprised by the bitterness, I stare at him from across the rectangle table that separates us. Is it totally crazy that I feel sorry for him? I mean, does that even make sense?

He's Roan freaking King, for goodness sake.

Unsure if I'm making a mistake, I tentatively reach out until my hand can gently cover his larger one. His gaze falls to our connected fingers in surprise. Mine do the same as the breath gets wedged in my throat.

What the hell am I doing?

The more time I spend with Roan, the more these strangely tender feelings inside me grow and flourish. If you had asked me a month ago, when I spilled my drink all over him, I would have told you that I wanted nothing to do with a football playing Neanderthal like Roan King. I would have said he was a dumb jock coasting through college on his football prowess and by nailing as much ass as he could.

Somewhere along the way, my opinion of him has changed.

I still think he's a player but now I'm kind of wondering if he uses women the same way they use him. I almost want to shake my head as that strange thought settles in my mind. Am I actually making excuses for his behavior?

Before I can say anything, he leans forward, the intensity of his blue-green gaze holding mine captive. "Do you realize that you're the only person who doesn't talk to me about football?"

When I stare in confusion, he continues, "Even my professors talk to me about the season and turning pro." His body strains toward mine. "There were two teachers last year who didn't bother to grade my papers. They just gave me A's."

My eyes widen at his hushed admission. "How do you know that?"

"I found a few errors and brought it to their attention. Both smiled and patted me on the back. They told me that I had bigger concerns to focus my energies on."

We fall into silence. I'm flabbergasted something like that could happen. Especially here at Barnett. This is a top-notch school. It's academically rigorous.

Tension fills every line of Roan's face. "You can't tell anyone about that, Ivy," he mutters. "I'm serious."

Even though I feel conflicted, I jerk my head.

That's not fair to everyone else who works their asses off to pull good grades. Maybe Roan isn't taking advantage of professors who are willing to hand out A's for being a top recruit on campus, but I'm sure there are other student athletes who get by because of it.

Once again, I realize how wrong I was to make a snap judgment about him.

Angling my body closer, I whisper, "I won't tell anyone." It goes against everything I believe in, but I don't want to break his confidence. "I promise."

His gaze holds mine for a long moment before finally sliding away. "I shouldn't have said anything to you. I'm not looking to jam anyone up."

"I know, but it's not right."

He nods solemnly, acknowledging the truth of my words. Then he yanks off his ball cap and plows his long fingers through his dark hair before pulling it back over his head, so his face is somewhat shielded from view.

Our extra-large pizza arrives as we sit in silence. Once we both take a slice, the strangely somber mood lightens. Uncaring that Roan is sitting across from me, I take a huge bite. My eyes flutter shut as the perfect mixture of crust, sweet yet zesty sauce along with pepperoni, mushrooms, and sausage slams into my taste buds. I think a little moan of appreciation slips out of my mouth.

God, but I've missed this!

It goes without saying that the food in Paris was a culinary experience. Fresh baked pain au chocolat (croissants filled with dark chocolate) in the morning along with un café noisette (an espresso with a little cream), croquet monsieur (grilled ham and gruyere cheese with a fried or poached egg on top) for lunch, crepes which they sell on the street, and escargot. My home away from home was a tiny cafe a few blocks from school.

So, yeah...I ate well while I was away. It's kind of unbelievable that I didn't pack on a ton of weight. Then again, when in Paris, you're hopping on the metro and walking almost everywhere.

But this pizza...I missed it. I can't help but shove another bite into my mouth before savoring the medley of flavors.

Like a total glutton, I gobble up the first slice within a matter of minutes. I hate to admit it, but I'm not even aware of Roan sitting across from me. I'm in a little place called pizza nirvana. As I reach for a second piece, my gaze collides with his. He sits across from me, staring with a look of astonishment.

When I quirk a brow, he says, "I've never seen anyone polish off a slice like that and I eat with three hundred-pound dudes who play football."

Unable to help myself, I chuckle. I've never been a shy eater. I have a fast metabolism that Lexie regularly talks smack about because I can eat practically anything and never gain an ounce while she looks at a slice of cake and gains five pounds. Although, I think that's an exaggeration because that girl can polish off cake like nobody's business. Especially chocolate.

I realize it's all the hours I spend in the studio that helps burn the calories and keeps me slim. And yeah, I won't lie—it probably has a lot to do with genetics as well.

Unashamed, I shrug. "I'm hungry."

"Clearly." He shakes his head before taking a big bite and swallowing it. "And here I thought I'd have leftovers to take home for breakfast."

"Oh, hell no. If there are leftovers, I'm calling dibs," I shoot back.

"Maybe we should order another pizza to go."

I give him a wink before taking another huge bite. "Make it two."

He laughs before we go back to polishing off the extra-large pizza. When I'm finally stuffed, I finish off my water before sitting back. There's no denying that my belly hurts. I can't believe I scarfed down three slices of pizza and did it in front of Roan King. Most girls probably wouldn't eat more than a few salad leaves and a carrot stick and call it dinner.

You know what?

I don't care. I like to eat. As long as I'm healthy and in shape, it doesn't matter. I kind of wonder if seeing me stuff my face is a turn off. Curiosity gets the better of me as I fish around for an answer. "I bet the girls you take out barely eat anything at all."

Almost quizzically, his brows draw together before he shrugs. "I wouldn't know how much a girl typically eats. I've never been out with one before."

My mouth falls open in surprise before I clarify, "You've never been on a date?"

He shakes his head. "Nope."

"Why not?"

He glances away, saying somewhat evasively, "Just haven't." After a moment or two, his gaze arrows back to mine. "I've never been interested in having a relationship and it wasn't necessary."

Necessary?

What the heck does—

Oh. I see...

He doesn't need to take a girl out and treat her nice to get what he wants at the end of the night. Women fall all over themselves to have sex with him.

I honestly don't know how to feel about that.

When I remain silent, Roan clears his throat and shifts on his seat. He looks uncomfortable. Well...good, he should feel like shit for acknowledging something like that. "You're the first girl I've taken out. This is my first date."

And just like that, the shield of ice that had fallen over me begins to thaw. "Oh."

Our gaze clings before he breaks the heavy silence between us. "How about I tell them to box up our pizza and we can head out?"

I hoist my smile, feeling sort of thankful that we dropped the conversation but at the same time, maybe wishing we had pursued it. Roan has me feeling all kinds of conflicted. And I hate it. I'm not used to being messed up over a guy.

Not even Finn affected me like this.

"I'm, ah, going to use the bathroom before we leave." I scooch out of the booth before heading toward the back of the restaurant where the restrooms are located. After I'm done, I run my fingers through my hair and slick on some lipstick before heading back to the table. My mind is so clouded with Roan and the feelings that have sprouted up that I slam into a hard body.

Embarrassed, I mutter a quick apology. "Sorry about that." The guy who I bumped into grips my upper arms, holding me steady. When my gaze lifts, I gasp in surprise, "Finn!"

His lips lift marginally but it's clear from the hard-edged glint in his eyes that he's upset. "Hi, Ivy."

It occurs to me that he probably knows who I'm here having dinner with. I've been so focused on Roan and...well...the pizza I was busy inhaling, that I didn't pay much attention to the people around us.

Apprehension ripples through me as I take a hasty step in retreat, trying to slip out of his grasp. "I, ah, need to—"

"Get back to Roan?"

The edges of my lips sink. His tone is just this side of shitty. In all honesty, he has no reason to be angry with me. We went out one time since my return from Paris. We're not together. He doesn't get to ask questions and expect answers or be pissed that I'm out with someone else.

I straighten my shoulders and arch a brow before glancing pointedly to where his fingers are digging into my upper arms. "Can you please let me go?"

A scowl moves across his face as his voice lowers. "I can't believe you're out with Roan King. That guy is a total douchebag."

How dare he? I grit my teeth in anger. "You know what, Finn? It's none of your concern who I spend time with."

Instead of releasing me, he hauls me closer. "I thought you were going to give us another chance. We were good together. Are you really going to throw away everything we had?" He cocks his head toward the main room of the restaurant. "For what? *That guy?*"

My mouth tumbles open.

I threw away our relationship?

That's rich!

"I think you're the one who threw me away instead of trying to make it work." I don't mention all the pictures Lexie sent me, but I want to.

He rolls his eyes before saying through clenched teeth, "We already talked about that. I couldn't hack a long-distance relationship. I'm more mature now." Frustration burns in his eyes. "But apparently you're more interested in being a part of King's pussy posse than having an actual relationship."

I gasp at his crude words. I'm about to let loose on Finn, when I hear—

"Is everything okay, Ivy?"

Finn and I turn toward the end of the hall. Roan stands fifteen feet away. Instead of letting go, Finn's fingers dig deeper into my arms. I can tell by the stiff set of my ex-boyfriend's chin that he's pissed off.

And probably spoiling for a fight.

I give Roan a slight smile as I wrench myself from Finn. "Everything's fine."

Even though he's talking to me, Roan's heated gaze never strays from Finn. "You ready to go?"

I suck in a deep breath to steady my nerves as my gaze slides to Finn. His eyes are blazing with both resentment and anger. "Yes, we're done here." I hope Finn realizes that it's not only this conversation... I'm done with him as well.

When Finn remains silent, I move toward Roan, who has turned out to feel like a safe place. As soon as I reach his side, one brawny arm slides around me as he holds two boxes of pizza with the other.

We're halfway to the exit when Roan asks tersely, "Are you seeing him?"

I can't help but glance up before answering, "No. We went out a couple of weeks ago. I haven't seen him since."

His arm tightens around me before we push out through the heavy glass doors. "Good."

I don't say anything to that because I'm not exactly sure what it means. And I'm not sure what I want it to mean either.

Or maybe I do...maybe I know *exactly* what I want it to mean.

CHAPTER TWENTY

Roan King with his arm wrapped around a female... and he's not leading her toward the bedroom? WTF??? Is it possible that our favorite Barnett football player is actually falling for someone? Speculation is running rampant.
KingOfCampus.com

As we're about to reach Roan's black SUV in the parking lot, his feet grind to a halt. Surprised, I glance over at him before searching the surrounding vicinity. But there's nothing. Nothing that should have him stopping so abruptly.

And certainly nothing to put such a strange look on his face.

Again, I scan the area before realizing there are two older men walking toward us. My guess is that they're in their mid-to-late forties. They're staring at Roan as they move in our direction. That by itself doesn't necessarily seem out of the ordinary.

People seem to gravitate toward the handsome football player. They think because he's a well-known athlete, they can stop and talk to him. I assume these two are fans like the elderly couple in the restaurant. Or the guy from the smoothie shop. But Roan's body has tensed which is definitely odd. I've never seen him be anything less than gracious and cordial when dealing with fans.

When the two men are about fifteen feet away, I murmur his name but it's as if he doesn't hear me. Or if he does, he doesn't bother to acknowledge it. Unfortunately, there's no time to question what's going on because a moment later, both men stop in front of us.

"Hey, Roan. How's everything going?"

"Good." Roan's shoulders relax a bit. "Everything's fine." As if suddenly remembering that I'm beside him, his gaze slides to mine before arrowing back to the guy directly in front of him. "We just grabbed something to eat at Peppino's."

"That's where we're headed." The older man's gaze encompasses the pair of us. "Been dying for a pizza all week."

A few seconds slip by as the conversation stalls. Not sure what to do, I hoist a friendly smile before thrusting out my hand. "Hi, I'm Ivy." I'm trying to make sense of what's going on here. It's definitely weird.

When the man with the inky black hair smiles, I realize he must be related to Roan. They're practically identical. Except he's older. By a good twenty years.

"Daniel." He nods to the man at his side. "And this is my partner, Linc."

Even though no one has acknowledged the connection, I'm wondering if this man is Roan's father. My mind cartwheels as I keep the smile firmly locked in place. I reach my hand toward Linc. "It's nice to meet you both."

"You, too." Linc smiles easily, his gaze turning mischievous. "So, you and Roan were having dinner together, huh?"

Heat fills my cheeks. "Um, yeah..." not knowing what else to say, I hastily tack on, "we're neighbors." But now my mouth is going, and I can hear myself talking. Because I'm nervous, I begin to babble. "And partnered up for a class project." Their smiles stretch wider which makes me feel desperate. "We're just friends," I blurt. I seriously want to kick Roan for leaving me to twist in the proverbial wind.

"What class do you have together?"

Since it doesn't seem like Roan will be contributing anything to the conversation, I answer, "Business Ethics."

"Sounds interesting," Linc says.

"Extremely." I might be overstating things, but whatever. I feel like I'm drowning over here. And Roan is standing there silently.

Daniel claps Roan on the shoulder. "I meant to call over the weekend. We were hoping you might be able to swing by for dinner next Wednesday night."

Since Roan has barely uttered a peep the entire time we've been standing here, I'm wondering if he'll respond. He surprises me by saying, "As long as it's after six, it shouldn't be a problem."

Again, I'm hit with how much these two resemble each other.

"Great."

Linc's gaze slides to mine before one side of his mouth quirks. "And bring your *friend*." The older man gives me a wink and I want to melt into the pavement of the parking lot.

What's worse is that Roan says absolutely nothing in response.

Oh my god, now I *really* want the earth to open up and swallow me whole.

We all say goodbye before Daniel and Linc disappear around the corner toward Peppino's Pizzeria. Roan hits the key fob and the locks on his SUV automatically unlatch. In silence, he opens the backdoor of the truck and sets the boxes of pizza on the seat as I climb into the front before slamming the door shut.

A few moments later, he slides in next to me. Even though he starts up the truck, he doesn't pull out of the crowded parking lot. He lets it idle. Unsure what to do, I sit quietly beside him as he stares sightlessly out the windshield. I'm not usually a fidgety person, but I can't help twisting my hands together, waiting for him to say something.

I want him to make sense of what happened back there. I've never seen Roan shut down like that before. It was weird.

The silence stretches until it turns oppressive. There have been times when the sexual tension simmering in the air feels so charged and heavy that I want to jump his bones. There have also been times when I've wanted to slap him upside the head because of an inappropriate comment that's come out of his mouth, but there has never been this kind of suffocating tension sitting uncomfortably between us.

I hate it.

Part of me wants to reach out and comfort him even though I have no idea why it's necessary. Something is weighing heavily on his mind. I also realize it has everything to do with the two men we ran into. Before I can overthink it, I place my hand on his thigh. He blinks a few times before glancing down at it. As I consider pulling it away, he covers my hand with his own.

"That was your dad, wasn't it?" My words are softly spoken because I'm not sure how he's going to react.

My voice is like the crack of thunder in the silence of the truck.

He jerks his head. "Yeah." Inhaling a deep breath, he forces it out slowly. "He's gay."

Unsurprised by the revelation, I nod my head. "I figured."

"Linc's a really good dude," he adds quickly, as if I might, for some reason, think otherwise.

"He seemed nice. They both did." Almost offhandedly I ask, "Your parents are divorced?"

"Um, yeah." He shifts on the black leather seat. "When I was fourteen, my dad dropped the bomb that he was gay." His gaze slides to the windshield again before he lowers his voice. "That he'd always been gay, and he was leaving because he couldn't continue to live a lie anymore."

"That must have been difficult." More like devastating.

"Yeah, it was."

I'm not sure if I should ask any more questions. Obviously, this is a touchy subject for him. "Are you two close?"

He searches my gaze carefully. "We weren't always. It really sucked when he first told Mom and me. I didn't get it." He shakes his head as if to emphasize his words. "*Like at all*. The whole thing pissed me off and I didn't want to be around him for a long time. *Years*. It took me a while to accept that he was the same guy he'd always been. The one I had idolized while growing up." Inhaling a deep breath, he continues, "Once I was able to wrap my head around the fact that he hadn't changed, we were able to move past it."

I can't begin to imagine what that was like for Roan. It couldn't have been easy for an adolescent boy to learn that his father was gay.

Not that I've cyberstalked him (okay, maybe a teeny tiny bit), but

I've tooled around on the website dedicated to all things Roan King and don't remember seeing anything about his parents or that his father was gay. Which is kind of surprising. It seems like everything else regarding his life is out there for the world to view, share, and comment upon.

I'm struck with a realization. "No one knows about this, do they?"

Once again, his gaze cuts to mine as the sun sets beyond the windshield. Even though I normally enjoy watching the sun dip beneath the horizon, I'm too focused on Roan to appreciate the beauty of the moment. "Nope. They don't know anything about my father."

"How have you managed to keep it a secret? Your life seems to be an open book. You can't go anywhere without pictures turning up or information being splashed across the internet."

He jerks his shoulders into a tight, almost defensive shrug. "It was never a concerted effort on my part to hide it. By the same token, it didn't seem like anybody else's business either." Yanking off his ball cap, he plows his fingers through his unruly hair before slapping it back into place. "He's gay and lives with his partner. After he came out, he never tried covering it up or hiding who he was, but my dad isn't the type of guy to ram it down people's throats either. It's one piece of who he is. It doesn't make up the totality of him. Just like me being heterosexual isn't the only thing that defines me. I'm a lot of other things as well."

He blows out a long steady breath. "I know exactly what the media would do if they got ahold of this. It would become a focal point instead of my talent and skill. I don't need that shit going into the draft. My dad is an architect and he's a damn good one. He owns his own firm. Once that information is out there, every time someone makes the connection between us, that's what will be uppermost in their minds. Not his talent, but his sexual orientation. If I were just a twenty-two-year-old guy looking to get a job in business after college, no one would give a crap about it. But like you said before," his gaze burns into mine, "I'm not anonymous. And everything that's put out there about me gets overblown. Neither of us want that to happen."

I can't help but squeeze his thigh as he runs out of words. "Not everything about your life needs to be made public." I think about the pictures of us that were posted and all the ugly comments. Even though being gay is nothing to be ashamed of, I also realize that not everyone is accepting. It's no one else's business if his father is gay. And it should be a non-issue if and when people find out about it.

Nodding, he puts the truck into gear. "We should probably get moving. I still have some work to plow through tonight."

"Okay."

As he pulls into traffic, I can't help but watch him from the corner of my eye. Roan has a strong profile. Even though his ball cap is still in place, I see the vibrant turquoise of his eyes as he focuses on the road stretched out ahead of him. His nose is straight, and his lips are full. His face is all chiseled angles and planes.

My heart skips a beat as I quietly study him.

Just when I feel like I've got a firm grasp on who Roan King is, something happens to change it. Every time it shifts, I'm surprised to realize that I like him even more than I did before.

CHAPTER TWENTY-ONE

The sexiest man at Barnett seems to be spending an awful lot of time with a tall willowy brunette. And yes...she's the same girl who has been previously photographed with him. Who the heck is this girl and how has she managed to capture his attention so completely??? Am I the only one who feels as if the world has completely fallen off its axis??? KingOfCampus.Com

Everything I learned about Roan tonight churns through my head. Even though I'm tired, sleep continues to evade me. I've spent the last twenty minutes debating whether to shoot him a quick text.

He was unusually quiet when we parted ways outside my apartment. I was thinking he might want to come in and talk but when I hinted at it, he didn't seem interested. And I kind of hated myself for the disappointment that surged through every cell of my being when we said goodnight before I shut the door, leaving him alone on the other side.

I've composed at least eight different text messages before erasing each one. I mean, it's not like we're going out or anything. I think it's already been established that a relationship between us isn't going to work. But we are kind of friends...*right*? And friends check up on each other. So, that being said, maybe I should make sure he's okay.

I grab the pillow from under my head and yank it over my face before screaming into it. I'm starting to drive myself crazy with this ridiculousness.

After a few contemplative moments, I toss the pillow from my face and pounce on the phone. Before I can give myself too much time to reconsider my decision, I stab out the words. Then I hit send before collapsing onto my bed and huffing out a breath.

Ridiculous.

I am acting totally *ridiculous*.

And I hate it.

This isn't me. I'm not one of these silly girls who obsesses about a boy or stalks them around campus. Unfortunately, I seem to be doing a damn good impression of one.

When my phone doesn't immediately ping with an incoming message, I nibble at my lower lip. Well, what did I really expect? It's midnight. He's probably sleeping. And I am acting like a total loser.

A Roan King groupie.

Ouch...

That stings.

Both my pride and sensibilities.

As I grab my pillow from the floor where I'd thrown it, my phone dings. And yeah, I all but fall on it in my haste.

I'm fine. Thx for asking.

Is he really fine? Does he want to talk for a while? Do guys even like talking when something is bothering them? I have no idea. I don't remember spending a lot of time with Finn conversing about stuff.

But still, I can't resist asking...

Do you want to talk?

One minute, then two, slowly tick by. When there's no response after three angst filled minutes, I set my phone on the nightstand before rolling over and curling up into a ball. Then I squeeze my eyes shut and hope that sleep will finally come now that I've reached out to him.

A light knock on our apartment door has my eyelids flying open as

I jump out of bed. It has to be Roan. Who the heck else would it be? I race to the door and yank it open. He stands on the other side, looking as rumpled as I probably do. Although Roan looks decidedly sexy in a pair of low-slung athletic shorts and nothing else.

Nothing.

Else.

Cue the saliva.

I gulp as my gaze crawls over the wide expanse of his bare chest.

Holy hell but he's gorgeous.

In much the same way I checked him out, his gaze skims over me and I'm suddenly reminded that I'm wearing a body-hugging tank top and boy shorts. A chill sweeps through me as my nipples harden into fine little points. As his gaze meanders its way back up to mine, heat fills my cheeks at his obvious perusal.

"Looking good, Ivy. Thanks for the invite."

Unsure what to say, I roll my eyes before grabbing his hand and dragging him into the apartment. I bolt the door before we head to my room. As I pass by Lexie's closed door, I can't help but wonder what happened with the pregnancy test. I'm sure they must have come out while I was gone, but the door was firmly closed when I returned from dinner and I didn't want to disturb them. I figure Lexie will tell me what happened when I see her tomorrow.

Carefully, I close my bedroom door before turning to Roan, who has made himself comfortable on my bed. He's stretched out on my side of the mattress next to the nightstand.

I cock a brow. "When I said—*do you want to talk*, it wasn't code for —*do you want to have sex*." If that's what he thinks is going to happen, then I'll kick his ass out.

Unfazed by my sharp tone, he chuckles before patting the space next to him. "Jesus Christ, Ivy, I'm not interested in boning you."

Oh.

I frown, attempting to wrap my mind around those words. "You're not?"

He laughs softly at my confusion. "All right, allow me to rephrase that—I'm not interested in boning you *tonight*. Tomorrow we can go back to me wanting to get you naked."

Snorting, I hesitantly make my way to the bed. And a very sexy Roan who is stretched out on it. "That is so damn romantic. It makes my heart go pitter-patter."

Since he doesn't move from what is technically *my spot*, I have to crawl over him to get to the other side. His hands graze the sides of my body before finding my hips. When I'm practically straddling him, he holds me firmly in place.

"Is that what you want, Ivy?" His voice turns decidedly husky, and my belly hollows out in response. "Romance?"

My mouth dries at the notion. There is no damn way I could resist him if he were to turn on that kind of charm. I would be putty in his hands. Even though it's dark, his gaze pierces mine. It skewers me in place, making it difficult to breathe.

When I remain silent, his grip slackens and I'm able to scamper over him to the other side. Now that I'm here, I'm not quite sure how to position myself. My bed is a double and when I'm in it all by myself, it's plenty big. With Roan filling it, it feels teeny-tiny.

I scooch over until I'm plastered against the wall. As I settle, Roan slides an arm around my body and hauls me against him.

After a few moments, he whispers, "Relax."

"I'm totally relaxed," I squeak, my body as rigid as a two-by-four.

"Yeah, right. You feel completely relaxed," he chuckles, "I came over to talk. Nothing more. Okay?"

Those words have my stiff muscles gradually unlocking before molding against his frame. After a few minutes of adjustment, I find myself turning toward him until I'm aligned with every hard part of his body. With his arm wrapped around me, my head lowers to the solidness of his chest. As I release a pent-up breath, my palm settles over his heart.

"Comfortable?" The huskiness in his voice has something hot sliding its way through me.

"Yeah." He feels so damn good. I probably shouldn't be enjoying this as much as I am. Even though I'm all but dying to run my hand over his chest and six-pack abs, I don't. It's been a long time since I've been this close to someone. And I miss it. Miss the intimacy of it.

"Good." He pauses before adding quietly, "Thanks for inviting me over."

I glance up, trying to read his expression. "You were quiet on the ride home. I was worried."

He stares at the ceiling for a long moment. "Yeah. Sorry about laying all that on you."

"You don't have anything to apologize for." I'm flattered that he trusts me enough to share the private details of his life. I get the feeling Roan doesn't confide in many people.

The silence that stretches between us feels surprisingly easy and comfortable.

"I like you, Ivy."

His words have my breath hitching and my heart pounding. "I...I like you, too."

After another quiet moment, he admits, "I feel like I can actually talk to you."

"You can tell me anything. I'll keep your secrets." Saying the words out loud feels important. *Necessary*. I've learned things about Roan that no one else knows and I would never break that trust. No matter what happens between us. Whether we stay friends, or we become more. Or we stop talking altogether. I won't betray him. That's not who I am, and I hope he realizes that.

He angles his head and even though the room is blanketed in darkness, I know his gaze is trained on me. I feel the burning intensity of his eyes. "I wouldn't be here if I didn't know that."

Something that feels suspiciously close to happiness bursts inside me like an overinflated balloon.

His arm tightens, pulling me closer. "You know," he murmurs, "I've never done this before."

Unsure what he means by the comment, I ask, "Done what?"

"Cuddled in bed with someone and just talked."

I guess that shouldn't surprise me. He might've had sex with a ton of girls but that has nothing to do with intimacy. Lying in bed with someone, opening up, and sharing the pieces of yourself that actually matter, *that's* true intimacy. Screwing someone is just that...*screwing*.

"I like it," he muses. "It's nice."

"It is." I can't believe how comfortable I feel with him. I like knowing that he feels the same way.

"I knew right away that you were different."

"Different?" I'm not sure how to take that.

"Different in a good way," he assures me. "I've never felt like you wanted a piece of me. Or that you're with me because I can do something for you."

"I can't imagine what that's like." I really can't. I suppose, on a very small scale, it's like when the photos were posted online and suddenly, I was inundated with friend requests and followers. Random people were calling my cell or saying hi to me on the way to class. I didn't really know any of them but suddenly they all wanted to befriend me because they thought I was close to Roan.

How could you ever let your guard down? How would you know if someone genuinely cared about you or was using you? That would really suck. And it would make it impossible to start a relationship.

It makes me wonder if Roan has anyone in his life that he can actually trust.

"It can be difficult. You don't make a lot of new friends. Not good ones unless they're in the same situation as you are. And you keep the ones you have close and hope they don't let you down." It surprises me when he chuckles. "I still can't believe you tried dumping me as your partner."

I bite my lip to stifle the soft giggles that try to escape. I'm embarrassed about that. "Hey, I've already apologized. I assumed you would be some meathead jock and I'd get stuck doing the entire project by myself." I peek at him before adding, "Obviously, I don't think that anymore."

He sounds strangely contented when he says, "Good."

As I lie against him, I want nothing more than to smooth my hands over his skin. To learn the map of his muscular body. Unable to resist, my shaking fingers stroke their way over the wide expanse of his chest. "Do you want me to stop?"

He shakes his head just once. It's almost as if he's holding his breath, not daring to suck in any oxygen. Only when my fingers flutter over one hard male nipple does a low groan escape from his mouth.

My teeth sink into my bottom lip as my fingers continue to dance over him. Roan is so hard and chiseled. I bet he's like this everywhere. As tempted as I am to explore further and find out firsthand, I know it would be a mistake. I want this to be more than a middle of the night hookup. A no-strings attached, easy lay. As difficult as it is, I still my fingers over his rigidly held abs. When my movements cease, his hand rises to cover mine.

For a few moments, we remain silent, our bodies entwined.

He picks up the thread of our previous conversation by saying, "I mentioned that my parents divorced when I was fourteen…"

"Mmm hmm." I'm surprised that he's bringing up the topic again. It means more than I'm willing to admit that he's opening himself up to me.

"I never knew. Never suspected that my dad was gay. He never seemed…" his voice trails off as if at a loss for the words he's trying to grasp on to, "like that…you know?" His brow crinkles as he moistens his lips. "He didn't fit all the stereotypes."

It would have been difficult to find out as a young teen that one of your parents wasn't who you'd always thought they were. That there'd been facets you had been shielded from.

He tenses beside me, admitting in a voice that is strung whipcord tight, "When people at school found out, I got a lot of shit. They started asking if I was a homo like my dad. There were guys in my gym class and on the football team who refused to change in the locker room if I was there."

My heart constricts. That age is hard enough without heaping questions about your sexuality on top of it. It's certainly no secret that kids can be cruel to one another. Especially at that age. No one wants to be pegged as different. If they are, they certainly don't want to be teased and ostracized for it. Unfortunately, those kids are the easiest ones to target and are tormented the most.

"I combatted it the only way I could." Inhaling a deep breath, he blows it out slowly as if it's physically painful to do so. "I got into a shitload of fights and I started screwing any girl I could and bragging about it."

Closing my eyes, I try to envision what it was like for Roan to fight against the world all so he could prove that he was his own person.

"All through high school…" As his voice trails off, I'm struck with the realization that this behavior didn't stop in high school. It continued into college.

With my heart breaking, I rise until my face is scant inches from his. "You have nothing to prove, Roan. I hope you've finally realized that. You are your own man now."

His gaze searches mine before he nods. It's a brisk movement. "I know. It's just been…hard to open up. I've been shut down for a really long time. People have always pigeonholed me. First, I was the gay guy's son and then I was the football playing stud. Even though I did well in school, people assumed I wasn't smart enough to earn those grades. I guess I got tired of trying to prove who I really was. When my dad moved here after the divorce, I decided Barnett was someplace I wanted to play ball at. They're a Division I school, and I liked the coach. I was also able to get a full ride, not only for football but academics as well. I thought moving here would be a fresh start, but I guess I'm still a meathead jock coasting through school on his athletic talent and looking to get as much ass as he can."

I wince. I'm just as guilty of assuming things about Roan as everyone else. Instead of being the guy I pegged him to be, he's turned out to be something else entirely.

"You don't have anything to prove. You just have to be the guy you were always meant to be. If people want to assume things about you, that's on them. That's their issue, not yours."

I think about how considerate and caring he was at my dad's. Not once did he leave my side. He constantly made sure I was okay. In hindsight, that's when my feelings first began to change, and I realized there was more to Roan than I originally suspected.

The corners of his mouth lift before his hand slides across my cheek. "Thanks, Ivy." Gently he pulls me toward him until our lips can brush. The caress is sweet and tender.

Just as I wonder if he'll deepen the kiss, he puts some distance between us before pulling my head against his chest. We stay like that until sleep finally has my eyelids feathering closed.

CHAPTER TWENTY-TWO

*Grab some Kleenex, ladies, I think Roan King has got himself a bona fide
girlfriend. We're talking actual handholding while walking around campus.
Goddamn it...where'd I put my tissue? KingOfCampus.com*

Bright sunlight pours through my unadorned window and hits me
square in the face. I roll to the side and take the pillow with me,
smashing it over my head. As I do, snippets of last night flash through
my head.

Texting Roan.

Him coming over.

Lying in bed together and talking.

The last memory I have is falling asleep with him.

Suddenly, I'm whipping the pillow off my head and bolting up in
bed. I shove the hair from my face as my gaze flies around the room
before realizing it's empty. Almost as if it was nothing more than a
strange sexy dream. After a few moments, I collapse onto the mattress.
I know it was real. His masculine scent clings to my sheets. The urge
to roll around in them all the while inhaling deeply is overwhelming.

Even though I try to close my eyes and go back to sleep, memories from last night race through my head. The pieces to the puzzle make so much more sense. All the random girls and hookups. Never opening up, never trusting anyone with the truth of who he really is.

I stare blindly at the ceiling as all of it tumbles around in my head. Fifteen minutes later, I've gone over the entire night from running into him in the apartment lobby to falling asleep in his arms at least a dozen times. There's no way I'm going to fall asleep now. Thinking about Roan has me all geared up. I throw off the covers and pad into the kitchen to get a bowl of cereal.

As I lift the spoon to my lips, my roommate's door opens, and Dylan and Lexie walk out. I give them a silent chin lift in greeting as he pulls her into his arms and holds her for a long moment. Before leaving, he presses a tender kiss to the top of her head.

When Lexie returns to the kitchen, I notice her eyes are puffy and red like she's either spent the night crying or hasn't slept a wink. Even though she remains silent, I set the bowl on the counter and pull her in for a quick hug.

"Do you want to talk about it?"

She inhales a shuddering breath before slowly blowing it out. "I took the test and it was negative."

I pull back and hold her at arm's length before searching her face. And yet she still looks upset. "That's good news...right?"

She nods. "Of course, it is. I'm twenty-one years old. I'm not ready to be a mom and Dylan certainly isn't ready to be a dad."

It's obvious that something is still bothering her. "What's the problem then?"

"I haven't gotten my period and I'm worried that maybe I took the test too early. Maybe I really *am* pregnant and it's like a," she pauses, "you know...a false negative." As soon as she says the words, tears fill her big brown eyes making them all shiny and bright. She shakes her head and pinches the bridge of her nose as if she has a sinus headache. "My parents will kill me if I'm pregnant. Neither of them finished college because my mom ended up getting pregnant. I'm the first to go to college. I can't drop out now." Thick emotion clogs her voice. *"I just can't!"*

I rub her arm with soothing strokes. "I think you're getting ahead of yourself. You took a test and for all you know, it was accurate, and you aren't pregnant."

"After Dylan finishes with his classes, we're going to the clinic on campus." She swipes at her eyes as tears trek down her cheeks. "I can get a more accurate test done there. What I can't do is sit around here waiting. I need to get this figured out."

"That makes sense. Do you want me to come with you?" I hate the idea of blowing off a class, but I'll do it for Lexie. We've always been there for each other and that will never change.

I hold her eyes for a long silent moment before she shakes her head. "No, it'll be fine. Dylan is coming with me."

My schedule for the day flashes through my head. It's almost nine o'clock in the morning. I have my Business Ethics class at ten and then French and dance. On Fridays, I teach two classes at the studio in town. It'll be after seven by the time I return home.

"Text me when you find out what's going on, okay?"

With a nod, she swings toward her room.

My voice is riddled with concern as I ask, "Aren't you going to class, Lex?"

She glances over her shoulder and meets my gaze before shaking her head. "No, I can't concentrate today. And I'm really tired. It doesn't feel like I slept at all last night."

I hate to see her hurting like this. "Okay."

After she closes the door, I finish the rest of my cereal. I can't stop thinking about Lexie and the potential situation she could be in. It sucks. What's worse is that they were trying to be careful by using condoms. Unfortunately, no matter how cautious you are, accidents still happen.

It makes me glad that I'm not intimate with anyone at the moment.

Of course, as soon as I think about sex, Roan's gorgeous face pops into my head. That's another sticky situation. It's entirely possible that I'm developing feelings for him. I'm not sure how smart that is.

Thirty minutes later, I'm showered, dressed, and ready to go. I checked on Lexie, who is sleeping soundly. As I open the door to head into the hallway, I have to stifle a yelp because Roan is there, blocking my way.

He's also holding two containers of coffee.

"Hey." His smile is bright and warm. It does strange things to my insides. "I was about to knock."

I can't resist returning his easy smile. "Hey, yourself."

He holds out an iced coffee. "Thought you might need a little caffeine this morning."

Absurdly touched by the gesture, I grab the tall cup. "That was really nice of you. Thanks."

My gaze holds his as I take a sip. I really shouldn't feel this gooey over him bringing me a coffee. But I do.

God, do I...

As I lock the apartment door behind me, I realize that I'm in huge trouble with this guy.

"So, I thought you might want a ride to campus," he says.

Again, I'm surprised and touched by his thoughtfulness. "That would be great." Our apartment building is located a couple of blocks from campus. Most mornings, I either walk or hitch a ride with Lexie. It's not that big of a deal but it's sweet of him to offer.

Such.

Huge.

Stinking.

Trouble.

As we arrive at the elevator, I press the button and wonder what the hell I'm going to do about all these feelings that are surging to life inside me. Before everything can circle around in my mind again, Roan says, "Thanks for letting me crash at your place last night. It felt really good to talk about all that stuff. To get it off my chest." His voice lowers. "You're the only one who knows about all that shit."

It's as if there's a magnetic pull between us and I find myself stepping closer to him. "I meant what I said last night, Roan. I won't tell anyone what you shared with me."

"I know." Confusion flashes across his face. "It's not like we know each other that well, but for some reason, I feel like I can trust you."

Strange as it is, I feel the exact same way. It's not something that makes the least bit of sense.

The spell is broken when the elevator dings before sliding open. After we step inside, it descends to the lobby. On our way out, Roan surprises me again by grabbing my hand and holding it in his larger one as we leave the building.

A few guys pass by. They greet Roan before giving me chin lifts in acknowledgement even though I have no idea who they are. Since they didn't seem to notice the handholding, something loosens in me and I tell myself to relax and enjoy the moment.

Holding hands is no big deal.

Right?

With anyone else, it certainly wouldn't be.

But with Roan, it feels huge. *Monumental.*

We climb into his truck. Five minutes later, he's sliding into a parking spot near Adler Hall where our class is located. Cutting the engine, he turns to me. Neither of us move to exit the vehicle even though we both need to get to class.

A look of nervousness flashes across his face which is completely un-Roan-like. "Grabbing dinner last night was nice." He pauses as if waiting for me to confirm his words. I jerk my head into a nod because he's right, it was nice. "Good." He gives me a brief smile before continuing. "I was kind of, um, thinking we could do it again."

My mouth falls open. It almost sounds like he's asking me out. Not that I doubt my hearing, but still, I need him to reconfirm this. "Are you asking me out on a *date*?"

His gaze holds mine. When it seems like he might scrap the idea and start backpedaling, his lips twitch into a grin. "Yeah, I guess I am. I want to take you out, Ivy."

My facial muscles are dying to break into a huge-ass grin. And maybe I'm even tempted to do a little happy dance right here in the front seat of Roan's truck. Even though I'm starting to fall for him, I'm not sure getting involved is a good idea.

Can a relationship between us end any other way than badly?

My guess is no.

When I don't respond, his face falls. "You're not interested?"

My teeth sink into my lower lip as his wide gaze clings to mine. I want to. I really do. I'm just afraid there's no point in starting something with a guy like Roan. He doesn't *do* relationships. And I don't do his brand of casual.

"I am..." My voice trails off.

His chin drops. "But?"

Shrugging, I ask, "Why?"

That's what I don't understand. Roan can have anyone he wants. Hell, he could have *lots* of somebodies. He certainly doesn't have to go out on a date with any of them either. That much has already been established.

"*Why?*" He seems confused by the question.

"Yeah." My brows slide together. "Why do you want to take me out? You've already told me that dating isn't your thing."

He contemplates me for a long moment that leaves my heart stuttering before slipping my fingers into his. "It usually isn't. I mean, it never has been before."

That doesn't necessarily answer my question.

"But why *me*? You could have anyone you wanted. There are thousands of girls who would love to date you." Even though that number sounds like an exaggeration, it's probably not.

He blows out a steady breath before admitting, "You're the only one I can be myself with. I've never experienced that before and, well...I like it. *A lot.* I like how I feel when I'm with you."

The walls I'm trying so hard to keep in place tumble down. How can I *not* take a chance when all he's done is open himself up to me? Even though I'm in no way convinced this relationship won't end up exploding in my face, I think that maybe...*just maybe*...it's worth taking a chance on.

Roan is worth taking a chance on.

"Okay," I whisper.

A silly grin slides its way across his handsome face. If my heart weren't already melting, that would totally do the trick. You'd have to be made of stone not to be affected by him.

And I am most definitely not made of stone. Especially where this guy is concerned.

"Okay?" The happiness lighting up his face intensifies. And god help me, so does mine in response. I can't help it.

His eyes are wide, brimming with excitement as he reconfirms, "We're really going to do this?"

"Yeah." The same excitement courses its way through my veins. "I guess we are."

"All right." He glances at the digital clock on the dashboard. "I guess we better get to class before we're late."

We exit the truck at the same time before meeting up at the hood. Roan nabs my fingers with his larger ones. For a moment, I glance at our clasped hands before my gaze lifts to his. I'm getting used to him doing that.

As we hit one of the main walkways that lead to Adler Hall, I notice other students staring at us. Some point and whisper. A few take out their phones. Most turn our way so they can wave or say hi to Roan. A few girls stop and openly stare at our joined hands as if they can't believe what they're seeing.

Roan smiles, greeting people along the way like he's some kind of celebrity. It's more than a little disconcerting. I've seen how strangers react to him but in a large group like this, simply walking to class, it's a little overwhelming the way they flock to him.

Before I know it, people are crowding around us, trying to get close. Even though I'm at his side, two or three girls wiggle their way in until they're pressed up against him. And don't think the chick who keeps rubbing her ridiculously big breasts against his bicep has gone unnoticed either. I shoot her a dirty look. Although it does absolutely nothing to deter her behavior. Her attention is trained solely on Roan.

The only thing that stops my temper from flaring is his lack of response to her. Questions are being shot at him. Greetings are called out. There are fist bumps and shoulder slaps as we progress to Adler.

The crowd surges and it almost feels as if I'm being pushed away from him. When I try to loosen my hand and move out of the way, Roan's grip tightens in response. His gaze touches on mine before he tucks me closer to his body and picks up the pace.

As we hit the cement steps of the business building, the crowd disperses.

Agitated by what happened, I mutter, "I don't know how you deal with that all the time." I hate it. "Do you even know those people?"

He glances at me before shaking his head. "There were a few guys I knew," he shrugs, "but otherwise—no."

"And the girls?"

Ugh.

Is this really what I've been reduced to?

A jealous shrew?

I don't like it. Not one damn bit.

"I don't really pay too much attention to them. There are always girls hanging around. That's just the way it is."

I suck in a breath and try to decide how I feel about this. Do I really want to deal with all the attention he garners every time he steps out of his apartment? Especially on campus. I'm not going to lie—it's a little daunting.

Roan squeezes my fingers to get my attention and my gaze arrows to his. "Having second thoughts already?" There's an odd note woven through his words. A tightness. As if he's steeling himself for my response.

It's on the tip of my tongue to lie. To tell him—*no, of course not.*

But...I am.

It's just so weird.

The way people fall all over themselves to be around him. I've never looked at Roan, or anyone else for that matter, like that. It's difficult for me to wrap my brain around that kind of fawning behavior.

When I remain silent, he stops before gently placing both hands on my shoulders and turning me toward him. His gaze impales mine. "Let's take this one date at a time, okay? There's no pressure."

I quirk a brow. It sounds suspiciously like he's thinking about multiple dates instead of one. He grins as if he can read my mind.

His brows rise across his forehead. "All right?"

When he stares at me like that, it's hard not to agree with him. I nod my head.

He leans forward and presses his lips against mine before pulling away. "Good. Now let's get to class before you make us late."

I laugh as he tows me the rest of the way.

CHAPTER TWENTY-THREE

Later that evening, after I return from teaching dance, I hear the low murmur of voices from the TV in the living room and breathe a little sigh of relief that Lexie isn't holed up in her room. Unfortunately, my phone died after French class, so I wasn't able to reach out to her. I hope she's okay.

Instead of finding Lexie in the darkened living room, it's Dylan I stumble across. He's sitting in the overstuffed armchair with his head cradled in his hands. From the way he's hunched over, I can tell something is wrong. And Lexie isn't anywhere to be seen.

Glancing at her bedroom door, I find it closed.

This doesn't bode well at all.

I set my bag down and close the distance that separates us before settling on the couch next to the chair. When Dylan doesn't acknowledge my presence, I wonder if he's even aware that he's no longer alone. Both his hands are tunneled through his golden blond hair as he cradles his head in his hands.

Tentatively I reach out, gently laying my hand on his shoulder before giving it a squeeze. "Dylan? Are you okay?"

When he glances up, I'm shocked to see that his eyes are red rimmed as if he's been crying. He doesn't say a word, just shakes his head in answer. My heart sinks. I can only imagine that the test results were positive if he's this upset, and Lexie has shuttered herself away in her room.

"What happened?"

His gaze holds mine for a heartbeat before dropping to his fingers which are clasped tightly in front of him. His elbows rest on his spread knees. He looks miserable.

"The test was negative."

I release a puff of air in relief.

Thank god she isn't pregnant!

But...why does he look like this?

And why is Lexie alone in her room?

None of this makes sense.

Before I can ask, he says, "She broke up with me."

"*She did what?*" Shock reverberates in my voice. Why would she do that? Lexie is crazy about Dylan and from all indications, he's just as crazy about her. They're perfect for each other. So perfect that it's usually nauseating to be around them. Like you've eaten-too-much-sugar sickening. But still, I love them together.

He spears me with a gaze that is full of misery. "She said she needed time to figure things out. That this has really scared her." He shrugs his massive shoulders as if he doesn't quite know what to make of her words.

He stares at me as if he expects that I might be able to explain her rationale for breaking his heart, but I don't have any answers. I'm as mystified as Dylan is by the situation. The silence between us stretches until the need to offer some small bit of comfort bubbles up inside me.

"I'm sorry. I think if you give her a bit of time, she'll realize that she's overreacting. I know how upsetting all this was for her."

He nods before going back to staring at his clenched hands. His knuckles have turned a stark shade of white. "It was hard on both of us, but the difference is that I don't want to throw away what we have because something life changing almost happened."

As I shake my head, my response gets stuck in my throat. He's right. As if in physical pain, Dylan carefully rises to his feet. "I stayed because I didn't want her to be alone in the apartment. Now that you're home, I'm going to head to my place."

His gaze slides to Lexie's bedroom door as if he's unsure what to do or how to proceed. I guess there isn't a playbook when something like this happens, you have to wing it and hope you're doing the right thing.

"Take care of her, okay?" His deep voice almost breaks. "You know she'll just lie in bed and wallow if you let her."

His words shatter my heart. What he's saying is true. Lexie *will* wallow in bed. She's always been like that.

"She'll come around, Dylan. Give it a few days. I'll talk to her."

With a look of dejection, he nods before quietly closing the door behind him. With my mind spinning, I hesitantly knock on Lexie's door. When there's no answer, I call out, "Lexie, sweetie? Can I come in?"

When there's still no answer, I knock a little harder. She needs to realize that I'm not going to leave her in there by herself. "Please, Lex, I want to make sure you're okay."

A small sob meets my ears and I decide to open the door regardless. If the situation were reversed, she wouldn't walk away. I push open the door and peek around the corner. She's curled up in a tight ball on the mattress. The light from the hallway slants over the bed. Her face is pale and streaked with tears.

My heart hurts for her and what she's going through. "Oh, Lex." I settle at the edge of the bed. Gently, I run my fingers through her hair. "Talk to me. Tell me why you're so upset. Dylan said the test was negative."

"Yeah," her voice cracks, "it was."

I wish I understood what was going through her head. I hate that she's breaking up with someone who cares so much about her. "Why did you breakup with him, hon?"

She squeezes her eyes shut and stays silent for so long that I begin to wonder if she'll respond. "What happened was terrible, Ivy. I can't take the chance that it could happen again. I don't want my life getting derailed because of a stupid ripped condom."

Unsure what to say to her rationale, I inhale a deep breath before carefully pushing it out. It feels like Lexie is overreacting to a situation that could have turned out disastrously but didn't.

"You still love Dylan, don't you?" Have I totally misinterpreted the connection between them? Maybe she doesn't feel as strongly about him as I originally thought.

A lone tear treks down her cheek before she nods. "I love him more than anything." She inhales a breath before forcing out the rest. "But I feel like we need to take a break. Pull back a bit. I didn't go to college to find a husband or baby daddy. I want to finish my degree and get some kickass job in fashion. That's the plan. That's *always* been the plan. Not getting knocked up at twenty-one and having to drop out." Her voice breaks on those last words.

"Oh, Lex." I honestly don't know how to comfort her. I thought she might be overreacting but maybe...maybe she's not. Maybe she's right to take a step back and get her priorities figured out. I've never had a close call before but what she's describing scares the shit out of me. All it takes is one moment for your life to change.

Even though Lexie has dodged a bullet, instead of celebrating her good fortune, she's breaking up with her boyfriend. I can't help but tug her into my arms. "Everything will be okay. You need to take some time and process what happened. If you truly love Dylan, then you shouldn't break up with him over this. He didn't do anything wrong. In fact, once you told him what was going on, he was there for you. Not all guys are like that."

"No, he's wonderful." She sniffs again before wiping her eyes. "But he'll want sex on a regular basis and I'm not sure if I can do that. I don't even want to think about sex right now."

"Okay, that makes sense, but maybe you need to go on the pill and continue using condoms. That way you're doubly protected. If one fails, you're still good."

"I tried going on the pill freshman year and it made me sick." Looking resolute, she shakes her head. "That's not an option."

I nod, suddenly remembering what she's talking about. For some reason, Lexie was sensitive to the estrogen and progestin hormones in the pill. She was nauseous all the time and didn't last more than two weeks on it.

"Maybe you should go back to the clinic and talk to someone about what other options are available. There has to be something else besides condoms."

Halfheartedly she shrugs. I can tell that no matter what I say, her mind is made up. "I don't want to think about it right now."

"Okay," I agree lightly, "just promise me that you'll talk with Dylan. He was really upset when I found him sitting in the living room, Lex." I can't help but remember that he was waiting for me to come home so she wouldn't be alone. I mean...she can't dump someone who loves her so much!

"I know, but I need to focus on my classes and be on my own for a while."

My gaze skims over her. She looks tired and pale and just as miserable as the guy she broke up with. "Have you eaten today?" There are dark smudges under her eyes. I'm betting that she hasn't.

"No, I wasn't hungry and after the appointment there was so much churning in my head. Then Dylan and I got into a fight."

"About what?"

She swipes at another tear. "He was so ecstatic that I wasn't pregnant and couldn't understand why I was still upset. He seriously wanted to come back here and have celebratory sex." Her expression morphs into one of horror. Like he asked her to murder a basket full of puppies.

I give her a slight smile. Because yeah, I get where she's coming from. But it sounds like he was just being a typical guy. "I'm sure he was relieved that everything was okay."

Her brows snap together as a spark of fire leaps into her eyes. "Don't make excuses for him! The guy thinks about sex twenty-four seven. Obviously, I was relieved too, but I wasn't about to jump back into bed and do what had gotten us into this mess in the first place!"

The aggravation bleeding through her tone has the edges of my lips twitching upward. "I'm not making excuses for him. I'm just trying to see it from his perspective, Lex. That's all. I'm trying to wrap my head around two people who love each other but aren't together anymore."

She closes her eyes as if exhausted by everything that has happened. Or maybe it's our conversation that is wearing her out. "I want time to sort through everything."

"Okay. It makes sense after the scare you've had. I get it." Changing the conversation, I ask instead, "There's some leftover pizza in the fridge from last night, how about I heat you up a few slices?"

The way she perks up is almost comical. "From Peppino's? Sausage, mushroom and pepperoni?"

"You know it," I laugh. It's always been our go-to takeout. It got us through finals and a few breakups freshman year. It's the best comfort food in the world.

"I'll have it cold." Flopping onto her pillows, she adds sweetly, "Two pieces, please."

Cold pizza sounds amazingly good right now. "You got it." I rise to my feet and head to our cramped kitchen, pulling out two huge slices for each of us. With plates held in each hand, I bring the pizza to Lexie's bedroom before retrieving drinks and napkins. Once I have everything we need for an impromptu picnic on her bed, we both dig in.

"You went out last night, huh?" She asks the question before taking a monster bite from her slice. Like me, her eyes nearly roll back in her head. "So, so good. It's even better cold the next day."

I agree, taking a large mouthful of my own. "Yup." I really hope she won't push the dinner issue any further.

Already I see the wheels in her head turning as her eyes narrow with speculation. I almost groan. Even in the midst of her own personal crises, she still wants to talk about my non-existent love life.

"Who did you go out with?" A devilish smile tilts her lips upward. "Let's look online and see if my hunch is right."

Crap. I kind of forgot about all the picture snapping BS. I'm almost afraid of what she'll find. Then again, maybe she won't find anything. I didn't notice anyone taking photos. Although, to be fair, I barely noticed there were people in the restaurant with us.

That's the effect Roan has on me.

She swipes her phone from the rattan nightstand next to her bed before tapping the screen. "Hmmm, looks like there are a hell of a lot more pictures of you and Roan posted here." She shoves the phone in my face. "And surprise-surprise, here you two are at Peppino's!"

She gives me a faux-shocked look, complete with a hand to her mouth and big wide eyes. "Here you two are walking to class this morning," one brow hikes up her forehead before practically hitting the ceiling, "and OMG, you're holding hands!" This time I think the stunned expression is legit. My face heats as she stares at the screen.

Unable to stand another moment, I nip the phone from her hand, my pizza all but forgotten as I scroll through the assortment of new pictures. This is un-freaking-believable! I mean, seriously! I glance at Lexie and shake my head. "Don't people have anything better to do than stalk him?"

She snorts. "Roan King sightings with a girl out in public are a rarity, my dear Ivy."

I'm still having a difficult time understanding this level of curiosity. It's just plain creepy. "But still...he's just a guy."

Lexie rolls her eyes as if I'm totally clueless. And maybe I am. All of this pseudo-fame he's got going on baffles me. "He's a hot football playing god who will hopefully win the school a championship this season before turning pro. So yeah, he's a major freaking deal around here. He has stalkers and gawkers aplenty."

Between mouthfuls, she fires off both questions and comments. "What's going on between you two? I didn't even know you guys were a thing." She shakes her head in disbelief. "I can't believe I'm even saying that! Roan King serious about a girl! Color me completely shocked!" She throws her napkin down. "And you didn't tell me any of this! You've been totally holding out."

"You're getting ahead of yourself, Lex. It isn't serious." Well, not yet, it isn't... "We're just..." I shrug, unsure what to tell her.

Do I want to get serious with Roan?

Maybe I do.

I'm still not sure it's a good idea. I really like when we're alone together but out in public? That's a different story. "Look, we're just going on a date."

She crows with delight. "Roan doesn't take girls out on dates!"

I laugh at the bug-eyed look she's casting my way. "It's one date. That's it."

The edges of her lips curl up and it's like the sun shining brightly after a thunderstorm. So maybe I'll let her bask in her delusions regarding Roan.

And maybe I'll bask in them as well.

CHAPTER TWENTY-FOUR

Roan King is playing the best football of his life. Does it have anything to do with the girl he's been linked to? Inquiring minds want to know...
KingOfCampus.com

"Are you sure you want me to tag along tonight?"

Roan slants a look my way. "That depends—does it make you uncomfortable that they're gay?"

I drill him with a hard look before rolling my eyes. "Absolutely not. I'm a dancer. Do you know how many gay guys I've worked with?" The answer to that question is—a whole hell of a lot.

A cheeky smile blooms across his face as he admits, "I like that you're surrounded by gay men."

"They're not all gay." I smirk. That would be a stereotype. An untrue one at that.

As we stroll up the sidewalk to his dad's house, Roan yanks me against his chest as his arms snake around me, pulling me close. He growls, "Are you trying to make me jealous?"

Even though I want to groan at the feel of all that delicious muscle pressed against me, I shake my head. "Hardly. And I'm not the one with all the stalkers, *Mr. king of campus*."

He winces as I tease him with the nickname. What I've learned is that Roan hates being referred to as *the king of campus*. It's like nails on a chalkboard. He might be used to the attention he attracts, but that doesn't mean he enjoys it. When fans focus on him, he always reminds them that Barnett's success on the field is a team effort. He might be looking to turn pro but there are several other players who intend to do the same.

There's no denying that Roan is the face of the Bulldogs. When ESPN talks Barnett football, Roan King's name is inevitably discussed. His stats are hashed and rehashed every Saturday. The closer we get to the draft, the more ramped up the attention becomes.

With our hands clasped—and yeah, I love the feel of him holding mine within his larger one—he gives a quick rap on the door before throwing it open.

Daniel and Linc live in a small bungalow in the heart of downtown where they're able to walk to the restaurants, coffee houses, and trendy little shops that line University Avenue, the major street running through the city that Barnett calls home. It's an old house that his dad bought, gutted, and remodeled after the divorce. Daniel is an architect and Linc owns his own construction company. They met through some business dealings they had together.

From the outside, it's easy to tell that a lot of love, attention, and detail went into restoring this house to its former glory. It's absolutely beautiful.

"Hello?"

Both Daniel and Linc appear from the back of the house. Right away, Daniel pulls Roan into a brief hug before Linc gives him a pat on the shoulder. It's obvious that there is a lot of affection between the three of them. And then I'm being swallowed up in hugs from both men. After everyone greets one another, we move onto a large deck overlooking a small, secluded backyard. Tons of trees border the property giving it a lush, private feel.

"This is beautiful." I can't help but admire how tranquil it is. A tiny slice of greenery in the midst of the city.

"Thanks, it's one of the reasons we snapped up the property when it became available. Great location. Secluded backyard. The house itself needed a lot of work but the bones and foundation were solid. Since the house had fallen into disrepair, that meant we could gut it, start from scratch, and make it exactly what we wanted."

"Wow. I'm really impressed." My gaze slides around the meticulously landscaped yard. There are vegetable and herb gardens along with several different flowerbeds dotting the leafy green area. It looks more like a well-cared for park rather than someone's backyard.

Pleased by the comment, Daniel shrugs. "It took a few years but the blood, sweat, and tears have been worth it."

Linc returns with a serving tray that holds two bottles of Vitamin Water along with two glasses of wine. He hands us the bottles. "Can I assume you've been laying off the alcohol?"

Roan shrugs. "For the most part. Every once in a while, I'll kick back with a beer, but that's about it." From what I've seen, that's probably true.

The blond-haired man levels him with a stern look. "The next couple of months are critical. Come January, you'll be entering the draft. You need to be in peak physical condition for the NFL Scouting Combine in February."

Tensing up, Roan nods before taking a drink from his bottle. "I know what needs to be done. It's not a big deal if I have a beer. I'm working with the team trainer on a daily basis and I'm stronger than ever. You don't have to worry, Linc. I've got everything under control. I'm putting in the time and seeing the results."

"I know." His expression softens. "We're so close to making this happen. And the team is doing so damn well. Three and zero. You guys keep playing like this and you could have a perfect season. There's a big game this weekend. Have you been watching film on UMass?"

"Hours of it. I think we found a few weaknesses that we'll be able to exploit."

Apparently liking that notion, Linc's smile widens. "We're still working on snagging some tickets for the game on Saturday."

"I spoke with your agent yesterday. Green Bay, the Bangles, and Jets have all put calls in to him."

The two discuss potential teams and which seem like the best fit. As I sit back and watch their interaction, it becomes increasingly clear that Linc is extremely involved in Roan's NFL prospects. More so than Daniel. Which is interesting. As nice as it is to see that the man in Daniel's life cares so much about Roan's future, his involvement seems a little over the top.

The conversation eventually circles back to the Barnett Bulldogs and their upcoming game schedule. After fifteen more minutes of football talk, Daniel shuts down the discussion with an announcement that dinner is ready.

Thank god.

My eyes were starting to glaze over.

Even though I've never been particularly interested in football, I'm trying to learn a little more about the sport. Clearly, it wasn't enough. With Linc firing off in depth questions, talking stats, and using a whole lot of sports terminology, I'm pretty much clueless as to what they've been discussing.

Dinner consists of a garden salad full of fresh vegetables and then a delicious pesto salmon grilled on a cedar plank set on top of a bed of nutty tasting wild rice. The salmon is so flakey and fresh that it practically melts in my mouth. I may love to eat but I have zero time to cook, so I appreciate a homecooked meal. And this one is excellent.

Linc shoots Roan a look. "Have you been eating a healthy mix of complex carbs and lean proteins?"

As soon as the question leaves Linc's lips, Daniel holds up a hand effectively silencing him. "No more talk about football, proteins, carbohydrates, or training schedules, okay?" He flashes a quick smile in Linc's direction before turning his attention to me. "I'm sure all this football talk is boring the hell out of Ivy."

With a mouthful of salmon, I shake my head. Quickly swallowing, I say, "No, of course not." Okay...pretty much.

His eyes twinkle with undisguised humor. "Are you a football fan?"

I'm guessing he already knows the answer to that question from the vacant look in my eyes when they had been discussing the draft and what Roan was doing to prepare for it. "Um, no...not really."

Hastily, I tack on, "I mean, I haven't been in the past. I'm trying to learn more about it now that Roan and I have become friends."

Roan squeezes my hand under the table. "She's coming to the next home game to help cheer us on." He gives me a wink.

I'm looking forward to watching Roan out on the field. He's obviously very good at his position or NFL teams wouldn't be scouting him. I think watching a Barnett game will be more fun now that I know someone who is playing. Over the last few weeks, I've gotten to know quite a number of the football players. They're all nice guys. Not quite the Neanderthals I assumed they would be.

All right...maybe a few of them are.

Daniel cuts into my thoughts when he says, "Roan tells us that you're a dancer."

I nod. "Yes, I've been dancing since I was three. I'm double majoring in dance and finance."

He looks impressed. "Wow, that's quite a combination."

"Well," I shrug, "I want to have something to fall back on in case it doesn't pan out. Being a professional dancer is highly competitive. And I've always been interested in business, so it seemed like a good fit."

"That's a smart way to approach it. Shoot for your dreams but have a backup plan in place in case it doesn't work out the way you hope it will. And you studied abroad last year?"

Feeling like a bobble head, I nod. "I studied at the Conservatoire de Paris for fifteen months."

"We were in Paris two years ago on vacation. The architecture is stunning."

"Yes." I smile in earnest, feeling a bit more at ease with the flow and direction of our conversation. "It's absolutely beautiful. There's so much to see and do. Cathedrals and gardens. Statues and arches. Everything is amazing. And you can walk almost everywhere."

His eyes sparkle as he warms to the topic. "You didn't even mention the Eiffel tower or Opera House."

"Or the Louvre!" Reminiscing about Paris and the time I spent there is usually enough to have sadness bubbling up inside me. Strangely, it doesn't happen this time.

He grins. "How about the Catacombs of Paris?"

I shake my head before shuddering. "I was roped into a tour when I first arrived. That's when I realized I'm a bit claustrophobic."

"It's certainly interesting."

"And spooky," I can't help but add. Long dark tunnels under ground with tons of old bones stacked on top of each other does not equate to a good time in my book. Call me crazy...

Linc takes this opportunity to steer the conversation in a different direction. "So, will you be graduating this year, Ivy?"

My gaze holds his inquisitive one. "No, I'm a junior. I have at least another year and a half after this semester. I'll probably need to take a few summer courses because I'm working toward a double major."

He nods, digesting everything I've said. "What are your plans as far as dance is concerned?"

"Well," I release a small breath, "I'm hoping to audition for a few ballet companies this spring. If I can get in somewhere, then I would leave school, otherwise I'll keep working toward my degree. One of my teachers has a few contacts in Chicago and Cincinnati, so he's been keeping an ear open for me."

From the corner of my eye, I notice Roan's dark brows shoot up. My plans, as far as dance is concerned, isn't something we've discussed. He probably assumed I would finish out my degree at Barnett. More than likely, that's what will happen.

"I didn't know you were planning to audition before you graduated."

I shrug. "I'm not sure if it'll actually happen."

With a thoughtful expression, he nods but doesn't say anything further on the subject.

Only now am I wondering if I should have told Roan about the possibility that I could leave Barnett before graduating. Although, it doesn't sound like Roan will be around after this year.

We've been spending time together and I'm hoping we'll continue to do that but still...it's all so new. It's not like we've sat down and exchanged life histories or talked extensively about our plans for the future.

The rest of the evening turns out to be mellower than the first half. There's no more talk about Roan turning pro or questions for me regarding my plans for the future. It's well after nine o'clock when we decide to head home. The evening turned out to be more enjoyable than I imagined it would.

When we're outside my apartment door, Roan asks, "How come you've never talked about auditioning this spring?"

I shrug. "Everything is so tentative right now. And nothing may come of it. There didn't seem to be a point in bringing it up."

"But if an audition comes along and you get a part, you would definitely take it?"

It's not a question I have to think about. "Of course, I would. That's what I've been working toward all these years. To be part of a company would be a dream come true." That's all I've ever wanted.

We both have dreams that we're set on pursuing and neither one of us are going to change the course of them because of a budding relationship. Roan could get drafted anywhere. And my future is equally uncertain at this point. I could spend the next year and a half finishing up my degree and then move to a bigger city where the possibilities for professional careers in dance are more plentiful.

Instead of firing off more questions, he leans in and covers my lips with his own. He strokes over them before sucking my lower lip into his mouth. A spark of heat ignites in the pit of my belly. It's always like that when he touches me. *Instantaneous.* No one has ever made me feel like that before.

A groan slips free. I've never met anyone who could take me from zero to sixty the way he does. With leisure movements, his lips slide across mine. It's as if he knows exactly how much I want him to take this deeper and he's toying with me. When his tongue finally slips into my mouth, I open fully for him.

Wanting more.

Wanting everything he's willing to give.

Our tongues tangle, caressing each other until he sucks mine into his mouth. It feels as if I'm going to come out of my skin.

My hands slide across his chest, feeling all the chiseled hardness under the pink polo he's wearing. It's a sexy color on him. With his sun-kissed skin, he totally owns it. I'm about to climb up his body when he draws away, breaking contact before resting his forehead against mine. It takes a moment for me to realize that he's panting as harshly as I am.

"You should probably go inside, Ivy." His voice sounds as if it's been roughed up and scraped raw. It arrows clean through me right down to my core.

I'm so turned on. Everything aches. I can't stop the husky words from tumbling out of my mouth. "Do you want to come in for a bit?" I *really* want him to come inside. I don't think I've ever wanted anything more in my life. It's been nine months since I've been with a guy. Normally, sex isn't something I dwell on.

That hasn't been the case since I've met Roan.

I've thought about sex more in the last month then I have in the last year. And it has everything to do with the way he makes me feel. The chemistry that sizzles and snaps between us. And the surprising way he's opened himself up to me.

It's so damn sexy.

He gives me a heated look that almost singes me alive before shaking his head. Disappointment surges through me and I realize that when I hit the sheets tonight, it'll be with a massive case of sexual frustration.

"That's probably not a good idea."

I stroke my hand from the top of his chest down to his rigidly held abs. My eyelids are at half-mast as I stare up at him. "Are you sure?" I'm not proud of the coy note lacing my words, but what else am I supposed to do?

I want Roan in the worst way possible.

Especially after that kiss.

A growling noise rumbles up from deep in his throat before he grabs my purse and rifles through it. I'm so stunned by his abrupt movements that it takes a moment to realize what he's doing. Before I can get the words out, he grabs my key and shoves it into the lock. Then he throws the door open and practically shoves me inside the small entryway.

"Night, Ivy."

With that, he slams the door in my face. I stare at the closed door with my mouth hanging open.

What the hell just happened?

I thought he'd want to come in and continue what we'd started in the hallway. Clearly, that's not the case. Which, for someone with his sexual track record, doesn't make a whole lot of sense. I can't ask him what the heck is going on because he's already gone. The door to his apartment opens before slamming shut with a resounding thud.

Umm, okay. I guess that's the end of that.

With a sigh of frustration, I slip off my heels before padding toward the bedroom. Noise from the TV hits my ears and I suspect I'll find Lexie asleep on the couch even though it's not quite ten o'clock. The last couple of days have been rough on her.

I'm quietly making my way to the bedroom when a tousled head pops up from the couch.

Her voice is low and groggy as if she's been sleeping. "How did your date go?"

Halting in my tracks, I spin toward her. "I don't think eating dinner with his dad and," it's on the tip of my tongue to say partner, but I quickly remember that no one knows about Roan's dad being gay, so I bite back the words and say instead, "Um, I don't think that qualifies as a date."

She ignores my verbal stumbling and latches onto the fact that Roan took me to meet his family instead.

"You had dinner with his dad?" Her eyes widen as wonder fills her voice. "I can't believe he took you to meet his family! Are you two, like, *a thing?*" It doesn't matter if she'd been sleeping moments ago, she's wide awake now.

"*A thing?*" I'm not even sure how to answer that.

"You know—going out or whatever the kids are calling it now-a-days." Her lips twitch. Mine do as well. "I mean, I know you're not hooking up." Her eyes narrow before reconfirming, "Right?"

Well...I *tried* hooking up with him tonight. Unfortunately, it didn't go so well. But I'm certainly not going to share that little tidbit of information with her. How humiliating...

The guy known for his one-night stands won't even fool around with me. It would be comical if I weren't so damn turned on at the moment.

"No hookup action has taken place. And I have no idea if we are *a thing*. So, chill on the labels, okay?"

Since she's sitting here alone, I'm guessing that Dylan and Lexie haven't worked things out between them. "Have you spoken with Dylan?"

Her smile dims before she jerks her head into a nod. "He texted and I told him that I needed more time and space."

"Do you feel any better about what happened?"

With a sigh, she shrugs. "A little bit, but I'm not ready to jump back into what we had. I didn't realize how serious we had become over the last eight months. I need time to figure out what I want."

"Was he understanding about it?" Not all guys would be. Some might even tell her to go fuck herself. Or be out screwing around since they're on a *break*. I don't think Dylan is like that. He seems fully committed to Lexie.

"Yeah, actually he was." A slight smile curves her lips. "He told me he'd wait and that we were in this together even if I wanted to be alone right now."

My heart melts. "Awww, that's so sweet, Lex. How can you not totally love him?" Hell, I'm not going out with the guy and *I* love him. He really is a sweetheart and if I ever doubted his feelings for Lexie, this has totally reconfirmed how much he cares about her. The fact that he's willing to give her room to breathe is all the proof I need.

She huffs out a breath. "I *do* love him, but I need to get my own shit figured out first. I'm going to make another appointment at the clinic and talk to them about birth control options." Her voice lowers. "I don't ever want to go through that again. It was so scary. It made me realize how careless I was being. I took for granted that a condom would be enough protection." With a look of irritation, she shakes her head. "It was really stupid on my part."

"Well," I respond lightly, "then something good came out of the situation."

She gives another shrug before her expression turns contemplative. "Yeah, I guess."

As we fall into silence, I jerk my head toward the bedroom. "Okay, I'm going to hit the sack."

Thirty minutes later, I'm lying in bed when my phone chimes. Almost immediately, I reach for it. I have the feeling it's Roan and a little flutter of excitement slides through me as I unlock the screen.

Yup, that's right. Passcode protected, baby. Thank you very much, Roan King. Lesson learned the hard way.

U asleep?

No.

Wanna talk?

Sure.

A few moments later, there's a light knock on the apartment door. I jump out of bed and sprint to the entryway before throwing it open. And there he is, looking adorable and mouthwatering in a pair of athletic shorts and a T-shirt that hugs his bulging biceps and chest.

I seriously love soft cottony T-shirts right now.

New.

Favorite.

Thing.

I raise my finger to my lips and give him the—*you-need-to-be-quiet* look. He smirks and nods before following me in. As Roan and I turn the corner into the short hallway that leads to the bedrooms, I skid to a halt, coming face-to-face with my roommate.

With a raised brow, she leans oh-so-casually against her doorjamb.

"Well, well, well," she drawls, a shit-eating grin plastered across her face, "good evening, Roan. Spending the night, I see." She hasn't looked this bright-eyed and amused in days. It would be nice...if it wasn't at my expense.

"Ummm..."

Yup, that's the best I got right now. I'm totally drawing mental blanks.

And Roan being Roan, flashes her a wide smile before adding in a wink for good measure. "Night, Lexie. See you in the morning." With that, he grabs my hand before towing me to my room and slamming the door shut.

"Don't think I'm unaware of him spending the night last week, too!" A hoot of laughter follows that announcement before she closes her bedroom door.

I cover my eyes with my hand and sigh. "Aw, crap."

He's quiet for a moment. "Does it matter if she knows I'm here?"

My hand falls to my side as my gaze arrows to his. Silently, I contemplate the question.

Does it matter if Lexie knows?

Probably not.

Although, this is new and I'm not sure if I can slap a proper label on it. I don't even know if I want to. Maybe I want to enjoy what's unfolding between us and take it one day at a time. I don't want to think too much about it. Which isn't my usual style.

As I open my mouth to say, "I guess not," he strips off his shirt.

My mind goes a little—oh who am I kidding? His bare chest has my mind going *a lot* fuzzy. I go a little bit stupid every time I see him without a shirt.

Not that I'm complaining.

Instead of waiting for an invitation, he climbs onto my bed before settling in. Kind of like he's been there a hundred times before and it's no big deal. He holds up the covers and silently gestures for me to join him. He doesn't make me scoot against the wall this time but backs up so there's enough space for me to nestle in front of him. I don't say a word as I climb in and he curls his body loosely around mine.

A contented sigh falls from my lips. How is it possible for this to feel so damn right when I don't know if anything will come of it?

"I'm glad you came with me tonight." He presses a kiss to the side of my face, and I can't help but snuggle against him as if this is exactly where I belong. Where I've *always* belonged.

"It was nice." I think about Linc and his laser focus on all things Roan and football. "Linc sure is..." My voice trails off. I don't want to offend him by sounding critical of someone who is part of his family.

Without skipping a beat, he says, "Intense?"

I turn my head until I can meet his gaze in the darkness. "Yeah, intense. A lot more than your dad."

He shrugs. "Linc played college ball. He knows exactly what I need to do to make it to the next level. My dad never played. I think that's why Linc is so involved in the process. He researched the colleges that were making offers and set me up with an agent."

"Wow."

"I appreciate everything he's done for me," he adds. "I wouldn't be in such a good position without him."

I can see how helpful that would be but still...it seems like a lot of pressure to heap on a twenty-two-year-old.

His warm breath feathers against my skin. "Other than all the football talk, did you enjoy yourself?"

I close my eyes and revel in the feel of him pressed against me. "Yeah, I did. They're both really nice. Your dad is so laid back. It seems like you two have a really close relationship."

"We do. It took a while to get to that point, but I can finally accept and appreciate that my dad isn't like everybody else's. Football is what Linc and I first bonded over. It gave us something to talk about."

I turn in his arms. "I'm glad you have people in your life who see you for the person you are," I whisper before pressing my lips against his.

After a few more gentle caresses, Roan pulls away before tucking me against his chest. "I like being with you, Ivy." His lips flutter against my forehead. "I like it a lot."

"Me, too," I admit.

For a long time, we lie tangled up in each other's arms, exploring one another with slow strokes. When we finally fall asleep, my head is nestled against the solid wall of his chest and I feel happier than I can remember being in a long time.

CHAPTER TWENTY-FIVE

There's a huge game coming up this weekend and everyone is expecting Roan King to lead the team to another amazing victory! Tons of people are caravanning to UMass for the game. If you're a true RK fan, you're not going to want to miss this one! KingOfCampus.com

I shake off the last remnants of sleep and roll toward Roan who is snoring soundly beside me. Sometime during the night, the sheet slid down so that it only covers the top of his low-slung shorts. The edges of the thin tan cotton are crumpled around his lean hips. Much to my delight, there's nothing but hot naked chest as far as the eye can see. To say that he's gorgeous is an understatement.

Every time I stare at him, my heart stutters in response.

It's doubtful that I could pull my gaze away even if I wanted to. Since he's still sleeping, I don't have to. I glance at the tips of his inky black hair that has a hint of curl to it to those ridiculously long lashes that are feathered across his cheeks.

Seriously...what guy has lashes so full and thick?

Ugh. It's so not fair.

And that mouth...

Total sin.

He has a strong profile. It would be a lie to say that I'm not tempted to nip at that jutting chin. Somehow, I manage to resist the urge as my gaze drifts down his body. Since he's not awake, I don't have to worry about him smirking at me for ogling him. You know he would. So, you better believe I'm going to take advantage of this while I can.

His body has a natural sun-kissed hue to it. His shoulders are wide, and his biceps are bulging. There is so much muscle that has been painstakingly sculpted. Almost as if it's been carved from marble. I can appreciate the level of dedication it takes to develop a body like his. It's a work of beauty.

His chest is solid and the swirl of dark hair on his torso only makes him sexier. He's so damn manly. My gaze meanders its way over strong pecs to his ribs and then onward to tight abdominals. Even in sleep, they're amazingly well-defined.

I can only stare at him in bewilderment. Someone needs to explain how Roan King ended up in my bed.

With me.

No, seriously. For the life of me, I can't wrap my brain around it.

Not that I couldn't eat him up with my eyes all morning, but the need to touch him pounds through me like that of a steady, insistent drumbeat. Carefully, I lean over before pressing my lips against his softly parted ones.

As I feather kisses across his mouth, Roan stirs as if he's fighting to surface from a deep slumber. With a groan, he stretches his powerful body. As I lower my mouth to his again, he kicks away the sheet before hauling me on top of him. I squeal in surprise as I find myself draped across him.

Oh my...

He growls, which has to be one of the sexiest sounds I've ever heard because it's all deep and rumbly, before grinding his morning wood against the apex of my thighs. Sharp shafts of desire slice clean through me with each purposeful stroke. An achy moan escapes from my lips. His tongue delves into my mouth before his arms snake around me, pressing me closer.

He matches the same rhythmic thrusting of his tongue to that of the thick erection sliding against my panties. I feel the rigid length of him through the athletic shorts he wore to bed last night. Every capillary in my body dilates with intense, bone-melting pleasure.

Before I can collect my scattered thoughts, he flips us over so that he's on top, settled between my spread thighs. I widen them, wanting him as close as possible. Little whimpers of pleasure fall from my lips every time his erection rubs against my slick core. My panties are completely soaked with arousal.

I want to rip off the clothing that separates us and feel his cock sliding deep inside me. What he's doing feels so damn good. Just as I'm about to suggest that we shed our clothing, he heaves himself away from me before rolling onto his back and throwing an arm over his eyes.

For a moment, I lie there, panting heavily, trying to figure out what the hell just happened. One moment, he's dry humping me and I'm feeling like I could explode with an orgasm and the next, he's pulling the plug and baling.

I kind of thought that maybe...you know...we might...well...*have sex*.

Trust me, I was totally on board with the plan. My nether regions are filled with so much aching pressure that I'm tempted to climb on top of him and see if I can convince him to take this further. Instead, I try to calm the hormones raging within me.

I don't think I've ever been this turned on in my life.

Once I'm under control, I roll toward him. I need to figure out why he put the kibosh on what was happening between us. It was feeling pretty damn good from my end of things.

With my hand propping up my head, my gaze slides over him. His chest rises and falls with every harsh breath he takes. I'm almost awed by all the tightly harnessed power contained within the confines of his skin. The need to touch him thrums through me. I reach out before carefully laying my hand on his arm. His muscles tense. The flesh beneath my fingers is hot to the touch as if his body is raging with fever.

"Just give me a moment. Okay, Ivy?"

My brows draw together at the gruff words.

What the hell is going on?

I thought he wanted me. It sure as hell *felt* like he wanted me.

Did I do something wrong? Touch him in a way he didn't like?

I know Roan has been with a lot of women. Tons of them. Hell, drunken bards have probably been written about the sheer number of his conquests. Maybe he finds me lacking in some way.

It takes another few tortuous minutes before he lifts his arm away from his eyes and peers at me. His gaze slices through me with its vibrant intensity. I remain silent, even though a thousand questions bubble up within me.

"I don't want to rush this," he says. "I like you way too much to ruin it by not taking my time with you."

And just like that, all those vicious thoughts that had been gaining traction in my head vanish. I close the distance between us until I'm able to press a lingering kiss against his lips. You better believe this guy's sexiness factor just shot through the roof.

"You're not going to ruin anything, Roan." My gaze sifts through his. I've never wanted anyone more in my life. "I like you. And I want to have sex with you."

Even though I just blurted that out, it's true. I *do* want to have sex with him, and I'm not embarrassed to admit it. At the moment, it's in the worst *I-haven't-had-sex-in-a-really-long-time* kind of way.

He doesn't crack a smile or smirk. There aren't any knowing or victorious glints lighting up his eyes. "I want that, too. I just don't want to move too fast with this. That's all I've ever done, Ivy. Screw around with girls without getting to know them. I don't want to do that with you." He pauses for a beat. "This is different." His gaze scours mine. "You know that, right?"

If I didn't like him already, those words would have pushed me completely over the edge.

"Yeah," I admit. Whatever this is between us, it *is* different. For both of us. "So..." I clear my throat. "No putting that morning wood to good use, huh?"

His lips quirk at the corners. It's such a sexy look. "Not today. But soon, I promise." He leans over so that his lips can glide across mine.

God...could I seriously like this guy more?

The answer to that question is an unequivocal—*no. No, I couldn't.*

Damn...

CHAPTER TWENTY-SIX

Uh-oh, Roan's new girlfriend better watch her back...some of these bitches have razor sharp claws. Especially when you're messing with their man...
KingOfCampus.com

"So...not gonna say one damn word about it, huh?" Lexie elbows me in the side as we make our way across campus. We've both finished up with classes for the day and we're going to grab lunch. After that, I need to head over to the studio to work with Eric, one of my dance teachers.

"There's nothing to say." Unless I mention how hard I'm starting to fall for Roan. Even thinking those words sends a little spasm of pleasure ricocheting through my belly.

"Oh honey, are you seriously telling me that he spent the entire night in your bed, and *nothing* happened?" Skepticism laces her voice. Since we're talking about Roan King here, I can't blame her for it. I would be dubious, too.

I rub my side where she poked me. That girl can really pack a punch when she wants to. I think she's way too used to elbowing

Dylan. "Nothing happened." It still blows my mind that he wouldn't have sex with me this morning.

"I don't believe you."

I skid to a halt before turning toward her. "I wouldn't lie to you. We just kissed. That's it." Okay, so maybe I'm omitting this morning's dry humping action.

She huffs out an exasperated breath. "You seriously have to be the only girl at Barnett who's actually slept in bed with him and not had sex!"

Her words only remind me of what he recently confided—that he's never slept in bed with a girl. That it's always been about the physical act and nothing more.

"Yes, well, I was more than willing," I mutter before I can think better of it.

"*What?*" Lexie all but screeches.

I wince as a few people passing by turn and stare in our direction. The last thing I want is to draw more attention to myself. Since my relationship status has become public knowledge, I'm no longer able to move around campus unnoticed.

I groan as my cheeks flag with color. "Can we drop the subject, please?"

For once, Lexie looks as if she might be considering my request. She holds up her hands in a gesture of surrender. "Fine. We'll table this discussion until lunch."

Great. Now I have something to look forward to.

"Ivy!"

My head unconsciously snaps in the direction of my name. When my gaze lands on a group of girls I don't know, I continue walking. My hope is that if I ignore them, they'll go away. I'm tired of girls coming up to me, asking a bunch of stupid questions about Roan.

Or worse...

"Hey, Ivy—wait up!"

This time, when I glance at them, they've closed the distance separating us. I stop and turn toward their small group. Lexie grumbles something under her breath.

Out of the three women, the blonde in the middle seems to be in charge. "Are you Ivy? The very same Ivy who's going out with Roan King?"

Trouble simmers in the air and Lexie quickly flanks my side. Before I can open my mouth to answer, she cuts in, "What do you want, Jillian?"

Rarely have I heard Lexie use such a shitty tone with someone. It tells me everything I need to know about this conversation. My gaze bounces from Jillian to Lexie before settling on the curvy blonde.

Going out might be overstating things a bit, but I don't correct her. It's none of this girl's damn business what Roan and I do.

Jillian's perfectly sculpted brows snap together as her gaze slides down my body before returning to my face. She looks none too impressed with what she finds standing before her.

That makes two of us.

"Is there a reason you wanted to talk to me?" In hindsight, this is the point where I should have turned around and walked away. Guess I'll know better next time. Although, I'm hoping there won't be a next time.

She smirks. "Yeah, I wanted to know how someone who looks like you managed to snag Roan."

My eyes widen. It feels like I've been bitch slapped into next week. I have no idea how to respond to that.

"What the hell kind of question is that?" my friend barks.

Thank god for Lexie.

The whipped-out words have me snapping out of the stupor I'd fallen into.

Before the other girl can respond, she snaps, "You're just bitter that Roan wasn't interested in anything more than nailing your ass."

The pretty blonde narrows her eyes. "Who the hell is even talking to you, Lexie? For god's sake, you couldn't even hold on to Dylan Sullivan. Seriously, how sad is that?" A mean glint enters her eyes. "By the way, I heard he was with Sloan Morgan at the Sigma house last night."

When Lexie's face pales, the other girl covers her pouty mouth with a manicured hand. "Oops, sorry...thought you knew he'd already moved on."

"You're such a bitch," Lexie seethes. Her hands tighten into fists that hang at her sides. I really hope she doesn't decide to throw a punch. I'm not sure we could take all three of these girls. I also hope for Dylan's sake, that he was nowhere near the Sigma house last night.

"I know." Jillian smiles sweetly before her gaze arrows to mine. Her lip curls with scorn. "I seriously have no idea what he sees in you. I mean, you're flat as a board." Arching a brow, she looks as though she's considering something. "Well, you must give one hell of a blow job. Enjoy him while you can, honey. It won't last long. In case you haven't noticed, Roan likes to spread himself around."

Lexie snorts. "You would know all about that. You like to spread yourself equally thin."

Jillian shoots Lexie a death glare before the three girls flounce away. As I watch them retreat, I realize that my hands are trembling. I've never experienced that level of bitchiness before. I notice a few people have stopped to watch the encounter and are whispering to one another with their heads bent together.

Not wanting to stand around as the speculation runs rampant through the crowd, I grab Lexie's arm before towing her to the parking lot where her car is located.

"Hey, I thought we were grabbing lunch at the caf?"

Hell no.

After that confrontation, my appetite has pulled a disappearing act. All I want is to get off this damn campus and away from the harsh glare of the spotlight. For god's sake, it's not even a spotlight that's shining down on me. The only reason that girl came after me is because of my relationship with Roan.

Unbelievable.

"Let's go somewhere else," I mumble.

Her expression softens. "Yeah, sure."

We find her Jetta and pull open the doors. I slump onto the front seat and throw my messenger bag into the back before turning to Lexie.

"What in the hell was that?" I ask with a shake of my head. "Did that seriously just happen?" I'm still reeling. I've never had a problem with anyone before. I try to treat people the way I would want to be treated. That's one of the lessons my mother taught me, and I try never to forget it.

That girl—*Jillian*—had a shitload of nerve to march up to me like that and say something so unbelievably rude. She doesn't know me. She doesn't know *anything* other than the fact that Roan has taken an interest in me. For that reason alone, she's decided to dislike me. How childish is that?

In all honesty, Jillian is gorgeous. Way more beautiful than I'll ever be. She probably has a legion of men trailing after her. And yet she wants one who isn't interested in her.

Lexie blows out a lengthy breath. "Jillian is nothing more than a skank who has a massive hard-on for Roan. When I started hanging out with Dylan and Roan second semester last year, she was always hovering around him." Lexie rolls her eyes. "I think she'd blow him in front of a room full of people if it meant that he'd give her the time of day."

That thought makes me physically ill. I can't imagine being so desperate for someone's attention that I would disrespect myself like that. Maybe I shouldn't, but I can't help feeling sorry for her. For the low self-esteem and self-worth she obviously struggles with.

Something tightens in the pit of my belly as I force out the realization. "She's been with him? They've had sex?"

Lexie eyes me for a long moment before admitting, "Yeah, he has."

Of course he has.

I stare up at the creamy white interior of her car because I don't know what else to do. Is this what I'll have to put up with from now on? These jealous women seeking me out, telling me to my face that I'm not good enough for him? I'm almost embarrassed when the hot sting of tears pricks the back of my eyes.

Damn it!

Lexie reaches out and rubs my arm. "She's a spiteful bitch, Ivy. Don't pay any attention to her."

I huff out a shaky laugh. "That's a little hard to do when she's all up in my face, spewing her garbage."

"I know" she sighs. "I went through a little bit of that last year when I got together with Dylan. After a while, it died down and then it wasn't such a big deal."

"I really like him." The words slip a little too easily off my tongue.

She gives me a sympathetic smile in return. "I know you do, sweetie."

I roll my head to the side until my gaze can lock on hers. "He's not the asshole jock I thought he was."

Actually, he's not an asshole at all.

Her lips curve up a bit more. "No, he isn't. I think," her words falter before she continues, "I think it's his way of dealing with all the attention. You've seen how people are constantly following him around, talking to him. And the girls...there's no shortage of them. They're always throwing themselves at him. Whether he wants them to or not."

"Yeah, I know."

In that moment, I realize that all Jillian wants from Roan is the status and attention that comes from being linked to him. It's appalling how many mercenary bitches there are on this campus.

It makes me sick.

And angry.

I don't give a shit if Roan plays football. I've never cared about it. In fact, I think I'd actually like him more if all this fame or whatever-the-hell-it-is wasn't attached to him. It's really pathetic that no one else feels the same way.

It may have taken a while, but I finally see the real Roan King.

The man beneath all the hype and bullshit.

I see the guy who drove me home and spent the entire day with my family, people he didn't even know. I see the guy who made sure I was okay because he understood how difficult the situation was for me. It's the same guy who wants to make sure we get to know one another before sleeping together. I see a guy who was able to move past his own prejudices and stereotypes to eventually change his ideas about what a father needs to be.

The Roan King I've fallen for has absolutely nothing to do with football or the NFL. He's smart and caring beneath all the protective armor he wears. It's only now that I understand why he needs to guard himself the way he does.

The guy I've gotten to know over the past month is someone I've come to care about. I wish everyone else could look past the pretty exterior to see the guy beneath the football hype. He's a really great guy.

One worth knowing.

Lexie interrupts the whirl of my thoughts when she asks, "Does this change the way you feel about him?"

I inhale a deep breath before slowly forcing it out. "Yeah, I think it does."

Her voice lowers as sadness fills it. "Being with an athlete isn't for everyone. It's definitely not as easy as people think it is."

With a shake of my head, I realize that she's misunderstood my words. "It actually makes me want him more because it seems like I'm the only one who wants him for who he is. Not the bullshit that comes from being with him."

A smile blooms across Lexie's pretty face. "There she is! That's the girl I know!" She gives me a wink. "Those bitches aren't going to know what hit them."

Well, I don't know about that, but sure...why not?

CHAPTER TWENTY-SEVEN

Roan King wandering around the fine arts building??? What's up with that? Hmmm...I can only imagine what he's doing there. I have the sneaking suspicion that a certain dancer has something to do with this... KingOfCampus.com

Roan

Even though this is my fourth year attending Barnett, it's the first time I've stepped foot inside the fine arts building. Ivy said she needed to stay late and work with one of her professors on a solo she's preparing for a show at the end of the semester. Since I finished up practice early, I thought I'd meet her so we could head back to the apartment together. I hate the idea of her walking home alone.

I head toward room 105...or maybe it's a studio. I have no clue. Throughout the corridor, there are framed photos of dancers. All the women are long and lean with builds similar to Ivy's. The men are muscular but not in a bulky, football-player-type of way. For a moment, I stop and study one of the posters.

Is this the kind of guy Ivy usually goes for?

Some artistic, scarf wearing, murse carrying dude who will cry at a foreign film?

The idea of having to sit through some boring movie with subtitles sends chills scampering down my spine. Okay...I did happen to catch *Crouching Tiger, Hidden Dragon* and that had subtitles, but it was the kickass fight scenes that got me through it.

And if you actually suggest a *murse* or a scarf, I'll pop you right in the nose. I'm not kidding, either.

It's not like I don't have a soft side...I do. Although, Ivy is the only one who has ever taken the time to unearth it which only makes me like her more.

I move on, walking down the long echoing corridor. I feel comfortable just about everywhere I go on campus. But here, in this building, I feel strangely out of place. As I pass by a group of people, their eyes flicker toward me but there's zero recognition on their faces as they continue talking. It's like I'm an ordinary dude.

It's a little strange but not unwelcome. I shove my hands deep inside my pockets and keep moving until I find the studio. It's the only illuminated room in a hallway full of closed doors.

As I get closer, I hear the music before I see her. My breath lodges at the back of my throat as Ivy soars gracefully through the air, legs stretched out perfectly. She lands on her toes before tucking into a somersault and leaping up. Her left leg swings out behind her and then she's spinning. Her upper body arrows toward the floor while one leg is held perfectly straight, pointed toward the ceiling.

My heart spasms as I watch her dance. She's unbelievably graceful. The way she's able to move and contort her body almost defies logic. The music ends and I almost clap my hands when a deep male voice cuts through the silence.

"That was very good, Ivy...*very good*. But there is still room for improvement. You need to extend your lines on your Jeté entrelacé."

The man emerges from the shadows where I didn't notice him before and moves toward Ivy, who is breathing hard in the center of the room. Her arms are settled on narrow hips as she watches him.

Like the posters and photos lining the corridor, this guy is muscular in a way that isn't bulky.

"Attitude devant," he snaps out.

Ivy rises on the toe of one foot while elevating her other leg waist high and bending it at the knee. One arm is raised above her head while the other is stretched out. She holds the position as the dude... who I'm guessing is her professor, runs his hand over the muscles of her rigidly held leg.

"Remember not to overextend." He moves her leg a fraction before holding it in place. "See? Better. Much better."

It's only when his hand falls away that I realize I'm holding myself whipcord tight. He gives her a few more instructions before sauntering back to the shadows where he's no longer visible. Ivy rises to her toes before extending an arm over her head and lifting her leg into the same position.

"Perfect," he calls out.

She breaks the pose before throwing a smile in his direction.

I can't help but clear my throat. Even though she's not facing me, her gaze arrows to my reflection in the mirror. I hold up a hand and give a hesitant wave. Her face breaks into a grin and a shiver slides through me.

Holy shit.

I'm in deep with this girl.

I rein in a snort. That is such a pussy-ass understatement. Meeting Ivy has been like getting hit with a two-by-four across the back of my skull. I've been trying to shake my head clear ever since that first encounter.

With an amazing amount of grace, she pads over before reaching up on her toes to give me a quick kiss on the lips. I want nothing more than to haul her close but I'm all too aware of the guy watching us from the corner of the room. My gaze slices to his. He doesn't look particularly interested in what we're doing. Although there's a hint of amusement etched across his face.

"Let me grab my bag and we can take off."

I give her a nod before she runs over to the mirrored wall to grab her bag from the floor. She gives the guy, who honestly doesn't look more than twenty-eight, a wave before saying, "Thanks for the help, Eric."

"Anytime. You have amazing potential, keep working at it."

She flashes him another grin and jealousy bubbles up inside me that he's able to coax a smile like that from her so effortlessly. Trust me, I know how ridiculous that sounds. The funny thing is, I've never felt this way about a girl before.

Protective.

Jealous.

Needy.

I've never allowed these kinds of feelings to take root and flourish.

But there's something about Ivy. From the beginning, she was different from almost everyone else I'd met.

"I will, thanks again!" she calls out.

I take her bag and sling it over my shoulder before nabbing her fingers with my own. She gives me another smile as we walk through the echoing corridor.

"You have a good day?" I ask.

Something flickers in her gaze before her smile brightens. "Yup. How about you?"

"Better now." Unable to resist, I tug her to me, hugging her lithe body to mine. I realize my day is so much better now that I've seen her beautiful face. And watching her in that leotard certainly didn't hurt either.

As we leave the fine arts building behind, I ask, even though I'm not necessarily jealous, "That guy is gay, right?"

Ivy laughs. The deep throaty sound has the edges of my lips tilting upward in response.

With a sly look, she hurtles a question back at me. "Would it make you feel better if I say *yes?*"

She's kidding, right? Of course, it would. "Definitely."

"Then yes, he's *totally* gay." Her slender shoulders shake with silent laughter.

My eyes narrow. "What you're really telling me is that he's not gay at all."

"Nope." She pops the P at the end of the word.

As we walk through campus toward the lot where my truck is parked, I nod to a few people along the way. My hand tightens around hers because I know the attention bothers her.

But tough shit.

To those people, not Ivy.

I'm starting to realize that her opinion is the only one that matters. Being with Ivy is so different than being with anyone else. There are times when I get the feeling that people agree with me simply because of who I am. And I don't want that. Half the time, I think she disagrees with me just to be obstinate.

That probably shouldn't be such a turn on.

I use the key fob before opening the passenger side door. Then I jog around the vehicle and hop in beside her. For a moment, I glance over as she slides the seatbelt across her chest before clicking it into place.

No, Ivy Kaster is definitely not my usual type. That's what makes her so special.

Her gaze settles on mine. There must be a look on my face that gives my thoughts away because I hear the slight intake of her breath.

She breaks the silence with a whisper. "Do you want to stay over tonight?"

Hell yeah, I do.

I sleep so well when I'm in her bed which is crazy because it's a tight fit. There's definitely not room to spread out but I love having her wrapped up in my arms. And I like shooting the shit with her before we fall asleep.

I've never felt this way about a woman.

I used to look at guys like Dylan, and even Sam when he's had girl-friends, and think they were crazy for wanting to be tied down to one specific female. I couldn't understand what the point of that was when there was so much more out there for the taking.

But I get it now.

Hell, we haven't even had sex yet and I'm totally fucking crazy about her.

It has me considering possibilities that I've never bothered to contemplate before. Possibilities that have to do with the future and wanting Ivy to be a permanent fixture in it. Although even I, who has absolutely no dating experience whatsoever, know that it's too early to talk about this kind of thing with her. For the time being, I'll keep those thoughts to myself.

Even though I don't want to, I shake my head. If I spend the night, I know *exactly* what will happen and I'm not ready for that. I'm actually enjoying all the anticipation we've got going on here.

That's just another thing I've never experienced before. In the past, if I wanted to get laid, I went out, found a willing chick (or two) and had sex. Or, at the very least, got a blow job to take the edge off. There wasn't any waiting. Or anticipation. It was more like scratching an itch. I never gave it too much thought.

The sex meant nothing to me.

And the girls meant even less.

What I feel now is the complete opposite.

Her brow lifts. "No?" She strains toward me but can only go so far with the safety belt harnessing her in place. That's probably for the best. At the moment, that belt is my new best friend. My willpower is dangling by a thread.

"I want to have sex with you, Roan." A rare vulnerability fills her words. As if she's taking a chance by putting herself out there with the admittance. "Don't you want that, too?"

Oh god.

Is she fucking serious?

It takes everything I have not to plow my fingers through my hair in agitation. There is so much pent-up sexual frustration brewing inside me that it's almost overwhelming.

Umm, yeah...of course I want to have sex with Ivy. And if I didn't care about her, I'd be tearing off her clothes and yanking her onto my lap right here in the middle of the parking lot before screwing her brains out, giving us both what we so desperately want. A memory from this morning flashes through my head. Damn but it felt good to grind myself against her. My cock twitches in agreement.

Down, boy...

Uncertainty flickers in her eyes as if she's bothered by the fact that I'm *not* trying to get in her pants. Doesn't she understand that I want to do this the right way? That what's happening between us matters and I don't want to fuck it up by moving too quickly? Ivy is the only person I can be myself with. The last thing I want to do is ruin that.

I reach out and stroke the side of her cheek with my fingers. Her gaze clings to mine. "I want one date." Her mouth opens and I know she's about to bring up the dinner with my dad and Linc. Yeah...that wasn't a date. "A *real* date. Just you and me."

The corners of her lips lift, and I wonder if she'll argue. What Ivy needs to realize is that this is going to happen. It's just not going to happen tonight.

"Okay," she says. "When? Right now?"

"No," I chuckle, "not tonight." I blow out a long breath before mentally running through my school and football schedule. I leave tomorrow for the UMass game and won't return until late Saturday night.

What I love is how much she wants *this*.

How much she wants *me*.

Just because I'm holding off doesn't mean I want her any less. I'd like nothing more than to hole up in her apartment for days and have my wicked way with the girl. But it's important to do this right. Despite the blue balls I'm currently sporting, that means waiting a few more days.

"How about Sunday afternoon?"

"I teach until one. As long as it's after that, it works."

"Great." A grin tips the corners of my mouth. "I'll pick you up and we'll have our date."

She nods as an answering smile lights up her face.

Since I'm not harnessed in by my belt, I cup her cheek with my hand before leaning over so my lips can slide across hers. As we kiss, I find myself experiencing yet another first—planning a date with someone I've developed feelings for.

CHAPTER TWENTY-EIGHT

Roan King just played the best freaking game of his life yesterday. He caught three passes before plowing his way into the end zone. The last of which won a tied-up game for the Barnett Bulldogs in the final seconds of the fourth quarter. RK is on fire this season and it's almost a sure bet he'll be turning pro when the draft rolls around. All hail the king of campus! KingOfCampus.com

Roan

I'm not going to lie, I'm nervous as hell. My palms are actually a little sweaty. It's totally ridiculous. Up until this point, I've pretty much screwed my way through high school and the first couple years of college. This will be the first time I've ever made love to a woman.

Shit. That makes me sound like a pussy, doesn't it?

Even in my own damn head, I sound like a little bitch. But it's the truth. Ivy will be the first girl I don't fuck just so I can blow my load without a second thought.

What happens today matters.

A whole hell of a lot.

So...no pressure there at all.

Hence the sweaty palms.

While planning this date, I tried to think of something that would be romantic yet wouldn't come across as cheesy. I hope I've come up with a winner. I cut the engine and watch as Ivy checks out her surroundings with interest before her gaze swings to me.

"Where are we?"

I point to the small cabin about fifty yards away. There's a private five-acre lake to the right that is surrounded on all sides by dense forest. "At my dad's cabin. He finished remodeling it a couple of months ago."

Once again, her gaze settles on the one-story log cabin. "Wow."

I nod toward it. "Come on, I'll give you a quick tour."

After we exit the vehicle, I take her hand as our boots crunch against the gravel of the drive. I unlock the front door and hold it open as she walks inside. She stops and takes everything in, silently absorbing it. I have to admit, Dad did a kickass job with the place. I love spending time here, tromping around in the woods. Doing a little fishing, swimming, and hiking. It's the great outdoors with all the modern conveniences of home.

And then some.

Big screen TV, state of the art kitchen with stainless steel appliances, and two bedrooms with king-sized pillow top mattresses. Hell, if this place were closer to school, I'd have no problem living here. It's way better than my apartment.

"This place is amazing." Her voice is filled with awe as her gaze flits around the space.

I grin with pride. "I know, right?"

Since the cabin is really just a kitchen, living room, bathroom with a waterfall shower, and two bedrooms, the grand tour doesn't take more than a few minutes. Once we return to the main living area, I tell her what the plan for the day is and hope she's onboard with it.

Since I haven't come up with an alternative, I'm screwed if she's not.

"There are a few trails we can hike and then I thought we'd go out in the canoe and have a picnic lunch in the middle of the lake."

Her eyes widen as she tilts her head. For a heartbeat, maybe two or three, she doesn't say one damn word. Nothing. She holds my gaze with a wealth of speculation in hers. Everything in me stills.

I don't realize I'm holding my breath until she says, "You put a lot of thought into this."

The air trapped in my lungs escapes in a rush before I give her a wink. "Nah, just threw some stuff together."

You're damn right I put a lot of thought into this date. I don't think I've ever wanted anything to be more perfect than the afternoon I'm about to spend with Ivy.

She glances at her Timberland clad feet. "Now I understand why you asked me to wear these." When her gaze slices to mine, there's a mischievous glint there. "I thought maybe you had some kink to you."

I bark out a laugh before tilting my head as if to assess how hot she would look in hiking boots and nothing else.

I have to admit, it's kind of a turn on.

"Don't want those dancing feet to get blistered." If I start imagining Ivy without her clothes, the rest of the day isn't going to go well for me. In need of a distraction, I head to the kitchen before grabbing two bottles of water from the fridge. I hand over one before snagging her fingers. I love the way they fit perfectly in mine. "Ready to go?"

"Yup, lead the way."

For the next hour and a half, we tromp through the trails that crisscross the twenty-acre property. I have fond memories of coming here as a kid. After my parents divorced, this is where my dad lived until he purchased the house near Barnett.

It never occurred to me that I would want to share this place with a girl. Being here with Ivy, enjoying the woods and the sunshine spearing down through the leafy canopy above us, feels right.

And being with her is so damn easy. I never imagined it could be this way.

We shoot the shit as we hike our way across the trails. We talk about our childhoods. Our hopes and dreams for the future. Ivy surprises me by opening up about her mother. She's never done that before. I listen quietly and hold her hand. I hate the slight tremor in her voice as she admits how much she still misses her. It's like a hole in her heart that refuses to fuse back together again.

By the time we return to the cabin, I feel like I know so much more about her. And it's not bullshit surface crap either. It's stuff that actually matters. It's the stuff that makes Ivy the woman she is today. As I pull her into my arms and kiss her gently on the lips, I wish there was a way for me to absorb all the hurt that pulses through her.

Once we pull apart, I grab the cooler from the back of the truck before heading down to the wooden dock. A red canoe is beached in the sand near the shoreline. I set the cooler of food on the middle bench before instructing Ivy to sit up front so I can take the seat in the back. As she stands in the boat, I pass an oar to her. After she settles, I grab another paddle before carefully making my way to the back bench. Then I use the oar to push off from the shoreline until we're steadily gliding through the water.

"We'll head to the middle. You start to paddle on the right side, and I'll paddle on the left and then we'll switch."

Just like our entire relationship, we find an easy rhythm until we reach the center of the lake. There's a slight breeze ruffling the tree-tops and the sun is high in the cerulean-colored sky. A few white puffy clouds float by. Frogs croak near the shoreline, breaking up the silence. A bass jumps at the edge of the lake where there's an abundance of waterlilies. There is a gray egret standing in the shallows where the cattails grow. The serenity found here is one of the reasons I wanted to share this place with Ivy. It's one of the few escapes I have.

"This seems like a good place to stop." I lay my paddle lengthwise in the canoe and Ivy copies my movements. "Why don't you turn around and then we can dig into our lunches."

Carefully, she swings her legs around as I pull out two sandwiches, a big bag of chips, two bottles of water, along with some fresh fruit.

Her expression morphs into one of surprise. "This is really nice, Roan. Thank you."

I grin, secretly thrilled. "Hungry?"

She takes a massive bite from her sandwich and I have to admit that I like the fact she's got a healthy appetite. It's hilarious because you would never think so by looking at her. Her body is tight and athletic. I've been with girls of all sizes but the majority of them have curvy bodies with a lot going on up top and a good-sized ass.

Ivy doesn't have much in the boob department and her ass is high and tight. The thought of squeezing it in my hands has my cock stirring in my cargo shorts. For whatever reason, this girl totally does it for me. Although, the last thing I need is to pitch a major tent. So, I slow track that line of thinking as she continues to chew.

"I'm starving. That hike was great, but it really did me in." She gives me another wide smile before attacking the rest of her sandwich with a single mindedness that I have no other choice but to respect.

As I work on mine, I ask, "So, what's going on with the whole audition thing?"

Popping a chip into her mouth, she says, "I haven't heard anything yet. Eric has a few contacts in some of the major cities." She shrugs. "We'll see if anything pans out. I'm hoping for a couple auditions when it gets closer to the end of the spring semester."

"But if something came along right now, you'd probably take it?"

She holds my gaze for a long moment before nodding. "Yeah, I'd have to. Dance is so competitive. And if I have a chance to get in somewhere, I need to take it. It's what I've spent my entire life working toward."

I nod, it's the same way I feel about football. Making it to the NFL has always been the dream. This is the first time my attention is divided between football and something else.

I had assumed that, if things worked out between us, we'd have the rest of this year to be together before I get drafted. I hate the idea that she could leave at any given moment. I'm not trying to get ahead of myself here, because this is really new, but Ivy is the first girl I've wanted to explore a relationship with. I don't want to lose her. "And your dad is cool with you dropping out of school?"

Ivy inhales a breath before pushing it out again. "He would prefer I finish my degree. But if I get an audition and make it, then he'll understand." She gathers up the wrappers and napkins before shoving them into the cooler before asking a question of her own. "Even though this is your fourth year, you won't graduate, right?"

"No, I switched majors last year and it set me back credit-wise. If I enter the draft this January, I won't have enough credits to get my degree."

"Is it pretty much a done deal that you'll enter the draft?"

Now it's my turn to suck in a deep breath. I'd thought I had everything planned out. It's only recently, as the draft looms closer, that I'm no longer certain about my future. "Linc thinks I should go this year. He's afraid I could get injured and hurt my chances of turning pro. I'm having the best season of my life, so it makes sense for me to strike while the iron is hot."

As I push out the words, Ivy does that thing where she tilts her head as if she's picked up on something important. "You're not sure if that's what you want to do?"

It shouldn't surprise me that she's so attuned to my thoughts and feelings, but it does. I've spent so much time burying my true emotions that I'm not used to sharing my inner thoughts with someone.

I rip my gaze from hers to stare out across the glassy surface of the lake and the greenery that surrounds us. Even though we're only a forty-minute drive from Barnett, it's as if we're a thousand miles away from the pressure that constantly shadows me. Every once in a while, I find myself needing to escape and clear my head. To forget, even for a few short hours, all the stress, all of the decisions that need to be made within the next few months.

Shit.

Now I sound like an ungrateful prick. I know how difficult it is to make it to the NFL. Hell, probably every little dude who picks up a ball in peewee football has dreams of making it to the NFL. The reality is that less than one percent of kids playing high school football will make it professionally.

Less than one percent.

So, I know how lucky I am to be in this position. It's not something I take for granted.

I have a lot riding on this. People who are pulling for me, supporting me, counting on me to go all the way. Family that I don't want to disappoint. Sometimes it feels as if everyone at Barnett assumes that I'll turn pro. That I'll be another success story they can tout for the Barnett University football program.

Part of me feels like Ivy can understand the pressure of pursuing an athletic dream. I like that we have that in common. I like that she's so focused on making it in dance. We both have the same drive and determination.

"Roan?"

Lost in thought, my gaze snaps to hers. "Sometimes I think it might be nice to finish up here and then enter the draft the following year."

Her expression softens as she considers the statement. It's almost as if she realizes how difficult that was for me to admit out loud. "Then why don't you?"

I shrug. Part of me wants to glance away from the inquisitive bright green eyes locked on mine, but I hold steady. If I've learned anything about Ivy over the last couple of weeks, it's that she's perceptive and tenacious. One way or another, she'll get to the bottom of the truth.

"I'm playing the best ball of my life. There's a lot of buzz surrounding the Bulldogs. I don't want to lose that momentum. And with the guys graduating or entering the draft this January, I'm not sure what the team will look like next year."

"All right, so why consider waiting?"

Restlessness slides through me and I jerk my shoulders. This isn't an easy topic for me to discuss. Maybe that's because I've never had anyone to talk to who wasn't pushing for me to commit after my fourth year.

Ivy has zero investment in my decision.

"I'd like to finish up my degree. Who knows how long I'll end up playing football for? I've worked really hard over the past three years to balance football and school. People may think that I've skated through academically, but I haven't. I've put in the time. Plus, I know everything will change once I turn pro. My life will never be the same again. The fame, attention, and money..."

"Most guys wouldn't feel that way. They'd want it all as soon as they could have it. They wouldn't give a crap about the degree they've been working on."

My gaze skewers hers. "Yeah, I know. I play with guys who feel that way. College is nothing more than a means to an end. It's a place to workout. To get bigger, faster, and stronger so they can make it to the NFL in three years. Instead of taking advantage of a free ride, they take bullshit classes that will go toward a useless degree they won't be able to do anything with." I can't help but shake my head at the stupidity of that logic. I've tried steering a few of them into something more meaningful, but most don't give a shit.

It's such a waste.

"Even though I get tired of the attention on campus, it's nothing compared to what it'll be once I'm picked up by a professional team. And I'm enjoying the season. The guys are in a groove. Playing in the pros...it's the next level," even though I tell myself not to say the words, they slip out anyway, "and just because I'm good here doesn't mean shit out there. I could end up crapping out."

I've seen it happen before.

"I can understand what you mean," she murmurs. "I have the same fears. Performing at Barnett is way different than competing against a dancer who was classically trained at Julliard or has been working professionally for years."

Like I said before—Ivy is perceptive. She gets it. I've never been with a girl I can chill with. A girl I connect with on more than a physical level.

And you know what?

I like talking to Ivy. I enjoy spending time with her. And god knows I love holding her in my arms when I fall asleep at night. It calms something deep inside me that I didn't realize was unsettled.

"You can't let your fears stand in your way, Roan. You're an amazing football player. There's always a learning curve when you move up to the next level. That's to be expected."

I run a hand through my hair as her words resonate within me. How can I not think about some of the players who have been hyped up by the media, were supposed to be a first or second round draft pick, and then got passed over until they went in the last round. Or couldn't hack it in the NFL.

I don't want to be one of those guys.

There's a lot of pressure on me and I realize that most of it is self-imposed. "I don't want to make a decision based on what everyone feels is best for me. I need to do what I think is right."

She nods before stretching across the middle seat of the canoe until she can lay a hand on my knee. Gently, she squeezes it before my fingers cover her delicate ones. I love touching Ivy and feeling connected to her.

I lean forward, needing to feel her lithe body pressed against mine. Almost as if we're magnets straining to connect, she attempts to close the distance between us. The shifting of our combined weight makes the canoe teeter.

It wouldn't be a big deal except Ivy's eyes flare with panic as she scrambles to steady herself. The rocking motion turns precarious as I attempt to stabilize the narrow boat we're sitting in. Water sloshes over the edges and splashes on our clothes.

Not wanting her to panic, I say calmly, "Ivy, sit back down."

She continues to scrabble for purchase as her fingers grip the metal sides. I'm trying to keep my amusement contained. She looks like a nervous cat who is intent on avoiding being tossed into a bathtub. When she leans to one side, I try to steady us by leaning the other way, hoping it will be enough to still the frantic swaying. Unfortunately, I overcompensate and when she shifts to the other side, I know it's too damn late to save us.

"*Ivy*—"

I get her name out before the canoe flips and we get dumped into the spring-fed lake. Even though it's late September, the water is still warm. Otherwise this would suck a whole lot more.

As I surface, Ivy sputters next to me as she treads water. There's a thin veneer of shock coating her expression as if she can't believe what happened.

"The canoe," she gasps. It's turned over and bobbing upside down in the water next to us.

A more pertinent question would be— "Are you okay? Do you know how to swim?"

A gurgle of laughter escapes from her lips. "You probably should have asked that before we went out in the boat!"

I grin. She doesn't seem angry over our current predicament. Some girls would be seriously pissed off at finding themselves floating in the middle of a lake. "You're right, I should have." Since she's treading water next to me like a champ, I'm pretty sure she knows how to at least doggie paddle. "I need to get this canoe turned over so we can get back to shore."

That turns out to be a ten-minute fiasco. It probably would have gone a lot faster if we weren't laughing and splashing each other like a couple of kids. When we finally get the canoe righted, climbing inside presents an entirely new, not to mention, difficult challenge. I hold the red boat steady while Ivy hoists herself over the edge before tumbling inside with a loud *oomph*.

My shoulders shake with silent laughter as she swears under her breath like a sailor.

"You better not be laughing!" she yells from the bottom of the canoe before her head pops up. She glares at me, looking very much like a drowned kitten.

I school my features. "I wasn't."

Her eyes narrow until they're slits. "Yeah, you were. You were *definitely* laughing at me."

Her hand shoots out, skimming across the rippling surface of the lake. She's got good aim, I'll give her that. It hits me square in the face. I shake it off and launch myself at the canoe before grabbing the metal rimmed edge and giving it a good shake. "Do you want to join me in here again?"

She squeals before crashing to the bottom of the boat. "Goddamn it, Roan!"

Still laughing, I steady the vessel. She crawls over to the middle bench before picking up the oars we found floating in the water. With one hand on the canoe, I tow her to the dock. Thankfully, it's bright and sunny out or we'd be freezing our asses off. Although she does have a pretty cute ass, so maybe I wouldn't mind seeing that.

I drag the boat onto the beach before helping her out. Once her fingers are firmly ensconced in mine, I don't let go. My gaze runs down the length of her. Her hair is slicked back, and little rivulets of water slowly trek their way down the side of her face before dripping onto her clothing. I can't resist reaching over and giving her a soft kiss.

As I do, her hand fists the collar of my shirt as if to keep me anchored in place. After a few heated moments, I pull back. We're both soaking wet. Water is pooling in my Timberlands.

"We'll have to borrow some of my dad's clothes and throw these in the dryer."

Her eyes hold mine before she says with enough heat to have my cock twitching in my shorts. "Or maybe we just throw them in the dryer."

Before I can process the words, she grabs the hem of her shirt and drags the drenched material over her head. My eyes widen. All I can do is stand there with my breath wedged in the middle of my throat as she unbuttons the tiny red shorts that are currently plastered against her tight tummy and hip bones.

Have I mentioned how amazingly long those sexy little shorts make her legs look?

Like they go on for miles and miles.

With her gaze holding mine, she steps out of the shorts until she's standing in nothing more than a lacy, pale pink bra and a tiny frothy scrap of material I'm going to guess are panties.

Holy shit this girl is hot. All the saliva in my mouth dries as my eyes eat her alive. Even though my cargo shorts are freezing cold, I'm now sporting a massive hard-on.

She glances at the boots still adorning her feet. "I guess it's not so sexy with these on, huh?"

My gaze falls to the tan leather Timberlands strapped to her feet before slowly traveling up her toned athletic body. "Actually," I swallow thickly, "its *way* sexier than you can imagine." I'm not lying either. I don't think I've ever been more turned on in my life.

One side of her mouth quirks up. Her eyes take on a sexy glint as if she's well-aware of her own sex appeal and enjoys flaunting it. And yeah...that's fucking hot as well.

"Would it be sexier if I took off the bra and underwear?"

Damn, I can't tell if she's fucking with me or not.

I'm barely able to choke out the words as I imagine what *that* would look like. "God, yes."

The smile fades from her lips as she reaches around her narrow ribcage and unclasps the lacy bra. As it snaps apart, the thin straps torment me by sliding oh-so-leisurely down her arms until her breasts are bared.

I'm not going to lie—I've been fantasizing about what Ivy looked like since she slammed into me on campus. What I find is even better than my imagination could possibly conjure. It's absolute perfection. I didn't think I could get any harder, but I was wrong. I'm so stiff it's painful. The last thing I need is to come in my shorts like a goddamn prepubescent teenager.

How humiliating would *that* be?

That was more of a rhetorical question, no need to answer.

Ivy's breasts are small, tight, and slightly rounded. They're topped with gorgeous little blush-colored nipples that are jutting out as if begging for attention. I want to wrap my lips around one of them and suck it into my mouth until she's moaning with the need to feel my lips everywhere. A groan escapes from me and heat leaps into her eyes as if she's as turned on and impatient as I am.

Which isn't possible.

Before I can babble out some kind of ridiculous nonsense about thanking god or her or *someone* for the amazing moment I'm having here, she wiggles her way out of that little pink scrap of fabric covering the only part of her my eyes haven't touched. As she kicks them off, I realize it's a teeny tiny thong.

Again, my gaze slides greedily over her body. Long and lean. A flat belly that dips in at her hip bones and—

I swallow thickly at the sight of her gorgeous pussy.

Two words for you—*completely bare.*

Which is sexy as fuck.

Barely do I resist the urge to plow my hand through my hair. Instead, I whip off my shirt before tossing it over my shoulder. My trembling fingers—yeah, for fuck's sake, my fingers are actually shaking —fumble around with my belt before unbuttoning and unzipping my shorts. They crash to the ground at my feet before I kick them away.

When I'm in nothing more than boxer briefs, I quickly unlace my boots.

When they've been tossed aside, I glance up and find her standing before me in nothing more than Timberlands.

Goddamn, that's one sexy mental snapshot.

"Come here, beautiful." My voice is low and gravelly. I don't want to scare her with how growly it sounds. She steps forward so that I can work on her knotted laces. In record time, I have her divested of those sexy-as-fuck boots.

I know...who would have thought?

Certainly not me.

Once she's totally bare, my fingers graze the smooth skin of her calves to the delicate undersides of her knees before moving past the lean muscles of her thighs to her gently flaring hips.

My hands slide to her ass and I pull her forward, pressing a kiss against the vee of her heated flesh. The way her breath catches is music to my ears. It only stokes the flames that are leaping and twisting within me. I want to spread her wide and lick every beautiful inch of her.

Ivy is, without a doubt, the sexiest woman I've ever been with.

Up until now, all I've done is screw around with scores of faceless, nameless women. Tons of them. So many that I've lost count. I stopped keeping track a long time ago. None of them were anything more than a quick fuck. At first, it was a way to prove to myself and others that I was nothing like my father. Then it was a way to release pressure. To turn off my mind and forget about the constant stress of performing with a few moments of mindless pleasure. And I enjoyed it. I mean, come on...of course I did.

A soft wet pussy and big bouncy titties...

What's not to enjoy?

In the back of my mind, I always knew why they were with me. They didn't give a shit about me anymore than I did about them. What's unfolding with this girl couldn't be more different than every past sexual experience.

I care about Ivy.

And maybe she cares about me, too. She wouldn't be doing this if she didn't have feelings for me. And that, I realize, makes this so much more special than almost any other moment of my entire life.

Suddenly, I'm glad that it's Ivy I'm experiencing this with. This isn't going to be some fast fuck or a faceless screw. I'm going to take my sweet damn time with her. I'm going to make love to this beautiful woman who is giving herself to me.

As I rise to my feet, I press my lips against her mouth, allowing my tongue to sweep inside, mingling with hers for a heated moment or two. Damn, but it would be all too easy to let the attraction burn hot and consume us. I need to slow this down and enjoy what's happening. Her fingers slip inside my boxers before stroking up and down the iron-hard length of me.

A low growl of need falls from my lips. It feels as if I'm holding on by a frayed thread. My balls are so tightly drawn up against my body that they ache for release.

"You gonna lose the boxers?" The huskiness of her voice sends me rocketing over the edge.

"Consider them lost," I whisper fiercely against her mouth.

In three seconds flat, I make good on that promise. The boxers have disappeared and we're both naked, embracing one another as the sun strokes over our chilled flesh. My skin might be cold from the impromptu swim, but I'm burning up inside.

Without another word, I wrap one arm under the back of her thighs as I hoist her into my arms. She can't weigh more than a buck twenty. She's so light. About half my weight.

She nestles close to my chest as I carry her to the house and through the front door to my bedroom. Gently, I place her in the middle of the king-sized bed. Her body sinks into the feather comforter as her gaze burns into mine. For a moment, it feels as if my heartbeat stutters before pounding into overdrive.

Again, I'm struck by the realization that this girl matters.

She matters more than anyone else ever has.

How's that for a kick in the balls?

I get lost in the heaviness of my thoughts until she stretches out her hand. When I place my fingers in hers, she tugs me to the bed until I'm sprawled over her. I capture her lips before our tongues tangle together.

Even though I'm dying to bury myself deep inside her heat, I don't. I want this moment to last. I want to draw out every ounce of pleasure that I can. This needs to be the sexual experience that all others get measured against.

And are found lacking.

It's a tall fucking order but I think I'm up to the task.

Hell, I know I am.

I spend a good ten minutes licking at her mouth, sucking on her tongue, tormenting her until she's as mindless and frenzied as I am. If the moans that fall from her lips are any indication, I think she's loving it. I could spend the rest of the day paying homage to that gorgeous mouth of hers, but I want to explore the rest of her slender body now that I have her exactly where I want her.

With teasing strokes, my tongue and lips slip from her chin to the hollow of her neck. I bathe the pulse that beats a steady thumping rhythm under her delicate flesh before sliding over narrow shoulders and her breastbone. I want to learn every curve and dip until I know her as well as I know myself.

When I reach the gentle swell of her breasts, I take my time, nuzzling her with my lips and teeth. Ivy arches as I circle my way closer to the tightened nipple. Unable to resist the temptation, I swipe over it with my tongue.

One stroke, then two before sucking it into my mouth.

Her body writhes beneath mine. Breathy little moans full of pleasure fall from her lips as her fingers rake through my damp hair. With a popping sound, I release the bud and stare at her with fascination.

Her body is absolute honeyed perfection.

I used to think that breasts needed to be supersized. Larger than life. Ginormous. With big button-like nipples topping them like cherries on a monster sundae. If a girl wasn't busting out of a lowcut shirt, I barely spared her a glance. I had zero appreciation for such high, tight globes of flesh.

I almost snort.

I am such a fucking asshole.

No. I *was* such a fucking asshole.

Ivy's breasts are flawless. Taut and perky. With beautiful little pink nipples that get so damn erect that I want to stroke, suckle, and play with them for hours.

My lips slide over to the other as I worship it in much the same fashion until Ivy is undulating against me. She squirms with pleasure. God, I love that her body is so damn responsive.

To me.

Only me.

You better believe that we'll discuss that after we're finished here. Although when that'll be, who the hell knows. Not for a while, if I have my way.

"Roan, I want you in me...*now*." She sounds as if she's burning up inside. I know exactly how she feels. "*Right now!*"

I raise my head from her breast until my gaze can drill into hers. Even though I'm hard as hell, a smile tips my lips upward. "Bossy much?" I can't believe I'm teasing her at a time like this. Being with Ivy is so damn easy.

She makes a growly noise deep in her throat. "Don't be an ass and make me beg for it."

I perk up at the notion of Ivy Kaster begging for anything, let alone my cock inside her perfect body.

Talk about hot.

She spreads her thighs wide as I settle between them. The thought of having those long, toned legs wrapped around me as I pound into her has me clenching my teeth, trying to harness and control every instinct that is hammering through me. My gaze arrows to her pussy.

Damn.

"I need to taste you, Ivy." With my gaze fastened onto the delicate pink folds, I lick my lips in sweet anticipation. I want to feel her pulsing against my tongue. I want to lap at her before sucking her clit into my mouth.

With a moan, she shifts restlessly beneath me. "Not now," she breathes, sounding as if her body is racked in agony, "later."

My gaze slides over the very core of her. The temptation to run my tongue over the length of her slit thrums through me like a heavy drumbeat. As much as I want that, the need to bury myself deep inside her claws at me. The throbbing head of my cock is nestled against her wet heat. As I hold myself rigidly above her, I can't help but admire the way our flesh connects. I want to see the precise moment I enter her.

Fuck.

Sweat pops out against my brow. The thought of being inside her has me on the verge of losing it. I almost want to squeeze my eyes shut so I can rein in my desire. At this rate, I'll blow my load before she has a chance to blink.

To be clear—that has never happened before.

Ever.

Even though my brain isn't firing on all cylinders at the moment, I remember to ask, "Are you on the pill?"

"No, we need to use a condom."

My gaze slices from her glistening lips, spread so beautifully for me, to her dazed eyes.

Shit. Shit. Shit.

I think that sentiment sums up the situation perfectly.

"Don't you have any in your room?"

Now why the hell would I have a stash of condoms here?

I shake my head as I rack my brain for a solution. If I don't come up with one fast, I'm probably going to lose my fucking mind. "I don't bring girls here."

Even though this feels like a dire predicament, a slow smile blooms its way across her flushed face. "I'm the first girl you've ever brought to the cabin?"

My gaze fastens on to hers. "You're the *only* one," I confirm. For so many things, but I keep that to myself.

All right, back to the situation at hand.

Condoms.

Do I have any?

I know there weren't any in the pockets of my shorts or wallet. I can't believe I forgot to bring the fucking condoms! Unbelievable.

Wait a minute...truck.

There might be a few in the glove compartment.

"I, ah, think there are some in the truck," I say. "I'll be right back."

Before she can blink, I'm up and racing through the cabin and out the front door. My junk is flopping around in the breeze. Then I'm racing across the gravel drive (that fucking hurts!) and yanking open the passenger side door before delving into the glove compartment like my goddamn life depends on it.

Three.

Hallelujah! Praise the lord!

With my fingers wrapped around the stash, I race to the house before diving onto the bed, ready to take up my previous position. Which was, in case you forgot, with my throbbing cock poised at the entrance of her gloriously spread pussy. The condoms are still fisted in my hand as if I'm afraid to lose one. When I meet her gaze again, she looks like she's on the cusp of losing it.

"I could hear you swearing a blue streak out there," she says.

Now that I have her in my arms and I'm absolutely one hundred percent certain this is going to happen, I huff out a relieved breath before my lips twitch. "Fucking gravel," I chuckle. "I think there might be a piece embedded in my foot."

With her gaze clinging to mine, her body shakes with silent laughter. I can't help but follow suit. Jesus Christ. Now we're both dying. Since the last thing I need is to stab her with my rock-hard cock, I roll onto my back. She curls up into a ball beside me, her body practically convulsing.

After a couple of minutes, our laughter subsides, and Ivy drapes her arm across my abs as her head rests against my chest. Moments ago, I was so jacked up, I thought I'd be a one pump chump. Now, Ivy is wrapped up in my arms. We're still chuckling about what happened, and I don't think I've ever felt more contented.

CHAPTER TWENTY-NINE

It's like the king of campus doesn't have eyes for anyone other than Ivy Kaster. I guess that old saying is true—when they finally fall, they fall hard...
KingOfCampus.com

"Ivy, can you stick around after class for a few minutes?"

I towel off my face before giving Eric a quick nod. We've spent the last hour and a half learning new chorography. It's always a challenge, but one I love. A few girls are trying to convince me to come out with them tonight and see a local band that's playing near campus, but I can't. Roan and I are adding a few finishing touches to our project which is due on Friday.

Once the other dancers head out, Eric approaches. "Remember when I said I've got a friend who is a choreographer with the Cincinnati Ballet?"

The question hangs heavily in the air between us.

My heart stutters for a few beats before rioting painfully against my chest. I want to say— *yes, of course!*

But I don't.

I can't do anything other than stare at him with eyes that are on the verge of popping out of my head.

A satisfied smirk nudges his lips upward. "So," he drawls, "they'll be holding an audition in two weeks. They've lost two dancers to injury from the corps de ballet." He pauses, allowing the bomb he dropped to fully sink in before adding, "I think you should go to the audition, Ivy. This could be the big break you've been waiting for."

When I'm finally able to wrap my lips around the words, I whisper, *"Are you serious?"* I can't believe it. This is just too amazing.

Eric was one of my professors at Barnett during my freshman year. He's the one who helped me prepare my audition when I applied at the Conservatoire de Paris. It's only because of his encouragement that I submitted an application for the study abroad program. I couldn't have done it without him. I didn't believe in myself enough as a dancer without him pushing and prodding me every step of the way. He's a demanding teacher but I'm a better dancer because of it.

He levels me with a hard look. "Of course, I am. Positions don't open up very often and when they do, they're highly coveted. And there are two of them!"

I nibble at my bottom lip. I know he's right. An opportunity like this won't come around again. Having spent the last year in Paris, studying and performing, I feel like there couldn't be a more perfect time for me to audition. I learned so much at the Conservatoire, my skills have never been sharper.

But I'm not sure if I want to leave Barnett. I just returned from Paris and I've finally settled in.

And then there's Roan...

Eric's eyes narrow as he watches me. It's as if he knows exactly what's rolling through my head. "You have to do this, Ivy. You have to go to Cincinnati and audition. You'll regret it for the rest of your life if you let an opportunity like this slip through your fingers. Trust me on this."

Doubt floods through me. I know precisely what kind of amazing dancers an audition like this will draw. "Do you really think I'm ready to compete for a position at the Cincinnati Ballet?" I can't believe I'm even asking the question. As if I have enough talent to be considered for a spot. Before he has a chance to answer, I start to ramble. My voice rises with the nerves that are prickling beneath the surface. "You know what kind of dancers I'll have to compete against!"

The very best.

My belly pinches and nausea rises within me.

Can I seriously compete against professional dancers of that caliber? Am I good enough to step foot on the same stage as them?

Eric reaches out, wrapping his fingers around my upper arms and giving me a little shake. When my gaze snaps to his, he says calmly, "I wouldn't have singled you out, Ivy, if I didn't believe that you had the talent, skill, and determination to become a soloist. That's my honest opinion."

As his words wash over me, they're somehow able to calm the jangled nerves that are spiraling out of control.

Eric believes in me.

He wouldn't risk his name or reputation, if he didn't think I could kill this audition.

His voice softens. "You don't need to make a decision tonight. Take a day or two and think it over, all right?" He gives my arms a light squeeze before drawing away.

I inhale a deep breath and nod. "I'll do that and get back to you."

As I leave the studio, it feels like I'm in a daze. *I can't believe this is actually happening!* It's like a dream come true. To become a dancer in a company is all I've ever wanted since I was a little girl with my first pair of ballet shoes. I almost shake my head because, honestly, I shouldn't even have to think about this.

Who has to consider such an amazing opportunity?

Ummm...no one. That's who.

But I *do* need to think about it.

Am I ready to leave school and move on with my life?

My jacket is tucked around me as I race down the cement stairs of the fine arts building. I'm operating strictly on autopilot. Everything, all of the pros and cons, are tumbling through my head at lightning speed as I move across campus.

I can't believe there are cons that even need to be considered.

But there are, and my relationship with Roan is one of them.

It's been a couple of weeks since that afternoon picnic at his dad's cabin. I never thought in a million years that I would fall for Roan King, but I have. We haven't dropped the big—*I love you* bombs yet. But the feelings are there. The words practically burst from my lips anytime I'm with him. It's getting more difficult to rein them in. I feel more for Roan than I ever did for Finn. Which is surprising, considering that I've known Roan for a little more than eight weeks and I was in a relationship with Finn for six months.

If I leave Barnett now, I'm not sure how we could make a long-distance relationship work. This whole thing between us is still so new. Finn and I were together for a lot longer and he certainly wasn't willing to stick it out. Then there's Lexie and the apartment we rented together. I would feel awful about ditching her halfway through the year.

Although, I'm probably getting ahead of myself. Even if I audition, the chance of me getting offered a position is slim. Inhaling a deep breath, I slowly force it out again.

"Hey, babe."

Roan materializes out of nowhere before tugging me into his arms. Startled, my heartbeat thumps painfully as I squeak out a response. "Hi."

A smile moves across his handsome face. "Did I startle you?"

Even though I'm conflicted about the audition, I'm always happy to see Roan and be nestled in his strong embrace. "I guess you did. I wasn't paying attention to where I was going."

He squeezes me to him before planting a kiss on the crown of my head. He winces as my arm slides around his ribs.

The smile falls from my lips as I glance at him with concern. "Are you hurt?"

He jerks his shoulders. "I took a few hits in practice. It's nothing to be concerned about."

Pulling away, my fingers skim under his sweatshirt to find the warm flesh beneath before I shove the material upward. A gasp falls from my lips as I stare at the ugly bruise already forming on the right side of his ribcage.

My gaze flicks to his and he gives me another little shrug. "Big game this Saturday. Bowling Green. Everyone wants to knock us from our number one seed. Gotta practice hard."

The Barnett Bulldogs haven't lost a single game this season. Bulldog fever has officially reached epic proportions on campus. Roan has been working hard to get ready for each game.

I never realized that playing football, or any sport at the college level, is more like a job. Especially when you attend a Division I school. You don't just show up for the games. There are practices, sometimes twice a day. Film to watch, plays to go over, and strength training. Between football and classes, Roan has little in the way of free time.

Once in a while, I catch a fleeting glimpse of the stress he's under and the toll it takes on him. In those moments, I want to make every-thing better. I want to be the safe place where big strong Roan King can let down his guard and simply be.

I slant my eyes up at him and whisper, "How about I kiss it and make it all better when we get home?"

A wolfish grin tilts his lips upward before he gives me a wink. "Only if I can do the same."

"Deal."

I soothe my fingers over the fresh bruises blooming their way across his flesh before tugging the shirt down. It's on the tip of my tongue to tell him about the audition as we walk to the lot where his truck is parked. As much as I need his advice, I know Roan has a lot on his mind with the Bowling Green game coming up.

The last thing he needs to worry about is me.

I glance at him and notice the faint smudges under his eyes. He's working so hard. Up and out the door before I wake in the morning to workout in the gym before practice. Then its classes, studying, watching game film, and yet another practice before falling into bed only to get up and do the same thing all over again the next day.

As much as I want to tell him to take it easy, I know it won't do a damn bit of good. He won't stop pushing himself until he achieves what he's set out to. His dedication and focus are only part of what I admire about him.

It's lightly that I say, "You look tired."

He smiles before pulling me close and sweeping his lips across mine. "I am." Heat sparks to life in his eyes as they crinkle at the corners. "But not *too* tired, if you know what I mean."

I laugh and roll my eyes. Roan is never too tired for *that*.

The only time we don't have sex is the night before a game. He's superstitious. Some ridiculous bullshit about sex sapping his strength and all that mumbo jumbo. Whatever...

"Yup," I reply drily, "I'm aware." He knows that my tone is a big act. I love what we do in bed. In fact, I'm pretty damn obsessed with his gorgeous body. I could spend hours in bed, exploring all those sculpted muscles. The thought of doing just that has my panties dampening with excitement.

Roan chuckles as we stroll along the cement pathway. A few people call out and wave as we pass by. They congratulate him on Barnett's winning season and ask how he thinks the Bulldogs will fair against Bowling Green. He's never anything less than courteous, always thanking them for their support.

It's almost hilarious how I thought he was such a conceited jackass. Now that I've gotten to know him, Roan is the furthest thing from a jerk. As we reach his truck, he pops open the door for me before moving around the hood and sliding in beside me. He starts the engine and pulls out of the lot. Once again, I find my gaze settling on him as he focuses on the ribbon of road stretched out in front of us.

Roan has turned out to be one of the best things in my life. I love being with him. Even if we're just hanging out or talking. I love the way he holds me in his arms. His presence makes everything better.

My breath catches as I'm struck with the realization that I love him.

Truly love him.

The thought of auditioning in Cincinnati and leaving school in December, maybe sooner, has brought all these feelings into sharper focus. I suck in a surprised breath and realize that I don't want to leave him. I'm not ready for our relationship to end. The alternative is to give up on something I've worked my entire life to achieve.

How can I do that?

Before I realize it, we're pulling into our apartment complex. Roan cuts the engine before turning to me. He winces as he twists his torso. Dance can be hard on your body, particularly your feet, but football seems to be brutal on everything. Especially when it's the job of some gigantic dude to tackle you to the ground. I've watched two games so far. I couldn't help but sit nervously in the stands, biting my nails, praying he wouldn't get hit and suffer a concussion or some other serious injury.

It happens.

All too often.

"You've been awfully quiet, Ivy." He reaches out, gently caressing my cheek before cradling it in his palm. "You gonna tell me what's on your mind?"

My shoulders sag. As much as I want to sit on the news of my audition, I can't hold back or lie to him. When I don't respond, his thumb strokes the delicate skin beneath my chin and my eyes feather shut as a sigh falls from my lips.

"What's wrong, baby?"

My insides pinch because this audition is fantastic news. It's a chance to dance professionally. And yet, I'm conflicted.

My eyelashes flutter open. "There's nothing wrong. Everything is fine."

When he cocks his head and stares at me, it feels as if he's sifting through my innermost thoughts for the truth. Before I can say anything else, his expression hardens. "Is someone giving you a hard time?"

"What?" My brows pinch together before I remember the website and some of the not-so-nice conversations I've had with a few of the women on campus. Although, it's been happening less often. People seem to be getting used to us as a couple. Even the photographs on that stupid website haven't been quite so harsh. In the beginning, they were mostly unflattering shots. Me without an ounce of makeup on. Bending over. In the midst of saying something and making a weird face. There was even one snapped in the studio while I was adjusting my boobs. I pretty much look like I'm feeling myself up.

That one really pissed me off. You can imagine the kind of comments *that* photo garnered.

"No, nothing like that." I take a deep gulp of breath and force out the words. "Eric told me about an audition for the Cincinnati Ballet. They've lost two dancers and he thinks it would be an amazing opportunity."

For a heartbeat or two, Roan doesn't say anything. He doesn't even blink. It's as if he has to give himself a little mental shake before his deep voice booms, "That's fucking fantastic news, Ivy!" Then he pulls me to his chest and kisses my forehead.

Now that the cat is out of the bag, a huge smile curves the edges of my lips in relief. "You really think so?"

He pulls away enough for our gazes to lock. "Damn right I do! When's the audition?"

Now that Roan knows and is happy about it, I feel my own excitement rise at the prospect. "In two weeks. That's all Eric told me."

"That gives you two weeks to prepare something to knock them dead with."

I blow out a breath as the realization sinks in. "Yeah." I need to focus on a solo as well as my classes. I can't let them fall to shit. More than likely, nothing will come from this audition.

"You're going to be awesome. I don't know much about dance, but I know how I feel when I watch you perform. Not everybody has that gift." He pauses, attempting to put his thoughts into words. "When you're out there, I can't take my eyes off you. It's like you're lit up from within and it shines on everything."

His words make my heart clench. That's probably the nicest thing anyone has ever said about my dancing. Absurdly touched, I whisper huskily, "Thank you. That means a lot to me."

I hate to even bring this up, but I have to. "If, and that's a huge *if*—"

"*When*," he cuts in. "It's *when*."

I smile and swat at his chest, careful not to hit the bruised areas under his shirt. "You don't even know what I'm about to say."

"I do. You're talking about getting the part."

The smile falters from my lips. "I'll be competing against professional dancers who are more talented and experienced than I am."

Frustration flashes across his handsome face. "Don't you get it?"

I can only blink. Apparently, I don't. "Get what?"

"Those dancers are competing against *you*," he says softly. "*You're* the one with all the talent. They need to watch out for *you*."

A thick sheen of tears fills my eyes. What he's saying means so much to me. It actually means *everything*. "Roan—"

He shakes his head. "It's the truth and obviously Eric knows it as well. That's why he told you about the audition." He inhales a deep breath before pushing it out. "You'll go to Cincinnati and you'll be brilliant. I don't have any doubts about it. If I weren't in the middle of the season, I would take you myself, but I can't."

I lean over and kiss him on the lips. God, if I hadn't realized that I already love him, this conversation would have done it for me.

I nip my lower lip with my teeth and hesitantly ask, "What about us?" Now, more than ever, I don't want to leave him.

He looks unconcerned as a smile tugs at the corners of his lips. "We'll be fine. Just focus on nailing this audition. There'll be plenty of time to work out the details after we know what's going on."

He's being so supportive. I feel so damned lucky. "Really?"

"Really-really."

I can't help but chuckle. "Okay, then."

I feel so much lighter and happier now that I've talked this out with Roan. I can finally be excited about the audition. And I realize, as those feelings wash through me, that I want it more than anything.

I want to go to Cincinnati and totally kill it.

CHAPTER THIRTY

*Who would have thought that our very own Roan King would actually settle down with a girl? And look so damn content doing it??? *Headshake* Mind totally blown... KingOfCampus.com*

I glance at the leaden-colored clouds overhead and hope the weather holds. The last thing I need is for the sky to open up and pour down on us. The day is overcast and there's a definite chill to the air. What else would you expect in Cincinnati at the end of October?

I'm tempted to pinch myself. It's difficult to believe that I'm here. Lexie squeezes my hand as we stand outside the Aronoff Center where the Cincinnati Ballet performs.

This isn't the first time I've been here. My mom and I spent a long weekend in Cincinnati and took in a show. The CBC performed the Nutcracker at Christmas time. It was nothing short of magical. The entire time I sat in the audience, my gaze stayed glued to the dancers on stage in their gorgeous costumes with their graceful sweeping movements. I remember whispering to Mom before the curtain closed that someday I would be up there performing the Nutcracker.

And now here I am, auditioning in two hours. I almost shake my head.

Is this really happening?

"Are you nervous?" Lexie squeezes my hand. "I'm nervous for you." She sucks in a breath before pushing it out in a rush. "There's a slight possibility I might throw up. That's how sick I feel."

"Don't you dare puke." I shoot her a glance before my gaze arrows back to the massive building in front of us. "But, yeah," I whisper, "I am."

I have no idea why I feel the need to hush my voice. It's kind of like being in church. Even though there is a ridiculous amount of noise coming at us from all directions, this moment feels sacred. Like I'm standing on the cusp of something amazing...something life-altering.

So yeah, I'm nervous, but also excited as hell. This moment is the culmination of all the dance classes I've taken since I was three years old, the long grueling hours spent perfecting choreography, the blisters and bruises on my feet, the muscle aches and strains. I wouldn't be standing here without going through all that.

I'm ready.

So ready to do this.

I've spent the last week and half learning new chorography with Eric. Other than going to class and cranking out whatever work needed to be completed, I spent all my free time in the studio.

I wasn't sure how Lexie would react when I told her about the audition, but she's been totally supportive. When she suggested we road trip here for the day, I wanted to hug and kiss her.

Actually, I *did* hug and kiss her. Too many times to count.

After the audition is over, Lex and I are going to walk around the city before driving back to Barnett which is about six hours away.

We stare up at the Aronoff Center with its gorgeous wall of glass. It's a beautiful piece of architecture. It's almost impossible to believe that in precisely one hundred and twenty minutes, I'll be performing on stage.

"You ready to head inside?" she asks, breaking into my thoughts.

We really should. I need to check in and stretch before running through my choreography. I should slip on my headphones and get into a good mental space. But I can't help wanting to stand out here and soak up the freaking awesomeness of this moment. I did the same thing when I arrived at the Conservatoire. I stood outside the building and took a minute to appreciate that I was there, that I'd actually made it happen.

This experience is another one of those life defining moments.

One I'll look back on in five or ten or maybe twenty years and still remember exactly what it felt like to stand here. In four hours or so, the audition will be over. Done with. I won't be able to change the outcome.

But right now...*right now*, anything can happen. The moment is chock-full of possibilities, dreams, and hopes.

In silence, I admire the theater, thinking about what will happen inside and on stage. I ponder how different the next year of my life could be if I impress the panel of judges.

I take one last deep breath and nod. "Yeah, I'm ready."

I don't think I've ever felt more ready for anything in my life.

"You're going to nail this, Ivy. I just know it. You're an amazing dancer." Her voice is filled with pride.

My gaze slides to her. "Thanks for being so supportive. No matter what, you've always been there for me. I couldn't ask for a better friend." In the good times and bad, Lexie has always been steadfast at my side. She was there to wrap her arms around me when Mom was diagnosed with breast cancer and she was there when we laid her to rest on a warm July morning. I bawled on her shoulder when Dad turned my world upside down again by announcing his engagement to Leah.

No matter what, Lexie has been an unshakable fixture in my life. I don't think I'll ever find another friend quite like her. Everyone should have a Lexie Abbott in their lives. I know how lucky I am to have her in mine.

"Hey," she says, voice sounding suspiciously thick, "we've been there for *each other* throughout the years. We'll always be best friends. No matter what."

I pull Lexie into my arms and hold her tight. "No matter what happens today, it means a lot that you're here to share this moment with me."

She gives a watery little laugh as if she's trying to rein in her emotions. "Like I said before—you're going to nail this. I have no doubt about it." Even though her lips slide into a pout, I can tell she doesn't mean it. "And then you'll be living an amazing life here and I'll be stuck at Barnett for another year and a half."

As the words escape from her mouth, it strikes me again that there's a very real possibility that could happen. Holy crap! How exciting would *that* be? To dance professionally on stage for a living?

"You'll have to visit me every single chance you get!"

"Damn right, I will!" she says as we start walking again.

As we reach the glass doors of the theater, my phone rings.

It has to be Roan. He wanted to be here so badly. Instead, he's sitting on a bus, headed to an away game. There's so much background noise, I have to press my hand against my other ear so I can hear him clearly.

"Hey, babe. Are you there yet?"

His voice is like being wrapped in a warm comfy blanket. Everything in me calms. "Yeah, we're about to head inside the theater and check in."

"You're going to be great. You know that, right?"

I squeeze my eyes tightly shut as his words pour over me. "I hope so," I whisper. It's awesome to have Lexie here but I wish Roan could have made the trip. I need him to wrap me up in his muscular arms, hold me tight, and give me a kiss for good luck.

When he chuckles, it's low. Not at all like his normal, lighthearted one or the sexy, gravelly laugh that sends little shivers scampering down my spine before arrowing straight to my core. This one is tinged at the edges with sadness. "I really wish I could be there with you. I'm glad you didn't have to make the trip by yourself."

"Me, too. Lexie and I are going to walk around the city after this. Do a little shopping before heading home."

"Sounds fun. Are you planning to drive all the way back tonight?"

"Yeah. The audition is at noon and we'll leave by six, probably roll in around midnight." I'm hoping it goes well or the rest of the day will be a complete bust for me. I won't be able to stop myself from mentally critiquing my performance. Over and over and over again. And Lexie deserves a shopping excursion after carting my ass here. We were tired and groggy when we hit the road this morning around four. She did all the driving so I could sleep.

"Sounds good, babe. Can't wait to see you tonight."

"Me, too. Have a great game."

"I'm planning on it. I'll call you after it's done to see how everything went but I know you're going to be amazing. You always are, Ivy."

I smile and whisper, "Right back at you, King."

It's on the tip of my tongue to tell him that I love him, but I rein it in at the last second. We're almost to that point but I don't want to do it over the phone. Not when he's so far away, sitting on a bus full of rowdy, jacked up teammates. When I finally tell Roan how much I care about him, it'll be when we're together. Alone.

He pitches his voice low. "I'm really hoping you'll slip into my bed later tonight."

That was the plan. "Sounds like a date."

"All right, I'm going to let you go so you can get ready. And I'm not going to wish you luck because this doesn't have anything to do with luck, it's about being prepared and talented and you're both, Ivy. I'm proud of you, baby."

"Oh, Roan," I whisper, heart expanding, "I can't wait to see you tonight."

"Right back at you, Kaster."

I laugh. "Okay, I'm hanging up now." As I glance at the building and the dancers filtering past us, obviously here for the same audition, nerves chew at my insides.

We say one last goodbye before I hit the end button.

"Ivy?" Lexie's wide eyes fasten onto mine as I pocket the phone. "You ready for this?"

I inhale a deep breath before gradually forcing it out. "I've been ready my entire life."

With that, we pull open the doors to the Aronoff Center and walk inside.

CHAPTER THIRTY-ONE

Another winning game where Roan King was literally on fire. It's as if every pass thrown to him couldn't have gone anywhere but in those big strong hands of his. Bulldog fever has never been more out of control. If you're not a Bulldog fan, you might as well pack your bags and get the hell out of town. Once again, RK has proven that he's NFL ready. And he's never looked so good doing it either...
KingOfCampus.com

"Have you heard anything yet?" Lexie asks.

Biting my nails, I shake my head. It's been three days since the audition in Cincinnati. I thought for sure I would have heard something by now. If not by the company itself, then by Eric who is friends with one of the chorographers. I've been on pins and needles ever since. Every time my phone buzzes, I find myself pouncing on it.

Even though there were over two hundred dancers at the audition, I don't feel like I could have performed any better. By the end of my three-minute piece, everything I had to give was left on the floor. No regrets. No second guessing myself. I was one hundred percent satisfied with my performance.

If I don't get it, so be it. I'll chalk it up to experience, do a few more auditions in the late spring/early summer and keep working toward my degree in finance. I'll be here with Roan for second semester. And I'll be able to live with Lexie for the duration of our lease.

So, it's a win-win situation.

But still, I really wanted this. I wanted to know that I could hold my own with professionals. People who actually make their living in the world of dance.

"What does Eric say?"

I blow out a steady breath before answering. "That it can take time. They record all the auditions, review them, narrow down the field, and then make decisions."

Lexie nods as if that makes perfect sense. I'm not saying it doesn't, but all this waiting is killing me.

As she opens her mouth to say something, there's a knock on the apartment door. She glances at me before hurrying to answer it. Since I'm sitting on the couch, I don't have a clear sightline into the entryway. All I hear are murmured voices pitched low.

When the door closes a few moments later, Lexie pads into the living room and...drumroll please...Dylan is a few steps behind her.

I bolt up on the couch. My gaze bounces from Lexie to Dylan and then back again. "Hey, Dylan." I'm not sure what this means, if anything. Dylan and Lexie still aren't together. He's been giving her the space she asked for. He used to drop by unannounced all the time. That doesn't happen anymore.

Since Roan and I spend time together at his apartment, I see Dylan with a fair amount of frequency. We've talked, but there isn't a whole lot for me to say. He no longer resembles the happy-go-lucky, affable guy I met the day before the semester started. Ever since the breakup, he's been a lot quieter. More introverted and melancholy. He spends more time in the gym working out and running outside. His body is definitely more fit and cut than it was before.

"Roan mentioned you had an audition in Cincinnati over the weekend. How did it go?"

"I haven't heard anything..." My voice falls away as I shrug. "Apparently not that well." There's no question about it—rejection sucks.

But that's the way it goes when you're pursuing a career in the arts. You have to believe a hundred percent in yourself, be persistent, constantly be honing your craft, and have thick skin.

He nods. "I'm sure it'll work out, Ivy."

I hoist a smile at his kind words. "It will," I agree, "one way or the other." At this point, that's all I can tell myself.

He gives me a slight smile in return, but it's not a full-blown Dylan Sullivan grin. As much as I understand why Lexie felt the need to pull away and get some perspective, my heart goes out to Dylan. He's a good guy and he's been a great boyfriend. I hope if Lexie decides she wants him back, he's still available.

As silence falls over the three of us, his gaze flits to Lexie.

She clears her throat and jerks her head to the bedroom. "We're going to talk for a bit." That being said, they disappear inside her room.

My fingers and toes are crossed that they'll work everything out.

Restlessness slides through me as I click through a handful of channels, unable to find anything interesting that holds my attention. As I shut off the TV, my phone buzzes and I all but fall on top of it. I almost swallow my tongue as an unknown area code flashes across the screen.

5-1-3.

That's a Cincinnati number!

I scramble to my feet and stare at the cell as it buzzes in my hand. An odd kind of paralysis seizes every muscle in my body. It's like I'm frozen in place. I've been waiting for this call for the past three days and now that it's happening, I'm scared to answer it. By the third ring, I know I have to hit accept or it'll end up going to voicemail.

I whisper a quick prayer and stab my finger at the screen before bringing the phone to my ear. "Hello?"

My heart skips a beat as I wait for the voice on the other end. It feels like an eternity slowly passes by before someone responds. "Hello? Is this Ivy Kaster I'm speaking with?"

All the saliva in my mouth dries. "Yes," my voice wobbles, "this is Ivy."

"Hi, Ivy, this is Carter Moliter from the Cincinnati Ballet." When I remain silent, he continues. "I'm calling in regard to the audition that took place on Saturday."

Oh god. This is it. *This is really it!* A shiver of apprehension scampers down my spine, making the skin on my arms prickle with goose flesh. My future comes down to this moment. To the next words that come out of his mouth.

Instead of sounding strong and confident, my voice comes out all breathy and whispery. "Yes?"

"As you know, we have two spots to fill for on pointe dancers in the corps de ballet. The turn out was excellent and we had two hundred dancers audition with us."

Nerves seize my belly. Maybe this call isn't good news. Is it really possible that I've been plucked from obscurity from a field of two hundred dancers?

"The judges were impressed with the sheer volume of talent that showed up. We couldn't have asked for a better pool of candidates to choose from. After watching the auditions and reviewing the video, we were able to narrow the field down to twelve dancers who we felt would be wonderful additions to the company."

This is bad. Maybe I'm talented but not enough to compete for a spot with the Cincinnati Ballet. My knees weaken and I fall onto the couch with a thud.

"It was an honor and privilege to audition." It's a struggle to keep my voice light even though there is so much disappointment trapped inside my chest. The talent that showed up for the audition on Saturday blew me away.

"As I'm sure you're aware, The CBC prides itself on the outstanding quality of its dancers and choreographers. We can only invite the most talented individuals to join us."

"Of course." And I, apparently, am not one of them. This hurts more than I imagined it would.

I've spent years auditioning for spots. I've had to audition for every dance team I was part of as well as Barnett and a few other colleges I was considering. Not to mention the Conservatoire. I put together a video and was critiqued by my instructors. So, I'm used to the process and realize that it's not going to work out in my favor every time. They could have been looking for something specific. Taller. Shorter. Blonde. Brunette. You just never know.

But the Cincinnati Ballet...

This was my first *real* audition for a professional gig.

And I didn't get it.

"Congratulations, Ivy, you were selected from over two hundred outstanding candidates for one of our positions. I hope you realize what an honor this is."

His words take me completely by surprise. "*What?*" I'm barely able to whisper the word. "You're saying," I have to gulp down all the thick emotion that is trying to claw its way into my throat, "you're saying I've been selected to dance for the Cincinnati Ballet?"

My mind spins. I was so sure he was trying to let me down easy.

The man on the other end chuckles. "Yes, you have. The judges were all very impressed. You're a talented young woman."

"I-I can't believe this." The hot sting of tears pricks the back of my eyes as I hold the phone to my ear.

The only thing that could make this moment better is if my mom was here to celebrate this achievement with me. She loved dance so much. She's the reason I started taking ballet classes in the first place.

"Thank you, Mr. Moliter. Thank you so much!" I still can't believe this is happening.

"You're welcome, Ivy. When can you be in Cincinnati?"

I take a deep breath as everything crashes around in my brain. I can barely think straight. "When do I need to be there?"

"The sooner, the better. I'm not going to lie, the first couple of months are going to be grueling. You'll have to learn all new choreography. It'll be long hours spent in the studio." He sounds like he's shuffling through a few papers. "I see you're attending college right now." There's a pause. "Is this going to be a problem for you?"

Even though he can't see me, I shake my head. "No. I just need to speak with my professors and the school to see if there's any way for me to get credit for the classes I'm enrolled in."

There's more shuffling. "The most I can give you is three weeks to tie up any loose ends. There are a number of girls who share apartments. I'll give you a few names to contact so you're able to get a place lined up in the interim."

Oh my god...I have to find a place to live and only three weeks to do it.

"Okay, that would be great."

"Wonderful, Ivy. I'm going to give you my number. Once you settle everything at your end, let me know when you'll be arriving in Cincinnati. I'm also going to send you some paperwork to look over."

"That sounds good." I scribble down the names and numbers of the girls.

"And Ivy?"

I blink. "Yes?"

I hear the smile in his voice when he says, "Welcome to the Cincinnati Ballet."

"Thank you." I can't help but squeeze my eyes shut and kick my legs in the air. "Thank you so much!"

We say our goodbyes and I sit there for I-don't-know-how-long just staring at the phone in my hand. My entire body vibrates with excitement.

I'm going to dance with the Cincinnati Ballet!

My first impulse is to race over to Roan's apartment and share the good news with him.

As I sprint to the door, doubt niggles its way into my brain. I mean...how will we make our relationship work when I'm six hours away and he's at Barnett?

Mr. Moliter said the first couple months would be difficult. Which isn't surprising. I'll have all new choreography to learn. An entire show worth. The hours will be long. Exhausting. It's doubtful I'll have any spare time to visit Roan. And with football, school, and getting ready for the draft, neither will he.

I inhale a deep breath and try to calm my racing thoughts. Even though I couldn't be more thrilled to receive such a coveted offer, there's a downside. I don't want to leave Roan behind. I'm afraid that I'll lose him. It's not like we've been together very long. Hell, it's only been a little over a month. Everything between us is relatively new.

I'll also have to leave school. I have no idea if I'll be able to salvage any of my credits for that fall semester which has been paid for with scholarships and financial aid. So far, I've earned A's in my courses, but there's still all of November and part of December to get through before the semester wraps up. I don't know if the school will allow me to complete the classwork from Cincinnati.

And then there's Lexie. After nearly a year and a half of separation, it's been so nice to room with her again. What kind of friend would I be if I baled on her after two months? I signed a yearlong contract for the apartment. Can I just take off and leave her high and dry? I hate that Lexie will have to scramble to find a new roommate.

With all of these thoughts churning in my head, I slowly lower myself to the couch. Was I seriously giddy only moments ago? How did being offered an opportunity to dance with the Cincinnati Ballet turn into a negative thing? It's almost mindboggling.

Unsure what to do, I head over to Roan's so I can share the news with him, and we can talk about how we'll make our relationship work. My step falters as I open the apartment door and step into the hallway.

What if he thinks it would be best to end things?

I can't blame him if that's what he decides. I was seeing Finn for six months and he probably started cheating as soon as my plane hit cruising altitude. I don't think Roan would do that, but he might not be interested in having a long-distance girlfriend who is never around.

By the time I reach Roan's apartment door, I'm a nervous wreck. An opportunity that felt like a miracle ten short minutes ago now feels like a mixed bag. If I leave—

Oh my god...I'm not even one hundred percent certain that I'm going to accept the position.

The negatives keep piling up and I can't seem to look past them.

What if I don't seize this opportunity and it never comes around again? Can I live with that? Confusion and nerves slide through me as I rap my fist on the door and wait. I can't stop from bouncing on the balls of my feet. When the door swings open, I find Sam on the other side.

Now that I'm with Roan, Sam is a lot friendlier. I'm not sure what his standoffish behavior was about, and I've never bothered to find out. My attention has always been focused on his roommate. "Hey, Ivy. You looking for Roan?"

Barely am I able to pull my lips into a smile. "Yup, is he here?" I want to find Roan and hash this out with him. I need his reassurance that everything will work out.

"He's in his room. You can go on back."

Sam holds the door open for me. A moment later, I'm heading down the short hallway to Roan's bedroom. Even though the guy's apartment has three bedrooms instead of two, the layout is the same as ours.

I knock lightly on the door before pushing it open and popping my head inside.

A smile moves across his face when he spots me, and it sends a spasm through my heart.

Can I really leave him behind?

"Hey, babe. I was hoping you'd stop over."

With a hurried step, I move toward the queen-sized bed where he's sprawled, reading a heavy tomb of a textbook. He tosses it aside before holding out his hand to me.

"You busy?" I need to unload everything careening around in my head.

"Nah. Just trying to get ahead. I'll miss Friday's lectures for the game this weekend, so I want to make sure I get everything done beforehand."

Roan has turned out to be one of the hardest working guys I've ever known. If he's not working out in the gym or on the practice field, he's studying. I wish everyone at Barnett realized how much effort it took to be a star athlete and student. From a distance, his success looks effortless. I'm sure most people assume he's blessed with good looks and natural athletic ability. But it's so much more than that. It's his internal drive and competitiveness that pushes him to be the best at what he does. Luck has nothing to do with it. He works his ass off to earn his success.

"Ivy?" His gaze searches mine as all these thoughts ricochet through my brain. "Everything okay?"

As I stare at him silently, a burst of love explodes inside my chest. The feeling slams through me, stealing my breath away. I shake my head and try to clear my thoughts. Somehow, when I wasn't looking, I fell in love with Roan King. I never meant for it to happen.

And now, I can't bare to lose him.

Panic seizes me, choking me from the inside out.

If I leave for Cincinnati, everything will change. Maybe he won't cheat on me like Finn did, but I can't imagine our relationship surviving so much distance. I have no car. No way of visiting him on a regular basis. And I don't have any money. As prestigious as it is to be a dancer for the Cincinnati Ballet, it doesn't pay much.

Maybe this isn't the right time to take this leap. Maybe I need to finish out this year or even earn my degree before I start the audition process. I can continue with my dance classes and hone my skills. Then I'll be more prepared to pick up my life and move to some unknown part of the country where I don't know a soul.

Roan scoots from his reclined position on the bed before grabbing hold of my hand. He gives me a light tug and I tumble onto his lap. His arms wrap around me, holding me close to the solid wall of his chest. God, it feels good to be nestled there.

"Ivy, tell me what's wrong."

What's the point of telling him about this opportunity? I'm no longer sure I want to accept the position. I'm not as ready for this next step as I'd thought. Three months ago, I would have jumped at an opportunity like this without so much as a second thought. And now...

Now I'm all tangled up inside.

I spent fifteen months in Paris, creating a new life for myself only to uproot it and move back to Barnett, where I've spent the last two months settling in, making new friends, working hard in my classes, and finding love.

How can I throw all that away?

Roan's fingers skim over the line of my jaw before sinking into my hair. "What's going on? It seems like something is bothering you. Tell me what it is. I promise, we'll figure it out together."

I take a deep gulp of air and open my mouth, ready to tell him about the offer when something else pours out, taking us both by surprise.

"I love you, Roan."

One side of his mouth hitches before his lips slide across mine. It only takes a moment before I'm opening under the gentle pressure. His tongue mingles with mine before he pulls away.

"I love you, too." His grin is so wide that he's practically beaming. "You beat me to it. I've been wanting to tell you for a while now."

I can't help but return the expression. "Me, too."

He shoves the books from his bed. They crash on to the floor before Roan sinks to the mattress, pulling me down on top of him. His hands wrap around my waist as if to anchor me in place.

He stares up at me with love shining brightly from his eyes. "I know we haven't been together long, but you mean more to me than anyone else ever has."

I lower my face until I can stroke my lips over his. "I feel the same."

"Are you going to spend the night?" He raises a brow. "Queen-sized bed."

With the Cincinnati Ballet dilemma forgotten, I smile. "Yup." There's nowhere else I'd rather be than right here with Roan.

"Good. Cause I love holding you in my arms at night."

And I love being there.

I sit up and yank off my shirt before tossing it to the floor. Then I unsnap my bra and throw that as well. Roan's gaze falls to my breasts before his calloused palms come up to cup them. For someone with such huge hands, he's incredibly gentle with my body. I may not have a lot going on up there, but he seems to love what I do have. The way he looks at me makes me feel beautiful. No one has ever made love to me the way he does. There's a fierce tenderness in the way he takes me.

The groan that falls from his lips is full of need. His hot length is nestled beneath me as I straddle him, rubbing myself against him.

"Damn, Ivy..." I love the hoarseness of his voice when he says my name. It's so freaking sexy.

Then again, everything about Roan is sexy.

And he's all mine, I remind myself.

I slide my fingers beneath his shirt and tug the material until it's bunched up around his chest. I stroke my fingers over his flat male nipples, loving the way they tighten under the gentle pressure. Roan growls as I lean down, sucking one into my mouth. His hands slide along my body until he's able to palm one firm ass cheek in each hand. He squeezes both of them before dragging me forward and then back again so that I ride his rock-hard erection.

Arrgghh.

A moan falls from my lips as he continues to torture me. The delicious friction has sparks of arousal igniting in my core. He does this a few more times before his hands disappear. He sits up enough to tug the shirt over his head and toss it to the floor.

"These need to go," he says, fingers delving inside my leggings before sliding both my panties and the black stretchy material down my hips. I stand and shimmy my way out of both garments until I'm completely bare. His T-shirt is gone and the athletic shorts he's wearing are tented in the front.

I raise an eyebrow. "You gonna get rid of those?"

Roan grins, sliding both the shorts and boxers over lean hips and muscular legs before kicking them off. My eyes arrow to the nest of dark curls as his cock springs free.

And what an impressive boner it is.

As I lower myself on top of him, Roan places both hands on my hips, halting my descent. "Oh no, you don't." He pulls me forward as he slides down the bed until my spread pussy hovers above his mouth.

My breath catches as I stare at him from my position on the bed. It is unbelievably sexy to see him between my legs. His gaze burns brightly as his warm breath feathers over the most intimate part of me. His hands drift from my waist to my spread thighs. Need intensifies as his fingers stroke over me, massaging slow circles that move closer to my core.

All I want to do is spread myself wider and feel the lash of his velvety tongue. What I've learned in the weeks we've been together is that Roan knows exactly how to please a woman.

His touch is addictive.

"Your pussy is so fucking pretty." His voice is husky, sounding as if it's been scraped low. "So pink." A whimper spills from my lips as he nibbles at my aroused flesh. "And smooth..." His tongue is back, slipping inside me before licking my silky folds. Heat floods my core as he laps at me.

I spread my legs wider, needing to feel his tongue glide over every part of me. My head lolls back as a moan builds in my chest. As Roan sucks my clit into his mouth, his hands slide from my thighs to my ass, cupping each cheek before squeezing them.

"You taste so good, baby. I could eat you up all night long." His low-pitched words are whispered against my throbbing flesh.

There is no way in hell I could last all night.

I don't know if I'll last five more minutes.

The way he plays with me is sweet torture. In less than a month, he's learned all the ways I love to be touched. I've done the same, discovering what drives him crazy. Like my bare pussy.

He loves it.

He loves nuzzling the soft smooth flesh. He loves running his blunt fingers over me until I'm slippery with need. Or my flexibility. I thought he was going to come in his jeans the first time I laid on my back and spread my legs completely wide. There are a few other gymnastic stunts I've perfected that have him frothing at the mouth.

Roan also loves the way I suck the blunt tip of his cock, swirling my tongue over the bulbous head. He loves the way I stroke my thumb over the little slit, spreading around the pearly drops of moisture until he's groaning with need before finally sucking him deep into my throat.

I've never felt as sexually free or open with anyone else before. And I love it.

His tongue slides over me again before he scrapes his teeth against my clit. It's like a firework exploding inside me. My hips undulate against him as an orgasm streaks through my body. Before the last ribbon of pleasure can fade, his hands are at my hips before he shimmies his way up the bed. He yanks open the drawer of his nightstand and grabs a condom, ripping open the package and sheathing himself right before plunging inside me.

"I can't wait any longer," he groans, pulling out and thrusting into me again. I moan as we fall into a rhythm. His breathing quickens as his hips move beneath me.

Even though I just came, everything inside me tightens, building with each and every stroke of his cock. I love the feel of him buried deep inside me. His fingers go to my breasts as he strokes my nipples until they're hard little points. He knows damn well that it drives me crazy.

My breasts may be small but they're sensitive. He continues to toy with them, pulling at the elongated little buds until I'm on the verge of climaxing all over again.

"Not quite yet," he grits out. With his hips thrusting against me, his thick cock slides in and out of my slick heat until it feels like I could splinter into a million pieces.

His gaze locks on mine. "I'm so close, baby."

I moan, feeling the same.

Any given moment I'm going to—

Roan shudders beneath me. His movements become frenzied as he strokes my body from within. It's enough to send me tumbling over the edge. As we finish, the sound of our breathing is harsh and labored. My heartbeat thumps against my ribcage as I lower my face until my lips can brush over his.

As they do, he whispers thickly, "I love you, Ivy."

"I love you, too." I echo the sentiment before collapsing against his chest. As I listen to the quick thudding of his heart, I realize I didn't tell him about the call.

I squeeze my eyes shut as all of the conflicting emotions from earlier tumble their way back into my brain. I'm no longer certain what the best course of action is. In the moment that is unfolding, what I want most is Roan.

I want *this*.

I'm scared that if I leave, I'll lose it.

I'll lose *him*.

What becomes apparent is that no matter what I choose, I'm going to lose something precious.

CHAPTER THIRTY-TWO

Awwww... Yet another ooey-gooey photo snapped of Roan King and his girl. Is anyone else getting sick of seeing these two lovebirds together??? I know I am.
KingOfCampus.com

"Babe, I'm so sorry you didn't get the part." Roan pulls me in for a hug and holds me close, gently rubbing my back. "You must be really bummed." He drops a series of light kisses on the top of my head. "Those bastards don't know what they're missing out on." Anger vibrates in his tone. It's like he's actually affronted on my behalf.

Which is so sweet...

I stare at the rolling lawns of Barnett and watch as people rush past on their way to class. Its early November and the trees are completely bare. The temperature has grown chilly making it necessary to wear a warm coat when heading outdoors.

Guilt floods through me and I clear my throat. "Yeah, I'm bummed about not getting it." That isn't necessarily a lie. I *am* bummed about not going to Cincinnati. Although, I feel like it would be worse if I went and lost out on the opportunity to have this relationship develop into something more.

Did I make the right decision?

I have no idea. I was panicked by the thought of losing Roan after I agreed to the position in the corps de ballet. Now that I've decided to turn it down, I can't help but wonder if it's a mistake. I've come to the conclusion that no matter what I choose, I'm going to miss out on something.

I haven't called Mr. Moliter back just yet because I wanted more time to mull over the predicament. That, unfortunately, hasn't gotten me any closer to feeling settled about my decision. I'm as conflicted as I was before.

To receive that call had been thrilling. Within five minutes of jumping for joy, I was crashing back to reality. After we'd made love and declared our feelings for each other, it had seemed like staying at Barnett would be the best course of action.

But that doesn't necessarily feel like the right choice either...

"I'm so proud of you for going to Cincinnati and auditioning. It takes a lot of courage to go after your dreams."

Even though he's trying to bolster my spirits, his words make me feel worse. And I can't even tell him that. I can't tell him that I was offered a position but plan on turning it down.

Instead, I say, "Thanks."

"You need to look at it as a test run. Maybe you can call and get some feedback on your performance." Again, he presses a kiss against the top of my head. "Constructive criticism is always helpful."

"Ummm, yeah...maybe." I bite down on my lower lip until it feels as if I'll draw blood. Any moment, I'm going to blurt out the truth. Before that can happen, I untangle myself from him. "I should probably get going. I need to talk with Eric before class starts."

"All right. I'll walk with you," he says, giving me another sympathetic smile. He's trying so hard to cheer me up. And it's all but killing me.

Even though I did this for the right reasons, it feels wrong to lie. I know exactly what will happen if I tell him the truth—he'll insist I go. He'll tell me that we can make a long-distance relationship work.

And that will be the beginning of the end.

All of these mixed up feelings roll around in my head as we silently walk to the fine arts building. Once we're outside the cement stairs that lead inside, Roan envelopes me in his arms. After a moment or two, his gaze searches mine. "I'm really sorry, Ivy. I know how much you wanted this. Rejection sucks. I guess it's just part of the process, right?"

Unable to open my mouth because if I do, I'm pretty sure the truth will pour out, I jerk my head into a nod.

"Everything happens for a reason."

I almost choke on my own spit. Oh god...he's been reduced to useless platitudes in an attempt to bolster my spirits. I love him for it, but I need to get away before I crack. "Okay," I croak before fighting my way out of his arms, "I've got to go."

"See you later, babe." He looks troubled as his eyes search mine. It's like he can sense that I'm holding something back from him.

Barely can I lift my lips in response before waving goodbye and dashing inside the familiar corridors of McKinley Hall. Once I make it to the studio, I throw my bag in the corner before collapsing onto the floor and drawing my knees up to my chest until I can rest my head on them. Even though class doesn't begin for another fifteen minutes, girls are already warming up at the barre. I should be doing the same, but my heart isn't into it today. Which is a first. Even my breakup with Finn wasn't enough to dampen my spirit to dance. In fact, that was one way I worked through my heartache.

What am I going to do?

I haven't officially turned down the position yet and already I'm being eaten alive by regret. I can only imagine how I'll feel once I call Mr. Moliter and tell him that I've changed my mind.

Oh my god...who does that?

Who turns down the opportunity of a lifetime?

"Ivy?"

I lift my head only to find Eric. Concern is etched across his furrowed brow. I give him a slight smile before resting my chin on my knees. Even though Eric is one of my favorite instructors, he's the last person I want to discuss the situation with because I know he'll be disappointed in me. And I don't think I can stand that right now. "Hi."

He arches a brow. "And here I thought you would be riding on cloud nine. What's going on? Have you spoken with your other professors yet? Are they going to allow you to finish up your courses?"

Not even for a second does he consider the possibility that I won't accept the offer to go to Cincinnati. We're both dancers. You don't turn down a professional opportunity. I'm suddenly wishing that I hadn't come so early to class.

When I don't respond to the fired off questions, he drops down onto his haunches until we're eye level. "What's going on?" His tone softens, turning gentle and that is so not what I need right now. Any moment the dam is going to break, and I'll be powerless to stop it from all pouring out.

"If a couple of your professors aren't willing to work with you, let me know and I'll talk with them myself. This is way too amazing of an opportunity to throw away."

Tears spring to my eyes. I inhale a shaky breath and force out what needs to be said. Sooner or later, I'll have to tell him. "I've decided not to accept the position."

"*What?*" His eyes widen as his face turns slack. I don't think I could have shocked him more. It would be comical if the situation wasn't so painful. There's about twenty seconds of stereo silence before he asks, "What do you mean *you're not going?*" He almost laughs except there's a sharp glint in his pale blue eyes. "Of course, you're going! This is an incredible opportunity, Ivy! It's not something that will come around again."

Unable to hold his penetrating stare, I glance away and mumble, "I can't do it. I'm not ready for this."

His expression hardens as he accuses, "This has everything to do with that football player!"

He rolls his eyes and shakes his head as if he's totally disgusted. As if he's lost all respect for me. Which stings. Eric won me over from the moment I walked into his studio freshman year. He's hardcore and demanding. He expects perfection from his dancers. He's one of those teachers who knows how to tease out a student's talent with a mixture of constructive criticism and praise.

Unsure what to say, I lick my parched lips. Frustration simmers in his eyes and it only makes me feel worse. "That's part of it," I hedge, "but, I don't know if I'm ready to pick up my life and move to Cincinnati. I just returned from Paris."

After another long silence that leaves me feeling twitchy, Eric's face softens. "Look, Ivy, ultimately you're the one who has to live with this decision. Personally, I think you're making a mistake. It'll be one you end up regretting." His gaze searches mine. "Did you already decline the offer?"

I shake my head. "Not yet."

He closes his eyes briefly as if sending up a little prayer. When he opens them again, they arrow straight to mine before he squeezes my hand with his fingers. "I know you're scared to jump into this. There's a guy you seem to be clicking with. Life at Barnett is familiar and comfortable. Trust me, I get it. The prospect of taking a chance and moving to Cincinnati, not finishing up your degree—it's all happening fast." He pauses for a beat. "But this is the kind of opportunity you've been working toward your entire life. You need to think it over carefully before you throw it away."

More confused than ever, I shake my head. "Part of me wants this so badly that I can practically taste it and then there's another part that wants to stay here. At least until the end of the year."

"I know." A sympathetic light fills his eyes as he squeezes my hand again. "Moving on and leaving everything behind while you grab hold of your dream with both hands is a scary prospect. If you do this, your whole life will change. This is it, Ivy. The CBC is huge. If there's one thing that I'm certain about, it's that you're up for the challenge. There were over two hundred dancers at the audition. You wouldn't have been chosen if you hadn't impressed them with your skills and ability. If they feel you're ready for the rigor and challenge that comes along with the position, then you should trust in that." His gaze sears mine. "Can you really walk away from such an amazing opportunity to live out your dreams?"

I shake my head in misery. "I'm not sure..."

"I think we both know why you're so willing to walk away from this." His eyes narrow. "Did he tell you not to do it? Is that why you're backing out?"

"Of course not! Roan would never tell me not to follow my dreams." I gnaw my bottom lip, silently debating if I should tell him the whole truth. I want to get it all out in the open and be honest with someone. I'm holding everything in and it's ripping me apart. "I didn't tell him that I was offered the position."

A deafening silence follows, and I cringe.

When I can't take another moment of his intense scrutiny, he repeats slowly, *"You didn't tell him that you got the part?"*

"I was going to and then..." My voice trails off.

A heartbeat or two passes before he prods, "And then what?"

In a tiny voice, I admit, "I don't want to lose him, Eric. He's the first guy I've ever really cared about." Is it so hard to understand that I wouldn't want to throw away a meaningful relationship? Doesn't Eric realize what a struggle this decision has been for me? "Everything is so different with him."

"Do you think he'd want you to walk away from your dreams? Would you want that for him? He's the one who will get drafted by the NFL, right? Would you want him to give that up for you?"

The words slide off my lips before I can consider them. "Of course not!" I would never want Roan to give up anything for me. Least of all the dreams he's worked so tirelessly to achieve.

"Then why don't you talk to him. Give him a chance to tell you what he thinks. If he cares about you at all, he won't want you to sacrifice everything you've spent your life working toward."

The bitch of it is that I know Eric is right. It's the reason I've kept this from Roan.

Eric straightens to his full height before jerking his head toward the barre where the other dancers are stretching. "What you need is to get out of your head for a while. And I can help with that." He gives me a smile.

An evil one.

I know all too well that Eric will work me over until Cincinnati and Roan are the last things on my mind. And that's exactly what I need right now. I need to lose myself in dance. In the rigor of choreography. I need to shut off my brain and feel the movement as it flows through my body, lighting me up from the inside out.

As Eric claps his hands together, everyone's gazes fall on him. "All right, everybody, time to get to work!"

CHAPTER THIRTY-THREE

Someone's looking good out there on the football field... All I have to say is that Ivy Kaster is one hell of a lucky girl. KingOfCampus.com

Roan

We're walking toward the locker room after a grueling two-hour practice when Dylan unsnaps the strap of his helmet and lifts it from his head. Then, like a goddamn dog, the asshole shakes out his wet hair. Since I've already removed my helmet, his sweat hits me like a spray of bullets.

With a curl of my upper lip, I give him a good shove. "Dude, that's disgusting. Get the fuck away from me!"

The asswipe actually chuckles. "That's man sweat. You wouldn't know anything about that. You mostly stand around looking pretty."

"Yeah," I snort, "that sounds like me. Once again, you've nailed it right on the head."

He smirks before looking me up and down. "Sure you shouldn't be playing quarterback?"

I give him the stink eye in return. "Fuck you, dude."

A wide smile spreads across his face. "Sorry, you're not my type. You're a little too meaty for my taste. I like a slimmer build."

I drop my shoulder and ram him from the side. The impact sends him stumbling a couple of paces. He laughs, knowing that he got to me. Dylan can be a real dick sometimes. "No wonder Lexie cut you loose."

I'm fully prepared for retribution. The verbal jab is below the belt and I damn well know it. Instead of doing the expected, he grins like he's not bothered by the comment.

"Didn't I tell you that we're back together?"

I glare before muttering, "She must be out of her fucking mind."

"Yup, that's exactly what she said—that she'd been going out of her fucking mind without me." He adds a little more swagger to his step.

I roll my eyes. I'm sure that's *exactly* how it went down. More like Dylan crawled on his hands and knees, begging her to take him back. If anyone has been out of their mind, it's that guy. Talk about mopey... "I'm glad you got your shit settled."

His expression sobers. "The separation was driving me bat shit crazy."

He's not kidding. "What are you talking about? You're always bat shit crazy. Don't blame it on Lexie breaking your heart."

Dylan's eyes narrow and he looks ready to retaliate when someone shouts my name.

"Roan King?"

It doesn't take long to find the owner of the voice. There are people dotting the stands watching practice, but this guy is leaning against the cement wall of the tunnel that leads inside to the locker rooms. As I hold his stare, it occurs to me that he looks vaguely familiar, but I can't place where I know him from. Which isn't all that unusual. People are constantly talking to me or introducing themselves. I meet hundreds a week. After a while, the faces blur.

Not really in the mood to shoot the shit with some dude after the punishing two-hour practice Coach put us through, I say in a clipped tone, "Yeah, that's me."

As his gaze holds mine, I get the feeling he's not a fan who has shown up to yap at me about the Bulldogs or the outstanding season we're in the midst of.

"Do you have a minute to talk?" he asks.

My gaze slides to Dylan, who promptly rolls his eyes before picking up his pace and disappearing inside the tunnel. "Catch you later, man," he hollers over his shoulder.

I run my fingers through my drenched hair as the guy lifts himself away from the wall before walking toward me and offering a hand. Since I'm sweaty and kind of dirty, I wipe my palm on my white pants before reaching out to shake it.

"I'm Eric Wexler," he says, "one of Ivy's professors."

That's when recognition slams into me. I give him a chin lift. "Yeah, I remember. You teach dance." I shift my helmet from one hand to the other and wonder what the guy is doing here on the football field.

The smile he gives me is tight as if he doesn't really want to be here talking to me. Which makes two of us, I guess. I'm sweaty and tired. I want to hit the showers, shovel some food into my mouth, study for a couple of hours, and then curl up with Ivy for the night. I need a little one-on-one time with my girl. I almost snort, seriously loving the way that sounds. Who would have thought that I'd enjoy being tied down?

I know...totally crazy.

"That's right." For a moment, he shifts under the intensity of my stare. Like he's not quite sure how to say what needs to be said.

Before he can bottom line it for me, I blurt, "Is something wrong with Ivy?" Even I can hear the threads of concern that weave their way through my words. Why else would this guy be here? "Is she in trouble or something?" The thought leaves me stone cold and a bit panicky.

After a long silent moment, his shoulders sag as regret flickers across his expression. "Look, she wouldn't be happy if she knew that I was here talking to you. But you need to know what's going on—"

I shift restlessly before cutting him off. "But Ivy's okay, right?"

His face softens as the words spill from my lips. "She's fine but there's something she hasn't told you."

My brows beetle together. I wish this guy would just spit it out. It feels like he's jacking with my head. If something is going on with Ivy, then I want to know about it. I can't imagine what this guy came all the way over here to tell me. And I certainly can't imagine what Ivy could be keeping from me.

His pale blue eyes skitter away before he mutters, "She's going to be pissed that I told you."

Frustration bubbles up inside me. "Dude, just tell me what the hell is going on!"

He straightens to his full height. "You know about the Cincinnati audition, right?"

Why the hell is he bringing *that* up? "Yeah, she was passed over for it."

Eric stares at me before shaking his head. "No, she wasn't."

What the fuck is this guy saying?

Thrown off guard, I rear back and fold my arms across my chest. My red and white helmet dangles from my fingers. "Yeah, she told me she was—"

As soon as I bite out the words, the implication of what he's saying sinks in. Filled with confusion, I shake my head. "Are you saying that Ivy lied about the audition?" I can't believe she would do that.

"That's *exactly* what I'm telling you."

"But why?" She wanted this so badly. "Why would she do that? She's been working her entire life for a shot like this."

He nods in agreement. "Yes, she has."

"Why?" My lips tug down at the corners. Only now do I understand the look filling his eyes. It's as if he's silently accusing me of sabotaging her budding career before it ever has a chance to get off the ground. I shift my hips and press a hand to my chest. "You think this has something to do with *me*?"

Unhappiness flits across his face as he sighs. "I think it has *everything* to do with you. A few months ago, Ivy never would have turned down an opportunity like this. She was with that other guy far longer than she's been with you and she didn't think twice about studying in Paris."

He cocks his head as if silently trying to take my measure. It has me unconsciously drawing up to my full height. Which is, by the way, considerably taller than this guy.

Professor or not.

It's as if he's trying to figure out what Ivy sees in me. Even though I'm pissed off she kept this from me, my chest swells with love for her. This dude can't possibly see what Ivy does. She's one of the few people who has taken the time to get to know me.

"Look, Roan," he finally says, "you can't let her walk away from this."

Like I want her to do that? Of course, I don't! My tone turns surly. "What am I supposed to do about it?"

"Don't stand in her way. You've seen her dance. She belongs onstage. Maybe she won't regret her decision right away, but she will. Eventually. Especially if she's not able to get in anywhere else. Or, god forbid, she injures herself and isn't able to dance at a professional level."

The saliva in my mouth dries. I only want the best for Ivy. She deserves it. The last thing I want is to be the reason she doesn't chase down a dream. And I sure as hell don't want her resenting me down the line for holding her back.

I like Ivy...hell, I love her, but who knows what will happen in the future. We haven't been together all that long. It almost defies logic that she would give up this kind of opportunity for me.

Me.

Again, emotion surges in my chest to the point of cracking wide open on the football field.

"Roan." His voice snaps me back to the conversation. "If you truly care about Ivy, you won't stand in her way. She needs to do this, and time is running out. She hasn't officially turned it down yet. If she does, she'll never get another chance to dance with Cincinnati again. They won't look at her. It's as simple as that."

"I told her that if she got the gig, we'd make it work," I mutter. "What more do you want me to do?" What more *can* I do? I don't want to hold her back, but I don't want to lose her either. It took me way too fucking long to find her. To find someone who sees me—*who loves me*—for who I am.

He stares at me for a long moment and what I see in his gaze sets me on edge. "Look, it's obvious your future is getting ready to unfold as well. Do you even know where you'll be after this year?"

I shake my head, not liking the direction this conversation has swerved in. "No. I won't know anything until April."

"I think Ivy realizes that if she leaves Barnett, the chances of your relationship surviving are slim. She'll be busting her ass in Cincinnati and won't have much free time and you'll be god knows where, also busting your ass." He allows those words to sink in before continuing. "Do you realize how difficult that will be? You'll both be starting high pressure, intensely physical careers in different cities all the while trying to make a name for yourselves."

My heart actually constricts because, damn him, he's right.

There's only one thing to do.

And we both fucking know what it is.

CHAPTER THIRTY-FOUR

Do you hear that? It's the sound of thousands of Barnett women rejoicing that Roan King is once again single. Ivy Kaster's loss is our gain. KingOfCampus.com

Roan

"Hey, I didn't expect to see you tonight. I thought you had—and I quote," she holds up her fingers to make little bunny ears, "a *shit ton* of work to plow through." Ivy smiles from where she sits on her bed. Now that Eric has filled me in on the situation, I see the heaviness of the decision that weighs her down. I'd thought it was the pain of rejection, but that's not the case. Even Ivy realizes that what she's set on doing is wrong and it only reinforces that I need to make it right again.

The fact that she is willing to sacrifice her dreams makes me feel completely unworthy.

I don't deserve that kind of love from her.

I attempt to hoist a slight smile but can't force the edges of my lips to tilt upward. It's too damn hard. My heart already aches. I'd be lying if I didn't admit that my heart is screaming for me to turn around and leave.

But I don't have a choice.

"Yeah, I do. So, I can't stay long." It takes effort to clear the thick emotion from my throat in order to force out the rest of the words before I do something stupid...like swallow them back down and pull her into my arms. "We need to talk."

With a slight frown, her gaze probes mine with more care. Ivy is so attuned to me. She realizes that something isn't right. I see it in the way her body straightens. *"We do?"*

A tidal wave of dread crashes over me as I nod. "Yeah." The nerves jangle beneath my skin and I run a quick hand through my hair. God, this sucks. What's worse is that I can't tell her I know about the part. I don't want her pissed at Eric. She needs him in her life. He's her biggest champion and has been instrumental in her career. I can't take that away from her. Ivy has already lost enough. She can't afford to lose him, too.

As difficult as it is, I push out the words. "You know how I've been thinking about putting off the draft for another year and staying at Barnett?"

It's clear from the confused expression that flickers across her face that she doesn't understand where I'm going with this. What I'm about to say will blindside the fuck out of her but I don't know any other way to do it. She jerks her head into a tight nod.

We've had many conversations about the ramifications of entering the draft this January or waiting another year and finishing up my degree. After talking with Eric, I made a decision. It feels like the right thing to do. I can't stay at Barnett without her. The memories will end up killing me.

"I've decided to go ahead and do it. I'm entering the draft in January."

A bright smile lights up her face as she hops gracefully from the bed before bouncing into my arms. "I'm so happy for you, Roan! If you think it's the right decision, then it is."

As much as I want to wrap my arms around her and hold her close, I don't. I'm afraid I won't be able to walk away after I finish this.

"I think so, too," I murmur.

My tone must give away that all isn't right. She pulls away to meet my somber gaze. Any moment, I'm going to crack.

"What's wrong?" she whispers.

I have to clear my throat as my gaze slides away from hers. I won't be able to look at her and recite the words I've practice a hundred times in my head. *I just can't.* "Here's the thing, I feel like I need to focus on football right now. I need to get bigger, stronger, faster. My agent thinks if I can improve my times at the combine, I'll generate more interest with the scouts. Then I'll have a better chance of going in the first or second round and securing a bigger signing bonus."

I let the words hang in the air.

For a long painful heartbeat, Ivy remains silent. I force my gaze to hers. She doesn't make a sound. Not one goddamn sound. She stares at me with wide eyes that swim with both hurt and shock. Like she can't quite believe what tumbled out of my mouth.

The pain filling her eyes kills me. I feel like such an asshole. I don't want her to believe for one fucking moment that football is more important than she is.

Because it's not.

And ball has always been more important than just about everything in my life.

But not Ivy.

Never Ivy.

In the short time I've known her, this girl has come to mean everything to me. No one knows me the way she does. And it's doubtful anyone ever will again. She sees the person I am beneath all the hype and bullshit. It'll kill me to let her go. The only consolation I have is that it would have slowly killed her to stay. To give up this opportunity to dance with the Cincinnati Ballet. I can't allow that to happen. It's that knowledge alone that has me following through with my plan.

"What are you saying?" Her voice sounds as if it's been strangled from her body.

Again, I plow my hand through my hair in agitation as I glance away. "I think it's best if we take a break so I can focus on the draft. I can't afford to have any distractions."

She makes a pitiful noise deep in her throat that cuts me to the quick. "You're saying I'm a...*distraction?*" There is so much devastation packed into those five little words.

No, god, no!

It takes everything in me not to reach out and grab hold of her, to soothe her with words of love as I wrap my arms around her. The last thing I want to do is push her away.

"For the time being—yeah. I have to give one hundred percent to this." I shrug. "All of my focus and drive needs to be concentrated on the draft. On adding muscle and cutting down my times. And then there's school..." I suck in a painful breath before adding, "It's important that I finish strong."

When she untangles herself from me, I know it'll be the last time I hold her in my arms. Already they ache from the loss of her.

She stares at me as if she has no idea who I am.

"How can you say that? I thought," she shakes her head, slender shoulders slumping before she swings away. She buries her face in her hands. Not a sound escapes from her lips. I don't think I could bear to hear her pain. I'm on the verge of crumbling as it is. One heartbreaking sound from her and it'll be over. I won't be able to stop myself from yanking her into my arms and telling her that I didn't mean one damn word of it.

This is more difficult than I imagined it would be.

Like a magnet, I feel the pull of her and can't resist moving closer. Even though I'm the one bent on inflicting pain, I want to soothe it away. I lay a hand gently on her shoulder. As soon as I do, she goes rigid. I hate that this will end up tainting our entire relationship.

"It's just bad timing." I gulp, "Maybe after the draft is over and I know where I'm going..." My voice trails off. I could end up in Seattle or Green Bay or Florida, for fuck's sake. And she'll be dancing in Cincinnati, trying to make a name for herself. Just like Eric said. She sure as hell doesn't need me anchoring her down. I don't even know if we could make it work regardless. Eric filled my head with so many doubts.

She inhales a shaky breath before saying quietly, "No, I don't think so, Roan. This is it for us."

Then she turns, impaling me with her emerald depths. They're like a sword going right through my fucking heart. "I'm really sorry, Ivy." More than she'll ever know. *I'm doing this for you,* I want to say. *You deserve this break. You deserve the chance to be out there, lighting up the stage. I can't hold you back from that. You would end up hating me for it. And I would end up hating myself for not being strong enough to let you go.*

She's riddled with so much pain that she doesn't see the sentiment lurking in my eyes.

"I know how much you want this," she says. "And I would never stand in your way or do anything to hold you back from achieving your dreams."

Her words give me the much-needed strength to walk away. She's absolutely fucking right about that. She would never stand in my way.

And I won't be the one to stand in hers.

CHAPTER THIRTY-FIVE

*Other than around campus, Roan King sightings have become a rarity...
Someone must be nursing a broken heart. Who would have thought that our
very own campus player had one buried beneath all that sexy muscle? Trust me,
I'm just as shocked as the rest of you. KingOfCampus.com*

"I can't believe you're really leaving." Lexie murmurs in a wobbly voice before crushing me to her. I can barely breathe.

"I know," I whisper, "I feel like a real shitbag for baling on you like this."

She pulls away until she can meet my watery gaze. "Don't you dare say that! What kind of friend would I be if I didn't support your dream?"

When I open my mouth, she cuts me off. "A pretty damn crappy one!"

My lips twitch. Lexie is my best friend. I think she always will be.

She gives me a big grin before adding, "Anyway, I'll be crashing at your new apartment over break. You're not getting rid of me that easily."

I roll my eyes. "You know I'm shacking up with three other girls, right? It's just temporary until I can find something else." Thankfully, I won't have to look for an apartment immediately. I can take my time settling in, get acclimated to the company and city before I look for my own place. I'll probably live there for at least four or five months. Maybe longer, depending on how everything goes. From what I hear, I'll barely be at the apartment. Rehearsals are long and demanding.

"I don't care, it's just so exciting!"

I can't help but bite back a small smile. She's right. It's exciting. I just wish things had worked out differently with Roan. We haven't spoken much since he pulled the plug on our relationship about a week and a half ago. I still see him in class and run into him in the halls every once in a while, but that's about it.

He seems to be doing what he said—working out, playing ball, and studying.

I try not to dwell on what else he might be doing...

The moment people sniffed trouble in the air, it was all over that stupid website. It's a relief that he hasn't been snapped in any pictures with other girls. Not that I've been, um, cyberstalking him or anything like that...

Okay, maybe a little.

Even though I wanted nothing more than to crawl into bed with a pint of Chunky Monkey ice cream, I couldn't. There was too much that needed to be done. I had to speak with my professors about finishing out my courses even though I would be in Cincinnati. Most of them were cool about it. My guess is that my perfect attendance, participation, as well as being an A student helped with that. There was only one professor who gave me a hard time, but Eric took care of it. It's doubtful he'll give me an A for the semester, but at least it'll be a passing grade. My plan is to come back for finals in mid-December. It'll be a lot of work with my new rehearsal schedule, but I've got nothing else going on. I should be able to handle it for the next month.

I also had to figure out what to do with all my crap. Which is, as we speak, being packed up in the small U-Haul truck my dad rented. I'm going to spend a few days with him and Leah before he drives me to Cincinnati on Saturday.

So, even though I would have loved to wallow, there wasn't any time for it.

The fact that Roan considered me a distraction that would only get in the way of his goals still stings like a bitch. I keep telling myself that we weren't meant to be. Bad timing and all that other BS. We're both busy, attempting to make our dreams come true. Even now, I only want the best for Roan. I'd like to think he wishes the same for me.

"Hey, babe, did you tell Ivy that you already found a roommate?"

Dylan sidles up behind her. There's a smirk on his face that has me narrowing my eyes at him before swinging my gaze to Lexie.

"You did?" Wow, that was quick! She never mentioned it. A blush heats her cheeks as one of my brows slides upward. Well, well, well... isn't this interesting. When she remains silent, I can't help but demand, "Come on, Lexie, tell me!"

"Go on and tell her, babe." Dylan is all smiles. He's practically beaming.

With a sheepish look, she rolls her eyes. "Dylan and I are going to give living together a test run."

My mouth falls open. "Oh my god!" I pull her to me, hugging her tight. "That's great!" When she says nothing, I push her away until my gaze can search hers. "This *is* a good thing, right?"

She glances at Dylan before the corners of her lips tug into a smile. "Yeah, it's a good thing."

As soon as I release Lexie, Dylan wraps his arms around her before giving me a wink.

Unable to help myself, I laugh, "Well, isn't that convenient."

A huge grin spills across his handsome face. "Totally convenient."

I feel so much better knowing that Dylan is moving in with Lexie. Even though they spent some time apart, it seems to have been good for both of them. I won't be at Barnett to see firsthand what's going on between them, but I know Lexie will give me the lowdown every time we talk.

My phone buzzes, letting me know that Dad is done rearranging the truck downstairs. He told me he'd get everything packed up while I made one final sweep of the apartment and said my goodbyes to Lexie and Dylan.

"I guess Dad is ready to take off..." My voice trails off as a big fat tear rolls down Lexie's cheek.

"Oh, Lex—"

She breaks free of Dylan's embrace only to hurtle herself into my arms. "I'm going to miss you, Ivy-girl," she whispers fiercely.

My heart clenches as I rein in my own tears. "I'm going to miss you, too. Like you said earlier, you're going to come and visit over Christmas break. We'll have a blast. Just like we always do."

"I know, but this has been fun, too. I'm gonna miss seeing your face every day."

"I'm gonna miss being here," I agree sadly. "But we'll talk and text all the time."

With a sniffle, she draws away from me until Dylan can enfold her again in his arms. His chocolate-colored eyes meet mine over her head. He gives me another wink and I know he'll take good care of her in my absence.

My phone buzzes again. "Okay, I better go."

I head for the door, swiping at the moisture that has gathered in my eyes before sucking in a ragged breath. I never imagined it would hurt so much to say goodbye to her...again. When I left for Paris, I knew I'd return to Barnett to finish out my junior and senior years. That's no longer the case. My time here is done and I'm moving on with my life.

As I close the apartment door for the last time, I come face-to-face with Roan. Our gazes lock as we both grind to a halt. We must look like deer caught in the blinding headlights of an oncoming car. It would be comical if it didn't hurt so damn much.

"Oh." We haven't spoken since he dumped me. No matter how hard I rack my brain, I have no idea what to say. "Hi." Worse than that, I can't stop eating him up with my eyes.

The corners of his mouth quirk. "Hi, Ivy." He sounds oddly subdued. No flirty tone is sight which is probably for the best. He doesn't make a move to leave. Instead, he shoves his hands into the pockets of his cargo pants as an uncomfortable silence settles over us.

It's kind of unbelievable how our relationship unraveled in the blink of an eye. I really thought he cared about me. I know how much he meant to me. I loved him. That thought is almost enough to have a gut-wrenching sob rise in my throat. As much as I hate to admit it, I *still* love him. Even after he told me I was nothing more than a distraction standing between him and the NFL.

I still love him.

With those thoughts churning through my head, I take a hasty step in retreat. What we had is over with and the best thing I can do is close this chapter of my life. It's taking everything I have inside not to reach out and pull him to me. I tighten my fingers so that I don't do just that. "Well, um, I have to go. My dad is waiting."

He closes the distance I've put between us by taking a step forward. "You're heading to Cincinnati?"

"Yeah. Everything is all packed up. I'm going to spend two days with my dad and Leah before he drives me there on Saturday."

He smiles, but it's strained at the edges as if this encounter is as painful for him as it is for me. "I'm really happy for you, Ivy. You deserve this opportunity. You've worked hard to get where you are."

As my gaze slides over him, I realize that I can't stand here for another moment shooting the shit with him like he's just some guy I used to know. Like he never carved out a special place in my heart. The pain sitting between us feels like a living breathing entity. And it's just too much.

"Thanks." I clear my throat. "I should go." The last thing I need is to break down. How humiliating would that be? I don't want to be that girl. I've already cried too many tears over him. I'm done with that. And talking to him, being this close to him, has all the harshly throbbing pain rushing to the surface again.

"Yeah, okay." Sadness flickers in his eyes before he jerks his head into a tight nod as if there's nothing more to be said. And maybe there isn't. Maybe we said our goodbyes after he broke my heart.

Impatient to escape, I turn away. As I do, his hand snakes out, wrapping around my arm before yanking me to him. A heartbeat later, I'm crushed against the solid strength of his chest.

"Roan," I breathe, knowing that all this will do is cause me further heartache.

His gaze locks on to my confused one before sifting through it.

There's a wealth of sorrow and regret lurking in his gorgeous blue-green depths. The normal twinkle is noticeably absent. "I never meant to hurt you, Ivy. I hope you realize that."

I shake my head.

Why is he doing this?

Doesn't he understand that it will only make the pain I've been desperately trying to tamp down flare back to life with a vengeance?

"Letting you go was the hardest thing I've ever done."

That doesn't make a damn bit of sense. "Then why did you do it?"

"I didn't want to stand in your way. You had to go to Cincinnati and pursue your dreams. I couldn't let you turn down the opportunity." His voice lowers until it sounds as if it's been scraped raw.

"I told you that I didn't get the part." My brows knit together. "How did you know I was lying?"

He compresses his lips into a tight line.

His gaze becomes shuttered as everything falls neatly into place. "Eric told you." I can't believe he would interfere in my life like that! He knew how much this relationship meant to me.

"I couldn't be the one to hold you back," he whispers.

Unable to meet his gaze, I lower my head until I can rest it against the chiseled planes of his chest. "Why didn't you tell me the truth?"

"For the same reasons you didn't tell me."

My mind works furiously. "So...you didn't break up with me because I was a distraction?"

Roan runs his fingers through my hair before feathering a light kiss against my forehead. "No. You could never be a distraction, Ivy. Not ever. If anything, you make me want to be a better man."

Just as my heart lifts, it crashes back to reality. "But I'm leaving, Roan. I'm leaving for Cincinnati."

He tugs my body closer until I feel every hard line of him. "I know." There is so much sadness packed into those two words.

All I can think about is how torn I'd been when I had received the call. "I love you," I whisper brokenly, "I didn't want to leave you."

"I know, that's why I had to let you go." Again, he presses a kiss to the top of my head. "I couldn't be prouder of you, Ivy. For everything you've accomplished. And everything you've yet to achieve. There's no way I could hold you back from doing that."

My heart thumps a painful beat as I squeeze my eyes tightly shut. "That was my decision to make, not yours." I understand why he did it. And I can't say that I wouldn't have done the same for him but still…I feel tricked into choosing Cincinnati.

It's like he knows exactly what I'm thinking. Instead of agreeing with the sentiment, he asks, "Wouldn't you have done the same for me?"

As difficult as it is, I gulp down the thick emotion that chokes me. I don't answer because we both know the truth. I never would have allowed him to give up on his hopes and dreams of playing in the NFL.

"Ivy?"

Tears seep into my voice. "I would never stand in your way."

He pulls away enough for the blunt tips of his fingers to slide under my chin before lifting my face so that my gaze can lock on his. "And I won't stand in yours. I've never cared for anyone the way I care about you."

Doesn't he understand that his words only make walking away impossible? It was so much easier when I thought he wanted to focus on his dreams. Now that I know the reason he broke up with me, the pain of our parting bubbles to the surface.

"So what happens now?"

The fierceness drains from his eyes only to be replaced by sadness. "I think you need to focus on dance. You need to throw yourself one hundred percent into this. And you won't be able to do that if you have one foot in Cincinnati and another back here at Barnett. The last thing I want is to let you go, but I think it's best if I do."

I squeeze him tight, giving him one last hug before untangling myself from him. As much as I hate what he's saying, I know he's right. We both have dreams and they aren't going in the same direction.

When my phone buzzes for the third time, I swipe at the tears rolling down my cheeks. "I have to go. My dad is waiting downstairs."

I back away, turning before forcing myself to move toward the elevator. If I don't leave now, I'm not sure if I'll be able to. Every fiber of my being is screaming for me to stay.

"Ivy?"

His voice is hoarse, almost as if it's been dredged from deep within. Even though it's painful to glance back, I do. I can't help myself. As our gazes collide, my heart cracks wide open before splintering into a million pieces in the middle of the thinly carpeted apartment corridor.

"I love you," he whispers.

I stifle a sob, spinning around before escaping into the stairwell that empties into the lobby. It's taking everything I have inside to walk away. To leave him behind at Barnett while I move forward with my life in Cincinnati.

CHAPTER THIRTY-SIX

Roan King is certainly lying low these days. Not sure what's going on with him. Is our guy just focused on winning more football games for Barnett or is it something more? If anyone has insider knowledge, please post!
KingOfCampus.com

Dad settles at the kitchen table with a beer in hand. He clears his throat before saying, "I'm proud of you, Ivy. For you to be selected at this audition is a big deal."

My gaze slides to his in surprise. "Thanks." A moment later, my attention returns to the tall glass of water I've spent the better part of twenty minutes staring at before admitting, "I wasn't sure you would be happy about this...about dropping out of college."

He takes a deep breath before slowly releasing it. "I've always thought finishing up your degree was important. I wanted you to be able to get a good job and have something solid and dependable to fall back on, something with job security if dancing didn't work out."

I focus on him as he continues. It sounds suspiciously like he feels the way I suspected he would.

"But I also know you love dance. You always have. Ever since you were a little girl. You were accepted at Barnett and the Paris program. And now you've been selected out of all those women to dance for the Cincinnati Ballet. I always knew you were good," he shrugs, "but you're obviously a lot better than *just* good. What I want, what I've always wanted, is for you to follow your dreams. And this is your dream, Ivy. So how can I not support you in achieving it?"

I shake my head, torn between the anger I've all but cloaked myself in for the last five years and the need for my father's love and approval.

Love wins out. "Thanks, Dad. It means a lot to hear you say that."

He shifts on his chair, looking decidedly uncomfortable. "Your mother would be so proud of what you've accomplished. The way you followed your heart and didn't let anything, or anyone stand in your way."

My eyes well with emotion. We never talk about Mom.

Not ever.

His gaze drops to the beer bottle in his hand. "The last seven years have been rough on you and I'm sorry for that. You were just thirteen when your mom was diagnosed with cancer and then she died two years later." He pauses. I can tell how difficult this conversation is for him by the way his throat silently works to get the words out. When he continues, it's in a much softer voice. "And everything just moved so fast with Leah..." He leaves the rest to hang in the air between us.

There's something that has been eating away at me for the last five years and this feels like the only opportunity I might have to ask it. "Were you cheating on Mom? Is that why you and Leah got together so quickly?"

My quietly uttered words are like a bomb being dropped in the middle of the table. Neither of us dare to move a muscle as a stifling silence descends. My heart pounds painfully in my chest as I wait to see what he'll do. Part of me wonders if he'll respond. We've never talked like this before.

And not just about Mom.

We don't talk period.

Not about the things that matter. When Mom died five years ago, she wasn't the only one I lost. Dad disappeared as well. The easy relationship we'd always had with one another changed. It became more distant. It was like the grief we each felt made it impossible to bridge the distance that separated us. Leah fractured our relationship further. In hindsight, I don't think it was her intention, but it was the end result.

Dad doesn't say a word as he lifts the bottle to his lips before taking a long pull. He practically drains the entire thing before gingerly setting it down again.

Leah and the twins aren't home, they're at swim class.

It's just the two of us.

His voice sounds strained as he asks, "Are you sure you want to talk about this, Ivy?"

Do I really want to talk about this?

Not really, but I have to.

I bite my lower lip and jerk my head into a nod. I need to know the answer. It's a question that has been stuck in my head for the last five years. No matter what it is, I need to hear the truth from him before I can move on. I'm tired of being angry at them. Five years is a long time to be consumed with bitterness and resentment. It's exhausting. And it's no way to live your life.

He breaks eye contact, lowering his head and staring down at his fingers. "I guess I'd always hoped you would move on so we wouldn't have to discuss it." His gaze rises, piercing mine. The agony is clear within his deep brown eyes. "But you've never gotten over it, have you?"

"No." I shake my head even though the answer couldn't be more obvious to either of us. "There was no way for me to move on. It hurt too much. I need to know the truth, Dad. Then maybe I can finally put it behind me where it belongs."

He nods as if that makes sense but still, I can tell he doesn't necessarily want to dredge up the past. A faraway look enters his eyes as he begins, "When I met your mother, we had just finished college and were looking for jobs. Once we got together, we were inseparable. We fell for each other so quickly. I knew within a few weeks of meeting her that she was it for me. After we dated for about nine months, I proposed, and we got married." He looks caught up in the past as the edges of his lips tilt at the corners. "We were happy. Especially after you came along. You were such a good baby. Such a joy to both of us." He shakes his head. "Your mother would have had a whole houseful of kids, if she could of."

His words catch me off guard. I'm an only child. Well, before the twins I was... "She wanted more kids?" I don't know why that surprises me so much. I'd never heard her mention wanting more children.

Sorrow fills his gaze before he nods. "Yeah, she did. We both did."

My brow furrows. "So why didn't you?" It seems so logical. You want more kids? Then you have them. But they only had one.

He inhales another breath before forcing it out as if what he's about to reveal is still tender and raw. "We discovered that your mom had something called fibroids when she was pregnant with you. After that, they got worse and eventually she needed a hysterectomy." He shifts uncomfortably before adding, "Which is to say—"

I hold up a hand to cut him off. "I know what it means, Dad. She had to have her uterus removed." My heart clenches as I whisper, "Which means no more kids."

"No more kids," he echoes.

I sit back and stare at Dad as my mind spins. "I never knew."

He shrugs, using his thumbnail to pick at the label on the brown glass bottle. "You were young when it happened. I'm not surprised you don't remember. It was a painful subject for your mom to talk about. She'd always wanted to have a big family, but I guess it wasn't meant to be. So, we contented ourselves with you. And I think teaching filled part of that void as well. She loved being around all those kids." His lips lift. "Even the mischievous ones."

My mom was a wonderful second grade teacher. Everyone adored her. She was warm and fuzzy but tough as tacks when she needed to be. She had dedicated her life to working with children. Instilling within them a love for reading, no matter what level they were at. I'd always admired how dedicated and passionate she was about her profession.

When she stopped working, so many of her former students and parents dropped by the house to spend time with her. Colleagues she'd taught with for more than a decade would come by, dropping off knitted hats when she lost her hair because of the chemo. Or blankets because she would get so cold. They would bring books for her to read and old photos of her teaching in the classroom to reminisce over.

Yes, my mom loved me. And she enjoyed the kids she taught at Harper Elementary School.

But that doesn't explain how he could move on from the woman he claimed to love after she lost her battle with cancer. If anything, it only confuses me more. "That doesn't help me understand what happened, Dad."

His gaze flicks away for a moment before arrowing back to mine. "The three of us were happy. We had a good life. It was devastating when your mom was diagnosed with breast cancer. But I thought, okay —we're going to beat this. She's a fighter."

I hate thinking about that particular time. How hard the chemo was on her. How sick my mom would get. The failed treatment plans. Always living for the next set of test results. Always worried about what tomorrow would bring. Then sitting by helplessly as she slowly deteriorated. Becoming weaker. Frail. Until she was a pale shadow of the vibrant, outgoing woman she'd once been.

He slides a hand roughly through his peppered hair as his eyes take on a glassy, faraway look. "It was difficult to watch. Hard to realize, and then accept, that the treatments weren't working, and we were losing the battle."

My heart cracks wide open as I silently listen to him talk about such a painful period in both our lives. At least he's opening up and letting me in. As much as it hurts to discuss the subject, I don't feel quite so alone in my grief.

"It was hard on all of us." I clear my throat and whisper, "Mom included."

He nods. "Of course, it was. She lost her life. She's missing out on seeing what a wonderful, smart, talented daughter she raised."

As soon as he says those words, my eyes flood with moisture.

"After your mom died," he gulps, "I guess I shut down. All that emotion felt too raw to deal with. I started putting in long hours at work. It was hard being at home where everything reminded me of her. Of the life we'd built, the life we no longer had. It was easier to stay away. You were only fifteen years old at the time. I didn't want to burden you with my grief." He pauses and wipes the dampness from his eyes.

"Leah was just a colleague at that point. She was someone I'd worked with for years. We weren't close. A couple of weeks after your mom passed away, she came into my office and told me about her mother dying from cancer. As weird as it sounds, we had that loss in common. She could understand everything I was going through, all the heartache, anger, and depression. It felt good to share my feelings. To open up with someone who wasn't involved in the situation." He jerks his shoulders. "I guess our relationship developed quickly from there."

All I can do is stare at him silently and try to wrap my brain around what he's telling me.

Before I have a chance to respond, he continues. "It's hard for me to regret what happened. If Leah hadn't gotten pregnant, we wouldn't have the twins. But I know that my relationship with her, and how swiftly everything evolved, was difficult for you. I'm sorry for that, Ivy. I really am. If there hadn't been a pregnancy, we wouldn't have moved so abruptly. We could have taken our time."

His gaze holds mine and I hear the sincerity in his voice. I know he's trying to be honest with me. "Leah is a good woman and she makes me happy. Maybe us getting together didn't happen the way it should have, but it happened, nonetheless. I hope at some point, you'll be able to accept that. The five of us, we're a family." He sucks in another deep breath before pushing out the rest. "We may not be the family you want, but we're the one you have. And we'll always be here for you, Ivy. No matter what."

As he finishes, a thick silence settles over us as everything he just divulged circles viciously around in my head. I'm not sure how to respond. For so long, I've been holding on to so much anger toward both of them.

Obviously, Leah was an easy target to focus on. It felt as if she moved right in and took over what used to be my mom's role in this family. And that was a bitter pill to swallow. It put us instantly at odds.

In hindsight, I can't say she ever tried acting like my mom. She always left all the parenting decisions to my dad. There were too many times to count when she tried striking up a conversation. I was so full of grief and anger that I couldn't see past it. She tried talking to me about the loss of her mother, but I hadn't been ready to listen. I hadn't wanted to hear anything she had to say. I didn't want to have anything in common with her.

It's been five years since Mom passed away and the ache is still there. Some days it throbs more than others. Sometimes I think the pain of her death will never fade.

Not completely.

There are so many moments I wish I could share with her. All the competition dance teams I made, prom, getting accepted to Barnett, going to Paris, falling in love with Roan, auditioning for Cincinnati...

I miss her fiercely.

No one will ever fill the void of her loss within me.

But I'm tired of carrying around all this anger. It feels like I'm constantly hauling around ten bags of luggage. It's exhausting. I know Mom wouldn't want me to live like that. She was always so positive and forgiving. I also think she would have wanted my dad to find love again. Maybe not as quickly as he did, but she would have wanted him to have more children. Kids she couldn't have.

That thought alone has a sob rising to my lips.

In the blink of an eye, Dad takes me into his arms. All the sadness and anger I've been holding onto finally breaks free. It's as powerful as a dyke bursting. I sob like a baby in my father's arms for a good fifteen minutes before pulling myself back together again.

"I'm sorry, Ivy," he whispers harshly, "sorry that I didn't take more care with your feelings."

I pull away and swipe at my eyes with fingers that shake before grabbing a napkin from the silver holder on the table. I dab at the wetness that clings to my eyelashes before blowing my nose.

God, I hate crying.

It's never been a good look for me. I'm not one of those girls who cries pretty. Nope. Big noisy tears, red rimmed eyes, splotchy looking skin, along with a runny nose.

Although, I have to admit that it feels good to purge myself of all this poison. My mom wouldn't want me hanging onto it. More to the point, *I* don't want to hang on to it anymore. At the end of the day, my anger won't bring her back. And it hasn't helped me move on either. If anything, it's probably impeded the healing process.

"I want to be able to talk about her, Dad. This is the first time in five years we've actually sat down and done it."

He bobs his head, looking remorseful. "I know...you're right. I'm sorry for that, Ivy. I didn't handle her death well." He glances at his hands. "And I didn't handle what happened afterward the way I should have either. I'm sorry for all the pain it's caused you."

I bite my lip and ask, "But you're happy, Dad?"

The edges of his lips lift. "I am, Ivy. You, Leah, and the twins make me happy."

Emotion wells in my throat. "I'm glad. That's what Mom would have wanted," I whisper thickly. It's my way of letting him know that I forgive him. I don't want to hold on to this anger anymore. I want us to move forward and be more of a family than we have in the past.

"She would want *you* to be happy, too. She loved you so much, you were her everything."

"I know." It feels so good to get everything out in the open. Almost amazingly, I feel lighter for it.

"Your mom would be so damn proud of you, of what you're doing with your life. She would have loved that you're following your dreams and not letting anything stand in your way."

"I hope so, Dad."

"Oh sweetheart, you have to know that she would be thrilled about your position with the Cincinnati Ballet. She would be bursting with pride. She always thought you had amazing talent." He smiles. "Even when you were three years old."

I can't help but chuckle. Mom was always my biggest champion. My loudest cheerleader. I suppose that's why the loss of her has been so devastating. It was like a bright beacon of light being snuffed out within me. And then there was only darkness. "Thanks for saying that."

"It's the truth. She was always proud of everything you did, everything you accomplished. Of the young woman you were growing into."

It's ironic...my dreams of dancing with a ballet company are coming true and I'm finally having this amazingly candid conversation with my dad. For the first time since Mom was diagnosed with cancer, I finally feel like a huge weight has been lifted from me. Like I can breathe again...

And yet something is still missing.

Or rather someone...

Without Roan in my life, my dreams can't be fully realized. Without him to share in my accomplishments, they don't feel as monumental.

"Dad," I push out the words before I can overthink them, "can I borrow your car? There's something I need to take care of."

That's the moment I realize that I'm doing exactly what would make my mom proud...I'm following my heart.

CHAPTER THIRTY-SEVEN

Sources confirm that Roan's ex-girlfriend has left Barnett. Does this mean we'll finally get our favorite player back? The one who has all the girls on campus happily dropping their panties with one sexy smile aimed in their direction? Here's hoping so... KingOfCampus.com

Roan

Today, like the last week and a half of my life, has sucked major ass. Thank god, it's almost over. My gym bag is slung over my shoulder. I can't sit around that goddamn apartment one more moment.

Thoughts of Ivy are pounding through my brain like a vicious headache.

That and the fucking mistake I made in letting her go in the first place. But what else could I do? Hold her back from making a go of her dreams?

Nah...no matter how much I love her, I couldn't do that.

I plow an agitated hand through my hair and click the key fob to unlock the doors of my truck. I swear I had to stop myself about ten different times from jumping into my vehicle and taking off to see her.

Of course, I want her to follow her dreams, but why couldn't we do it together?

Maybe we could beat the odds and make this relationship work. Every time those thoughts gained traction in my brain, reality would crash down on me. Letting her go, letting her pursue her dreams in Cincinnati without worrying about me is the right thing to do.

I never realized how much it could hurt to love someone. It forces you to put that person ahead of your own selfish wants and in the end, do what's best for them. Even if that means letting them go so they can achieve everything they were meant to.

Love sucks, man.

It sucks the big one.

I'm hoping a couple of hours of working myself over will exhaust me enough to fall straight into bed and not think about how damn much I'm going to miss her.

How much I already miss her.

Fuck!

She's all I can think about, all I see, all I hear—

"Roan!"

I have to shake my head because her voice refuses to stop filling it. I don't know how I'm going to make it through the next semester. Memories lurk around every corner of campus.

"Roan, stop! Wait!"

Even though I know it can't be Ivy who is shouting my name from the opposite end of the parking lot, I spin around. As my gaze collides with hers, my mouth falls open.

"*Ivy?*" Even as I say her name, my eyes eat her up. Her cheeks are flushed and she's breathing hard. "What are you doing here?"

Silently, she jogs toward me. It takes her a couple of seconds to close the distance that separates us. When she's about three or four feet from where I stand, her feet grind to a halt. Her gaze flickers with uncertainty as it locks on mine.

It takes everything I have inside not to reach out and grab her. I have to jam my hands in the pockets of my athletic shorts in order to resist the temptation. If I touch her for even a moment, I won't be able to let her go. Not ever. It practically killed me to let her walk away this morning. I'm not strong enough to go through that kind of heartache again.

"Ivy?"

She sucks in a deep breath as her eyes search mine. "I couldn't just leave."

My heart speeds up, thudding painfully against my chest. "What do you mean?" Hope rises inside me.

"I couldn't leave without telling you how much I love you. I've never felt that way about anyone. I can't let it go." She inhales a big breath before forcing it out steadily and straightening her shoulders. "I don't want to let it go." Her voice grows stronger. More resolute. "I don't want to let *you* go."

As much as I long to hear those words, they only make everything within me ache. It's like throwing salt into an open wound. I can't allow her to lose sight of her goals. "You have to go to Cincinnati, baby. You have to follow your dreams. I refuse to stand in the way of that."

She closes the remaining distance between us before raising her fingers to my cheek and cupping the side of my face with her palm. My eyelids feather shut as my breath turns ragged and broken. Her touch, even as small as it is, kills me.

"You're part of that dream now. Without you, the rest of it doesn't mean a damn thing." She sounds so sure of herself, of what she wants. "We can make this work, Roan. I know we can."

My eyes open, sifting through hers for the truth. "It won't be easy," I warn softly, "I don't know where I'll end up next year." But what she's saying—I want it too. I want *her*. I want to make this happen because the idea of a future without her is too painful to consider.

Ivy steps closer until our bodies are almost flush. "I don't care. I just know that I need you in my life. And I want to be part of yours. I've never wanted anything more."

I drop my gym bag to the ground as my arms snake around her, hauling her closer. My lips hover over hers for a moment as I whisper, "Are you absolutely certain this is what you want? I won't be able to let you go again."

Her lips slide up into a relieved smile. "That's good to hear because I don't plan on ever letting you go either."

As soon as those words hit the air, my mouth crashes down on hers and, goddamn...nothing has ever felt so good.

So right.

One and a half weeks.

I went without the taste of her for one and a half weeks. Ivy is the only girl who took the time to see me for the guy I am beneath all the bullshit. From the first moment I saw her, I knew there was something different about her. Something that called to me and had me coming back for more. After knowing her for a couple of months, I can't imagine my life without her in it.

Thank god, I won't have to.

It will suck to be without her when she heads to Cincinnati but I'm confident that we'll get through this. We'll find a way to mesh our two worlds and make it work. The alternative is to say goodbye and move on.

I can't do that.

Ivy is the only girl I've ever loved. Loved enough to let go of when I thought it was in her best interest.

"I have a couple of hours before I need to head back to my dad's." Her eyelids lower and something deep within me stirs at the sexy look on her face. Already I know that a few hours won't be nearly enough to satiate the need I have for her, but if that's all I'm going to get, I'll happily take it.

She squeals as I lift her into my arms and carry her up to my apartment. I don't bother to let her go until we're locked inside my bedroom.

Hell...I may never let her go again.

EPILOGUE

Was there anyone who doubted, even for a moment, that Roan King, Barnett's very own king of campus, wouldn't turn pro this year? Nope...don't think so. The man is a total god. Barnett won't be the same without him. Farewell, RK, we'll still have Sunday afternoons during football season... KingOfCampus.com

June

My feet ache as I ride the elevator up to the twentieth floor. I'm used to it now. The rehearsal schedule for the CBC is just as demanding as I imagined it would be. Every muscle in my body has been completely worked over and the thought of soaking in a hot bath sounds like absolute bliss right now.

I was hoping to make it home earlier tonight so I could cook dinner, but practice ran longer than expected. We're in the middle of learning new choreography. The entire week has been grueling. I've been with the Cincinnati Ballet for more than six months now.

Rehearsals are long and expectations are a mile high. Perfection is the standard. If you can't hack it, you can exit stage left.

That being said, I love every single, gloriously punishing moment of it. Leaving school and moving to Cincinnati was the right decision. Sure, it took a month or so for me to get acclimated, but each day that I'm here, I get to live my dream. Not many people can say that.

I pull out my key and turn the lock before pushing open the door. As soon as I'm standing inside the entryway, I throw my keys into the ceramic dish Lexie gave me as a going away gift. She figured I would need it more than she did, and she was right.

It's just one more reason why Lexie Abbott is, and always will be, my best friend. That girl knows me like no other.

I drop my bag to the gray marble tile and pad into our spacious apartment. "Hello?"

Roan swings away from the oven with a huge smile lighting up his handsome face. "Hey, babe." He throws the potholders onto the black granite countertop before eating up the distance between us. "Missed you today."

He doesn't say another word before taking me into his arms. For a moment, I inhale a big breath of him. It feels good to be home. That's exactly the way our apartment feels—*like home.*

Together, we made it happen.

I'm so thankful that we were able to make our relationship work. The winter and spring were difficult with me in Cincinnati and him finishing up at Barnett, but we called, texted, FaceTimed, and visited as often as our schedules permitted.

You name it, we did it.

I'm not even going to talk about all the sexy phone calls that took place late at night. Since we couldn't see each other very often, you better believe there was a whole lot of that happening.

As soon as I left for Cincinnati, Roan spoke with his agent about making a push for the Cincinnati Bengals. Even though any team could draft him, that was the focus. Roan went in the first round.

Drumroll please...to the Cincinnati Bengals.

Once Roan knew he would be moving, we started hunting for an apartment and were lucky enough to find this one after a few weeks. It has two spacious bedrooms and a gourmet kitchen and living room. It was the gorgeous floor-to-ceiling windows that look out over the city that sold us on the place. With Roan's signing bonus, we were able to afford it. I moved in first and then, after finishing up in May, Roan followed.

We've been living together for over a month now. Even though, we've been a couple for more than nine months, we haven't lived in the same city for most of it. At first, I was worried that once he got here and we were together twenty-four/seven, our relationship wouldn't be as good as we thought it was. Maybe we wouldn't get along as well as we used to. Or maybe our feelings changed with all the distance.

That hasn't turned out to be the case.

If anything, it's the complete opposite.

I couldn't love Roan more.

We're both busy and it'll only get worse once Roan begins training camp in July. But it can't be any more difficult than living in two different cities and not seeing each other at all.

"I missed you, too." As I whisper the words, his lips crash onto mine, stroking over them in a way that drives me crazy. One single touch—hell, one single look and my panties are flooding with heat. I'm like one of Pavlov's dogs.

And someone just rang the dinner bell.

My lips open under the gentle pressure of his caress so that his tongue can sweep inside my mouth and tangle with my own. I may be exhausted, but I'm never too exhausted for this.

After a good five minutes, Roan pulls away before smiling at me. We're both breathing hard and there's a heated look filling his eyes that has me wanting to strip down in the middle of our living room.

"If the lasagna wasn't going to be ready in a couple of minutes, I would carry you off to the bedroom and have my wicked way with you." He nips my bottom lip before giving me another quick kiss.

Well, someone just said the magic word.

I perk up. "You're making lasagna?" Cue the salivating dogs again.

Sex, believe it or not, is all but forgotten in the blink of an eye. I absolutely love, love, love Roan's lasagna. By the way he's grinning at me, he knows it.

His eyes narrow. "Are you throwing me aside for lasagna?"

I give him a coy smile. "That depends—is there garlic bread?"

"Duh. Of course there is. How could I serve lasagna without garlic bread?"

"Then yes...you've been thrown over for lasagna." My belly growls in agreement. "I'm starving. Today was completely exhausting." But a good kind of exhausting. The kind of exhausting you get from doing something you love.

"Awww, poor baby." He leans in and presses another kiss against my lips. "How about you go and fill the tub and I'll bring your dinner when it's ready."

My eyes nearly cross with the idea of having a piece of lasagna while soaking in our gigantic tub. Hands down, this guy is the absolute best. Roan once told me that he wouldn't ever let me go, well...I feel the same way about him.

Since Roan hasn't started training camp yet, he spends a lot of time puttering around in the kitchen. He's been watching a ton of cooking shows and trying out new recipes. And I'll tell you what—he's damn good at it.

I cook out of necessity. Because, well, I like to eat. Roan actually enjoys it. It relaxes him. And the stuff he's able to whip up is almost as mouthwatering as he is.

A sigh escapes from my lips. "I think I love you, Roan King."

He smirks. God, but I love his smirk. It's sexy as hell. Just like the rest of him. "As long as you love me, I don't care what the reason is."

The list of reasons why I love this guy seems to grow longer with the passing of each day. He's such an intelligent, thoughtful caring man. And so not the meathead, skirt-chasing-jock I thought he was when we met.

All right, so maybe he was a bit of a skirt chasing player.

What matters is that he's not anymore. The only skirt he chases now is mine.

I think Roan was simply waiting for the right girl to come along and look past the gorgeous face, brawny muscles, and amazing athletic ability to see the guy lurking beneath.

He kisses my lips one last time before swatting my ass. "Go start your bath and I'll be in as soon as the lasagna is ready."

I lower my lashes. "Any chance you'll be joining me?"

Heat flickers in his vibrant turquoise-colored eyes as they drill into mine. "Already planning on it, babe."

I lean on my tiptoes and nip at his chin. "Good, because I'm dying for a hot sudsy bath, a long slow fuck, and some lasagna." My gaze holds his. "In that order, please."

The heat flashing in his gorgeous depths ignites into a veritable inferno. "God, I love when you talk like that." He growls out the words before pouncing on me.

Now it's my turn to smirk. "I know."

This is exactly what six months of phone sex will get you...

A dirty mouth and a very, *very* happy man.

The End

FRIEND ZONED

Violet

Sam slides onto the chair parked next to me about thirty seconds after class begins. His jean-clad leg presses up against mine as he settles in. Not taking my eyes off the professor, who has already launched into the lecture for the day, I whisper from the corner of my mouth, "Nice of you to join us, Mr. Harper."

Even though I'm not looking his way, I know he's grinning from ear to ear. I can all but feel it. His smiles are as blinding as the sun. Heat radiates from them in heavy waves. Any minute his warm breath is going to feather across my—

"I had to haul ass all the way from the stadium." He snorts before adding, "Coach scheduled a mid afternoon practice just for the fun of it."

Well...that last comment is debatable. It's early November, and damn chilly out. The Bulldogs have been on an incredible winning streak this season, which means ramped up practices and workout schedules so they can keep their number one seed going into the play-offs. At this point, everyone in their conference is looking to tear them down.

I glance at him, and notice that his dark blond hair is all shiny and wet from the shower he must have just taken. His bright blue eyes spear mine with a sparkle of mischief simmering in them. His cheeks are flushed, and his breathing is just a bit labored.

I'm slammed with the realization that this is probably how Sam looks right after a rowdy bout of sex. Something hot slides through me before settling deep in my core. Not knowing where the hell *that* thought sprang up from, I abruptly shift my body away from his. My brows pull together in bewilderment.

What the heck is that all about?

Not that I want to dwell on what it means, but those kind of pesky thoughts regarding Sam have been cropping up with a disconcerting amount of frequency lately. It's like I blinked one day and suddenly he looked different to me.

That being said, I need these feelings to go away.

Sam and I are friends.

Good friends. And I don't want that to change.

We met when I moved in with my grandparents who live next door to his family. That was eight years ago, and we've been tight ever since. Somehow, we lucked out, both of us choosing to attend Barnett University.

I wanted to stick close to my grandparents since I'm all they have, and Sam plays football for the Barnett Bulldogs. He was offered full rides to play at half a dozen other Division I programs, both in and out of state, but chose to stay local as well.

Needing to refocus my runaway thoughts, I murmur under my breath, "I'm hoping for your sake that you finished up the paper that's due today on the *power of the judiciary over the legislature.*" I keep my gaze focused straight ahead. The last thing I need is to incur the wrath of Dr. Rickets.

"Yup. Freshly printed with references cited up the ass."

I almost snort but rein it in at the last moment. References had better be cited or Rickets will come after you with both barrels blasting. He's flunked people in PS 345- *the Judicial Process* for less. Since Sam and I are both in the pre-law program, we have a lot of the same classes. Although, this is the only one we have together this semester. We end up hunkered down at the library on a fairly regular basis.

Rickets continues droning on as Sam gets his laptop up and

running. After about fifteen minutes, he leans toward me again, breaking my concentration. Unfortunately, laser focus is required because this class takes dry to a whole new and challenging level. "Are you planning to hit the Sigma party tonight?"

I'm on the verge of responding when our professor's sharp voice slices through the stale air of the classroom.

"An answer if you please, Mr. Harper."

My belly drops about eleven stories. Even though I try not to let Sam distract me, I hadn't been aware of a question being thrown out.

Sam, however, doesn't miss a beat. "Within limits, judges do, in fact, make law. Common law is their creation, and statutes require their interpretation. All law must continually be aligned with the Constitution. But at the end of the day, the Constitution means what judges decide it does."

If Rickets is at all impressed by the fact that Sam answered without even blinking, he doesn't let on. Although, by the way our professor presses his fleshy lips together, I'd have to say he's disappointed not to have caught Sam by surprise. He continues lecturing in a monotone voice, biding his time before springing yet another complex question on some unsuspecting student just trying to muddle their way through this class so they can graduate.

Almost leisurely, Sam stretches out his body in the seat next to me. As he does, the bottom of his soft gray cotton T-shirt rides up giving me a distracting view of rock-solid abdominals before I force my gaze away.

I seriously don't understand what's going on with me lately. I mean, it hasn't been *that* long since I've been with a guy. Certainly not long enough to warrant me noticing the taut ridges of my best friend's six-pack.

But I am.

I am *so* noticing them right now.

And that is all kinds of wrong.

"So, you in or out for the party?" he asks.

Annoyed by the unwanted feelings that keep popping up within me, I shake my head before muttering, "Can we discuss this after class? I'm trying to focus here."

The key word is *trying*.

Clearly, I'm having a difficult time with that. Which doesn't make the least bit of sense.

There is no way I should be having these kinds of thoughts about Sam. It feels, I don't know—incestuous.

Sort of.

We've known each other since we were fourteen years old. For goodness' sake, I used to crawl into bed with the guy when we were in high school. Sam was the only one who could chase away the nightmares. That being said, nothing ever happened between us. There certainly weren't any wandering hands during the middle of the night. No copping a cheap feel. No I'll-show-you-mine-if-you-show-me-yours. He would simply hold me in his arms while I slept.

That was it.

Up until recently, I never thought of Sam as anything other than my best friend.

Which is precisely why these thoughts are disturbing on so many different levels.

Unperturbed by my abrupt tone, he shrugs before slouching further onto his chair. "Sure."

Sam has—for all intents and purposes—a photographic memory. So, chit chatting the class period away is no biggie for him. All he has to do is read something once and it's locked in for life. I'm not going to lie, it's annoying to people like myself who have to study their asses off to pull decent grades.

Even though Sam doesn't face the same academic challenges that I do, he lets me borrow that big brain of his anytime I need it. He's pretty great about studying with me or re-explaining concepts that I don't have a firm grasp on.

After another thirty-three minutes, which is precisely three minutes past the end of class, Rickets finally releases us back into the world. People scatter from the room as if they're fleeing for their very lives. Rickets dearly loves a captive audience and is always reluctant to turn them loose when his time draws to an end.

As soon as we clear the door of the classroom, Sam slings his muscular arm around my shoulders as we make our way out of the polisci building. It may be bright and sunny out, but there's a cold north-easterly wind whipping its way through campus. I'm bundled up in my silver North Face coat and Sam is wearing his football jacket.

"I hate this weather," I grumble right before Sam tugs me closer. The guy radiates heat like a furnace. That being said, I can't help but snuggle into his warmth as the wind continues to slap at us with icy cold fingers.

"Better?" His lips are so close to my ear that the husky cadence of his voice sends an unexpected shiver skittering down my spine. My gaze flies to his, praying that the hitch in my breathing has gone unnoticed.

He flashes a brief smile but doesn't seem any wiser to what's going on within me. A little sigh of relief escapes from my lips. I don't understand why I keep reacting to him this way. It's disconcerting. Not to mention, embarrassing.

The first couple of times it happened, I shrugged it off as a fluke.

Unfortunately, we're moving past fluke and toward—

Nope. Not going to go there. Because I definitely don't think about Sam like that. Furthermore, I don't *want* to think about him like that.

"Much," I squeak as my heart continues to jackhammer painfully under my breast.

He glances around and asks, "So, where's what's-his-face? Hasn't he been meeting you after class?"

I send him one of those *I-don't-really-want-to-talk-about-it* looks, and he immediately chortles, which isn't a good look on him. "Jeez, Vi, ran another one off already, huh? That was fast. Even for you."

"Eight days," I confirm reluctantly. Which is par for the course where I'm concerned. My relationships have absolutely zero staying power. I've had cartons of milk sitting in my fridge that have outlasted some of these guys.

Which is...yeah...just plain sad.

"I don't know why you bother."

I shake my head and agree with the sentiment. "Me, neither."

"Off to sociology?"

I'm not even sure why he asks. The guy probably knows my schedule better than I do.

"Yup, then I'm done for the day." Although I do have a ton of studying to plow my way through this afternoon, which is pretty standard. There is no shortage of books that need cracking and papers that need writing.

"I have philosophy at one, film review, and then another practice to run through. So, are you heading to that party or what, Winterfield? There's not much else going on tonight." His arm tightens around my shoulders, drawing me closer until I'm able to get a whiff of his cologne. My insides do a little impromptu dance.

That reaction nearly sends me stumbling.

Seriously...WTF?

"After all the parties we missed because of Rickets class, not to mention studying for the LSAT, we've earned it." Trying his best to cajole me into attending, he adds, "Come on, Vi, it's supposed to be a huge monster bash. No one does it better than the Sigmas."

He's not lying about all the parties that have been missed because of writing that paper for Rickets' class and studying for the law school entrance exam, which we took in September.

Hmmm. I have to admit that he makes a damn good argument. Maybe we do deserve to cut loose, if only for a night.

That being said, I still hedge. "I have to see if Mia is up for it, but yeah, we'll probably stop by at some point." Mia is my roommate as well as best friend. We met freshman year in English 102.

You know when you meet someone, and right from the get-go it feels like you've known them your entire life? That's the way it was with us. We fell into an easy camaraderie. Sam is the only other person I've ever clicked with like that. Normally, it takes time for me to warm up and feel comfortable.

But not with Mia.

This is our third and final year rooming together. I'm really going to miss her after graduation. Mia's plans are to move to Philadelphia where her boyfriend, Carter, lives and right now, I have absolutely no idea where I'll end up studying law. Worse, I won't know until the spring when my (fingers crossed) acceptance letters start rolling in.

Sam squeezes me closer so that I'm pressed up against all the hard lines of his body. I hate to admit that my pulse skitters at the contact.

"Cool. Text me when you're heading over," he says.

Ha!

I give him a noncommittal response because I know *exactly* why he wants to nail down my ETA. This is nothing new. Samuel J. Harper considers himself to be my unofficial big brother. Even though I haven't asked him to look out for me, he insists on doing it anyway.

End result—the guy is a major cock blocker.

He could lay off with the whole big scary brother act he's got going on. I'm twenty-one years old and certainly no timid virgin. Sometimes, I have to wonder if he's under the misconception that we're living in Victorian England...

And he needs to safeguard my virtue.

Too late, dude.

Much too late.

What I suspect is that he enjoys frightening off potential suitors.

I almost snort.

Fine, we're talking more like one-night stands. I'm not exactly looking for a life partner at this point. I'm focused on finishing out my senior year of college before heading off to law school.

But still...a girl has her needs.

I should be allowed to blow off steam just like he is. Unfortunately, because of his height and sheer muscle mass, it isn't difficult for him to deter prospective candidates. I've yet to find a dude who will stand up to him. And if they're not willing to do that, then they probably aren't worth my time.

The guy definitely needs a girlfriend to preoccupy him. Maybe then he would leave me alone.

"All right, Vi, I'll catch you later." With that, Sam drops a quick kiss on the side of my face before taking off.

As I watch his long-legged strides eat up the concrete pathway, two girls sidle up next to me. For just a moment, all three of us silently watch Sam's retreating figure until he disappears into the thick crowd.

They sigh in total male appreciation.

The blonde wearing a beanie on her head clears her throat as my eyes swing curiously to her. "We were wondering what the deal is between you and Sam Harper."

I raise a brow.

Yeah, I know *exactly* what kind of intel these girls are after. They want to know if Sam and I are sleeping together. Since we tend to spend a lot of time hanging out, people naturally assume that we are.

I may not be into Sam that way—I'm really not—but I'm well aware of his finer points. He towers a few inches over six feet with a body honed by both football and weightlifting. He's got thick, dirty blond hair and bright, piercing ocean-hued eyes. The real draw, in my opinion, is that he's a seriously nice guy.

One of the best you'll ever meet.

When I moved in with my grandparents, Sam was the only kid who went out of his way to pry me from my shell. We spent that entire summer playing video games in his room, going to the movies, hanging out at the mall, and swimming at the country club his family belongs to.

The blonde's gaze darts to the brunette at her side. "You know, is he your boyfriend?"

Since I recognize them from Rickets' class, and they both seem like nice girls, I decide to let them off the hook. "Nah, we're not together like that."

Surprised by my answer, the blonde clarifies, "You have absolutely no interest in him? Because I don't want to poach someone else's man."

See? I like her even more now. This chick has just solidified her position as the number one girl I'm planning to push in Sam's direction.

"Nope, we went to high school together. We're nothing more than good friends."

With a shake of her head, she reveals a row of bright white teeth. "How are you *just friends* with someone as hot as him?" She stares at me as if I'm crazy.

That's the moment an image of his shirt riding up during the middle of class, revealing those rock-solid abs, nudges its way back into my brain. I clear my throat uncomfortably and force the memory away. "We don't think about one another like that."

Seriously...I don't.

I mean, we don't.

Is it really a big deal if I feel a little zing of attraction between us every once in a while? My guess is that it's completely normal. Certainly nothing to get bent out of shape over.

The brunette elbows her curvy friend before waggling her eyebrows. "Well, her loss is your gain, Allie."

My eyes quickly skim down the length of her.

Long blonde hair and deep brown eyes—check.

The thin, body hugging coat she's wearing shows off a rather impressive sized bust. Another check.

I can't help but smirk, feeling good about what I'm intent on doing. "Actually, you couldn't be more his type if you tried. Here," I decide on the fly, "I'm going to give you his number. Text him and see what happens." Sam seems to favor girls with long blonde hair, big brown eyes, and curvy little bodies.

He is such a typical dude.

Her eyes widen like she just won the lottery. "Really?"

I give her a wink. "Absolutely."

Maybe hooking him up with someone else will put the kibosh on all these strange bursts of attraction that keep zipping around inside me. What I need is for everything to slide back to normal between us. And maneuvering this girl in front of him is the perfect way to do it.

She beams. "Thanks! I'll definitely text him." Shaking her head, she introduces herself, "I'm Allie, by the way." She cocks her head toward her sidekick. "And this is Lanie."

"I'm Violet. Just tell him that I gave you his number. He won't mind at all." I give the pair a little wave. "Okay, well, I've got to hustle to sociology. Good luck with Sam."

"Thanks again!" They wave in return before our small group splinters apart.

My guess is that Sam will appreciate me steering this chick in his direction.

Added side benefit—it gets him off my ass.

Which is clearly a win-win situation in my book.

. . .

There are three books in The Barnett Bulldogs Series- King of Campus, Friend Zoned, and One Night Stand. If You Were Mine is a spin-off from characters from One Night Stand. Want to read more?

Buy Friend Zoned here -) https://books2read.com/friendzoned

Buy One Night Stand here -) https://books2read.com/jsonenightstand

Buy If You Were Mine -) https://books2read.com/ifyouweremine2

Or...buy all four books- The Barnette Bulldogs boxset for $9.99

-) https://books2read.com/barnettbulldogs

CAMPUS PLAYER

Demi

"Morning, Demi!" Gary, one of the stadium custodians, calls out with an easy smile and wave as he saunters toward me. "Up and at 'em bright and early this morning, I see."

My heart jackhammers beneath my ribcage from the twenty-minute run as I flash him a grin. "Always!"

"You have a good one! I'll see you tomorrow!"

Since I've already moved past him, I holler over my shoulder, "Same place, same time!"

Even with *The Killers* pumping through my earbuds, I almost hear the deep chuckle that slides from his lips. Our morning greetings are a ritual three years in the making. I've been running through the wide corridor that leads to the stadium football field since I stepped foot on campus freshman year. This will be something I miss when I graduate in the spring. Five days a week, I'm up at six, logging in a four-mile run before returning home, jumping in the shower, and heading off to class.

At this time of the day, the stadium is still relatively quiet, with only a few people wandering the hallways. There's something both serene and eerie about it. I've been here on game days when there are thirty thousand fans packed shoulder to shoulder, rooting on the Western Wildcats football team. Three-fourths of the stadium filled with black and orange is an amazing sight to behold. Football is a religion at Western. Unfortunately, the same can't be said for the women's soccer team. We're lucky if there are a couple of hundred spectators in the stands.

I've come to terms with it.

Sort of.

I keep my gaze trained on the light at the end of the tunnel and push myself faster. As soon as I burst out of the darkness, bright sunlight pours down on me, stroking over the bare skin of my arms and shoulders. It's late August, and summer is still in full swing. A whistle cuts through the silence of the stadium, and my gaze slices to the field. Nick Richards has been head coach of the Wildcats for the last decade. He also happens to be my father.

Two days a week, the guys are up at six in the morning for yoga. Dad is a big believer in flexibility. Even though I'm winded, a smirk lifts the corners of my lips. Watching two-hundred-and-eighty-pound linebackers contort their bodies into Downward-Facing Dog, the Warrior II Pose, and the Cobra is enough to bring a chuckle to my lips. Some of the guys actually like it, but most grumble when they think Dad isn't paying attention. Little do they know that he sees and hears everything.

My father catches sight of me and flashes a quick smile along with a wave in my direction. He has a black ball cap pulled low and aviators covering his eyes. There's a clipboard in one hand as he paces behind the instructor.

When I point to the field, he shakes his head. He might make the guys do yoga, but he refuses to participate. Something about old dogs and new tricks. Every once in a while, I'll tell him that he needs to get out there and set a good example for the team. He usually shoots me a glare in return.

Every Wednesday night, Dad and I get together. Our weekly dinners became a thing when I moved out of the house and into the dorms freshman year. He's busy coaching football, and my schedule is packed tight with school and soccer. Getting together once a week is the best way for us to stay connected. It doesn't matter if we're in the middle of our seasons; we always make time for each other. Especially since Mom lives in sunny California. After eighteen years of marriage, she got fed up with being a distant second to the Western University football program. She packed up her bags and walked out. I hate to say it, but Dad didn't notice her absence for a couple of days. Which only proved her point. Now she's remarried, learning to surf, and is a vegan. I visit for a couple of weeks during the summer before soccer training camp starts up at the end of June.

Even though it's only the two of us, our weekly dinners are set for three people.

I tell myself to stare straight ahead and not glance in his direction.

Don't do it!

Don't you dare do it!

Damn.

My gaze reluctantly zeros in on him like a heat-seeking missile. Long blond hair, bright blue eyes, sun-kissed skin, and muscles for miles. And he's tall, somewhere around six foot three.

I'm describing none other than Rowan Michaels.

Otherwise known as the bane of my existence.

My dad discovered the talented quarterback the summer before we entered high school and took him under his wing. Which has been...aggravating. In the seven years since, Rowan has become an irritatingly permanent fixture in my life. He's the brother I never wanted or asked for. He's the gift I wish I could give back. He's the son my father never had but secretly longed for.

On a campus with over thirty thousand students, one would think that avoidance would be easy to accomplish. That hasn't turned out to be the case. Somehow, we ended up in the same major—Exercise Science. I get stuck in at least one class with the guy each semester. This time it's statistics, which is a requirement. Three times a week, I'm forced to see him. And then there are the weekly dinners at Dad's house.

Every Wednesday, Rowan shows up without fail.

It's so annoying.

No, *he's* annoying!

Our gazes collide, and electricity sizzles through my veins before I immediately snuff it out and pretend it never happened.

I am not attracted to Rowan Michaels.

I am not attracted to Rowan Michaels.

I am not attracted to Rowan Michaels.

Maybe if I repeat the mantra enough times, it'll be true. That's the hope I cling to. I've made it through the last seven years trying to convince myself of this. I only have to get through our final year together, and then we'll go our separate ways—me to graduate school or maybe to the Women's National Soccer League, and Rowan to the NFL. He's one of the most talented quarterbacks in the conference. Hell, probably the country. There is little doubt in my mind that he'll be a first-round draft pick come next spring.

Trust me when I say that Rowan Michaels fever is alive and well at Western University. His fanbase is legendary. The guy is a major player.

Both on and off the field.

Girls fall all over themselves to be with him. They fill the stands at football practice, show up at parties he's rumored to be at, and basically stalk him around campus.

It's a little nauseating. Don't these girls have any self-respect when it comes to a hot guy?

I wince at that unchecked thought.

Fine…I'll begrudgingly admit it; he's good-looking.

I shake my head as if that will banish the insidious thoughts currently invading my brain. Enough about Rowan. It's time to focus on the reason I'm at the stadium at this ungodly hour. I rip my gaze from him as I hit the cement staircase. After half a flight, all thoughts of the blond quarterback vanish from my mind. How could they not when my quads, glutes, and calves are on fire, screaming for mercy as I force myself to the nosebleed section. By the time I finish, my legs are Jell-O, and I still have a two-mile run back to the apartment I share with my best friend off-campus.

I give Dad a half-hearted wave before leaving. It's the most I can muster. His lips quirk at the corners as he shakes his head. He thinks I'm crazy. At the moment, I can't argue with his assessment of the situation. Although, it's the extra training I put in that helps me run circles around the other team in the second half of the game.

The jog home feels like it will last forever. By the time I unlock the apartment door, I'm ready to collapse. I beeline for the shower and jump in before it's fully warm. My skin prickles with goose flesh, but it feels so damn good. Twenty minutes later, I'm dressed and ready to take on the day. My hair has been thrown up in a messy bun, and I'm making a protein smoothie that will fuel me for my morning classes.

Just before taking off, I poke my head into Sydney's room. I know exactly how I'll find her, and that's buried beneath a small mountain of blankets. She doesn't disappoint. We met the summer before freshman year in training camp and have been besties ever since. She's the yin to my yang. The peanut butter to my jelly. The Thelma to my Louise. Where I'm more introverted and cautious, she's loud and boisterous. She's been known to leap without necessarily looking at what she's jumping into. Every so often, it gets us into trouble. Sydney and I have lived together since sophomore year. I gave up trying to cajole her ass out of bed for a six o'clock run after the first week of us cohabitating when she nearly took my head off with an alarm clock.

"It's that time again," I sing-song obnoxiously, "rise and shine."

There's a grunt and then some shifting from under the blankets that tells me she's alive.

When I chant her name repeatedly, each time escalating in volume, she growls, "Get the fuck out!"

"Awww," I mock, "that's so sweet. I love you, too."

Sydney snorts before a hand snakes out from beneath the blankets to give me a one-fingered salute. Then she grabs a pillow and tosses it in my general vicinity. It falls about five feet short of its mark.

I stare at the dismal attempt. "If you're trying to cause bodily harm, you'll have to do better than that."

"Piss off."

"All right then." I shrug. "See you after class." With that, I close the door behind me.

My farewell is met with another indecipherable mouthful. If this weren't something we went through on the daily, I'd worry she was in the midst of a stroke. Sydney is definitely not a morning person. She's more of an early afternoon person. Another thing I've learned over the years? The action of waking up to a brand-new day is a gradual process.

She's like a bear rousing prematurely from hibernation. It's not a pretty sight. She's lucky I don't take her insults personally.

I grab my backpack from the small table crammed into the breakfast nook area along with a coffee before heading out the door. The apartment I share with Sydney is located three blocks from campus, which is highly sought out real estate. We're fortunate Dad is friends with the guy who manages the building. It's probably one of the only perks of having a father who is a head coach of a college football team.

You'd think there would be more, but you'd be wrong. Honestly, being Nick Richard's daughter is more of a hindrance than anything else. People assume you receive special treatment on campus, from professors, or that you have an in with all the football players.

Or worse...

Much worse.

After a bunch of ugly—not to mention untrue—rumors circulated freshman year, I've done my best to distance myself from the Wildcats football team. They're a great bunch of guys, but I don't need all the ugly gossip and speculation that comes along with being friends with them.

As I reach Corbin Hall, the mathematics building for my stats class, my gaze is drawn to a clump of students standing around outside the three-story, red-brick building. In the center of that crowd is Rowan. I don't have to see him physically to know that he's close. The muscles in my belly contract with awareness. It's like a sixth sense. One I wish would go away. He's the last person I want to be cognizant of.

As I jog up the wide stone stairs to the entrance, my gaze fastens on him. A smirk twists the edges of his lips, and my eyes narrow before I drag them away and yank open the door to the building. Relief rushes through me as I step inside the air conditioning and disappear from sight.

"Hey, Demi, wait up!"

I turn at the sound of my name before slowing my step. The dark-haired guy jogging to catch up smiles before falling in line with me.

Justin Fischer.

He's a baseball player and teammates with Sydney's boyfriend,

Ethan. We've been seeing each other for about a month. It's still casual at this point. With school and soccer, I don't have a ton of time to invest in a relationship. He seems to understand that and isn't pushing to be more serious.

When he leans in for a kiss, I angle my head. At the last moment, he tilts in the opposite direction, and we end up bumping teeth instead of locking lips. With a grunt, I pull away and chuckle. My fingers fly to my mouth to make sure I haven't chipped a tooth.

Maybe I've been reluctant to admit it to myself, but that kiss sums up our relationship perfectly.

Awkward and a step out of sync with each other.

"Sorry," he murmurs with a slight smile. I search his face and wait for any telltale sign of sexual chemistry to ping inside me. Unfortunately, my insides remain completely unfazed, which is disappointing but not altogether unexpected. I had a sneaking suspicion when we first got together that it might turn out this way.

"No problem," I say, hoisting my smile and brushing aside those thoughts.

"I haven't seen you for a couple of days," he remarks as we turn a corner and continue walking.

"It's been busy." Which isn't a lie. School might have recently started, but the academics at Western are rigorous. And being a Division I athlete is more like a job. If you're not ready to put in the work, don't bother showing up. There's no half-assing it around this place.

"When's your next game?" he asks.

"Tomorrow at six." My gaze flickers in his direction. Not that I expect him to come, but...

Fine, so maybe I do. If he wants to be my boyfriend, then he needs to show a little support.

His dark brows draw together. "That sucks. I've got a mandatory study hour I have to attend."

I shrug off the disappointment. It's another nail in the coffin of this relationship as far as I'm concerned. "That's cool. It's not a big deal."

"But I'll see you tonight?"

Oh. Right.

Tonight.

Well, damn. In a moment of weakness, I threw out an invitation to join our Wednesday evening dinner. It's one I now regret. If only there were a gracious way to rescind the offer.

"If you're busy, I totally understand—"

"Are you kidding? No way." With a grin, he shakes his head. "I wouldn't miss it for the world. I'm looking forward to meeting Coach Richards."

Great. So this is more about my father than me? Exactly what every girl wants to hear.

I force a brittle smile. "Awesome. He's excited, too."

That might be something of an overstatement.

Justin nods toward the end of the corridor. "I better get moving. Professor Andrews is a real stickler for punctuality."

"Yup. See you later."

This time, when he leans in, our lips align perfectly. The kiss is nothing more than a fleeting caress. There and gone before I can sink into it.

And I'm left feeling...absolutely nothing.

I bury the disappointment where I can't inspect it too closely before giving him a wave as he takes off. For a moment, I stand rooted in the hallway and watch as he disappears through the crowd. There's nothing to distinguish Justin from the thousands of guys who look exactly like him on campus. He's of average height and build with dark hair and espresso-colored eyes. He's nice enough. Although, if I'm completely honest, he's a little self-absorbed. He talks about baseball all the time. If Ethan hadn't introduced us, he's not someone I would have looked twice at. We don't have a ton in common.

As much as I hate to admit it, this relationship has probably reached its expiration date.

Now it's a matter of pulling the plug.

Ugh. I hate breakups. Although, it's doubtful this will end up destroying him. I'll have to make it through tonight and figure out the rest.

With a sigh of resignation, I head to the classroom and find a seat tucked away in the far corner of the small lecture hall. A lanky guy I recognize from a few of my other classes settles beside me. He flashes a dimpled smile as we empty our backpacks.

The tiny hair at the nape of my neck rises seconds before Rowan enters the room. It's like my body knows when he's within a thirty-foot radius. I glance at him from beneath the thick fringe of my lashes before shifting away. Air becomes wedged in my lungs as I wait for him to take a seat. And it won't be next to me because I'm—

"Hey man, would you mind moving?"

Surrounded on both sides.

Damnit. I'm hoping the cutie next to me will tell Rowan to go take a flying leap.

What? It could happen. Not everyone at this university is enamored of the football-playing god. Although I realize the odds aren't stacked in my favor. Rowan is the most recognized athlete on campus. People fall all over themselves to accommodate him.

It's a little sickening.

Okay, maybe more than a little.

"Sure, no problem, Michaels." The guy next to me hastily packs up his books before vacating the desk. Unable to ignore him any longer, I glare as Rowan slides onto the seat next to me.

"Did you really think you could evade me that easily?" Laughter brims in his deep voice. A voice, I might add, that does funny things to my insides.

"One can always hope, right?"

"Oh, answering a question with a question." He leans closer, eating up some of the much-needed distance between us. "I like it."

I roll my eyes as his lips stretch into a satisfied grin. Irritation bubbles up inside me when sexual tension blooms at the bottom of my belly. Or maybe that tension has settled a little lower.

It's definitely lower.

I'm tempted to swear like a sailor. How is it possible that I feel nothing for the guy I'm actually dating, and yet my pulse skitters out of control for someone I don't even like? It's so freaking ironic. It's been this way since we met, and nothing I do stomps it out. I can try to fool myself into believing it's not there, but that doesn't make it any less true.

It's a relief when Professor Peters takes his place at the podium and clears his throat. Once he's captured everyone's attention, he delves headfirst into the probability of dependent and independent events.

Grateful for the excuse to ignore Rowan for the next fifty minutes, I open my textbook and concentrate on the lesson. Just as the blond boy fades into the background, his bare knee bumps into mine. Electricity ricochets through my entire being. I glance at him to see if he's noticed the strange energy we always seem to generate and find his ocean-colored gaze fastened to mine.

My guess is that he does.

Damnation.

Want to read more of Campus Player? Do it here! -) https://books2read.com/u/mYAxqV